ABOUT THE AUTHOR

Sarah Barrie is a bestselling Australian author writing suspense in rural settings. Her debut bestselling print novel, *Secrets of Whitewater Creek*, earned her a spot as one of the Top 10 breakthrough authors of that year, and her next three books, the Hunters Ridge series, also reached bestseller status.

Sarah has also worked as a teacher, a vet nurse, a horse trainer and a magazine editor.

Her favourite place in the world is the family property, where she writes her stories overlooking mountains crisscrossed with farmland, bordered by the beauty of the Australian bush, and where, at the end of the day, she can spend time with family, friends, a good Irish whiskey and a copy of her next favourite book.

Also by Sarah Barrie

Secrets of Whitewater Creek

The Hunters Ridge Trilogy
Legacy of Hunters Ridge
Shadows of Hunters Ridge
Promise of Hunters Ridge

Bloodtree River
Devil's Lair

DEAD MAN'S TRACK

SARAH
BARRIE

FICTION
HQ

First Published 2020
First Australian Paperback Edition 2020
ISBN 9781489255310

Published by
HQ Fiction
An imprint of Harlequin Enterprises (Australia) Pty Limited (ABN 47 001 180 918),
a subsidiary of HarperCollins Publishers Australia Pty Limited (ABN 36 009 913 517)
Level 13, 201 Elizabeth St
SYDNEY NSW 2000
AUSTRALIA

A catalogue record for this book is available from the National Library of Australia

www.librariesaustralia.nla.gov.au

Printed and bound in Australia by McPherson's Printing Group

MIX
Paper from responsible sources
FSC www.fsc.org
FSC® C001695

This is book is dedicated to the extraordinary men and women who risk their lives every day to save others.

CHAPTER 1

'I'm sorry I got you into this!' Charlie Reynolds shouted over the gusts of wind blasting them with icy sleet. 'It's the stupid weather! I don't know where it came from. I can't see how to get down!'

Neither could Tess. She held on to a shelf of slippery rock on a narrow ledge high on the cliff face with frozen, aching fingers. Beneath them was absolutely nothing. She tried for a smile, for encouragement, because the cute but stupid twenty-three-year-old was close to panic, but in her head she was swearing: at him, the mountain, the weather, the whole messed-up situation. He had no right to be here. He'd been warned. No—he'd been *told*. Repeatedly. The Federation Peak climb belonged only to those with the experience to tackle it and enough respect for the extreme Tasmanian conditions to know when not to. And he'd climbed up anyway.

Now this.

She clung to her anger as desperately as she clung to the cliff, filled herself with it so there was no room for fear, for any of Charlie's panic to creep in. Panic, and the effects it had on the body, would only increase the chances of them falling to their deaths.

She wriggled her tingling toes in her boots and willed them not to lose sensation. 'Don't worry about that right now,' she called, cautiously sliding her foot down to the next small jut of rock. 'Just put your hand there for me. Right where mine was. That's it … Now just a small step down … Go steady.'

She watched Charlie's exhausted, unsure movements and sucked in an anxious breath as his fingers struggled to grip the ledge. The steady stream of water rushing off the cliff wasn't helping, and he was shaking so hard his coordination was poor. Tess wasn't much on praying, but she sent one up.

'How many rescues have you done?' He just wouldn't shut up. Nerves, she knew, but damn it, she was trying to concentrate.

'Plenty,' she answered. 'Haven't lost anyone yet.' But her voice wanted to crack from tension.

It was true that since joining the Search and Rescue team she'd participated in some emergency rescues, and not losing anyone was accurate. But *plenty* was a stretch, and this was not a textbook rescue. Wasn't even close. If conditions had been better the chopper would have come in. The police cliff-rescue team would have hooked Charlie up and brought him down safely. If this had been a rescue call-out she'd have a partner up here with her, with proper climbing gear. But she wasn't on a rescue. Charlie and his photographer mates had booked a guided hike for a nature documentary. A couple of days in the Southwest National Park to see Federation Peak, photograph some wildlife and head back out. Tour guide was as much as she'd prepared herself for—a quick climb up a stunningly dangerous mountain in a winter storm had never been part of the itinerary.

As Tess's mind wandered her foot slipped, catapulting her heart around her chest before she found traction again. *Stay focused, Tess. Or die.*

A few more steps and she felt safer ground underneath her. 'Okay,' she said loudly. 'Stop for a second, rest.' She needed a moment herself. They were off the main face, but there was still a lot of mountain to navigate.

Huddled, shivering, Charlie pulled off his beanie and wrung the water from it with shaking hands before returning it to his head. His thick mop of blond hair was as soaked as the beanie. 'I'm sorry,' he stuttered again. 'Last night's rain had stopped and I didn't want to miss a chance at the summit. I was sure the sun was coming out. I thought if I went up early I could be back before we headed out this afternoon. Lots of people do it without ropes, right? Hikers do it all the time. I wanted to sign the book at the top. I was just unlucky with the storm.'

He was rambling, wanting her to say it was okay, but damn it, it wasn't. 'Looks like we might get a short break in the weather,' she said instead, as the sleet eased to rain and a distant patch of blue penetrated the fog. 'It'd be a good idea to get going again while it lasts.'

'I didn't think you'd come up after me. I thought at best you'd call for a rescue.'

Which is exactly what she should have done. She shook her head. 'I called it in, but in these conditions they can't fly. They'll be en route as soon as they can, but you could have been up here a long time.' And looking at him, at the hypothermia and the fatigue, she knew he wouldn't have lasted more than a couple of hours. 'Right now, you're stuck with me.'

'I'm not complaining,' he said, and she saw the gratitude. 'I couldn't have held on that long. I can keep going now though, if you want.'

'Okay, let's go.' As they continued their descent, heath and sedge clung to crevices in the prehistoric quartzite where the rocks' jagged shapes provided better footholds.

'Where are we?' Charlie asked. 'I don't recognise anything.'

'Chockstone Gully's not too far below us. It's going to be slippery.'

He took a few exhausted breaths and blew into his gloved hands. 'Piece of cake, right?' he joked weakly.

They climbed under the enormous stone wedged in the wall of the gully and made their way down a near-vertical waterslide of slippery rock and moss before shuffling across its width to climb the adjoining pandani-dotted gully. 'Well, that's pretty nice,' Charlie said, indicating behind and below them to where the gully sharply dropped into empty space. The fog had cleared just enough to show off glimpses of Lake Geeves, six hundred metres below, its shores engulfed by ancient trees—mere pinpricks from their current height. Nice that we didn't end up down there, she thought with relief.

'I'm sorry, I need another break,' Charlie said, and propped himself against a crevice in the rock, but she could see some of his normal self returning. That bone-numbing fear had worn off.

She needed to warm up; despite her best gear she was soaked through. Every extremity stung with pins and needles, her face was frozen, her nerves were shot and, without the exertion of the climb, she was starting to shake.

Charlie rubbed his hands together to warm them. 'All this drama and not one photo,' he joked. 'I don't seem to have had a chance to get my phone out of my pack.'

Relenting, Tess unzipped the waterproof pocket of her hiking pants and took out her phone, moving around and above him. 'Okay, then, got the energy to smile?'

He did, and she caught a snap of him with a bit of the view in the background, but visibility was becoming poor again. 'I'll send it to you,' she said.

'Thanks. An eternal reminder of my own stupidity.'

A shout from above had both of them looking up. Damn it, she'd left the other two hikers, Ken and Patrick, at Béchervaise Plateau, hoping they'd have the sense to stay put. But they were coming down.

Charlie sent another apologetic glance at Tess. 'I bet the guys have got the shits with me.'

'They were very concerned,' she answered tactfully, remembering the outbursts of 'Irresponsible knob!' and 'Selfish prick!' that had exploded from their lips several times after realising where he'd gone. 'I'm not sure why they're coming down. We need to get up there.'

A fist-sized rock broke away from the mud and moss under Patrick's foot and tumbled past them. Tess kept an eye on its descent until, with a final high bounce, it disappeared over the edge.

'You're all right,' Patrick said with relief as he slid down beside them, closely followed by Ken.

'Fine.' Charlie brushed the comment off with a ridiculous amount of bravado.

'I wasn't talking to you!' Patrick snapped with a ferocious scowl. 'What the hell were you thinking?'

Charlie's face fell. 'I just wanted—'

'Yeah, you always *just want*!' Ken said. 'It's always about what *you* want. Tess could have died up there because of you!'

'I know,' Charlie said more sombrely.

'It's not the right time for this, guys,' Tess interrupted over a sudden gust of wind that brought a fresh lash of rain. 'We need to get back to camp. The weather's coming back in.'

'I could do with a hot chocolate,' Charlie said.

'Then come back to the tent and have it,' Patrick said. 'But you've gone too far this time. Never again, Charlie. Once we get out of here, that's it.'

'What do you mean?'

'You're off the project,' Ken snapped then, with a nod at Patrick, he started back up the gully.

'What? You can't be serious!' Charlie said, stunned. Then on a burst of desperation: 'Wait!' He made to bound up the slope, and the ground gave way underneath his feet.

Tess lunged, grabbing hold of his jacket.

And went with him.

They toppled, one over the other, down the steep gully.

She threw out her arms and legs, hoping for something to stop her fall. Her gloves were ripped from her fingers as her hands clawed, desperate for a hold. But the sharp, uneven ground bruised and sliced her frozen fingers, destroying them. She struck her head and her vision dotted. She hit the cold hard ground again, again, while one panicked thought screamed in the back of her mind: *The drop-off.*

She managed to get her legs in front of her and dug her heels in hard. It slowed her descent, then brought her to an awkward stop. Water running down the gully soaked into her clothes and threatened to dislodge her. Heart pounding, everything aching and stinging, she carefully turned her head. She was centimetres from the edge. Charlie was dangling from it, one hand wrapped around a jagged pillar of rock. Water cascaded off the cliff past him into nothing. His fingers were slipping.

More stones pummelled Tess as Ken and Patrick made their way towards them, frantically shouting.

'Stay still!'

'Hold on! We're coming!'

Terrified, she gingerly shifted to better brace herself, wedging one arm against Charlie's lifeline rock before offering her other hand. 'Take it!'

Terror etched every feature of his face, but Charlie eyed the distance to her hand. He lunged and his fingers brushed hers, almost held. She felt the tug of them, felt herself move. Her eyes left his for a split second as she searched frantically for somewhere to better brace her foot. Then a scream pierced the air as his grip slipped from hers. When she looked back, Charlie was gone.

She stared in horror at the emptiness of the space he had occupied, feeling herself slipping towards it. She clawed the ground with torn fingernails as her feet disappeared over the edge and her speed picked up.

'Tess!'

Something soft hit her face. Giving up her useless hold on the mountain, she snatched desperately at it and swung out into oblivion.

CHAPTER 2

Detective Senior Sergeant Jared Denham pulled the police car up behind one already at the scene and looked around. Hobart's Salamanca Markets were setting up for a big day of trading. Despite the lightly falling rain, people were milling with phones and dogs, and kids of all ages held parents' hands and gawked from the edge of the park. A disaster waiting to happen.

'We need to get these people back,' Detective Inspector Indiana Atherton muttered as she climbed out of the passenger side. Approaching sirens promised backup so she walked behind the car and flagged down more police and began shouting directions. Jared hurried across the park to where the new probationary constable who'd called the incident in stood partially protected by the cover of a tree.

'Emily.'

'Hey, Jared.' Behind the casual greeting was plenty of tension. 'I think she's wearing goods reported stolen last night from a break and enter.'

He looked around the tree. Seated on the shoulders of a statue a few feet in front of them was a visibly inebriated middle-aged woman in not enough clothing. She sported a handbag, a couple of sparkling necklaces, what looked to be expensive sunglasses and a short red dress that had shimmied up to her waist due to the way she was straddling Tasmania's twenty-eighth premier. In one hand was a mostly empty bottle of Jack Daniels, in the other was a Glock semiautomatic handgun.

'The guy hanging back by my car knows her. Says her name's Ruby.'

'Yeah, we know Ruby,' Jared said, recognising the woman. 'She spends half her life sleeping off big nights in our holding cells. I'm surprised you haven't had the pleasure yet.'

'Dangerous?'

'Wouldn't have said so. Until now.'

'She's as likely to fire that thing by accident as on purpose. There's too many people around.'

'We're dealing with that,' Indy said, coming in from behind them. 'How the hell did she get up there?'

'No idea. But she's—'

The gun raised above Ruby's head went off. Chaos ensued from the crowds at the police boundary. A child fell or was knocked over, her high-pitched wail echoing over the general noise. Ruby gave a 'Whoop!' and a pump of her JD into the air before bursting into an off-key rendition of *The Lone Ranger* theme.

'One of those bullets can travel a hell of a lot further and faster than we can clear this area,' Jared said and, ignoring Indy's 'Wait!', he stepped out.

'Hi, Ruby,' he said casually. 'How's it going?'

A smile erupted on the woman's smudged red lips. 'Hi, handsome!'

'That's Detective Handsome to you, Ruby.'

'Me and Mr Ogilvie here are having a party!' She knocked the bottle against the statue's head as though in cheers.

'Yeah, about that … It must be getting uncomfortable up there.'

She eyed him wickedly. 'Dunno. Kinda enjoying having a man between my legs. Specially one this hard! Get it?'

He forced a smile onto his face as she cackled at her joke and did what he could to keep his stance and expression relaxed. 'You gonna let me help you down?'

'Then what? You offering to take over?' Another 'Whoop!', another wave of the gun.

Silence had descended around them. Though they were further away, crowds still watched, many with phones up, recording. Media had arrived too.

'Okay, here's the deal,' Jared said. 'That gun is dangerous. There's kids around, Ruby. You don't want to accidentally hurt a kid. You need to hand it to me, okay?'

'Or what? You'll shoot me? Taser me? *Spank* me?' she asked, wide-eyed and enjoying herself.

'I don't want to do that. Neither does she,' he added quickly when Ruby's head whipped around to find Indy behind her. 'Because any of those options would mean lots of paperwork, and you know how cops hate paperwork.'

'Aw … she ain't gonna shoot me. She gets me coffee in lock-up.'

'There'll be no more coffee deliveries, Ruby,' Indy said. 'Not if you don't come down right now.'

'Also,' Jared continued to get Ruby's attention back on him and off his partner, 'being shot hurts. *A lot.* I can't stress enough just how bad it really does hurt. On top of that, you might fall down and, look, you're a long way up there. That's gonna hurt too. So, lots of pain. Instead, why don't you do us all a favour and hand me that gun, okay? Then I can help you down.'

Ruby considered that for almost too long, then her arm lowered.

'Don't point it at me,' Jared said quickly as Indy tensed. 'Finger off the trigger … great. Awesome job.' He closed the distance and took the gun then held it out to Emily, who stepped up to take it. 'Okay, let me help you.'

'My, my. What big muscles you have.'

'Thanks,' he muttered, wrestling Ruby to get her down safely. God, she stank.

Back on the ground, Ruby got her feet under her then ducked as an eruption of cheering broke out from the crowd. Jared got a better hold, thinking she was going to make a dash for it, but Ruby was simply bowing, still too drunk to realise how much trouble she was in.

'They want to take our picture, Detective Handsome,' she slurred. She tried to raise herself up and leant towards him with, if the pouty lips were any indication, every intention of kissing him. He avoided it, just, and Ruby cackled, coughed and, doubling over again, vomited on his shoes.

'Geez, Ruby!' Disgusted, he passed her over to Emily and wiped his shoes off on the grass as best he could.

'See ya back at the cells, eh?' Ruby called. 'Might need that coffee!'

'She's not our POI,' Emily confirmed outside the interview room at the station. 'Sorry, should have made that clear back at the park.'

'You're sure?' Indy asked.

'Yep. Constable Perry and I responded to a break and enter out on Kelly Street at around 2 am this morning. Owner was out, but a neighbour noticed a torch flashing around in the home when he got back from nightshift. We arrived at the scene just in time to see our thief bolt. He's a hell of a sprinter.'

'He?'

'Yeah. We chased on foot. We thought we had him at the Brick Factory but he tossed a black backpack over the fence and disappeared. We split up, couldn't find him. When we went back for the goods, the bag was gone.'

'Ruby couldn't have been drinking there. The place would have been closed.'

'She had the bottle with her,' Indy reminded him. 'She was most likely drinking on the street as usual. Got lucky.' She gestured to the interview room. 'You two have such a sweet relationship going, Detective Handsome. I'll let you talk to her.'

'Ha,' he muttered, but stepped through the door.

Ruby looked a lot worse for wear than she had at the park. The dark circles that were parked permanently under her eyes stood out more than usual against the pallor of her skin, and her dishevelled hair was limp and clasped in the fists currently holding her head up. The smeared, heavy makeup that had settled in the lines on her face made her look older than both the twenty-something she was trying to pull off and the fifty-two he knew her to be.

Indy pulled out a chair and sat back to listen, one leg crossed over the other. Jared stayed on his feet.

'So, Ruby,' he asked. 'Where'd you get the stuff?'

'I really need ta sleep this off, handsome,' Ruby muttered.

'Then let's get this done. Where?'

She dragged her fingers across her eyes. 'It just kind of … landed in my lap.'

'You see who put it there?'

'Nup.'

The way she averted her eyes gave him a small ray of hope she was lying. This was the third break-in in as many weeks and they needed a lead. 'That's a shame. You've gone a bit too far this time, discharging that weapon. You won't be walking out of here. Not before you've gone before a magistrate, anyway. The court might be more lenient if you assist us in our investigation.'

Ruby studied him through narrowed, bloodshot eyes, before muttering, 'Doesn't do a person any good to go dobbing. But maybe I do know a bit of something.'

He perched on the edge of the table. 'A little bit of what kind of something?'

'Coffee?'

'In a minute,' Indy said.

'Promise?'

Indy sighed loudly and got to her feet to stick her head out the door. 'Hey, Emily, can you run next door for an extra-large double shot latte with three sugars? Ta.' With a pointed look at Ruby, Indy sat back down.

'Okay, well,' Ruby said, her eyes back on him, 'I might know how your thief is scoping out his victims.'

'How would you know that?'

'Seen him at the Mobius a couple of times, and the Observatory ... pretty much all the nightclubs. Hangs around, talks to the chicks with the pretty jewellery.'

'You sure?'

'I paid attention. He's hot. I mean young and built with a kinda cheekiness about him. Not as built as you, Detective Tall, Dark, and Gorgeous, but his eyes are the same colour.'

'You could tell he had blue eyes in a split second in the dark?'

'When he tossed the bag I recognised him as he went round the corner, past the security light. Know from the club how blue those babies are.'

'Did he see you?'

'Dunno. Don't think so.'

There was a brief knock on the door before Emily appeared. 'Sorry, just had a call come in,' she said to Indy. 'There's been a fatality out on Fedder. Tess's group. Search and Rescue said to make sure you got the message the fatality isn't Tess, but she is injured. Went over a cliff.'

Indy's chair scraped back, and she was gone.

CHAPTER 3

Tess stared unseeing at the scenery beneath the chopper as it approached Hobart. It had taken another couple of hours for the weather to clear enough for rescue. If only it had been sooner.

Charlie's scream refused to stop reverberating in her head. She closed her eyes, saw him hanging from the edge, his eyes begging, his fingers slipping from their hold on that rock. She felt the scrape of his gloves, felt that sinking moment of not quite reaching far enough to hold on. Then the scream, over and over, like an echo. And he was gone. Just … gone.

She pressed her eyelids together hard. Was this her fault? Was there something else she could have, should have, done? A photography trip with experienced hikers. A short expedition through Moss Creek to Béchervaise Plateau for a look at Fedder. Plenty of panoramas, plenty of stunning gullies and ridges. Plenty of wildlife. And, as it turned out, plenty of mud and rain and swollen creeks, leeches, wet boots and cold weather. They'd said the weather made their photos more atmospheric, so they tolerated the cold and the wet more happily than most. It hadn't been until they arrived at the plateau that Charlie had even mentioned the possibility of the climb. He'd asked if she'd climbed it, she'd said she had, in good weather. She'd told him, when he'd asked, that yes, there was a way up without ropes. That most hikers did tend to do it that way. That the view from the top was breathtaking. Extraordinary.

She should have shut up. The conversation had just spurred his enthusiasm. Even when she told him a few of those hikers had died, that the climb was too dangerous in bad weather and that even if he reached the top without killing himself, he wouldn't see anything due to fog, he hadn't seemed entirely deterred. 'Not this time,' she'd said again over their last cup of tea for the night, 'not in these conditions.' She'd reinforced that. And then she'd crawled into her tent and curled up in her sleeping bag and slept.

How could she have known?

She should have known, when she'd woken the next morning to the sun creeping up, that he would have seen a few minutes of clear morning sky as the chance he needed. But she had already been feeling less than enthusiastic about the hike back to Farmhouse Creek to be picked up, and was preoccupied as she took her time emerging from her warm tent to get the camp stove going. The cloud was rolling in by the time the water boiled, and she'd been wondering how, if the predicted amount of rain fell, she was going to get them safely back across the creeks that had already been close to impassable on the way in. So she'd gone about getting breakfast sorted, decided, as the fog enveloped them in earnest, thick and spiked with icy rain, that she should ask them to cut their day short and pack up early. It was beyond atmospheric; they'd be lucky to see their hands in front of their faces. It wasn't until she heard the raised voices in the men's tent arguing over whether to go after the idiot that she realised what Charlie must have done.

All that time mucking around at camp when she could have been out there earlier, after him faster. Would he still be alive?

If only his friends hadn't brought the argument to the mountainside. If only they could have waited. She looked at them, strapped in in front of her. Their faces had been saying the same thing since they pulled her back over the ledge and saved her life, then walked back to camp without their mate.

Damn it!

She should never have headed out without ropes. It didn't matter that they weren't supposed to be doing any climbing. She'd pack them from now on. It was more room to find, more weight in the pack. But she'd take them. If she ever did this again.

The numbness that had protected her all morning was threatening to crack. Aaron Jackson, fellow Search and Rescue volunteer and tour company owner, pushed a bottle of water into her damaged hands. She took it, not because she wanted it but because arguing required too much energy. It was easier to just accept. She drew her lips up in what she hoped passed for a smile and lifted the bottle. The water lodged in her throat like concrete.

Aaron put a hand on her knee, squeezing it in understanding. Even before they'd started seeing each other he'd been someone Tess had known she could count on. He'd been an amazing mentor during her SES training and she'd seen him save lives first-hand. He was such a great guy. Now he'd come to get them in conditions that should have grounded the choppers much longer. He'd tended to her cuts and bruises, warmed her up, got them packed up and safely on their way home. But she was glad the noise of the chopper had put an end to conversation. She couldn't deal with any more advice. She'd already endured the gentle lecture on how important it was to remember her training, about what constituted acceptable risk and how it helped no one if she died trying to save someone else. She'd nodded in silent submission as he'd reminded her she should know when to wait for assistance, when to step back. *There are always consequences for our actions, Tess. You need to think, be smart.* She'd wondered several times if she'd have felt worse if she'd waited for that assistance and Charlie had fallen anyway. She'd decided she probably would.

And God, it all rushed in again: his petrified face, the feel of that brief tug of his fingers against hers. Then his scream in her ears and her own in her mind as she slipped into a gaping space that had wanted to swallow her whole. *If only, if only, if only …*

Feeling sick, she screwed the lid back on the water bottle and concentrated on keeping down the bile in her throat. Shock was wearing off. She needed to hold on to it a little bit longer. Just until she could find somewhere private to grieve and rage.

'What is with the traffic today?' Indy muttered from the passenger seat as they made their way to the heliport.

Jared sent her a sympathetic smile. 'It's the rain, slows the sensible ones down. We'll beat the chopper back, don't worry.' But he could tell she was worried, saw it etched in her face. 'She's okay, right?'

Indy dragged her fingers through her light brown hair. 'That's what she told them to tell us. But this is Tess, so who knows?'

'If she's capable of convincing everyone she's okay, that's got to be a good sign.'

'She's stubborn enough to fall over dead, still proclaiming she's fine.'

'I happen to like that about her,' he said lightly. 'I remember that attitude well from the time she saved my life.'

He saw some of the tension ease as her lips turned up into an almost-smile. 'You were bleeding to death on the floor but we had a serial killer in the building so I told her to go outside and call for help.'

'And she did. But then she came back in.'

'I know,' she said wryly.

He remembered how Tess had flown back in the door of the police station and dropped to her knees. Jared let his memory drift back …

'I'm Tess,' she said. 'Hi.'

The bullet wound hurt like a bastard and breathing was an effort, but he took in the serious brown eyes on the sun-kissed face as the long dark hair she'd contained in a ponytail fell forward. He thought he probably said hi back, but then he had to gasp as she pressed on his wound to control the bleeding. He was more sure he got out, 'Jared.'

'Nice to meet you,' she replied with a smile that said she realised how absurd the conversation was under the circumstances.

Pain and the threat somewhere from within the building stopped him smiling back. 'You were told to go outside.'

'I did. I called for help. It's on the way.'

'Great job. I'm fine. Now get out. There's a serial killer in here.'

Her face closed into a frown. 'If you're so fine, get up and walk out with me. Otherwise, would you shut up?' Then, mimicking him perfectly, 'There's a serial killer in here.'

He dragged in a few ragged breaths. 'Are you always this stubborn?'

'Do you always make this much noise?'

There should have been other noise. It was too quiet. He needed to get Tess out of harm's way. 'Listen, being young and beautiful doesn't mean you're invincible. If this arsehole comes out and shoots you, you'll be just as dead as anyone else.'

'Seriously? You're bleeding all over me and you're flirting?'

'I'm appealing to your ego. Nothing else is working.'

'How about going with the grateful?'

He was getting cold, his mind fogging. 'I'd be very grateful if you'd leave.'

She simply shook her head. 'Me and my ego are staying put.'

A sudden gunshot had his heart leaping in his chest. He felt her flinch, the pressure on his wound waver. Either it was over, or it was about to get a lot worse. But the seconds ticked on without another sound.

'I think I should take a quick look—'

He held her arm. 'If you leave, I'll bleed to death, remember?'

'I thought you were fine. Where's your gun?'

'The serial killer you want to go looking for has it.' Unconsciousness threatened. He fought it back. 'How would you know how to shoot, anyway?'

'Farm girl.'

Sirens wailed and commotion erupted outside. Tess stretched up to look out the window. 'Reinforcements have arrived.'

'I'll give you this, you know how to keep your head.'

'I'm pretty attached to it.'

Wouldn't be difficult to become pretty attached to it, he decided as his vision swam with black dots. The door burst open, jolting him back to consciousness as police swarmed in and Tess was replaced by two paramedics.

He looked for her outside, once he was on the stretcher. She was talking to Indy near where the killer's body was being wheeled out. 'Tess?' he called, got her attention. 'Thanks for hanging around.'

'Oh, now you're grateful?' she teased. 'I won't say, "Anytime," but it was interesting.'

'You saved my life.'

Her smile upped in wattage. 'Get better.'

He managed to nod before he was put into the ambulance.

'Earth to Jared?' Indy said in a tone that suggested it wasn't her first attempt to get his attention.

'Yeah, sorry. Was still thinking about that incident at the station. I'm not sure I ever really thanked her.'

'Yes, you did. It was years ago. Why worry about it now?'

He made the turn to the helipad. 'It was just a thought. You always think there's time, but you never really know when that time is going to be up. I'm thirty-four, but I could have been dead for years by now. Then there's Tess. She's how old?'

'Are you actually asking?'

He pulled a face. 'I just mean, you don't tend to think too much about time running out. But it does, sometimes. For that poor guy on the mountain today, it did.'

They looked up at the same time to see a chopper arriving. 'But not for Tess, thankfully,' Indy said. 'Let's go get her.'

The chopper landed in a whirl of wind and sound. Jared stood by the car as Indy ignored the steady rain and headed straight for the chopper, keen to check on the condition of her sister-in-law.

Tess was out first. Scratches and dried blood marred her face, a blanket falling from her shoulders as she spoke to someone inside. Two men in equally filthy hiking clothes emerged. Gear was dropped off the chopper by a tall, light-haired figure in Search and Rescue gear who didn't seem to want to take his eyes off Tess. He hadn't had much to do with Search and Rescue, but the guy was vaguely familiar.

Indy reached them and wrapped Tess in a hug, then pulled the blanket back up over her shoulders and steered her towards the car.

Once they were closer, Jared got a better look at Tess. The creamy complexion he'd always admired had drained to a translucent bluish-white save for the dark circles under eyes that looked shocked and blank. He'd only ever seen her hair in a sleek, dark ponytail. He had a suspicion it may have started out that way, but most of it was plastered to her face in tangled strands or hung limp around it. Her pain was evident in her hollow cheeks and tight mouth.

'Jared … Hi.'

'Hey, Tess. Glad you're okay.'

'Thanks.'

The blond guy was a couple of steps behind, and he sent Jared a hard stare before laying a hand on Tess's lower back. 'Indy, I know you'll want to talk to everyone, but I think Tess needs to go to the hospital first.'

'Yeah, of course. Thanks, Aaron, we've got her,' Indy said. 'Is there any chance you could take care of these guys and get them to the station for us?'

'I was going to take Tess,' Aaron said with a frown.

'I don't need a hospital,' Tess said wearily.

'Sweetheart, you need to get checked over,' Aaron said. 'Some of those cuts are deep. And you banged your head and your hands are ripped to shreds.'

The smile Tess managed for Aaron looked forced. 'It's just bruises and bumps and a couple of torn fingernails. We should all go to the station first and get it over and done with.' When she walked to the car, Jared opened the door for her. She smiled slightly. 'Thanks.'

'Welcome.'

'Tess.' Aaron all but barged Jared out of the way as he helped her into the car. 'You really should see a doctor.'

'We'll reassess at the station,' Indy said, sliding in beside Tess from the other side.

Jared waited for Aaron to move then closed Tess's door, went back to the driver's seat and started the car. 'Good to go?' he asked. Indy gave him a nod. Tess was staring out the window, features tight.

As he drove away, both women seemed content to remain silent. He guessed Indy didn't want to make Tess relive the experience again just yet. Not when she was about to go through it all officially.

'Do my brothers know?' Tess asked.

'I called Logan,' Indy said of her husband, 'and told him to let Connor know. We knew you were out that way and the media's already got hold of the incident. I didn't want them to worry.'

'And Connor will let Callie know.'

'Of course he will. She cares about you, too.'

'I know. It's just … They'll carry on.'

'We love you,' Indy said simply. 'We're supposed to carry on.'

'Oh God.' Tess's voice cracked on a quiet sob. Jared glanced into the rear-view mirror. Tess's face was buried in her hands. 'I couldn't save him, Indy,' she mumbled through the bandages. 'He was so scared and I couldn't get hold of him.'

Indy slid an arm around her and let her cry it out. Feeling helpless, Jared returned his attention to the road.

CHAPTER 4

Jai Wharton stood behind his boss's desk, perspiration prickling his temples, a lump of lead weighing his stomach down. Under Tank's simmering anger, the little office space in the back of Hobart's biggest pawn shop had suddenly become stiflingly hot.

Vince 'The Tank' Finlay shoved the sales docket across the desk and got to his feet. 'That was a five hundred dollar necklace and you sold it for fifty bucks!' Age was catching up with Tank, and he moved like a man who'd taken one too many beatings to his tree-stump torso. Old tattoos crept up his neck from beneath his 'I ride so I don't kill people' T-shirt and hugged the loosening skin on arms still sporting enough muscle to defend his nickname. The lines on his face made his eyes seem even smaller and his silver goatee wasn't as sharply manicured as the photo on his desk showed it had been when he'd ridden with his gang. But he was still a scary bastard when he wanted to be.

'What?' Jai picked up the receipt with an unsteady hand and tried to think back to yesterday's sale. It had been late in the afternoon, just before close. A guy had come in, nice jacket, cheap shoes. He'd had a woman with him, the fiancée. He'd paid cash—fifties. Jai risked a look at Tank and shook his head. 'No. I didn't. Maybe I stuffed up the receipt, but I got the cash.'

Tank lifted his hands, palms up, his face dark. 'Then where is it? 'Cause it isn't in the till.'

Jai thought about it again. He'd put that money in the till, he knew he had. Unless … 'I—I don't know why it's not there. Did you ask Pax?'

'Pax?' Tank's hands dropped to the desk and he leant over it, his scowl increasing. 'When was Pax near the till? He's just started working here. He hasn't been on the register, has he?'

'Um, not on purpose but …' Jai stared at the floor. He knew better than to keep arguing with Tank. He needed a moment to catch his breath, to figure it out. 'Guess I stuffed up. Sorry, boss.'

Tank continued with that stare for several more nerve-racking seconds. Eventually he nodded. 'When you make a mistake, you man up to it. You owe me four-fifty. You can't pay it, I'll take it out of your wage.'

'What?' A fresh explosion of anxiety hit Jai. He was barely scraping by as it was. 'But, boss, I can't afford—'

'Neither can I!' Tank snapped. He gave a heavy sigh. 'Look, I know it's tough at home, kid, and I respect what you're doing for your pop … so we'll make it twenty bucks a week.'

The heaviness in Jai's stomach turned to an anxious rattling. Tank didn't have a clue just how tough it was. Something out of his tightly managed budget was going to have to go, and most likely it would be food. But he nodded, turned and walked out of the office into the shop.

There was only one way he could think of that the money had gone missing. Pax was nowhere to be seen—probably bludging out the back with a cigarette as usual. Nothing had gone right since that dickhead Pax had walked in a month ago, handed Tank a letter and been given a job. If it hadn't been for Riley, he would have quit and tried his luck somewhere else, but Tank's daughter was the only good thing in Jai's life, so he was sticking it out as long as he could.

I respect what you're doing for your pop. Ha, Jai thought bitterly. Tank's so-called respect didn't mean anything. If he really respected him, he would have believed he hadn't made a mistake with that money. The more Jai thought about it, the more that anger built inside him, festered.

'I'm ducking next door for a pack of smokes,' Tank said from behind him. 'Back in five.'

Jai watched him go. As soon as Tank was across the road, he charged out the back to find Pax. The six-foot-two tattooed giant was reclining against the fence in the sun, legs crossed at the ankles, phone to his ear as he smoked a cigarette. No surprise.

'You took that money!'

Pax eyed him with curiosity then ended the call, put his phone in his pocket and took a long drag of his cigarette. 'Don't know what you're talking about.'

'Bullshit! That necklace yesterday! You watched me make that sale then I asked you to mind the front of the shop while I went to answer the phone in the office. You took the cash out of the till and changed the sale price on the computer.'

The cigarette hit the ground and Pax took his time very deliberately grinding it out with his foot. There was something threatening in that move and Jai tensed, but he was too worked up to back down.

'And how could I have done that?' Pax asked with a smirk. 'I mean, unless some fuckwit left the sale open on screen when he raced back to answer the phone.'

Jai risked a step closer to glare up at him. 'You need to put it back!'

Pax bent down and got in his face. Though physically tougher, with a few years on Jai's twenty-two, it was Pax's eyes that scared the crap out of Jai, even when their general coldness glittered with dark amusement. 'Or what?'

Jai clenched his fists, scrambling for something to say. 'Screw you!' exploded from his lips.

'Okay, pencil dick,' Pax said, and straightened up. 'What ya got? Wanna take a swing?'

Jai wanted to hit the bastard. He wanted to smack that smug smile right off his pretty face. But he wasn't stupid, and his rage-fuelled bravado was quickly fading.

'No? Didn't think so.' Pax's hand shot out and grabbed the front of Jai's shirt. He drove him back against the fence. Hard. Jai's spine blasted with pain and he bit his tongue, tasted blood. 'Ya sure?'

Jai nodded, shrinking back from the expression on Pax's face.

Pax laughed, released him and strode out the side gate.

'Hello?' Riley's voice echoed from inside the shop. Jai pulled himself together and brushed his clothes off, then went to find her.

He heard Tank's voice float out from the office. 'You're not going.'

'What?' Riley shrieked. 'Dad, you can't be serious! You were fine with this last week!'

Jai could smell lunch and saw four boxes of steaming fish and chips on Tank's desk as he approached the office. His mouth watered, even as he decided it could be a while before he got to eat any of it. Riley was standing in front of her father, hands on hips, short brown hair tucked back behind her ears. She was wearing jeans and one of the jumpers that were her preferred university wear and her heart-shaped face was set for battle. Riley and Tank rarely ever went head to head, but they were both as stubborn as each other so when they did it was huge.

'You heard what happened to that guy out at Federation Peak yesterday?' Tank asked. 'He was an experienced hiker with a guide and he's still dead.'

'We're not going to Fedder, Dad,' Riley said in exasperation. 'It's just the South Coast Track.'

'The fact you put a "just" in front of a week and a half long wilderness trek tells me how unprepared you are. I looked it up after hearing that news report. It's too dangerous.'

'Hundreds of people do it every year. It's fine.'

'You're not hundreds of people,' Tank said in his very reasonable, I'm-not-budging tone. 'You're a young woman with only a couple of easy day hikes under your belt.'

'A twenty-year-old woman who can make her own decisions!' Riley snapped, then sabotaged herself by stomping her foot like a child.

Jai shifted, his shoes scraping the lino, and her head swivelled in his direction.

'Hey!' She beamed, her face losing most of its scowl as she stepped in for a kiss. 'I called in with lunch.' She snatched one of the containers from their favourite fish and chip shop off the desk and handed it to him.

'Thanks.'

'Something smells good,' Pax said, ambling in. 'Hi, Riley.'

'Hi, Pax,' she said. 'I got you some too.'

Jai caught Tank's glare and found himself in agreement with the man for the first time that day. He wasn't sure Tank really liked Pax at all. The whole situation made no sense.

Completely at home, Pax sat down in a spare chair and kicked his legs up onto Tank's desk to open his container. Jai took another seat, thought he might as well get started on his lunch before Tank ordered them back to work.

'What've ya got there?' Pax asked of the folder Riley picked up from Tank's desk.

'Hike stuff. I thought if the shop wasn't too busy Jai and I could take a look at what I've organised. But Dad's forgotten I'm all grown up and is pretending he can stop me from going.' She looked from Pax to Tank.

'I can stop you from going,' Tank said. 'Jai has a job here. He hasn't applied for leave.'

Riley stared dumbfounded. 'Seriously? We told you about this!'

'And you have uni, which I'm paying for.'

'And uni is on break next month, which is *when we're going*,' she said.

'Where's the hike?' Pax asked.

'South Coast Track, the southernmost coastline of Tasmania,' she said with a wistful expression. 'I've wanted to do it for ages. It's pure wilderness. Just you and what you can carry on your back.'

'I hope you're taking someone with a bit of muscle. Someone who can step up if there's trouble.' Pax smirked at Jai.

Jai felt his fingers tighten around the fish and chip box and wished it was Pax's throat.

'She's not taking anyone because she's not doing it,' Tank said.

'Dad, we've already booked the flights to Melaleuca. They weren't cheap. And Jai went to a heap of trouble to get Evan into respite that week.'

Jai kept his attention on Riley. 'I thought we were flying back, not out.'

'The flight company said it's better to fly over and walk back, because bad weather can ground flights. I'd rather be delayed at this end than at Melaleuca, where we could be stuck for days in a basic hut waiting to be picked up. It should only take eight or nine days but we'll pack for a couple more, in case the creeks are up or we need to bunk down for a bit if the weather gets nasty.'

'Ya sound very prepared. You've obviously done ya research.' Pax looked at Tank expectantly.

A 'humph' came from Tank and with it a glower Jai hoped meant Pax was in for it later.

'All in all,' Pax said as he got to his feet, 'it should be quite the adventure.' He popped a chip in his mouth and winked at Riley before heading out with his lunch.

'More the merrier!' Riley called to his back.

Jai clenched his teeth so hard his jaw ached, then let out a sigh of relief when Pax laughed and said, 'I prefer civilisation. I did all that stuff during military training.'

'Military training?' Riley repeated in surprise, but Pax was out of sight and Tank was staring at her with a stern but thoughtful expression.

'How many people are supposed to be going with you on this thing?'

A sinking feeling hit Jai's stomach. *Don't let Pax be the one to change Tank's mind!* Riley already seemed to think the sun shone out of the bastard.

'There's six,' she said.

Tank nodded slowly. 'Make it seven and I'll consider it.'

'Seven?'

'Hire a guide.'

Riley's eyes widened. 'That'll make it way too expensive!'

'I'll cover it. Consider it your birthday present. A twenty-first should be special and I was wondering what I was going to get ya.'

'It would cost thousands! I already looked. How can you afford it?'

'Let me worry about that. Your lunch is getting cold.'

'He won't budge,' Riley complained as Jai let them into his house after work. 'How am I supposed to find a guide with this sort of notice?'

'That's what we're about to find out.' They walked into the kitchen, where his grandfather's carer was putting a casserole pot in the oven. 'Hi, Bev.'

Bev, a wiry woman in her late sixties with more energy than he had, closed the oven and smiled. 'Afternoon. How was work?'

'Okay. How's Pop?'

'He's got the footy on. He's had a good day, not so mad at the world as yesterday. Hi, Riley.'

'Hi.'

'There's mail on the counter for you.'

'Thanks.' A quick glance showed him they were bills so he chose to ignore them.

Bev drained her cup of coffee, then closed her crossword puzzle book and shoved it in her oversized handbag. Then she smiled, waiting.

'Thanks. Oh—um …' Jai dug into his pocket for his wallet and handed over some cash. 'Thanks. See you tomorrow.'

'See you then. I've left Evan some supper.'

Riley cracked the oven door open as Bev let herself out. 'Another casserole.'

'It's easy for him to swallow.' He walked into the lounge room. The thin, bedraggled form of his grandfather, Evan Wharton, sat on his favourite old recliner, staring at the commentators on the television. The buttons on his shirt were askew. 'Hi, Pop.'

Evan turned his head, nodded cheerfully. 'Jai.'

Jai stood perfectly still, a lump in his throat as emotion swamped him. Riley's hand on his shoulder helped him find his breath. 'Who's winning?' he asked casually.

'All over. Think I might go have my … thingamajig.'

'Your shower?'

'What I said, wasn't it?' Evan hoisted himself out of his chair. 'Would you get my nip of whiskey ready?'

'Okay.' Then as emotion overcame him: 'Love you.'

'Love you too, Jai,' Evan replied as though unsure what he was on about. 'Why don't you take that pretty girl of yours out? Got my dinner in the oven. Gonna have my whiskey with it and a sleep after my … thingamajig.'

Take Riley out? He'd be lucky to scrounge them up baked beans on toast, maybe some two-minute noodles. 'We're going to eat here. Let me know when you want your dinner and I'll sort it for you.' He stared after his grandfather as, humming, Evan limped towards the downstairs bathroom.

'He remembered your name,' Riley said. 'Hold on to that for a minute. Enjoy it.'

He nodded slowly. His grandfather's dementia had been getting worse with every mini stroke, and those moments of clarity were becoming fewer and further between. 'Yeah.' He wrapped his arms around her. 'Thanks.'

'For what?' she asked, linking her hands behind his back.

'For getting that.'

'Of course I get it. You love him. You're so good to him. I know it's hard. Lots of people wouldn't cope.'

'Lots of people wouldn't have coped with what Mum did to him, dumping me on him before I could even talk. I'm only doing what I need to do. Like he did. It's no big deal,' he muttered, embarrassed.

'And I'll talk to Dad about the money. You can't afford to lose any pay.'

He looked around. The house hadn't had a makeover since before he was born and it was about that long since they'd bought new furniture. Just paying the mortgage and keeping it running took most of his pay. The rest generally went on petrol and enough cheap groceries to get them through each week. Evan's care and medication wiped out the small pension he received. Whenever an appliance broke down it was a major disaster, so Jai had learnt how to tinker, to fix things. At least until it became impossible to get parts. But they survived. Just.

'I'll sort it,' he said. He still had some pride. 'Besides, you've already won a battle today. I'd stick with that.'

'Not unless we can find a guide, I haven't.'

'We will. Hey.' He put his hands on her shoulders and gave her a gentle shake, then smiled. 'Don't worry. Let's boot up the computer and get started.'

'Okay.' She kissed him lightly on the lips. 'You really are an amazing guy, Jai Wharton. I'm going to marry you one day.'

He never quite believed it but he never got sick of hearing it. He slid his arms around her waist and drew her closer. 'You're going to finish your degree.'

'Mmm hmm. And when I've found a perfect little school to teach at, you're going to get into TAFE and do that mechanics course you've wanted to do forever.' She lightly kissed his neck.

'And then we'll get that little house by the beach you've been dreaming about,' he murmured, kneading her hips with his fingers.

'And have a million kids.'

He drew his head away to stare down at her, amused. 'I thought it was two million.'

'Forgot.' She smiled. 'That's a lot. We should probably practise.' She slid her fingers under his shirt, the light rake of her nails making him shudder. Riley made everything bearable: his grandfather's cruel fate; his ex-con, arse-riding boss; Pax's bullying; the bills; and the house intent on falling down around him. She kept him grounded, kept him going. He gazed into her aquamarine eyes, and despite all of it, all the shit in his life, wondered how someone like him could possibly have gotten this lucky.

CHAPTER 5

Tess's horse shifted under her as it stretched down to graze. Its chomping accompanied the gentle stirring of the trees and the odd low rumble from one cow to another. She gave the glossy chestnut's neck an absent stroke and released the reins full length to allow the mare better access to the pasture. There was no rush. Around her, cows grazed peacefully, enjoying the sunshine. It was better, much better, to be out here than in the confines of her apartment. She'd slept through most of yesterday, and again, fitfully, during the early hours of this morning. So she'd risen early, struggling against her aching body. By lunchtime she'd been stir crazy and sick of well-meaning sympathy so she'd forced herself down to the stables and into the saddle.

It was an abnormally warm afternoon for a Central Highlands winter, a dramatic contrast to the freezing weather that had necessitated yesterday's mountain rescue. The changeable weather never ceased to amaze her and reminded her of what her father had taught her: *Never assume anything's predictable out here.* Murphy Atherton's words echoed in her mind as she looked over everything he'd achieved at Calico Mountain. The guesthouse, the stables, the sprawling paddocks.

He had been a practical man in many ways, and a tough one when it came to working the land, to building his own little empire. He'd turned a ramshackle inherited settler's hut on the wild edge of nowhere into a modest home. He'd married the love of his life. They'd planted vegetables, cleared paddocks, collected a few sheep at first, because they were cheaper than cattle. Every daylight hour—and many that weren't—had been for working. Dogged determination combined with a run or two of good luck had made the property viable, then seen it flourish.

The paddocks had been graced with several hundred fat, lazy cattle when the market crashed. Undeterred, Murphy had simply changed tack and plotted out a new course. He risked everything he'd built on a hefty bank loan and the guesthouse had been born. Locals had whispered that old Murph had finally lost his mind. But he'd turned his hand to tourism with the resolve he'd shown every other project and guests had come. He'd shared his love of the land with as many city dwellers as would grace his doors for the last two decades of his life. Nothing had slowed Murphy, until hard work had stopped his heart. Today would have been his seventieth birthday.

He'd raised his kids to respect the mountains, the climate, the conditions. To work with the land, not just on it, to appreciate it for what it was, and not take any of it for granted. His head for business had mostly passed to his eldest son, Connor, and his love of farming to Logan, the son he'd only known as his own for the last couple of years of his life. But Tess had inherited a decent enough helping of both, along with what some said was more than a generous scoop of her father's determination—or as Connor called it: block-headed stubbornness. She smiled as she thought about her brother and his new wife, Callie.

Both brothers were settled and happy. Marriage suited them, and their wives had quickly become more like real sisters than in-laws. A secret part of Tess wished for what they had, but she wasn't sure she was built for it. She'd skipped the whole teenage crush stage—had never fully understood the allure of imagining herself in love with rock stars or the hottest guy a grade or two ahead in school. She supposed she'd found it all just a bit … foolish. Perhaps it was the common sense she'd been raised to take pride in, or the demands of the land she'd worked for as long as she could remember. Maybe she'd simply been too wrapped up in horses and competing and, when she'd felt her feet itch, the wilderness adventures she'd indulged in. The land was her first love, the freedom of it, the challenge. Still, she and Aaron had something good, something promising. So maybe, just *maybe*, she could have it all.

Her mobile shrilled, breaking her reverie. A woman enquiring about a week-long hike, wanted to go immediately. No, not at this time of year, sorry. If she could wait until September, Tess would be happy to arrange it for her. She ended the call nicely though the woman wasn't happy. Taking two people out at that time of year wasn't worth the cold, wet and challenging conditions.

In the distance, the shuttle bus crawled to a stop in front of the rambling, two-storey timber guesthouse of Calico Lodge. A new load of tourists from one or more of the afternoon flights into Hobart. She should probably head back, see if Callie needed any assistance getting everyone checked in. Assuming she was allowed. Connor and Logan had been carrying on like the big brothers they were, fussing to the point of driving her crazy. Even Callie, who'd been doing more than her own fair share of fussing, felt sorry enough for Tess to chase them off more than once. Tess smiled again because she loved them, but being out on a horse in the fresh, cold air was better than any cup of tea or pillow behind her back.

She gingerly picked up the reins, arranging them loosely in her least damaged hand. 'Let's go, Flash.' The mare took one last cheeky dive at the grass before trotting off in the direction of the stables. Tess's body ached, complaining at the movement, but she ignored it, pressed on. She needed to work out the stiffness, get herself back to normal. There was too much to do.

She drew Flash up alongside the paddock gate and unlatched it, walked the mare through and closed it. Guest numbers traditionally dropped off in winter, though this year bookings were fuller than they had been for years. Her hiking business had started out as an extension of the day hikes they'd always offered at the lodge but had become so popular it was now a business in itself. Running it while helping out with the lodge was a near-impossible juggling act at times.

The sound of Logan's ute slowly approaching had her moving Flash off the drive and turning in the saddle. 'Hi.'

'Hi. How are you feeling?'

'I'm fine,' she assured him.

'Tess, it's a hell of an ordeal. You can tell the truth.'

'Okay, how's this: being out here on Flash has made me feel considerably less shitty than I was yesterday. Work for you?'

'Better. How are you riding with those cut-up hands?'

'It's Flash, Logan,' she scoffed. They both knew the mare was so well trained she didn't need to rely on rein control.

'Hmm,' he said. Then, 'Callie's looking for you at reception.'

'I'll put Flash away and head up.'

'Give her to me, Larissa will take care of her,' he said.

'Righto.' She slid carefully from the saddle to avoid the worst of the bruises, gathered up the reins and handed them to Logan through the open window. 'Make sure she gets some sugar.'

'You know what Larissa's like, she's more likely to give her diabetes than let her miss out.'

Tess gave the mare a pat before Logan crept the ute forward. 'Let's go, girl.'

'See ya,' Tess said as he drove off steadily, Flash following at a gentle trot. She turned for the guesthouse. The proud timber facade and wide verandas stood against a backdrop of stunning mountains and countryside. She walked up the steps through glass doors and into an inviting reception area with high ceilings, dual staircases and windows showcasing the mountains. She glanced left to the desk where Callie was checking in a guest. Another staff member was assisting. On Tess's right, guests enjoyed the large lounge with its twin fireplaces, comfy seating, tables and chairs. Books and magazines were scattered around, encouraging guests to relax. Enormous rugs covered the floors and led towards the bar, which offered everything from hot chocolate to fancy cocktails.

'Tess.' Callie tucked her red curls behind her ears as she ducked behind the desk to pick up a huge bouquet of pink and peach roses, alstroemeria and something green Tess couldn't name. 'Two things. First, these came for you.' Callie's smile became hesitant. 'Flowers from Charlie's family.'

Tess found herself holding her breath as she opened the card. It had crossed her mind they might blame her for the incident, even consider legal action. The card simply read, *Thank you for trying.*

'Oh, hell.' Tears instantly spiked as emotion choked her. She sucked in a steadying breath and pressed her fingers to her eyes, willing the tears back. She showed Callie the card.

'He would have pulled you both over. You know that,' Callie said gently.

'Yep.'

'And you tried your best to catch that hand anyway.'

And in last night's dreams, the worst of those dreams, she'd fallen with him. She sniffed. 'I'm okay.'

'Tess—'

'And second?' she cut in, because if Callie made one more sympathetic noise she'd lose it in front of all these people.

'Aaron is waiting for you in the bar.'

'Oh … thanks.' He'd wanted to see her yesterday, but she'd only wanted to sleep, to be alone, so she'd promised to call him today. She'd just needed the ride more than another dose of sympathy. 'Can you do something with these in reception?' she asked of the flowers. 'They're lovely, but if I have to look at them every time I go up to my apartment …'

'Sure.'

'Thanks.' She handed them back, then swiped at her eyes one last time and walked through the lounge. Aaron was seated at a table under one of the huge windows.

He got to his feet when he spotted her. 'How are you feeling?' he asked. He put his arms lightly around her. She felt the rise and fall of his chest before he let her go and smiled. 'You're up and about. That's good. Are you okay?'

'I'm getting there. You didn't need to come all the way out here. I would have called. I've just been—I wasn't quite ready to go over it all again. Sorry. Thanks for your help out there.'

'Where else would I have been?' He drew her over to sit down. 'I'm just so relieved you're alive.'

She sat down. 'So am I.'

The concern on his face was replaced by a trace of annoyance. 'You should never have done that. Risking your life for an idiot. You weren't set up for rescue.'

Again? she thought, instantly irritated. 'I know that! And if I'd have followed protocol he would have fallen before you got there. I had to try, and damn it—I got him down off that face! If that one last thing hadn't happened …' She pulled back when she heard her voice rise, threatening to crack. 'He would have been okay,' she continued more quietly. 'I couldn't just watch and wait. I know I should have, but I signed up to save people's lives, not watch people lose them.' Surely, she thought, Aaron could understand that?

'I hear what you're saying, but I trained you better than that. You need to keep your head out there,' he said, and covered her hands gently with his. 'Let's not fight. I don't agree with what you did, but I'm proud of you.'

Proud of her? If he was trying to be supportive, why did he sound so damn condescending? She set aside her resentment because she knew his words came out of concern. 'I got flowers from the family. I wouldn't have thought they'd be up to anything like that. There was a lovely message. They don't blame me.'

'No one blames you, Tess,' he said. 'You did more than anyone else would have. I spoke to the family—there's a lot of them. The sister would have sent those, I'd say. I told her what you did.'

'Oh. I didn't think to … I spoke to Charlie's friends. They called yesterday.'

'What did they have to say?'

She shrugged. 'Nothing new. They're devastated. Blaming themselves. Charlie put them in a couple of tricky situations over the years and they wanted to teach him a lesson. They didn't want him to die.'

'Of course not,' he said, then shifted in his chair, looking solemnly into her eyes. 'I wanted to tell you in person that Charlie's body has been located by chopper. I'm heading out with the team to bring it back shortly.'

'At least that's something,' she said softly. 'Better for the family to be able to bury him.'

'Unnecessary deaths are always very difficult. Why don't I come back tonight? Let me take care of you, take your mind off things.'

She considered it, but shook her head. Right or wrong, his lecture was still grating on her. 'Thanks, but I'm not very good company at present.'

'That doesn't matter.'

'It does to me. I need to be working.' She took a deep breath, released it with a smile that took some effort. 'Keeping busy. Then it'll be another early night.'

He looked like he was going to argue, his mouth a thin line of disapproval, but it widened into a smile as he looked over her head. 'Callie.'

'Hi, Aaron, sorry to interrupt. Tess, Jared's looking for you. I left him at reception in case you two needed a few more moments.'

'Oh, it's okay. We're done.'

'Jared?' Aaron snapped. 'As in Denham?'

'I guess he's following up on Charlie's death,' Tess said.

'Can he not just leave you alone? Surely you said everything that needed to be said.'

Surprised, Tess studied his face, wondering where the animosity had come from. Protectiveness, she decided. He wanted to distance her from the police follow-up. 'It's fine. I'm sure it's nothing to worry about.'

'I'll stay,' Aaron said. 'We'll talk to him together.'

'No,' she said more firmly than she'd meant to. 'But thanks. I'd feel better knowing you're out bringing Charlie back.'

His expression softened. 'Are you sure?'

She nodded. 'Yep.'

'Then I'll call back tomorrow.' He kissed her lightly.

'Sure. Great.' Tess saw Callie's brow lift in question before she led Aaron back out towards reception, conversing lightly.

Why did Jared need to see her again? Why couldn't Indy have spoken to her? She pressed a hand against the jump in her belly. She found Jared Denham intimidating. From their first dramatic encounter, with his blood all over her hands and his mind still on the job, she'd never quite shaken that larger-than-life heroic image she'd formed of him. Perhaps she'd even built on it, romanticised it in her mind over time to more than it had been.

She laughed at herself. *God, Tess. Cut it out.* She was an emotional disaster today. Perhaps she should have let Aaron stay. She dropped her head into her hands and gave herself a silent talking to. Aaron was so caring, so considerate. Why couldn't she just enjoy being taken care of?

She groaned quietly and dragged her fingers across her eyes. 'What is wrong with me?'

'Other than some impressive cuts and bruises, I would have thought absolutely nothing.'

She jerked her head up. Jared. He had a half-smile on his face, a glimmer of humour in his generally serious blue eyes. 'Sorry. I was just questioning my bitchy mood,' she said, clearing her throat.

'I'd cut myself a bit of slack if I were you.' He looked her over, making her all too aware of her untidy appearance.

'I wasn't deliberately keeping you waiting. Just needed a minute.'

'No problem. Actually, Callie was filling me in on her progress on the halfway house at Waldron Park.'

She smiled as she thought about Callie's beautiful family home. 'She wanted to help people suffering mental illness. Not hard to understand after what she went through.' Her smile dropped at the memory of what Callie's sister's mental illness had cost in terms of lives. 'She has a foundation running it and they're busy making the place the best it can be.'

'It's a good thing.'

In contrast to his easy tone, his eyes were sharp and probing, as though examining her every scrape and bruise. She shifted uncomfortably under the weight of it. 'So … is something wrong?'

'No. I just need you to sign this.' He took a folder from under his arm and handed her a copy of her statement. 'It somehow didn't get done when you were at the station.'

'Oh, right.' She grimaced as she straightened in her chair.

'I'm not going to ask how you're feeling,' he said with a grimace of his own.

'Really? Wow, you get the gold star. You have no idea how much I appreciate that.'

'Just self-preservation really. I've heard stories.'

The comment dragged a laugh out of her. God, it felt nice to laugh. 'Guilty. My ride this morning helped clear my head.'

'Shouldn't you be resting?'

She sent him a look that had him smirking. He lifted his hands in truce.

'I did that yesterday. Resting doesn't loosen me up.'

'And sitting around thinking about it doesn't help either,' he guessed more seriously.

'Would you mind telling everyone else that?' She took the document and signed it clumsily with her taped fingers. 'Here.'

'Thanks,' he said, and put it back in the folder.

Not sure what else to say, Tess got to her feet and walked with him back to reception. 'Thanks for coming,' she said when they reached the doorway. 'I'm sure Indy could have called in with it when she got home, saved you the trip.'

'Yeah, but I thought I should see how you were feeling.'

'You—why?'

'So I didn't need to ask.' He winked. 'See ya.'

Caught off guard, she managed a smile as she watched him walk out.

'He really is impressive,' Callie said, coming to stand beside her.

'Huh? Oh, Jared? He's a … nice guy.'

'Yeah, "nice guy" wasn't what was printed all over your expression just then,' Callie teased. 'Might Aaron's little possessive moment have been warranted?'

'Possessive?' Tess asked with surprise. 'He just wants to make sure I'm okay.'

'He doesn't like Jared,' Callie said. 'He sent him a dirty look as he was leaving.'

'I don't think Jared would care either way. He was just here to get a signature.'

'And to check up on you,' Callie said in a sing-song voice. 'I heard.'

Tess rolled her eyes and sighed. 'Cut it out.'

'So many big, strong heroes, so little time …' Callie taunted as she headed back to reception.

Hah, Tess thought with a roll of her eyes. Her phone alerted her that she had a message so she pulled it from her pocket. Aaron reminding her to rest. He was thinking about her, he was looking forward to seeing her tomorrow. He must have sent it from his car. She closed it, then pressed the photo gallery icon.

Charlie's smiling face appeared on screen. She stared at it, as she had so many times since arriving home, wondering if she should send it to his family. Not now, not yet. Maybe soon. She swiped at a tear working its way down her cheek, then another. God. She wasn't a crier. She didn't cry. But the tears just kept coming back. She walked out into the sunshine to clear her head.

Aaron's car was crawling down the long drive a few lengths behind Jared's. She frowned, wondering why it had taken him so long to get going. Had he been waiting for Jared to leave?

CHAPTER 6

'I'm sick of porridge,' Evan complained to Jai from his chair in the kitchen.

'I know, Pop. I bought you Weetbix.' Jai took another sip of his coffee and pulled the Weetbix out of the pantry.

There was a grunt. 'Weetbix sticks in my throat.'

Since when? Jai wondered, but didn't bother to argue. 'How about some toast then?'

'Sticks in my throat.'

'Okay … I'll cut you up some watermelon.'

'Don't like watermelon!' Evan snapped with a thump of his fist on the table.

Jai took a deep breath. Fruit was expensive, but when Pop was in a mood it was generally his only reliable go-to. 'Okay then.' He kept his tone cheerful, hoping that in five minutes Evan would forget his new dislike and watermelon would be his favourite again. 'Here, have some juice, eh?'

Bev walked in just as he put the full glass down. 'Morning!' she said brightly.

'I don't like juice!' Evan yelled. The glass and its contents flew across the room, catching Bev on the forehead with a sickening thud. She dropped like a stone, glass shattering around her. Evan got awkwardly to his feet and half stumbled, half stormed towards the lounge room.

'Bev! Are you all right?'

She was propped up against the kitchen counter, a dazed look on her face as blood poured freely from a cut above her eyebrow. Jai grabbed the only thing within reach—a tea towel—and scrunched it up. 'Hold this, I'll get something better,' he told her, then jumped to his feet and dug into the bottom drawer for the first aid kit. He wrenched it open, found some swabs, a soft bandage and sterile strips and crouched back down in front of her, hissing in a pained breath when he knelt on a shard of glass.

'Oh, love, I'm afraid I'm feeling a bit dizzy,' Bev murmured.

'Stay still, okay?' He retrieved a dustpan and broom and did his best to clear the glass before returning to Bev. Her hand dropped from where it had held the towel and it was clear from the gaping piece of skin she was going to need at least a couple of stitches. Her clothes were ruined and her eye was swelling.

'I'm so sorry,' he stammered. 'I'll … I'll get you some help.' He couldn't take her to the hospital because he couldn't leave his pop, so he called for an ambulance.

Half the street appeared out the front as the ambulance loaded Bev on board. Some who knew she looked after Evan watched Jai with judgemental eyes and hard expressions, as though this was somehow his fault. Stuff 'em, he thought miserably. Why should he care what they think? As soon as the ambulance pulled away he went back inside, away from the petty people in their pretty houses who had no clue how hard he was trying.

It wasn't until he was safely back in the privacy of his house that it occurred to him to wonder, what now? There was an agency he'd used on a few occasions when Bev couldn't make it, but they were more expensive. And he didn't like his chances of finding someone on the spot.

'Damn it!' He slapped his hands on the door and banged his head against it in frustration. It never stopped. Every time he thought it couldn't, it got worse. He couldn't afford not to work, but leaving his grandfather alone was unthinkable. He was likely to walk down the street naked and forget where he was, or break his neck trying to reach the locked liquor cabinet. Jai had paid Bev for the entire week; he wasn't going to get paid again until Friday and it wasn't like he had spare money floating around. If he used the grocery money he could afford a nurse for today. If he could get one. But then what? Maybe he could get Pop reassessed. He might be able to get the government-funded respite nurse an extra day or two a week. But that didn't help him today.

He got up and scrambled around in the top drawer for the respite company's card and called the number.

He got lucky. A nurse had a cancellation and would be there as soon as possible.

He was an hour and a half late when he finally pulled up outside work. Evan hadn't had that particular nurse before and there were routines and medications to explain before he could leave his grandfather with a stranger—trained or not. He knew it was going to cost more for the nurse for the day than he was going to get paid for his. Did he really need the car? That would get him a couple of grand. Maybe. But then how would he get Pop to the doctors?

'You're late!' Tank barked from the counter.

'Sorry, boss. I had to—'

'Getting a bit sick of hearing that, Jai.'

The anger Jai had managed to swallow back earlier rose from his chest to the back of his throat. 'Whatever,' he muttered and walked past him to put his coat and keys in the office.

'I'm sure I can find someone else if you don't want to be here,' Tank continued.

It was just too much. Jai needed help, not a lecture. It wasn't like he'd been out partying. He tossed his jacket and keys on the office desk, chest heaving with raw emotion. 'So fire me then!' he snapped, coming back into the shop. 'You say you respect what I'm doing for Pop, but you don't give a shit what that means!' He stormed out the back, took some ragged breaths and stared at the sky, then punched the wall, hard. His knuckles detonated with pain and tears spiked behind his eyes.

'Bad morning?'

'Damn it!' It burst from his mouth like an explosion. Pax was the last thing he needed. He spun, threw his arms out in invitation. 'You want to have a go too, huh?' When Pax chewed on a grin Jai shoved him back, almost hoping for the punch.

'Whoa,' Pax said in a tone that almost hinted at admiration. 'What's up, pencil dick?'

'Nothing a few grand wouldn't fix,' Jai muttered as he stalked away. He was going to have to apologise to Tank, but he just wasn't sure he could do it yet.

'Hold up.'

'Why?' Jai demanded, hand on the door. 'What could you possibly want?' If Pax didn't stop laughing at him he was going to risk it and thump him.

'Ya grandfather's some kind of psycho, right?'

His fingers curled back into fists. 'What did you call him?'

'I've got to say, this you is an improvement.' Pax took out his cigarettes and lit one. 'Riley mentioned you were taking care of him. Dementia or something, yeah?'

'Yeah, and he took out his carer this morning, so I'm stuffed.' Jai turned around again, fell back against the door and leant heavily on it. 'I'm sure that's made your day.'

Pax slowly nodded, considering something. 'I reckon I might be able to help ya out.' He stuck his cigarette in his mouth long enough to pull his wallet from his back pocket. He sorted through some notes, pulled a wad out and shoved it towards him. 'Take it.'

Jai looked at Pax blankly. 'What?'

'I said take it.'

Jai watched the cigarette burning between the man's fingers as he held out the cash, and hesitantly lifted his hand. Pax smacked the notes into it, ash sprinkling Jai's palm.

'When you're finished feeling sorry for yourself, come and talk to me. There's plenty more where that came from.'

Jai looked at the pile of fifties. 'More than this? Then why'd you pinch …'

'Just wanted to stir ya up.' Pax grinned and slapped him on the back. 'Like I said, come talk to me. I'll get ya out of trouble.'

Plenty more where that came from. I'll get ya out of trouble. The conversation stuck in Jai's head for the rest of the week. It was more likely Pax would get him into trouble, he thought as he rearranged stock on shelves on Friday afternoon. But Pax had handed over five hundred bucks—enough to pay the agency carer for the rest of the week. He didn't want to think about what that meant, because people like Pax didn't do things out of the kindness of their hearts. There had to be another way. But what? Jai had gotten through this week, but he had no clue how he was going to get through the next one.

'Hey, Jai!' Brock called as he came through the door with his girlfriend and Riley. Brock was a good mate, but they were polar opposites. Brock was fast, strong and ridiculously talented at anything to do with sport, and Jai had spent most of his high school years wishing they could trade places. The new girlfriend, Jasmin, was hot. If Jai hadn't been completely in love with Riley, he would have been wildly jealous. Jas reminded him of a Barbie doll, pretty and feminine, with long blonde hair and big blue eyes, though some of the stuff that came out of her mouth annoyed him. Like last week, when she'd tried to convince everyone she remembered a past life, or the month before when she'd decided her car was haunted. She was a bit loony sometimes.

'What are you guys all doing here?'

'Riley and I finished uni at the same time, and Jasmin has a day off,' Brock said. 'So we thought we should look at what we're going to need on this hike we're supposed to be doing. You in?'

'Not the hike we're *supposed to be doing*,' Riley said, 'the hike we *are* doing.' Then her face lit up as she shared her news with Jai. 'One of the guides we emailed got back to us. He's going to take us!'

He smiled, pulling her in for a hug. 'That's great news! Told you it would work out.'

'Is there a party I don't know about?' Pax asked. The guy had an annoying habit of turning up whenever anything was happening. It was the only time he bothered to be in the shop.

Jai noticed Jasmin's eyes widen with appreciation. What did the girls all see in him, anyway? 'No,' he said, then felt like an idiot. It was pretty obvious there was no pawn shop party going on.

'Shame,' Pax said, looking Jasmin up and down. 'Gonna introduce us?'

'I'm Jasmin,' she said before Jai could open his mouth. 'And you are?'

'This is Pax,' Riley said. 'He works for Dad.'

'Nice to meet ya,' Pax said.

'I didn't know Jai had a hot friend,' Jasmin muttered sideways to Riley but with a coy smile entirely for Pax.

Riley bumped Jasmin's hip with her own and shot a telling look towards Brock. 'You're *dating* Jai's hot friend, Jas.'

'Yeah, remember me?' Brock said, peeved.

'Just being friendly,' Jasmin said with a shrug. But her eyes remained on Pax longer than they needed to.

Brock put a proprietorial arm over Jasmin's shoulders and stared hard at Pax. 'We should get going. We have a hike to prepare for.'

The door chimed and Jai spotted Bev's daughter Karen coming through the door. His stomach lurched. 'Why don't you guys go on ahead? I'll catch up.'

Riley hesitated, but looked from Jai to Karen and nodded in understanding. 'Okay, see you at Kathmandu in about fifteen?'

He nodded. 'See you there.' Then to Karen he said, 'Hi.'

Karen's smile seemed genuine enough. 'Hi, Jai. I thought I'd call in, let you know Mum's doing better. The stitches are healing quite well.'

Relief flooded through him. 'I'm so sorry. Pop was having a bad morning and it was bad timing. He wasn't throwing the glass at her, he was just throwing it. Do you think she'll be right to come back soon?'

The woman's smile fell. 'About that,' she began, and the sick feeling returned to Jai's stomach. 'Mum's very fond of Evan, but she said he's been getting worse. This is not the first time he's hurt her. He pushed her over a couple of weeks ago, did she tell you? Got himself into a state and thought she was his long-dead sister tormenting him.'

'Yeah, I knew,' he admitted. 'I didn't realise he hurt her though.'

'Bruised her arms, knocked her hip—not that she wanted to worry you. Jai, she wants to help and the cash is handy, but Mum's getting older and she doesn't have his strength. He needs someone younger, fitter and better trained.'

He felt himself starting to sweat. 'Karen, please. I'll talk to the doctor about his medication. Anything you like. I need someone with him. I can't work and—'

'Mum said there's a respite company in town. They can send staff out who are much more qualified than she is. They have a whole team of nurses.'

'Yeah, I know. I do use them when I have to, and they're very good. But …' He trailed off when he saw the look on her face. What was the point? Karen wasn't going to budge. 'I understand. Tell Bev I hope she feels better soon.'

'I will.'

He watched her walk away. That was it. He was going to have to sell the car, maybe try and work two jobs. If he could get another one. He'd left school early and wasn't qualified at anything. Five minutes ago he'd been stupid enough to have been dreaming about new hiking clothes. 'Idiot,' he muttered to himself.

'You're in the brown two-storey on the corner, three streets down, right?' Pax asked from behind him.

Jai turned, wondering how much of the conversation Pax had heard. 'How'd you know?'

'Tomorrow night. I'll pick ya up at midnight.'

Warning bells clanged in Jai's head. 'What for?'

Pax's grin just got bigger. 'To have some fun. Trust me.'

Trust him? Jai almost laughed, thought he probably shouldn't. 'What kind of fun?'

'The best.' Pax thumped him on the back. 'The kind where ya get some cash in ya pocket.'

Without waiting for a reply, Pax disappeared back through the shelves.

CHAPTER 7

Tess slipped out of bed and headed for the bathroom. She didn't bother with her robe, she'd always been comfortable in her own skin. The unresolved ache Aaron had left her with made her restless enough to move with purpose. She slid the door closed and turned on the hot water. It cascaded over her, its warmth seeping into her skin. The bruising from the accident was slowly taking on more of a yellow tinge and the cuts and abrasions were close to healed. The fingernails she'd ripped so badly would take longer to recover, and the memories longer to dull.

She sighed heavily. It wasn't that the sex with Aaron was bad, exactly. But the only earth-shattering finale—as usual—had been his. Maybe that would improve with time. They'd work on it. Sex wasn't the be all and end all of a relationship, was it? She was probably still a little uptight about his reaction to the accident, because although he was right and protocol was there for a reason, she'd thought he'd be a bit more understanding. Then she'd tackled him over his late departure behind Jared last week, and he'd told her he'd been caught up on a business call as he was leaving. The perfectly reasonable excuse had left her feeling petty for asking. She wasn't back to her old self yet, that was all it was. Things would return to normal. Things would get better.

When she came out again, Aaron was propped on one elbow with a satisfied smile on his face, watching her. She'd hoped he would have gotten himself up. He hadn't spent an entire night yet but he was pushing for it and she wasn't sure she was ready to go there.

'Even all bruised up you're so freaking hot, Tess.'

She snatched her robe from the end of the bed and swung it around her shoulders, pushing her arms into the sleeves as she went past him to the kitchen and flicked on the kettle. 'Want a tea?'

He came over to stand behind her as she retrieved her favourite mug. 'Nope.' He kissed her collarbone, working his way up to her jawline. 'You smell so good.'

'My new body wash. The water is still hot if you want a turn,' she said.

'I had something else in mind.' His hands slid over her as he pressed himself against the small of her back. 'Want to go again?'

Despite her frustration, she really didn't. 'I'm pretty tired, Aaron. I took a guided hike out to Mount Field today and the guys were super fit. I had to push myself to go at their pace.'

There was a brief silence. She could almost see his brow furrowing in disapproval as she got a tea bag and popped it into her mug.

'I thought you were going to take a break from all that for a couple more weeks.'

'I'm actually feeling pretty much back to normal,' she said. 'Besides, it was booked. I thought a few hours in the national park would be good for me. Are you sure you don't want a tea?'

'No, thanks.' He began massaging her neck. 'You know, you should really be careful who you go out there with. We already know young men don't always think they have to listen to a woman. You also need to consider that they might be tempted to take advantage.'

God, really? 'I can take care of myself.'

He turned her around and drew the hair back from her face to stare at her with what she thought of as his serious expression. 'Everyone thinks that until they can't. That's some serious wilderness you head off into alone with strangers.'

'The wilderness is the whole point,' she said with a smile. She linked her arms around his waist. 'That's what people pay me for. You do it.'

Whatever temper that had simmered in his voice disappeared as he placed a light kiss on her nose. 'But I'm not a beautiful young woman.'

'No, you're definitely not,' she said, letting go of her growing edginess.

A grin slid onto his face as he pulled her back against him. 'Let me prove it.'

Tess wasn't sure he'd really proved much at all. As she stood in the stables the following morning, stroking a brush over her mare's glowing coat, she wondered again if the fault was with him or with her. Perhaps they wouldn't ever be a good match in that department. And then there was the discussion about how she ran her hiking business. They didn't seem to be on the same page with that, either. She'd turned Aaron's words over and over in her head. Could he have a point? After the accident at Fedder, she was beginning to question her competence and decisions. It was an uncomfortable track to walk.

She unzipped her jacket as she began to warm. The day was shaping up to be clear and cold, perfect for the ride she and Indy had planned. Tess was looking forward to it, but she couldn't quite shake her mood.

'You're very broody this morning,' Indy said, grooming her own mount. 'You sure you're up to this?'

'Feeling better every day.'

'Physically maybe, but the emotional stuff might take longer to get over.'

Tess stopped brushing. Huffed. 'It's not the accident—it's Aaron. He doesn't think I should take groups of male hikers out into the park.'

'What? Why? Because of Charlie?'

'Not entirely, though my ability to control a group of young men came into it. He's worried some of them might be tempted to take advantage of the situation.' She dropped the brush into the grooming bucket and picked up another to remove the knots from Flash's tail.

'Are you worried?' Indy asked, jumping straight into cop mode. 'Did something else happen out there?'

'Huh? No. *No.* Nothing like that has ever happened.'

'So what's the problem?'

Tess shrugged. 'It's more of a "just in case". It never even occurred to me. Perhaps it should have. It's annoying me.'

'He certainly seems to have a lot of opinions on what you should and shouldn't be doing.' Indy stroked the brush over her mare's dappled coat several more times before asking, 'What did you say to him?'

'I told him I could take care of myself. And before you ask, he told me that's what everyone thinks, until they find out they can't. Maybe he has a point.'

Indy's expression became doubtful. 'The Tess I know doesn't let anyone tell her what she can and can't do.'

'Which is a big reason why my relationships don't work,' she said, frustrated. 'I'm used to doing things my way. I always have. And I don't like being told what to do. I never have. But I nearly got myself killed. So … I don't know.'

'Yeah, you did. And I would never suggest I'm comfortable with you risking your life like that, but the fact is, you think you feel bad now? Just imagine how you'd feel if Charlie had died and you *hadn't* tried to save him. Hadn't done a thing to help. Logan has seen me risk my life more than once while doing my job and it terrifies him. You don't think he wants to keep me safe? But he's never once asked me to stop, never questioned my need to do it or told me what I can and can't do. He knows it's who I am, and he loves me enough not to try and change me. That's why we work.'

'Trying to figure out how much compromise needs to be involved in this relationship deal is driving me nuts. But Aaron's a good guy, Indy. I think he's worth it.'

'Hmm … I hear doubts creeping in,' Indy teased, then smiled wickedly. 'How's the sex?'

Tess hesitated, then shrugged. 'It's okay.'

Indy pulled a horrified face. 'Call it quits. Now.'

Tess grinned at that. 'I've decided we need to work at it.'

'You're—what? A month into this relationship? This is supposed to be the fun part.'

'But that so-called fun part wears off, right? Then you're left with the rest of it. That's what you're supposed to worry about. The forever part.'

Indy shook her head in disgust. 'Sometimes you're too practical for your own good.'

'I'm thirty years old and looking for a life partner not my next crush. Except I don't feel very adult. I think I'm actually sulking.'

'He's treating you like a child, so maybe that's appropriate.'

Tess dropped the brush back into the grooming kit. 'I'll talk to him about it. Come on. Let's get saddled up or we'll never get our ride in.'

'And then you're going to help me vaccinate and drench Monte, remember?'

'Yeah. Is that before or after you fix the mower and I work those breakers Logan's too busy getting ready for his campdraft to get worked?'

'How are you riding breakers today? I can see how stiff you still are.'

'Riding's helping with that.'

'Lucky,' Indy said, heading to the tack room for her saddle. 'Got to love our lazy days off.'

They rode up onto the mountain trails, raced along stretches of the colourful, heath-covered ground that bordered Mount Field National Park and ambled along steeper, heavily wooded areas complete with crystal-clear streams, tree ferns and towering swamp gums. They were riding back down to the stables before they'd spent half as much time up there as Tess would have liked.

'Rory needed this,' Indy said, pulling her big brown mare up next to Tess's as they dismounted. 'She hasn't been up on the trails for weeks. And it's fun, riding together.'

'We rarely hit a day off at the same time,' Tess said. 'You want to put the girls away and do Monte now?'

'May as well.' They glanced up as Aaron's car crawled to a stop. 'Unless someone else has other ideas.'

'Shut up,' Tess murmured, rolling her lips together so she didn't grin.

'Tess, there you are!' Aaron said, climbing out of his Prado. 'I thought you said you had the day off.'

'I do. Sort of. I just have to ride a couple of horses for Logan and help Indy—'

'I've been calling you.'

'Oh, sorry. I left my phone at the stables. What's up?'

His mouth twisted in exasperation. 'I'd planned to take you out. You've had a rough few days. I wanted to spoil you.'

'Sorry,' she said again. 'You should have lined it up with me.' Some of the irritation left his face as she put her arms around his waist and dropped her head back to smile apologetically.

'Doesn't matter.' Then he dropped a kiss on her forehead and bundled her close under his arm. 'And sorry for snapping. I was worried when I couldn't get hold of you. Are you free now?'

'Not quite,' Indy said. 'We still have a couple of things to do. Hi, Aaron.'

'Hi, Indy. Enjoy your ride?'

'We did.'

He beamed at Tess. 'You do what you need to do. Then how about we go out to dinner tonight?'

'Sounds perfect.'

Indy didn't say much as they got the equipment together and headed for Monte's yard, but Tess could almost hear her thinking. 'What?' she asked eventually.

'He's quite possessive, isn't he?'

'You too? Callie said the same thing.'

'It's something to think about. Some women like being smothered in attention. Others prefer their own space.'

'I thought we were supposed to want to be in each other's pockets at this stage. Are you sure you don't want to run Monte across to the crush?'

'For one little jab and a pour on? Nah. He'll be fine.'

Monte walked to the fence when he saw them coming and called out in greeting. Indy's hand-raised baby might be close to half a tonne but he didn't know it.

'I suppose you want me to do it so you can remain his favourite person?' Tess asked Indy.

'I'll always be his favourite person,' Indy said with a grin. 'But yes, please. I feel horrible jabbing him.'

They went into his yard and Indy gave him a scratch. 'Hi, bud.' Monte rubbed his head into her chest with enough force to send her back a step, then licked her arm. 'Sook,' she crooned.

'Spoilt brat, more like,' Tess teased. She reached up high on his neck and quickly injected the vaccine. As a surprised Monte stepped sideways, away from the short, sharp sting, one hoof landed squarely on Indy's toe.

'Ouch! Monte, get off!' Indy shoved at the steer, who took some convincing to move before burying his enormous head back into her chest for another rub. Despite the look on her face and the words being muttered under her breath, Indy hugged him before hopping to the fence and clutching her foot.

'Are you okay?' Tess dropped the used needle into the box and closed the lid.

'I am. My foot, however …'

'Steel-capped boots,' Tess reminded her with a pained expression. 'And the cattle crush. Both were designed for good reason.'

'I thought my riding boots would be fine. He wasn't being naughty, exactly. It was just bad foot placement.'

Tess laughed at that. 'Yours or his?' She helped Indy through the gate, where Indy pulled off her boot and sock with a relieved sigh. Tess cringed. Indy's big toe was already turning purple. 'We'd better get some ice on that. We'll leave the drenching for later.'

'It's not that bad,' Indy grumbled, and limped to the ute. When they were buckled in she said, 'Guesthouse. Bar. I need a cold drink as much as that ice.'

'All right.' Tess parked in the staff carpark and walked Indy slowly up the steps through the side entrance, a shorter walk to the bar. The area was only sparsely dotted with guests at this time of the day, so they sat by the window in the corner. 'Wait here.'

She asked Callie to get Indy an ice pack, then went behind the bar to get them a jug of lemon squash and some glasses.

'Here you go,' Callie said.

'Thanks,' Indy said and gently placed the ice on her toe, grimacing. 'Stupid big baby he is.'

'You think it's broken?'

'Looks like it,' Tess said.

'I'll tape it up, it'll get better,' Indy said. Then to Callie, she said, 'Monte hasn't been through a crush in his life. He'd stress more about that than the injection.'

'Yet you don't seem to have told him climbing into your lap is no longer an option.'

Indy grinned into her glass. 'He didn't mean it.'

Logan walked in and pulled a chair next to his wife before leaning forward and lifting the ice pack to examine her toe. 'Ow. Tess getting too much sympathy, was she?'

Indy slapped at him playfully. 'Monte was being a sook.'

'Anyone for steak?'

'Not funny.'

Logan smiled. 'Put the ice back on.'

She did so reluctantly. 'What are you doing here? Aren't you supposed to be packing for the campdraft?'

'On my way back to the house. Spotted you limping in.'

'Thank you.' She kissed him briefly. 'Go pack. I'm fine.'

'It's so easy with you two,' Tess complained as Logan headed out again.

'Easy? Mostly it is. We drive each other nuts occasionally, have the rare but sensational argument, disagree from time to time. But mostly, yeah, it's better than easy. It's amazing.'

'Hmm.'

'Is this about Aaron?' Callie asked.

'He's telling her what to do.'

Callie's brow lifted. 'And you're what? Listening? Wow, must be love!'

'I'm not so sure,' Tess said. 'I'd like it to be but …'

'Well, that's easy. Does he tie you up in knots?' Callie asked breathily. 'Make you pine for him when he's not around?'

'Think about him when you're supposed to be thinking about other things?' Indy continued sweetly. 'Make you weak when he looks at you a certain way?'

'Okay, stop.' Tess laughed. It sounded as though they were just getting warmed up. 'My life is not a cliché. That stuff is all exaggerated rubbish.'

'She can't be serious?' Callie asked Indy.

'Miss Practicality, over here? Don't be so sure. Logan told me once that Murphy Atherton took one look at Rosalie and decided that as she had a strong constitution, a good face and knew how to brand a steer, she'd do. So, who do you think this one takes after?'

'Oh, rubbish,' Tess scoffed. 'Dad was head over heels for Mum.'

'Yeah, but unless your brother is lying, that was how he did the looking. You're doing the same thing. What did you say before? Compatible, solid, dependable?'

'Do you ever forget anything?'

'Not in my line of work.' Then to Callie, she said, 'And the sex is no good.'

'Would you shut up?' Tess said with another laugh as she checked to make sure no one had heard.

Callie shook her head. 'Tess, you have a whole family of solid and dependable people around you. You can afford to fall head over heels for someone, practical or not. When I first came down here, I was never going near a man again and then Connor walked into the staff room and every cell in my body just about—'

'Okay! Seriously! Stop! I don't want to hear about my brothers' love lives. To be honest, it sounds a bit flaky. I don't think it's in me.'

Callie's eyes danced. 'I'm tempted to say you could very easily have come across as flaky the way you looked at Jared the other day.'

'Jared?' Indy asked. Then she said with a secretive smile, 'Interesting.'

'Oh, please, would you drop that?' Tess begged Callie.

'What time is dinner with Aaron?' Indy asked.

'You know what? I didn't ask. I'll find out.' She opened her phone and frowned. 'Hey, he really did try to call me. Like, twenty times.'

'Hmm,' was all Indy said.

Tess got to her feet, not wanting to analyse the number of missed calls because it really was a bit over the top. 'You rest that toe. I'd better go get Logan's horses worked.'

CHAPTER 8

Jai paced the small space of his kitchen, chewing his fingernails. Pax had said he'd pick him up at midnight to have some fun and put some cash in his pocket. It was already midnight, wasn't it? Why hadn't he said no right there and then? He should have backed out while he had the chance. This wasn't going to be good. He wanted to believe that whatever Pax had planned was somehow legal, but he wasn't naïve enough for that. If he'd had a phone number for Pax he would have called it and stumbled through an excuse. Everything was telling him not to go through with it. But he'd booked Pop's agency carer for next week and had no idea how he was going to pay for it. None. And the week after that there'd be another bill, and another, and the damn hike—he needed stuff for that. He had to do something. And that was why, deep down, under all the excuses that he should have, could have, would have gotten out of this, he hadn't.

He checked on Evan and found him snoring soundly in bed. Going out with Pax was risky on more than one count. Jai had given his grandfather just a touch more whiskey than usual so he was almost certain to sleep through. But what if he didn't? What if he woke up and did something stupid?

Light outside caught his attention, so he went back to the kitchen window and peered through. Pax had pulled up.

Shit. Jai's stomach sank. He didn't break the law. He never broke the law. What was he doing? He scratched at his back where nervous sweat was running from the base of his neck and seriously considered hiding in the house, pretending he wasn't here.

I need the money, he reminded himself. Whatever this is I have to pay for Pop's care. He slowed his breathing, fought down the nerves bouncing in his stomach. He could do this, because he had to. Before he could change his mind, he grabbed his jumper and stepped outside, quietly locking the door behind him.

'Hop in,' Pax said. 'Hurry up.'

Jai walked around to the passenger side and slid in. Pax was dressed completely in black: jeans, jumper, jacket. Scrunched together in the centre console were what looked like a beanie and a pair of gloves.

He barely had the door closed before Pax edged back out onto the road. 'Any reason ya decided on a white shirt?'

'I have a dark jumper,' Jai said. 'I don't know what we're doing.'

Pax tossed him a sideways glare. 'Shit, man. Ya can't be that stupid. We're not packing shelves at Woolies.' The car abruptly pulled over. 'Ya want to go home?' he asked, as though reading Jai's mind. 'Back to Grandpa?'

'What?'

'I don't have time to help out a gutless wonder that wants cash for nothing. Ya can go home and cry poor me, or ya can make some serious money. But make up ya fucking mind. Now.'

'I—I just can't afford to get caught,' Jai said more bravely than he felt. 'Pop needs taking care of.'

'Fuck me! Pop, Pop, Pop! Can't you just dump him in a home or something?'

Dump him in a home? 'It's not that simple. They cost so much money and there's never enough beds—'

'Would ya shut up?' Pax snapped in frustration. 'I don't care. I couldn't give a flying fuck. I just need to know if you're in or out.'

'Yeah, yeah, I'm in.'

Pax jerked his head in a nod. 'Ya do what I say, when I say and it'll be sweet. Easy money for Pop or whatever ya want, got it?'

'Okay.'

They drove for a few more minutes, through some gates and down a couple of dimly lit streets. Then Pax pulled the car up behind a shed on the side of a small road. 'Let's go,' he said, and climbed out of the car. 'Close the door quietly.'

Jai took a moment to pull himself together then stepped out, looking around. 'Where are we?'

'At the uni.'

'Why?'

'Plenty of ways in and out, plenty of cover. Here.' He opened the back door and took out a backpack, tossed it at Jai. 'Take this.'

Jai slipped it on as Pax took out another for himself.

They cut through the campus, joined back up with the road and followed it out towards a row of homes by the waterfront. The house Pax stopped at looked modest but well kept, with a tidy front yard and a white picket fence. A light was on somewhere inside.

'How do you know no one's home?' he whispered urgently.

'I know the owner, saw her at the club just before I picked ya up. Let's go round the back. I made sure the laundry door wouldn't lock.'

'But what if the chick comes back?'

'I'll deal with it. Relax.' Pax wandered casually past the house, looked around, then quickly ducked through the front yard to the side gate. Nerves bouncing in his stomach, Jai followed suit.

'Where are my gloves?' he asked when Pax opened the door.

'Ya won't need them. Come on.'

Jai had never broken in to a house before, but he thought it should be done a lot more quietly and carefully. Pax just didn't seem cautious enough—he headed straight through the house like he owned it and stopped in an untidy bedroom full of a woman's things.

Uncomfortable, Jai kept watch by the window as Pax took some jewellery from a drawer by the bed before rifling through more drawers, tossing the woman's things all over her floor.

'Go through the wardrobe,' he ordered. 'Check the shoes, socks, boxes. Ya never know what people hide where.'

He used a sock Pax had chucked to open the wardrobe door and pulled clothes off the racks. The woman had some nice stuff. He spotted a dress that looked about Riley's size, discarded the idea of taking it. He wasn't sure the feeling in his gut was all nerves. A large chunk of it felt suspiciously like guilt. Then he realised something. 'Hey, half the stuff in here is guys' stuff.'

'Yeah. The husband's overseas. Ya found anything?'

'Nah.' Jai kept searching, picked up a sock, felt the weight of it. He shoved his hand in, pulled out a large roll of money and several little bags of white powder. 'Hey, wow.'

'You found it. Excellent.' Pax pounced on the powder, shoving it in his bag.

'You knew this was here?'

'Somewhere, yeah. You keep the cash.'

'What—all of it?' Jai asked, astounded.

'Yep.' Pax looked around. 'I think we're done here. We should check out the other rooms then head off.'

Jai shoved the cash into his bag and followed Pax into a small study. A computer sat on a desk at one end of the room, a chair pushed neatly underneath it. There were a couple of photos on the wall of a pretty blonde with a broad-chested, shaven-headed man wearing camo gear. Jai was relieved to know the guy was somewhere far, far away.

'Come on, help!' Pax said, as he rifled through the desk drawers.

Jai opened a few plastic containers that were stacked in the corner of the room, found only paperwork in the first, spare bedding in another. 'You didn't tell me the chick was a drug dealer.'

Pax shrugged. 'Low-level shit. Nothing big.' Pax went to the display cabinet on the wall behind them. Jai hadn't seen it at first, but now his eyes widened in surprise.

'That's a lot of weapons.'

'Pretty impressive, huh? Husband's collection. Like any?' Pax opened the cabinet, chose a couple of small folding knives and shoved them in his bag.

'Nah.' Headlights swept through the hall, sending a spear of panic through his system. 'Hey! I think she's home!'

Pax went down the hall, came back. 'Yep. Taxi. Grab that knife with the bone handle for me before we go.'

Trembling with the need to escape, Jai scanned the shelf, found the knife and snatched it, then dropped it into the bag Pax held open. 'She's going to catch us. Shit. I can't get caught!'

'Calm the fuck down,' Pax said, as though they had all the time in the world, though he was moving quickly. 'Follow me.' They walked quietly through the house to the back door. As Pax closed the laundry door, Jai heard the front door open.

'She's gonna know we've been in there,' he whispered. 'What do we do?'

Pax crouched low in the shrubbery. 'You can run right out in front of that taxi if ya like, or you can keep it together for another few seconds so we can get out of this without being spotted.'

Sweating and trembling, Jai waited next to Pax while the taxi driver fiddled around in his cab. Lights were coming on all over the house, one by one. *She knows. She's calling the cops.* Why had he let himself get caught up in this? He knew it was a bad idea. Why didn't the damn driver leave? They were going to get caught.

'Okay, he's going,' Pax whispered. 'Ya ready?'

The fear was so great Jai couldn't speak, so he just nodded, and when the cab pulled away, he sprang up after Pax. He wanted to run, to bolt. But Pax dragged off his gloves and beanie, and walked with a purposeful yet relaxed stride.

Jai forced himself to keep pace, all the while imagining the police would turn up, but they got back to the car without any trouble. Once inside, he closed his eyes and took a long, relieved breath. When he opened them, Pax was grinning at him.

'What?'

'Ya fucking did it, pencil dick. I thought you'd bail for sure.'

He pulled the wad of cash out of his pack and stared at it. 'You weren't bullshitting me, were you? I can keep this?'

'All yours, mate.'

Mate? What happened to pencil dick? Jai undid the elastic band and carefully counted out almost two thousand dollars. His heart leapt and some of the weight of the last couple of weeks lifted. He bound it back up and put it away, not quite keeping the smile off his face. The guilt was still there, but it was overtaken by tear-jerking relief. He would have had to work a month for that. And it wasn't for him, it was for Pop. He needed it more than some drug dealer. Just for a little while, he wouldn't have to stress.

CHAPTER 9

Jared took one look at Indy as she entered the station's meeting room on Monday morning and made her a coffee. 'You're in early. What have you done?'

'It's nothing.' Indy limped over to a chair and sat down. 'Did you hear there was another break-in over the weekend? Owner came home in the early hours of Sunday morning and called it in.' She dragged out the chair next to hers and put her foot up on it. 'Four break-ins in six weeks, same night of the week, same area, same method of entry, same goods targeted.'

'Same thief …'

'And if so, I think Ruby could be right about how he's picking houses. I showed our latest victim, Caitlin Tilley, the sketch we got from Ruby and she said it looks like the guy she took home last week, only she remembers him having a small scar at the left side of his mouth, so it's been added.'

He looked at the sketch pinned to one of the boards. There were other images too, stolen goods, houses, a map with a large red radius and thumbtacks pinned within it.

'So, he's targeting single females. Picking them up, getting them to take him home, scoping out the houses before coming back, taking whatever he wants.'

'You can take out the single,' Indy said. 'Caitlin Tilley's married. Husband's away with the military. She's lonely … blah, blah.'

'Right. I'm guessing she doesn't want her hubby checking out the police report. We should ask the other victims if something similar has occurred.'

'I'll get Emily on it this morning.'

'I don't suppose he gave Tilley a name?'

'He said he thought it would be more fun if they remained anonymous. Joked that it was less likely a jealous husband would come looking for him.'

'Can't call him stupid.'

'We'll need to get that sketch out to all the clubs, get the staff to keep a lookout for him.'

'Right. It's good to finally be getting somewhere.'

'Actually, there are yet more upsides to this latest robbery. This time we might have a print. Side gate. And while our POI helped himself to the usual—jewellery and cash—he also pinched some knives from a collection belonging to the husband. Some of them are pretty rare and one of them is a one-of-a-kind Damascus folding knife. Very distinctive.'

'I revise my view on his intelligence. Must be getting cocky. Do we have a photo of it?'

'Yep.' She pointed to the board behind her. 'White one, bone handle.'

He took it down. 'I'll show it to local pawn shops, check Ebay, Gumtree, anywhere he might try to sell it.'

'Hopefully something will come back on that print. It'd be nice to make an arrest on this today. Wouldn't that be something?'

'I love that you still believe everything can fall into place that easily,' he said. 'And now that you've told me all that, want to tell me why you're hobbling around?'

She sighed impatiently. 'Monte stood on my foot.'

It took a moment before what she was talking about clicked. 'Monte your cow?'

'Monte my steer, yes. My big uncoordinated overgrown calf more like it. I think he's broken my damn toe.'

'I thought he was friendly.'

'Too friendly. No idea of personal space. My darling husband seemed to think I was after some attention because Tess is copping it all.'

He laughed and sat down to study the photo of the knife. Indy was right, it was distinctively marked. As a one-of-a-kind, it wouldn't be difficult to identify if it popped up somewhere. 'How is she?'

Indy rolled her eyes. 'Ready for the next adventure.'

'Right. How is she really?'

'She has a low tolerance for sympathy and while the sensible part of her brain is telling her there wasn't anything more she could do, the Tess part is giving her a hard time. I don't think she'd truly believe she'd done enough unless she killed herself trying.'

'She certainly seems to try hard enough.'

Indy sent him a puzzled frown. 'Harsh. Are we back to the incident with you at the station? You're really stuck on that at the moment.'

'Guess so.'

'I suppose she saw something in you worth saving.'

'If she ever lets you know what that was …'

'Pass it on?' Indy asked. Her eyes lit up. 'Why?'

'Shut up,' he said without heat, and drained his coffee before standing, ready to head out.

Indy didn't move, just sat in the same spot with her interrogation face on. It made him laugh.

'Maybe I thought about asking her out, but from the exchange last week I gather she's seeing that Aaron guy, right? So forget it.' He ducked his head down to speak to her directly. 'Indy, forget it.'

He left her drinking her coffee. Armed with a few copies of the photo of the knife, he took himself outside and pointed the car towards the biggest pawn shop in town.

The shop had had a repaint in army green since he'd last been in, and he was pretty sure it was larger, as though the premises that had been next door had moved and made room for an extension. Splashy gold writing announced he'd found Quick and Easy Cash, promising the best loans in town, a free cleaning service on pawned jewellery and great bargains. There was a display of jewellery in the window. It all looked brand new. Though the shop beyond was packed with goods, it was organised and tidy. He had to hand it to the owner, who had only completed probation a handful of years ago, he'd made good use of his time.

Jared pushed open the glass door and went inside. The owner, who liked to go by the name Tank, was talking to an elderly woman on a walker. The woman was wearing a look of consternation that reminded him of his old school principal. Tank's expression was pure exasperation.

'Mrs Ted, I gave you four hundred dollars for your pendant, you signed a contract to pay it back within six months, that contract was extended twice, to twelve, then eighteen months, and you never paid a cent, never came near me for another six months after that. Yet the moment it's out front cleaned up and ready to sell, you're back in here demanding I return it.'

'You can't sell it—it was my mother's! I just need some more time.'

Tank sighed and rubbed his forehead. 'Can you put down any money on it today?'

She hesitated. 'Well, not exactly …'

Tank glanced up, noticed Jared and smiled distractedly. 'Okay, look. Perhaps there's something you can replace it with? Something you're not so attached to?'

Mrs Ted thought about that. Her face transformed from worried to thoughtful then happy. 'Well, maybe I can at that. Would you hold it just a little longer while I go home and check?'

'Sure, Mrs Ted,' Tank said in a long-suffering tone that suggested he was accepting some sort of defeat. 'Of course. I'll pop it away again for you.'

'Thank you, Tank. You're a good man. I'll be back.' The woman shuffled slowly towards Jared on her walking frame, so he opened the door to let her out and got a smile and a very proper 'Thank you, sir.'

'Difficult customer?' he asked Tank as he approached the counter.

'That "going home to check" will be another six-month adventure,' Tank grumbled. But he took the pendant from the counter and put a lid on it, tucking it under the desk. 'If she manages to bring anything in at all, *anything*, I'll write off the loss and hand it back over.'

'You're a soft touch.' But it gave the guy points in Jared's mind. And the shop seemed to be doing well.

'What else can I do? She only pawned it to help pay for her husband's funeral.'

'Some people wouldn't care.'

'True. What can I do for you? Still looking for your thief? I had a Detective Constable Roberts around here last week with a list of missing items.'

'Yeah, we've got more missing stuff. You haven't seen this guy around, have you?' Jared showed him the sketch.

Tank looked at it carefully. 'No, sorry. I'll keep an eye out.'

'One of the most identifiable things stolen last weekend was a Damascus folding knife. Unique. This is it.' He passed him a photo. 'Shouldn't be too difficult to ID.'

Tank took the picture and studied it. 'Nice work. I doubt anyone smart enough to pull off all these successful robberies would be dumb enough to turn up in here with something as identifiable as this. But you never know.'

'They were dumb enough to take it in the first place—and leave prints at the scene, so it's worth a shot.'

'Can I keep these?' Tank asked, picking up the sketch and the photo.

'Yeah, I've got plenty of copies.'

A wiry young man with short dark hair, torn jeans and a handful of small boxes appeared from behind a row of shelves. He stopped in his tracks and eyed Jared nervously before hesitantly approaching the counter.

'Sorry to interrupt, boss. Pax said you wanted this stuff up front.'

'Thanks, Jai. I need you both to take a run out to deliver the mini kayaks. On the way back you can call into Bunnings and load up the new pallet racking.'

'No worries. Now?'

'Yep.'

Jai hesitated a second longer, shooting his boss one more nervous glance before making an awkward exit.

'Who's that?' Jared asked, suspicious of the guy's behaviour.

'Jai? Works for me. He's my daughter Riley's boyfriend,' Tank explained with a roll of his eyes. 'Took him on a couple of years back.'

'Is he okay? He looked pretty uncomfortable just now.'

Tank chuckled. 'Yeah. Riley's been at him about doing a big hike through the Southwest National Park. They've been out back practising pitching their tents. Looked like a bit of a disaster. Bit of a wuss of a kid, but heart of gold. I think he's stressing about the whole so-called adventure. I'd be pretty stressed myself if they were going alone. Made them use a guide.'

'Yeah? They're not booked with Tess Atherton, are they?'

'Nah, some bloke … Aaron Jackson, I think Riley said. She's referring to him as their babysitter.'

'Young and invincible, huh? Aaron also does Search and Rescue work, he knows what he's doing.'

'Good to know.'

'I hope they have a good time. Let me know if you spot any of this.'

'Will do.'

CHAPTER 10

Tess gave the young buckskin filly a soothing pat and hopped off. 'Well done, sweetheart. You're going to be a super campdrafter, aren't you, huh?' The three-year-old with the bright, inquisitive eyes was fast becoming a favourite. Maybe Tess could talk Logan into letting her campaign her for a while before offering her for sale. She wouldn't mind carving out some time for a few competitions.

She led the filly out of the arena and back to the stables. Larissa appeared to take the reins.

'How'd she go?'

'I think she might have to stay a bit longer than the others.'

Larissa grinned. 'Logan said you were bound to pick her as your favourite.'

'Did he?'

'Mmm. Because you wanted a buckskin out of Flash but then she wouldn't go in foal. And he'd already earmarked this one as pretty special. Reckons she's the best Rex has produced,' Larissa said, stroking the filly's face, 'and that's saying something.'

'Where is my devious brother?'

Larissa laughed. 'He's taken some guests on a trail ride.'

'I'll catch up with him later. I've got a group of my own to take out.'

'Riding? Logan didn't tell me. I don't have any horses ready.'

'No, relax. My group's going skiing.'

'Right,' Larissa said with relief. 'Let me take her for you. Enjoy the snow.'

'Thanks, and oh, I suppose I should ask … does my new horse have a name?'

'I think Logan was waiting for you to come up with one,' Larissa called over her shoulder.

Tess chuckled and walked back through the islands of gardens that flanked the driveway to the guesthouse. Logan and his big heart. It couldn't have been more than a week ago that she'd mentioned she missed campdrafting and suddenly he'd needed breakers worked. Now it looked like she was going to be competing again.

Her phone rang and the screen told her it was Aaron. She stopped under a large conifer and leant against it. 'Hi.'

'Hi, beautiful. I heard there's a good amount of snow on the ground up at Mount Mawson. Feel like heading up there?'

That he was asking her to go on an outing to the same place she was already headed was almost too coincidental. And for some reason she'd had it in her head he didn't like skiing. 'Aren't you working?'

'There are some benefits to being the boss. It's too nice a day for office work.'

'It is, but I can't, sorry. I'm already booked to take some guests out there. They want to try some skiing.'

There was a pause, then, 'Who are they?'

'A group of three friends from Far North Queensland.'

'A group of three men?' he asked quietly.

She looked skyward, mentally preparing herself for the argument. 'Yeah.'

'Tess, we talked about this.'

She smiled at a couple of passing visitors before answering. 'Yes, we did. And I told you I can take care of myself.'

The silence on the other end of the line stretched, but when the doubts would have crept in, Indy's lecture came to mind and strengthened her resolve.

'Look, Aaron. They're a nice bunch of guys. Nothing to worry about. If you want to do something later, I'll be back by five. Or we can go out tomorrow, just us. I've got some time in the morning.'

'Okay,' he finally said, his tone short and sharp. 'I'll see you tonight. Five o'clock.'

'Don't put yourself out,' she muttered at the phone when he'd ended the call.

She went into the guesthouse on her way to her apartment. She'd change, make sure all the equipment was loaded up, take water bottles, some—

'Tess!' Callie called out from reception. 'Did Aaron get hold of you?'

'Ah … just then. Sorry, he must have tried to call while I was riding. He wanted to go skiing but I had to tell him I was already taking a group out.'

Callie's face reflected her confusion. 'I already told him you had that on this afternoon.'

Annoyance washed through Tess. His choice of destination hadn't been a coincidence at all. 'Which was probably where he got the idea to take me himself, thinking I'd pass the all-male tourist group to someone else. Thanks, Callie.'

'Enjoy,' Callie said. 'Be careful of those big, bad tourists.'

'Funny!' she called back, but she didn't think it was. Aaron's attitude was really starting to bother her.

Mount Mawson basked crisp and white under a vivid blue sky. The snow covering wasn't as good as it would be in another couple of weeks, but it was enough for her tourists to be having fun. Neither Joe, Damien nor Duncan had ever tried skiing before, so a gentle slope was all they needed. The group had her in stitches with their attempts to stay upright on the skis, mostly because they were trying to 'mogul it' over an uneven patch of snow by a tumble of rocks. And failing. Tess watched them muck around. It was an entertaining and easy outing, and their location, just away from the scattering of serious skiers who were checking out the conditions, was at the edge of a pretty gully of snow gums and pandani, making for nice photographs.

'Hey, Tess!' Damien called out. 'Can we go over there?' He pointed to an area lower on the mountain where another cluster of rocks poked through the snow.

'Not sure how deep the snow is there,' she called back, and pointed her skis down the slope, cruising across to the spot. 'It's okay just here, if you want to come down.'

Damien and Duncan wobbled down with their skis crossed in an attempt to go slow. Joe, who'd had the least amount of success mastering them, had taken his off and trudged down. He stopped on a large rock, jumped into the snow and all but disappeared—only a hand waved out of the pocket he'd fallen into.

'Hey, it's really … white down here!' he said, sending his friends into a fit of laughter.

Grinning with them, Tess edged closer to try to help him out. They ended up in a tangle of body parts in the snow as they both fell, struggled up, fell again. She got one foot underneath her, then a knee. 'That's possibly the only deep area of snow on the entire mountain and you found it,' she said with a laugh.

'What's going on?' The voice was loud and familiar.

'Aaron?' Tess's smile faltered at the angry colour in Aaron's cheeks as he ploughed down the hill towards them. She regained her balance and found a safer spot to stand while Joe joined his mates. 'What are you doing here?'

'I thought I'd surprise you. Lucky I did. Are you all right?'

'Absolutely fine,' she said, both confused and embarrassed by the scene. She fought to keep a smile in place, her tone casual. 'We hit a deep pocket of snow, that's all.'

'I saw him drag you down under him!' As Tess shook her head, Aaron turned his anger on Joe. 'You grabbed her!'

Joe's expression went blank with surprise, then darkened. 'Mate, I don't think I like what you're implying.'

'I saw what I saw!' Then to Tess, he said, 'Give me your gear. We're leaving.'

'I'm not going anywhere. What's wrong with you?'

'Wrong with me?'

She didn't know where his anger had come from, but she desperately needed to calm this down. 'Okay, look,' she said, 'I'm fine and I'm working. We'll talk about this tonight.'

'Doesn't matter, Tess,' Damien said over whatever Aaron was going to reply. 'Time's just about up anyway. Let's call it a day.'

'I'm so sorry,' Tess said. 'I'll take you up.' They'd had such a good time she didn't want to leave it like this.

'We'll meet you at the car,' Damien said. 'As long as you're okay to deal with him?'

'Deal with me? You—'

'Yes, of course,' she cut in. 'Thanks.'

The men picked up their skis and trekked towards the carpark, occasionally glancing over their shoulders.

Humiliated, Tess spun on Aaron. 'What was that?'

'Tess, you don't know those guys from a bar of soap! You're so trusting! I saw the looks on their faces. There was nothing innocent about their behaviour!'

'I told you I was fine! This is my *job*. My *reputation*. Those guys are staying at the lodge for a week. Do you honestly think they're going to want to do any activities with me after this?'

His mouth pressed into a tight line. 'I'd say that's for the best, wouldn't you?' He took her skis in one hand and her arm with the other and began towing her up the hill. 'I'll take those men back. You can drive my car.'

'Let go!' She ripped her arm from his grip only to have him turn on her, his enraged face too close to hers.

'Stop causing a scene!' he hissed.

Her heart thudded once, her breath hitching at the venom in his tone. 'I'm not the one causing—' She broke off when his phone rang and he answered it.

His face was grave as he looked to the skyline. He ended the call. 'We'll have to talk about this later. We've got three hikers somewhere out at Cradle Mountain. A child is injured and there's only a rough idea of where they are.'

She bit back her anger. The last thing she wanted to do was spend any more time with Aaron today, but someone needed their help. 'I'll get the guys back to the lodge and meet you at the chopper.'

His glare moved up the hill to the carpark, leaving her in no doubt as to what he thought of that plan, but he nodded, then charged ahead of her.

She did her best to apologise to the tourists on their way back, and they assured her it was no big deal and that they'd like to go out again. Their generous attitude went a long way to cooling Tess's temper and by the time she was sitting in the helicopter over Cradle Mountain National Park, searching for the missing trio, she had it under control. But she still didn't understand where Aaron's rage had come from, and she didn't like that he'd managed to scare her.

He sat beside her, staring into the rapidly darkening landscape. They hadn't said much to each other since boarding the chopper but she could tell he was still angry. She scanned the track. In front of them, Cradle Mountain loomed large over its surroundings. The ancient monolith's dolerite peak stretched up from the rainforest- and pandani-covered mountainside to dominate the skyline, its reflection just as powerful in the quiet glassy water of Dove Lake resting beneath it. But there was no sign of the hikers.

She drew her eyes back to the track as the chopper moved on and Lake Lilla came into view. The track here went downhill into thicker forest and was more difficult to see, and the fog was rolling in more heavily.

'We're going to have to head back shortly,' the pilot warned. 'Visibility's poor.'

'There's an injured child out here somewhere,' Tess pleaded. 'Just a few more—there! Directly below. Someone's waving!'

The chopper circled around and she got a better look. A lone figure waving a red parka was trying to get their attention. The pilot radioed the other chopper, hovered. 'I'm not going to be able to land down there. It'll have to be a hover drop. I'll keep the chopper as steady as I can.'

Aaron tossed her a pack and she dropped it off the chopper, then jumped out after it. She hit the ground hard, took the sled from Aaron then got out of his way. The ground underfoot was thick with vegetation and loose with rocks. She did her best to negotiate it as the man who'd flagged them down approached.

'You radioed for help?' Tess asked as Aaron caught up.

'Yeah. I'm John. Our son's hurt. Meg, my wife, is with him.'

'Where?' Aaron asked.

'They're over here. He slipped, fell. Got himself wedged between two large rocks. The ground just seemed to give way.'

'How old is your son?' Tess asked.

'Twelve.'

'What's his name?'

'Leo. But he won't hear you. He won't wake up.'

Tess relayed the information over her radio, then followed the men to a steep area of mountainside. Aaron dropped his pack and began unloading equipment. Tess cautiously approached the edge to look for some sign of the wife and son. At the sight of the drop in front of her, her legs trembled and the ground seem to tip under her feet. She took some dizzy steps backwards, sank down onto the rock.

Aaron stepped straight past her. 'I can see them!' he said. Then to the woman below: 'Hi, we're here to help. How is he?'

'Breathing but unconscious! His leg's twisted underneath him. I'm trying to keep him as warm as I can. Please hurry!'

Tess tried to move. She was still close enough to the edge to feel unsteady. The wind was blowing out over it. The breath locked in her lungs, her muscles refused to work except where her fingers clutched at the smooth rock for some sort of hold.

'Tess!' Aaron called out. 'Get the ropes out! We can tie off to those trees and stick a chock in that crack in the rock.' He pointed somewhere behind her.

She managed to drag her unsteady legs back under her and stood up, got her breathing back under control. Turning, she saw where he was pointing. Yes, that would work. This part she could do. She pulled out her equipment and got started.

'You ready?' Aaron asked a few minutes later, harnessed up with his gear as she fumbled into her own.

She nodded, walked back to the edge and looked over. She'd be okay this time. She could do this. The wind whistled, became Charlie's scream. It burst into her head, rendering her helpless. She stared at the drop. Saw it moving, coming closer. She was going over.

'Tess!'

'Huh?' Another chopper swung into view, bringing the paramedics.

'I'll go first. You can lower the sled, then …' Aaron's voice faded in and out as her vision swam. She shook her head. Moved out of his way.

'I can't do it,' she whispered.

'What?'

'I'm sorry! I can't go over.'

'Of course you can, just go!' he snapped.

She turned away with another shake of her head then felt a shove from behind that catapulted her towards the ledge. Terror rocketed through her as she fell awkwardly and grabbed desperately for the rope. Clinging, pedalling her legs back from the ledge, she fought for safety.

'Hey, are you okay?' John asked, helping her to her feet.

She swung around on Aaron. 'What was that?' she yelled in disbelief.

Aaron's face reflected surprise. 'What?'

'You pushed me!'

'I—no. Tess, I tripped over your rope. Sorry if I bumped you.'

'Is there a problem?' John asked. 'Because my wife and child really need your help!'

Aaron's gaze was intense as he looked her over. 'Just sit down, right here. You look like you're going to pass out.'

'Hey!' one of the paramedics said as they rushed in. 'What have we got?'

She could have sworn … She staggered out of the way to let Aaron and the medics work.

CHAPTER 11

From his kitchen window, Jai watched a car cruise slowly down the dark street, make a turn and disappear. Not a cop car, he reassured himself, not looking for him. He'd been checking over his shoulder all week, expecting Detective Denham to turn up. He'd been sure he'd get sprung, especially knowing they'd somehow gotten Pax's likeness. He'd seen the detective show it to Tank and had wondered why Tank hadn't said anything, but he wasn't quite game enough to ask.

He'd pictured it all in his head, over and over: the arrest, the criminal record and the sick panic of trying to get Pop looked after. And maybe the worst one of all: losing Riley. She'd never look at him the same, wouldn't want to be with him. And how could he blame her?

So he'd almost said no when Pax had approached him with another job offer earlier in the day. But after a brief wrestle with his conscience, need had won out. That last lot of cash had bought a decent amount of food and paid Evan's new nurse David and two bills. They'd only pinched some stuff from a drug-dealing cheat. Why should he feel bad about that? It wasn't fair people like her had that sort of money when he had a pop like his and the bills just kept coming.

So this time, Jai didn't hesitate when Pax pulled up. He grabbed the pack Pax had left with him after last week's robbery. He was dressed in black from head to toe and had bought his own gloves while shopping with Riley, a pair of warm black ones that would prevent the chance of any more fingerprints being left behind and keep his fingers from freezing off at the same time. He'd had a good excuse to pick up the balaclava too: it would be useful on the South Coast Track. Riley had laughed and said he'd make a good bank robber. He was damn glad she had no clue how close she was to the mark. He was already starting to feel like a pro.

'Hey,' he said, climbing into the car.

Pax nodded, glanced briefly at him. 'Better,' he said of Jai's appearance, before pulling back out onto the road.

'I got gloves and a balaclava, too.'

'Great.'

There seemed to be a tension about Pax there hadn't been last week. It made Jai's stomach curl and his earlier confidence plummet. 'Is everything okay?'

'Yeah—yeah, it's good. Just planning.'

'It's a boat, right?'

'The chick that owns it is loaded. I want the diamonds, but you can have whatever ya want from the rest of it. There should be a decent amount of cash on board.'

Jai nodded and looked out the window. It was a quiet night. The supermarket had closed and the twenty-four-hour Macca's was open but the drive-thru was empty. Everyone who was out at that time of morning was no doubt in the city, not in the suburbs. Pax turned onto the boulevard, passed the deserted Short Beach carpark and pulled over, killing the lights and idling the car.

'Can ya see anyone?' Pax asked.

The houses that lined the other side of the road were dark and quiet. A sign warning they were in a neighbourhood watch area was attached to a streetlight, but there was no indication anyone was taking a late-night stroll or peeking out from behind closed curtains.

'Nup.'

'Me neither.' Without turning the headlights back on, Pax drove off again, this time to duck into an unnamed road that led to a protrusion of land in the bay containing a park, scout hall, boat sheds and the local rowing club. He swung the car into a space behind the park's public toilets, hiding them from the road.

'Isn't this a bit dangerous? There's only one way in and out.'

'We can't be any further away on this one. If anyone calls the cops, they'll go straight to the yacht club, not here.'

There was that jump in Jai's gut again. 'Okay.' He got out of the car, pulled on his gloves, wore the balaclava pulled up like a beanie and followed Pax at a jog along the rock wall to a small jetty. A dinghy was tied to one of its pylons.

'Here.' Pax pulled a gun from the back of his jeans and handed it to him.

'Whoa!' Jai jumped away. 'What's that for?'

'Would ya keep ya voice down and grow a pair?' Pax hissed. 'My contact said there might be a dog. A big bastard of a thing.'

Jai's head was shaking of its own accord, his hands raised as though in surrender. 'I don't want to kill anyone's dog, man!'

Pax shrugged and grinned. 'Then let's hope it's friendly.'

'What's on the end of it?' It looked like Pax had attached part of a torch to the barrel.

'Homemade silencer.' He spun Jai around, shoved the gun into the waistband of his jeans. 'Remind me to take the safety off when we get there.' Pax climbed down to untie the dinghy. 'Let's go,' he ordered, when Jai just stood there.

'Where'd this boat come from?'

'You ask a lot of questions, ya know that? Get in.'

Jai awkwardly managed to get in without getting wet and felt the gun dig into his back as he sat. He nervously shifted a bit. Just how safe was it there?

Pax took a long look at the boats moored at the nearby yacht club then began rowing. 'Keep ya eyes open. If ya see anyone, tell me.'

The oars made little noise as they slid through the black water. Ahead, impressive rows of yachts loomed over their moorings, their tall silhouettes sparkling in the glow of the half moon. Pax aimed the dinghy at the largest of them all.

'That doesn't look like a yacht,' Jai whispered.

'It's a motor yacht. Now shut up.' Pax let the dinghy drift to the dock and tied it off.

'Why not just walk in?'

'I told ya to shut up!' he whispered. 'There's probably a guard somewhere, so eyes open.'

'Right.'

Pax pulled out a mobile and opened an app. 'The boat's security needs to be turned off,' he explained before Jai could ask, then, apparently happy it was sorted, he climbed onto the dock. Jai wondered how Pax had gotten the app, but he wasn't going to risk making another noise to find out.

Keeping low, he followed Pax onto the most luxurious boat he'd ever seen. It shone silver and white, boasting comfort and class. Pax seemed to know exactly where he wanted to go: through a galley, up a small set of stairs, then down a longer one and into a small hallway illuminated only by the reflection of the moon on the water. A few more steps then Pax stopped at a doorway, took the gun from Jai, fiddled with it and put it in Jai's hand. Mouth to Jai's ear, he whispered, 'If anything comes at ya, shoot it. Don't wait until you're mauled to put a hole in it. Ready?'

Jai swallowed hard. He couldn't do it. *Shit.* He couldn't. Pax was gonna spit but his hand was already trembling so hard he knew he'd never be able to pull the trigger if he had to. He shook his head violently, stepped back. Pax's eyes rounded in anger then narrowed menacingly. Still, Jai shook his head, tried to turn, bumped into the wall.

Thump.

Pax grabbed hold of him and turned him around. 'Fuckwit.' It was a barely discernible whisper. Then a rustling behind them had Pax lunging into the cabin.

'Look out!'

Something slammed into Jai as he lifted the gun. His finger convulsed on the trigger. The gunshot was muffled as he stumbled back, felt the weight slip from him to the ground.

No. He stared at the dark blur at his feet, heard a groan, then a choking, gurgling sound followed by utter silence.

That was a person.

The gun slipped from his hand. His whole world tipped on its axis as he stared, fighting the darkness to see, to prove himself wrong. He couldn't have shot a person. He *couldn't* have.

The room flooded with the soft, warm light of a bedside lamp. A muffled scream made him look up. Pax was covering a woman's mouth, holding her from behind on the bed as she too stared at the figure of the dead man on the floor. Then her eyes moved up, up, and she was staring at Jai like he was a monster.

'I—I didn't know!' he said. 'I thought it was a dog. I thought … They're not supposed to be here!' he almost shouted at Pax in confusion.

'Relax,' Pax said calmly. 'And shut up. Everything's cool.'

'I shot someone!'

'He had to die, mate. Now get out of here.'

Jai's head was shaking again, his body shivering. He needed to pee. To be sick. 'What—what about you? What are you going to do?'

The woman fought to scream again, eyes bulging. Pleading.

'I'll be right behind ya.'

Jai looked from the eyes of the terrified woman to Pax's cold, hard expression. 'I didn't mean it. I—'

'Get back to the boat,' Pax ordered. 'I'll get the stuff.'

'But—what—you can't hurt her.'

'Under control. Now get the fuck out!' Pax's voice was still low but urgent, more threatening.

Jai took one last look at the man at his feet, the woman on the bed. 'I'm sorry. I'm …' His voice cracked. He was strangely numb, but turned and walked robotically back the way he'd come in.

The cold air of the dock hitting his face was like the breaking of a spell. Great gulping sobs rose up and choked him, erupting violently from his throat. He'd shot someone. It had happened so fast. His stomach sank then rose, full of bile. He vomited into the water, couldn't seem to stop retching. When he brought it under control, he checked all around for signs anyone had been alerted by the noise he was making and, scared witless, scrambled down onto the dinghy.

He waited. The boat rocked gently. What was Pax doing in there, anyway? How much stuff was he taking? They needed to get away! What if there was a security guard? What if he was on his way over right now to see who'd made all the noise puking into the water? No one could be allowed to see them. He'd have to go into the water. Swim for it.

Then it occurred to him: the woman. She'd seen their faces. They were already screwed. Pax had to know that, didn't he?

Shit.

What was Pax going to do to her? He stood up to go back in, ducked for cover again when a boat puttered past further out in the bay. He should run to the police station, confess and get help. Screw Pax. He'd said no one would be there. But he'd accidentally killed someone. He'd go to jail. He couldn't think straight.

And then he ran out of choices. Pax was back. He sat down and picked up the oars. 'Untie us. Let's go.'

Every splash of the oars in the water sounded too loud, every second felt like hours, but no one came after them. No one stopped them. Jai had questions, but he was too scared to utter them. So he sat in silence, trying not to think too much about anything.

Back at the jetty they climbed out of the dinghy, Pax pushing it out to float away. Then he removed the phone from his pocket and smashed it before kicking the pieces into the water.

'What did you do to her?' Jai finally managed to ask as Pax reversed the car out of the spot.

'Best ya don't—fuck!'

An old man with a fishing rod and a thermos was illuminated by the headlights as the car turned. Pax fishtailed the car with a screech of tyres. 'I don't think he saw much,' he said, checking the rear-view mirror. 'Looks about a hundred. Bloody night fisherman.'

'Did you kill her?' Now that Jai had gotten the question out, he really needed to know.

'She'd seen us, mate. It would have been all over. Thanks for saving my arse back there.'

'You shoved that guy at me on purpose. You wanted me to shoot him!'

'You were the one with the gun. It was quicker and easier. I've thanked ya once, ya looking for a medal?'

'I thought he was a dog!'

'So ya said. Mate, ya should have seen ya face.' Pax laughed, hit the steering wheel with a 'Woo hoo!'

'I'm going to be sick.'

'Hey. Hey!' Pax slapped him hard on the chest with his bag. 'No, you're not. Take a look at the spoils!'

Jai couldn't care less about the spoils but he didn't want to piss off Pax again so he opened the bag and caught the glitter of diamonds in the streetlights, lots of them in various pieces of jewellery, a phone, some cash.

'There's not much money,' Pax said. 'A couple of hundred out of the guy's wallet, but I'll give ya a fair cut of the gems. Man, we'll be cashed up for years!'

'What about the gun?'

'Huh?'

'I left the gun.'

'Oh, yeah—nah, don't worry. It's sorted.'

Jai had never seen the guy on such a high. He'd known Pax could be nasty, that he didn't give much of a toss about anyone but himself, but he hadn't known, not until just then, just what a monster the guy really was.

How was he ever going to get himself out of this?

CHAPTER 12

'I can't believe how beautiful it is out there, thanks for taking us.'

Tess smiled at the pretty young woman and her fiancé. 'It was a pleasure, I'm glad you enjoyed it.' The pair wandered towards the guest lounge and she quickly scanned it for any sign of Aaron.

'Another beautiful morning out at Mount Field?' Callie asked from the reception desk.

'Yeah, they're a nice couple. The fiancé is training to become a park ranger. He was keen to learn about the plants and animals out there. Tested my knowledge.'

'Got any time free?' Callie stretched her arms above her head. 'I could do with some lunch.'

Tess pressed a hand to her stomach when it growled at the mention of food. 'I'd love to, but I agreed to meet Aaron for coffee.' She frowned at the thought of the uncomfortable conversation to come. 'We have a few things to discuss.'

'Sounds ominous.'

Tess looked around. Aaron hadn't appeared yet so she filled Callie in on the argument.

'Wow,' Callie said with a frown of her own. 'I can't believe he went off like that. He's probably calmed down and realised he went too far. I'd be surprised if he's not panicking.'

'I hope so. I never saw so much as a hint of that side of him before we started seeing each other. His temper was off the scale yesterday. I probably did misinterpret the push out on the rescue, but I didn't mistake the humiliation of him all but accusing those guys I took out to the snow of molesting me.'

Callie's face reflected shock. 'Hold on—what push?'

'It wasn't. I mean, it felt like it but—forget it. I was having a moment over the heights thing and not thinking straight.'

'Tess—' Callie bit back whatever she was going to say as her gaze moved past Tess's shoulder. 'We'll talk later,' she said quietly.

'Tess,' Aaron said as she turned to face him. 'Callie, hi.'

'Hi, Aaron,' Callie said with a touch of coolness that had his brow lifting in enquiry.

'Everything okay?'

'I don't know. Is it?'

Tess groaned inwardly. She shouldn't have said anything. 'Everything's fine.'

'Then shall we?' he asked. She nodded, then was held up by a hand on her arm. 'Let's not worry about coffee. We should head outside, take a walk.'

'Okay, sure,' she said, not missing the disapproving stare he directed at Callie.

She followed him outside and in silence they went into the gardens overlooking the mountains. She wondered if Aaron was framing his words carefully or simply waiting for her to say something first.

'Thank you for talking to me today,' he finally said.

She wasn't sure if she imagined the slight admonishment in his tone or not. 'I was too tired to go through it all last night. I needed to get my head around everything.'

He stopped walking to face her. 'What's there to get your head around? I was concerned about you.' His expression softened into a smile. 'I'd hate for you to get hurt.'

'You don't need to be that concerned. You were way out of line.'

He sighed and nodded, then gestured to a bench under the bare branches of an old oak tree. She sat beside him.

'Look, I didn't tell you, but the real reason I wanted to get out of the office yesterday was because I'd had a shitty start to the day. A phone call from an unreasonable client that ended in an argument. I thought I'd come and surprise you and clear my head. Then I arrived in time to see what I saw and … I overreacted. I was over the top. I'm sorry. You're the most capable woman I've ever met. I'll work on remembering that.'

Everything inside Tess gave a long sigh of relief. 'Okay.'

His face brightened. 'Then we're good?'

One last chance, she thought, to see if he means it, to see if this really can work. 'Yeah, we're good. And I know I've been a bit touchier about everything since the accident at Fedder, but I'm getting back to myself.'

'You're not there yet, though, are you?' It wasn't really a question. 'As far as Search and Rescue …' He took her hands in his. 'Tess, you need to take a step back for a while.'

'What? No. Look, I agree I should probably stay away from cliffs for the time being but for everything else, I'm fine.'

'It's too dangerous. We're not playing out there,' he continued patiently. 'We had a child in serious need of medical attention and you hampered the rescue. You freaked out at the edge of that small drop and held us up by accusing me of trying to kill you.'

She stiffened. 'I'm sorry, but it sure as hell felt like a shove.'

'Because you weren't thinking straight. I spoke to Craig. He agrees you should be off the list until you're back to your old self.'

'You did what?' she gasped, pushing to her feet. 'You had no right to—'

'Yes, I did,' he continued in that same infuriatingly calm tone. 'I know when a team member isn't up to the job and I can't give you special treatment because we're in a relationship.'

'I met with the counsellor as per requirements,' she said. 'I was cleared.'

'You shouldn't have been. You're very good at making people believe you're okay when you're not. I think you know that.' He took her hand and gently tugged her back down, his smile warming when she huffed but dropped to the seat. 'I'm sure you'll be back to yourself in no time. Let's just make sure you're safe, okay? You have to believe me when I tell you losing you is not an option.'

She stared sightlessly at the mountains, silently processing. She wanted to believe this was just Aaron being overprotective again, but the truth was he had a point. She didn't have a right to be out there if she couldn't do her job. 'All right.'

He skimmed his fingers down her cheek, eyes glowing with approval. 'Good. You just need to let me take care of things for you and everything will work out. You'll see.'

CHAPTER 13

Jared signed the register and stepped under the police tape onto a pathway that led to the jetty. Behind him a sturdy and sleek two-storey clubhouse boasted the title the Royal Yacht Club of Tasmania and he guessed from what he'd seen through the large glass windows that the restaurant would be worth a trip. Though it wasn't open, there were a few people inside, milling around, talking, watching with sombre expressions and coffees in hand. Club people, he supposed, a small gathering created by whoever his people had called to get access to the marina.

In front of him rows of moored yachts rested on water so still the morning sky reflected flawlessly on its surface. He imagined how peaceful it would be at this time of the morning, if not for the flashing lights of police vehicles and the steady stream of personnel traipsing on and off the jetty.

'Detective!'

Wonderful. The media had arrived. He spotted the local news reporter and his sidekick with the camera waving at him from the police line. He nodded in greeting, then deliberately turned away again to prepare himself for the scene he was about to walk into. Emily was nearby, talking to a balding middle-aged man in a cheap suit with a complexion that suggested he was most likely the one who'd found the victims. Jared caught her eye and she motioned him over.

'This is Warwick Snell, the personal driver to one of the victims. He found the bodies.'

'Hi, Mr Snell, I'm Detective Senior Sergeant Jared Denham.'

Snell was clutching a bottle of water, crinkling the plastic in his fingers. He stopped and put it at his feet in order to shake Jared's hand, then didn't seem to know what to do with his hand once it was freed, eventually sticking it in his pocket. 'It's been a bit of a shock. I—it's awful.'

'Can you tell me what happened this morning?'

'I was supposed to pick them up at seven. They had a nine o'clock meeting with investors at Claremont Golf Club and were going to breakfast together at The Source first. It's in Berriedale, Mr Sash's favourite.' He bent down and picked up his water bottle again, played with the lid. 'I was to call them from the car and they were going to walk out to meet me, but Mr Sash's phone continued to ring out. I wasn't really sure what to do. At that time of the morning if their plans had changed or I'd somehow made a mistake I didn't want to wake them up but I thought I'd better. So I walked out to the boat. I thought it was strange the door was open, but I knocked a few times. I called out, didn't get a reply. Then I saw the blood.'

'Blood?'

'Yeah, a bit on the floor, like part of a footprint. I got worried so I went in, found more and ended up downstairs. I probably shouldn't have rushed in there, I know that, but I wanted to see if they were somehow still alive. It was pretty obvious, I guess, thinking on it now, that they weren't. I called the police and I waited.'

'Can you think back for me and try and remember if anyone was here when you arrived? Anyone near the boat, on the jetty, out here, in the carpark? Anyone at all.'

Snell stared into space, shook his head slowly. 'No, sorry. I mean, there could have been. I wasn't paying attention.'

'No problem. When was the last time you saw the victims alive?'

'Saturday night. I dropped them at the carpark just after midnight. I sat in the car for a minute, texting my wife to let her know I was on my way home. She likes to know, you know, how far away I am, so I saw them go through the gate and towards the boat. Then I left.'

'Anyone else around?'

'No. I don't think so. It was late.'

'Has anyone asked you anything regarding Wilde or Sash since they've been here?'

'Not really. I mean, a few people have said hellos as we come and go. It's a nice place, you know? Friendly.'

'Okay. So you dropped them off on Saturday night, sent a text to your wife and …?'

'Went home. Lindy waited up so we had a tea, went to bed. You don't—you don't think I did this?'

'We're just following protocol, Mr Snell. We'll need to verify your whereabouts, and because you went into the crime scene to check the victims for signs of life, there's some procedure we need to go through so we can eliminate you against any evidence that we might collect.'

'That's okay. I can do that.'

'Appreciate it. Emily, would you take care of it?'

'Of course. You'd better get out there. Indy's tapping her foot.'

'Which boat?'

'The Riviera 68.'

He looked out towards the chaos of people doing their jobs. 'That hasn't made it any clearer. There's police all over that dock.'

She smirked. 'It's the one you can't miss. Three storeys and sixty-eight feet of out-and-out luxury.'

'You a boat fan?'

'I sail. I like boats, and when they come like this, absolutely.'

'Thanks, Em.' He walked past rows of assorted boats and caught sight of Indy at the back of a sparkling white yacht in the last row, talking to another officer. She spotted him and beckoned him over. Emily was right, she looked impatient.

He walked briskly, noted the strain on her face.

'Get you out of bed, Denham?' she called as he approached.

'Yeah, actually. What do you know?' And he knew it was going to be bad, because it took a lot to put the snap in her voice and that look on her face.

'The two victims are Madison Wilde, of *the* Wilde family—you know, casinos, resorts, racehorses? Mega-rich Melbourne mob. And Brandon Sash, a corporate exec from a company Wilde Enterprises was working closely with over a proposed development down here in Tassie. Both deceased for approximately twenty-four to thirty-six hours. No one missed them yesterday, but they had a car organised to pick them up early for a meeting this morning. You spoke to Snell?'

'Yeah, Em's taking him back to the station for follow-up.'

'Great. The boat has a skipper but we've been unable to locate him.'

Jared stepped on board into an outdoor galley area and up a few steps into a bar. Then he was walking through a kitchen proper and saloon. Everything gleamed and reeked of wealth. He was starting to understand Emily's enthusiasm. This boat was nicer than most people's houses.

There were stairs leading up, he guessed to a flybridge and whatever other opulent space designers had deigned appropriate, but Indy led him down a different set. The large starboard cabin at the end of the hall directly in front of him looked untouched, its bed made up neatly, as were the twin beds in the room to his left, and from the glimpse he caught the ensuite was equally clean and tidy, then they turned abruptly right, past another bathroom and down a couple more steps into what could only have been the master suite. It should have been breathtakingly opulent. Instead it was a bloodbath.

The first victim, Sash, was somewhere in his mid-forties, with a tanned, trim physique and untidy, sleep-ruffled chestnut hair. He lay in the doorway in a pair of jade-green boxers, one hand still resting over a wound to his chest. Jared left him to take a look at the other victim. Madison Wilde, her features frozen in terror, had been a beautiful woman. But her long, lustrous blonde hair was now tangled and caked in blood, her green eyes cloudy. Her slim figure was sprawled on the king-sized bed with her chemise torn from it, the thick, white cover underneath her drenched in blood from a neck wound inflicted by the knife still embedded in her carotid artery.

'Looks likely she was raped,' he said almost to himself.

'There appears to be some bruising to the inner thighs, but we'll know more after the autopsy.'

Not much turned his stomach anymore, but his gut was rolling in protest and the smell added to his urgent need to escape the room made claustrophobic by death.

He looked away to give himself a moment, spotted the electronic equipment on the wall. 'You said the skipper's missing?'

'Yes,' Indy said. 'He has sleeping quarters on board but he's not there, bed doesn't appear to have been slept in. Also, there's no sign of forced entry, and the boat has an excellent security system which never activated. There's also that security gate at the end of the dock they would have needed to negotiate—unless whoever did this had water transportation. I have an officer checking on which boats were here in that time frame, whether any have left since, as well as who they all belong to.'

'The couple were in nightwear and the other bedrooms are untouched,' he said. 'Even if they did know their killer, they weren't expecting them. We need to find this skipper.'

'Yeah, we do. But I don't think we'll discover he's responsible. Take a closer look at the knife.'

Not really wanting to, he checked it out. 'Son of a bitch.'

'I got hold of Davis,' Indy said by way of greeting as she came into his office carrying two extra tall—thank God—cups of coffee. She handed him one. 'He's right to do the autopsies as soon as we've got the bodies formally ID'd. Want to be there?'

'Not particularly. How long do you think forensics is going to take with that knife? I want it confirmed as our stolen weapon as soon as possible by the owner.'

'It's got to be the same knife.' Indy blew on her coffee, as desperate for that first sip as he was. It was only nine-thirty but it felt like late afternoon. 'The chances of two identical distinctive weapons like that—minuscule. Tilley said it was unique.'

'You're the one who always says truth is stranger than fiction. We going to get this meeting done?'

'Yep. Just waiting on …' She walked out into the corridor and smiled at Emily, who appeared from the front desk. 'How did you go with Snell?'

'Got a written statement, spoke to his wife. Her story lines up with his. He's cooperated fully.'

'Anything else from the crime scene?'

'Nothing yet. The divers are out there now, in case the skipper's body went into the water. I've told them to call you directly if anything's found.'

'Good work,' Indy said, before going to the meeting room where the rest of the team was assembled. 'Morning.'

There was a round of greetings. Jared knew the four other detectives sitting around the table: Roberts, Perry, Frazer and Johns all had different specialised skill sets. The mix should be a good one.

'We have two victims, both deceased,' Indy began. 'First is Brandon Sash, forty-three years old, owner of Smart Moves Developments here in Hobart, and Madison Wilde, thirty-seven years old, of Wilde Enterprises from Melbourne, down here on business. They were discovered early this morning in the master suite of Wilde's motorised yacht by Sash's personal limo driver. Initial forensic data suggests they were murdered somewhere between 1 am and 4 am Sunday morning. Sash died from a single gunshot wound to the chest, Wilde from a knife wound to the neck following a suspected sexual assault.'

'Has the driver been questioned?' Sergeant Henry Roberts asked. Roberts was a rotund fifty-something with a pristine service record, mostly because he'd never had a case tough enough to mar it. But he was smart, and Jared admired his methodical approach to police work.

'He appears clean. We need to check and double-check everyone who knows and has been in contact with Sash and Wilde during their trip down here,' Indy said. 'This is going to be a very high-profile case. Everyone needs to be their absolute best, no slacking, no cutting corners. We can't afford to miss anything.' She exhaled sharply. 'It shouldn't need to be said, but under no circumstances does anyone provide sensitive details of this case to the media, or anyone else. We stick to the official statement I'll release shortly. I've already got media breathing down my neck.'

'Who's the guy on the board?' Sergeant Ralph Perry asked in his usual clipped manner.

Indy walked back to the pinned paper and rapped her knuckles against the sketch of their POI. 'This is the best sketch we have of our suspect in the spate of local jewellery thefts. He's been picking up women at nightclubs, taking them home then going back later to rob them. A knife taken during last week's robbery looks very much like the one used to murder Wilde. We'll know more when we get a solid ID from the owner. We also need to speak to this guy,' Indy said. She scraped a picture from the desk behind her and pinned it to the board. 'The skipper of the boat—George Fitzgerald. Fitzgerald has worked for the Wildes for seven months. Not so much as a parking ticket to his name. He's the only other person we know of capable of getting past the boat's security and he's currently missing. In case Fitzgerald is a third victim, we've got divers searching the water.'

'I'll see what I can find in terms of any security footage and CCTV of the surrounding area,' Emily said.

'Okay. As well as talking to the victims' family and friends, we need to get our POI's sketch around town. We've already posted the likeness in pubs and clubs, but we should follow up, talk to staff. We also need to piece together a clear picture of Wilde's and Sash's every move from the second they arrived up until the murders, and try and track down Fitzgerald's last movements.'

'I have the contact details for Wilde's parents,' Emily said. 'Sash's parents are deceased. He has a sister living locally. I have a number for her, too.'

'Thanks.' She checked her watch. 'Let's get moving. We'll reconvene in the morning. Thanks.'

Chairs scraped and an eruption of chatter followed Jared and Indy out into the hallway.

'All ready with the press statement?' he asked.

She nodded absently. 'The media have aired images from the yacht club. Someone leaked basic information on the murders, so I'm in damage control. I need to ensure the families are notified immediately.'

'You want me to talk to Sash's sister?'

'Thanks. Take Emily for that.'

He headed for his office, a long list of things to do churning through his mind.

'Jared?' Emily called from behind him.

'What's up?'

'Sorry, this should have been chased up already. Darren Crew from the coffee shop over the road called late yesterday afternoon. Apparently, he also bartends on weekends at the nightclub Caitlin Tilley frequents. He saw the sketch we put out and he reckons he's seen our POI.'

Hope shot through him. 'Thanks, Em. Have you got that address on Sash's sister for me? We'll take care of that first, then I'll drop you back here to start on surveillence footage while I pay him a visit.'

The streets were busier at this time of day and it took longer than he would have liked to get out to Rowena Sash's waterfront home. It was never pleasant informing relatives of a murdered loved one, and he and Emily had left Rowena with her partner to come to terms with the loss, to think about anything that might help with finding the bastard who took her brother's life. He hoped, he really hoped, his next stop would bring something helpful to light.

The coffee shop was doing a roaring trade. He stepped around the queue, copping a few annoyed glances as he waited at the steaming coffee machine where a frazzled young barista was churning out coffees, a long line of orders waiting on small dockets. Darren appeared from behind a display cabinet full of pastries and sandwiches. He looked anything other than frazzled as he slid several plates of food onto trays awaiting hot drinks; his heavily gelled dark hair was stylishly cut and plastered into place, and his light beard was just as perfectly manicured. He smiled, showing off shockingly white teeth.

'Detective, that was fast. Can I get you a coffee?' The comment garnered more glares from waiting customers, a mumbled objection.

'I'm fine, thanks. Is there somewhere we can talk?'

'Yeah. Come in.' Darren flipped open a fold-up counter door and Jared followed him into a tiny office filled with paperwork. 'Sorry about the mess. Not a lot of room in here and tax time, so … You got my message.'

'You think you've seen the guy in the sketch.'

'Yeah. Not at the club. I mean, I might have but it gets pretty hectic in there and the light's not great. But the boss at the club took a photo of the sketch, messaged it to all the staff, so I had it on my phone. Anyway, I was in the pawn shop on Harrington Street yesterday, enquiring about a treadmill they had in the window. Almost ran into him walking in as I walked out. I checked the sketch again and I don't know—it's just a sketch, right? But he was similar. A big bastard with that little scar at the side of his mouth.'

'This was at Quick and Easy Cash?'

'Yeah, that's it. You guys think he's been doing the break-ins, right?'

'Yeah, possibly,' Jared answered vaguely. 'I'll look into it.' He got to his feet carefully to avoid causing an avalanche of delicately piled paperwork and shook Darren's hand. 'I appreciate the call.'

'No worries. You sure you don't want a coffee to go?'

'And risk a riot?' he asked. 'I'll pass.'

CHAPTER 14

'Can I help you?' Jai asked a young man in a McDonald's uniform.

'Yeah, I need to make a payment on my Xbox. Thirty bucks.'

Jai took the cash—a couple of small notes and a stack of change. 'No worries, I'll just—' He stopped talking as the radio news echoed in his ears, much as it had every hour since he'd turned up for work.

'Police have confirmed the victims of the weekend's double homicide are Madison Wilde, daughter of Keith and Julia Wilde of Wilde Enterprises, well known for her commitment to several children's charities, and Brendan Sash ...'

'Um ... get you a receipt,' he finished.

Tank looked over his shoulder. 'Remember to count the money back with the customer,' he said when Jai began dropping it straight into the till.

'Early reports suggest the double homicide could be the result of a robbery gone wrong, however the vicious nature of the attack ...'

'Oh, right. Yeah. I was just …' His hands shook as he drew out the couple of two dollar coins he'd already put in, and in collecting them he dropped the rest. They clattered noisily on the counter, into the till and onto the floor. 'Damn it,' he muttered, then to the customer, 'sorry.'

Tank swore under his breath. 'What is wrong with you today?' he demanded, shoving Jai aside to work up the receipt.

'*Police are chasing up a number of leads and appealing to the public for information …*'

Leads? Shit. The old man? Just how good a look at them did he get? Had someone else been around? Where was Pax anyway?

Almost on cue, Pax ambled through the door and handed Tank some cash.

'Thanks.' Tank sent him a distracted glance and sorted out the customer. When the kid walked out, he turned his attention back to Pax. 'Took you long enough.'

'Got the bike unloaded then the guy wanted to try to talk me down. Cheeky bastard.'

'Glad you're back. There's plenty to do, considering this one's been about as useful as a third armpit all morning.'

Jai stared at Pax, hoping to see some sign he wasn't as unaffected by it all as he seemed. But Pax was … Pax. It was as though nothing had happened.

'Jai, what's the matter? Are you sick?' Tank asked.

'Huh? Oh. Just … maybe a bit.'

'You look like hell. Go get some water, sit down for a minute.'

Pax's warning glare made a thin sheen of nervous sweat erupt on Jai's face. 'Thanks, boss,' he managed.

He went into the office and grabbed his water bottle, then sat and placed his forehead on the cool surface of the table for a long moment before having a drink. He'd only taken one sip when Pax appeared in the doorway.

'You right?'

'Yeah. I'm okay.'

'Good, come give me a hand out the back.'

Shit, Pax was going to get up him about keeping it together. Resigned to getting it over with, Jai got to his feet but glanced at the CCTV when the bell sounded. His already upset stomach flipped. 'Quick,' he whispered to Pax. 'Don't let anyone see you.'

'What the fuck?' Pax muttered, but he went, didn't speak again until they were outside. 'What was that about?'

'The detective just walked in.'

'What detective?'

'The one that's got your picture!'

Pax looked confused. 'Mate, I don't know what you're talking about.'

'Tank didn't tell you? He came in a few days ago looking for stolen stuff, had a sketch of your face. He said it was a picture of the person they think is behind the recent robberies.'

'Are you fucking joking?' Pax laughed, but there was something dangerous in his expression that had Jai stepping back.

'Nah, there's a copy in the drawer under the till. Tank said he didn't know who it was, shrugged it off, said he'd let him know if any of the goods turned up.'

'Okay …' Pax's eyes darted around as though thinking. 'Go in and see why he's back.'

'But he was suspicious of me last time. Kept looking at me funny.'

'So don't let him see ya. Get in there! I need to know what he's saying.' Pax shoved Jai towards the door.

Reluctantly, Jai went inside, decided he'd be pretty safe if he stayed at the back of the shop. He swiped at his brow again, dragged his palms down his work pants and turned away from the counter, pretending to be tidying up.

'Yeah, I heard about it,' Tank was saying. 'All over the news. Shocking stuff. I guess you're hoping some of the goods turn up here.'

'There's that, and I've had a report the guy from our sketch has been spotted here,' the detective replied.

Jai almost dropped the drill he'd lifted to dust under, fumbling it to the shelf with a crash. He quickly moved further away.

'I don't remember seeing anyone in here that resembled that sketch,' Tank insisted. 'Let me take another look.'

'It was yesterday morning, early.'

Jai peeked through the shelf, saw Tank shaking his head. 'Nah, don't think so.' At the same moment, as though aware of the scrutiny, the detective turned and locked eyes with him.

'Hey … Jai, isn't it?' he asked. 'Come over here for a minute?'

Jai dragged his sweaty palms down his pants one more time before walking over. 'Yeah?' Then, at Tank's glare, 'I mean, can I help you?'

'I'm Detective Jared Denham. Remember me?'

'Uh, yeah.'

'You look a bit stressed out. You okay?'

'Sure. Just … got a cold.'

'That's no good. You didn't look well last time I was in here, either.'

Jai waited, feeling increasingly uncomfortable. He shifted from one foot to the next, felt the perspiration tickling his back. And the damn detective just stared at him like he *knew*. 'So …' he managed. 'Do you need something?'

'Yeah. I don't suppose you saw this guy come in yesterday?' The detective showed him the sketch of Pax on his phone.

'Nup,' he said, and cursed himself when it came out too fast. 'I mean, maybe. But a heap of people could look like that.'

'Lots of people duck in, look around and take off again,' Tank said easily. 'They don't approach the counter unless they have something to pawn or sell, or see something they want.'

'Of course,' the detective said, still watching Jai. 'I'm sure that's it.' Eventually those damn cop eyes turned back to Tank. 'You've got some pretty good cameras. Mind if I take a look at yesterday's footage?'

Jai couldn't help the look of distress he sent Tank. What the hell were they going to do now? If Pax got sprung, no doubt he was toast, too.

Tank shook his head. 'They're not recording. Damn things don't work properly. Course, I'd rather that little piece of information stayed between us. They're a good deterrent, that's about it.'

Jai felt his chest relax. Tank was good at this. He'd never really put too much thought into Tank's life in prison and before that, with his gang. He'd never brought it up. But now he was curious, found himself wondering about details that hadn't interested him too much in the past.

'Shame,' the detective said. 'Never mind. Keep an eye out?'

'You know it,' Tank said.

Jai watched the detective leave, then relaxed. Maybe he could talk to Tank about what had happened. He could be the right person to unload to, ask his advice. But as the thought of the incident flooded back into his mind, the idea of talking about it had him going outside for some much needed gulps of fresh air.

'Mate. You're gonna have to calm down,' Pax said from behind him.

'Tank just lied for you. Again. The cop was here about you. If he finds you, we're both screwed. I—the murder was all over the news. I didn't mean to kill that guy, but you killed the woman. And you don't care at all, do you?'

Pax's hand shot out and grabbed his shirt, dragged him in. 'You're gonna have to think real hard about what's gonna happen if ya stuff this up. Like prison. Ya want to go to prison?'

'No. No! I didn't mean it! Maybe if I just tell them I didn't mean it.'

'Ya broke into a boat, pointed a gun at an unarmed man and shot him. That's the reality. Wake up! The only way out of this is to keep ya mouth shut! Keep it together, understand?'

Jai jerked his head. 'Okay. Okay.'

'What was his name?'

'Huh?'

Another shake. 'The cop! Who was it?'

'Um … Denham. Detective Denham. He has a sketch, that's all. He knows you did the other robberies.'

'Fuck.' Pax released him roughly. 'Must have been that drunk bitch from the news. The one that pinched my stash. Denham, huh? I'll deal with the detective. Now toughen the fuck up and get on with it.'

'What are you going to do to the detective?' At Pax's glare, he nodded. 'I will. I—' Jai turned to the door at the same time Pax did.

Tank stood in the doorway, face thunderous. 'Get inside. Both of you!'

This just got better and better. Now Tank would fire him, probably dob him in, and his life and Pop's were both completely stuffed.

Tank turned over the 'Closed' sign on the door before heading for the office. Pax swaggered in in front of Jai, who felt like a student headed into the principal's office and twice as sick.

'You got him wrapped up in those murders?' Tank asked, coming in behind them.

'Chill, man,' Pax said. 'We're good.'

'It—it was an accident!' Jai stammered. 'We were just pinching enough cash so I could pay for Pop's care. They weren't supposed to be there.' His voice broke as he choked.

'I suppose this dickhead told you that?' Tank asked.

'Watch it,' Pax threatened.

'That's what this has been about all along, isn't it?' Tank asked Pax. 'This was never about Cochrane setting himself up with Madison's diamonds. He wanted her dead. Payback.'

'What's he talking about?' Jai asked Pax.

'I'm saying he damn well did know they'd be on that boat,' Tank snapped. 'That was the whole point.'

Jai stared hard at Pax in disbelief. 'You … what? Wait—you planned this?'

Pax shrugged. 'Would ya have helped out if you'd known the plan?'

'You bastard!' He launched at Pax, his fist slamming into his face with enough force that Pax took a few steps back.

Pax moved his jaw from one side to the other, dabbed at the corner of his mouth. 'Suddenly we've grown some balls,' he said, eyes boring into Jai's with threat. 'Ya do that again, I'll cut 'em off.'

'Why did you have to get him involved?' Tank demanded.

Pax shrugged. 'He needed cash, I needed a wingman.'

Tank swore viciously and paced the length of the office and back, fists clenched, expression grim. Finally, he stopped in front of Pax. 'I'm not touching that jewellery.'

Pax's eyes narrowed. 'You'd really fuck all this up over one sweaty-palmed little snowflake? I was doing him a favour!'

'You turned him into a thief and a murderer. That's no favour!'

'Yeah? And what do ya call not telling me the cops have a fucking sketch of my face? I've been walking around without a thought to it and you've known for fucking days! What were ya hoping would happen? Ya think the boss would have been happy if this had all gone to shit? How do ya think he would have repaid ya for that?'

'I lied to the cops twice already!' Tank growled back. 'The deal was to provide you some cover while you stole the diamonds, to get 'em clean and hand them over. That's it. No murders, no dragging anyone else into all this.' Tank's face flushed red as he closed in on Pax. 'You killed Madison Wilde!'

'Yeah. And you've got diamonds to process. I wouldn't want to have to tell tales. Do ya really think it'll be you the boss takes it out on if he doesn't get what he wants?'

Jai saw the colour leach from Tank's face before he nodded. 'I'll get it done, then you go. You get the fuck away and you never come back.'

Pax gave Tank a heavy pat on the back. 'Good choice, old man. Do it fast.' Then he swaggered out, reaching for his cigarettes.

Tank rubbed his forehead and resumed swearing under his breath.

Jai stood quietly, in shock, trying to process what had just happened. 'What were you both talking about?' he eventually asked. 'Did you know those two on the boat?'

'Jai, sit down,' Tank said wearily. 'You need to tell me exactly what the hell happened.'

He sat, not sure how to begin, but when he started talking it poured out of him. He didn't stop until the last bit, then he couldn't seem to get that out. 'He said there was a dog. I would never shoot a dog on purpose, let alone a person. I wanted to leave but I made a noise and then it all just … happened. It was so dark and there was movement and something hit me so I—the gun just went off.

I heard this terrible noise, this gurgling, gasping breathing and then it just stopped. I don't even remember pulling the trigger. Pax told me to leave, so I did. I left her with him. Oh God, what have I done?' He broke down into a fit of choking sobs. 'I didn't mean it. I swear I didn't know. I didn't know. I just needed the money for Pop. No one was supposed to be there. No one.'

Tank sat down heavily in his chair and stared at the roof. 'Okay. All right. Hell.' For an age he didn't say anything more, just stared into space. Then he looked at Jai and cleared his throat. 'I'm sorry you got wrapped up in this. Pax is a dick, but there's one thing he said that I'm going to agree with. You have to pull yourself together.'

He wanted to argue but Tank held up a hand to silence him. 'It's unfortunate, but it's done. Nothing can change what's happened and no one can know anything's up. You're going to keep your mouth shut, do your job and pretend this never happened.'

'I don't know if I can!'

'This isn't a choice, Jai. It wasn't your fault, but you won't walk free from it if anyone finds out. You have to find a way to live with it. Is there any way the cops are going to be able to tie you to this?'

'No. I don't think so.'

Tank leant forward, elbows on knees. 'Which is it? "No" or "I don't think so"?'

'That cop that came in said he found fingerprints at the robbery last week. I think they could be mine. And there was an old guy fishing when we took off in the car, but Pax reckons he wouldn't have seen much.'

'If they had your prints on record for anything they'd already have you under arrest. There's no reason for them to come looking for you unless you were spotted. That old guy, you didn't know him?'

'No.'

'What happened to the gun?'

'Pax said he took care of it.'

'Were you driving your car?'

'No.'

'What'd Pax do with the one you were in?'

'Don't know, didn't ask.'

Tank dragged his hand along the back of his neck and stared into space. 'I know he's good at covering his tracks.'

'Then I'll be okay.'

'I said his, not yours.'

'What does that mean?'

Tank levelled a sobering stare at him. 'It means Pax doesn't do people favours. He let you touch stuff without gloves, had you shoot that gun and, as far as you know, he didn't bring it back. Cops said they're looking for a knife—some special one. Did you touch that?'

He thought back to the first robbery he did. 'There was one knife … Pax asked me to put it in his bag. He had gloves. I didn't.' Tank was right. Pax had done all this on purpose! 'He had it on the boat with that woman!'

Tank nodded slowly. 'That and any other leads the police are working on will point straight to you. Pax didn't need a wingman—he needed a scapegoat.'

CHAPTER 15

'I think this was nicer than going out for lunch,' Aaron said. He was reclining on the hillside, looking as relaxed as Tess had seen him in ages. Around them, a dozen horses grazed peacefully while their riders explored the surrounding bushland of Calico Lodge's back boundary.

'This *is* going out for lunch,' she said with a smile. She heard splashing and wondered why anyone would be in the freezing water of the creek, but whoever it was sounded as though they were having a good time. 'Just with ten strangers and leftover food from a picnic to pack up.'

He chuckled. 'I'll do that in a minute while you round them all up, if you like.'

'Thanks.' She'd expected him to be annoyed when she'd cancelled their plans so she could fill in for Logan leading a guest ride. Instead he'd suggested he come along and help, and all morning he'd been nothing but the considerate, attentive, humourous guy she'd fallen for.

She watched him relocate a bug from his leg to the grass. Smiled. Maybe she'd invite him to stay tonight. They hadn't spent a night together since their argument, and he hadn't asked, but he'd dropped a couple of hints earlier.

He turned and propped himself up on his elbow. 'We should do this more often.'

'I don't see how. We're both busy with our own businesses.'

'Well, it just so happens I've had a brilliant idea.'

'Oh, yeah? What's that?' she asked, mirroring his smile.

'I think we should merge your hiking business with my tour company.'

'You think we should what?' she asked. 'Why?'

'Because it makes sense. We'd get to spend so much more time together. I can give you an assistant to take care of all the paperwork you hate doing, and we can pick and choose which groups you take out. Of course, the business would stay in my name but you would still be your own boss in every other sense. What do you say?' His expression was so hopeful, so excited.

She didn't share his enthusiasm. 'It's not that simple,' she said carefully. 'I have an equal share in the lodge with my brothers, and my hiking business is tied up with that.'

'So sell them your share. You don't need it. We'll build up our own business together.'

'Sell my share of the lodge?' she asked, stunned.

'It'll give us some serious capital to take the tour company to a new level.'

'*Your* tour company,' she said, suddenly annoyed. 'Because it would stay in your name, be your business, you said.'

He waved away the objection. 'We can work out details later. I just want what's best for you. Which is doing all the parts of your job you love without having to worry about the rest.'

Tess placed her elbows on her knees and pressed her fingers to her temples. 'I like things the way they are. I thought you said you were going to back off, give me some space to do my own thing? I'm the most competent woman you've ever met, remember?'

'Of course you are,' he crooned. 'It's not about competence.' He got to his feet, helped her up and framed her face in his hands. 'I want to marry you, Tess. I want us to be together forever. Let me take care of you.'

Marriage? Their relationship had been so short and, lately, tenuous at best. The business proposal was ridiculous enough, but this? What was he thinking?

Voices were getting closer and she looked over her shoulder to see four of the guests returning. A couple more came through the trees. She stepped out of Aaron's reach.

'It's okay,' he said conspiratorially. 'It can be our little secret for now.'

The ride back was anything but relaxed. She kept her attention on the guests, giving instructions as required, sharing information about the area and just generally chatting to anyone who wanted to talk. Marriage? The conversation echoed in her head in a constant loop. How could they be so disconnected from each other as to be on totally different pages where their relationship was concerned? And there was no way she was giving up the lodge and her own business to pour herself and her assets into Aaron's. She was beginning to doubt he'd ever be happy until he was running her whole life.

Once they reached the stables she was kept busy helping the guests unsaddle and cool down their horses, then a couple of teenage girls talked at her incessantly during the walk back to the lodge. She smiled and nodded occasionally, but her thoughts were on what to say to Aaron. He was staying quiet, but she could feel his eyes boring into her. It was like trying to think in a straitjacket. Then they were heading up the front steps of the lodge and she was almost out of time.

'Let's grab a cold drink,' Aaron suggested, leading her towards the bar after she farewelled the group.

'Okay.'

The first thing she saw was Indy talking to Callie. They were seated in the lounge, with one of the lodge's ploughman platters and glasses covering their table. Indy glanced at her and smiled before her gaze moved to Aaron thoughtfully. Indy had already bailed her up over the comment she'd made to Callie about the push out on rescue. Though she'd explained, she didn't think Indy had been convinced, and since Indy was suspicious by nature, it didn't look like she was giving Aaron the benefit of the doubt. Since then, Tess had lectured herself several times for even bringing it up. Aaron wanted to marry her, not kill her.

Aaron placed a hand at the small of her back and steered her towards Indy and Callie.

'How'd it go?' Callie asked.

'We had a wonderful day,' Aaron said, and beamed at Tess. 'Everyone's drinking soft drinks. Should we make it Champagne?'

Tess's heart leapt with panic. Surely he wasn't thinking of announcing— 'No!' she replied sharply and saw the warmth leach out of his face, 'I really need a large glass of water. I'm thirsty. Maybe we could go sit over in the corner for a while?' She tried to smile, knew it came off more like a grimace.

'All right,' Aaron said, eyes narrow. 'I'll get it. You go find a spot.' But he didn't move, just stood there until she walked away.

She spotted Joe and Duncan, two of the guys she'd taken to the snow, having beers in the corner and chose a table as far away from them and the other guests as possible. She didn't want anyone overhearing, even if she felt better knowing Indy and Callie weren't far away. She glanced at them and found their gazes fixed on her.

Indy said something to Callie then stood, moved over to Tess's table and sat. 'What's up?' she asked.

'I have to sort out something with Aaron.' She wondered why she didn't just tell Indy what was going on. But Aaron's frown from the bar kept her mouth closed.

'Something that involved Champagne?'

'Quite the opposite. Indy, I don't really think he wanted you following me over here.'

Indy flopped back more casually as though settling in. 'He didn't want you talking to us without him, which is why he waited for you to walk away from our table before he did. So, what? He's got you scared of upsetting him?'

She opened her mouth to object as Aaron started back across the room. Her stomach dipped at his disapproval. Maybe Indy had a point. Aaron's moods were getting under her skin. 'We have to have a bit of an awkward conversation. It'd be better if he wasn't annoyed before we started,' she said honestly.

'You're being manipulated into being controlled.' Indy got up. 'Just think about that.'

'What are we thinking about?' Aaron asked, placing a glass of water in front of Tess.

'I'll be over there with the others,' Indy said and walked away.

'Oh, just some … girl plans,' Tess managed while pondering Indy's words. Was she pandering to Aaron to avoid his temper? 'Thanks for the drink.'

'No problem.' He sat. 'And I'm sorry. I should have realised you wouldn't want to make an announcement about our engagement until it's had a chance to sink in and you have a lovely ring to show off. It was premature of me.'

'We're not engaged!' she blurted.

'Tess, I'll get you that ring. We can go now if you like, pick one out before the shops close.'

'Aaron, stop.' She rubbed her temples as the headache that had been teasing got more serious. She took a deep breath and one more look at Indy. Hell, when had she become such a wimp? 'It's not happening. I'm sorry, but I can't do this anymore. I can't be in a relationship that feels this claustrophobic.'

Aaron sat up straighter with that disapproving, tight-mouthed expression she was getting used to. 'I thought it might have been too soon, even though this afternoon you seemed more like yourself than you've been in ages. But I was wrong. You're still not back in your normal state of mind.'

'You're not *listening* to me. I can't marry you. I can't be the person you want me to be.'

'Oh for goodness' sake, Tess. You don't have to be anything other than who you are.'

'We're not a good match. You need to find someone who wants to be looked after, taken care of. That's not who I am. I need space, I need to be able to challenge myself, I need to make my own decisions.' She softened her tone. 'Before all this we were great mates, weren't we? Let's just go back to that.'

The anger returned, fast and sharp. 'I don't want to go back to that.'

She jolted when he grabbed hold of her wrist, tight enough to be painful.

'There's someone else, isn't there?' he snarled.

'What? No!' She needed to end this, now. 'I'm sorry. But this isn't going to work.' She pushed up from her chair and was nearly pulled over when he didn't let her go. Her wrist felt like it might snap.

'You're wrong!'

She glanced past the people pretending not to watch and saw Indy and Callie heading towards them. 'Please don't make this uncomfortable.'

'You might want to let her go,' Indy suggested. 'Now.'

Aaron finally released his grip, leaving a visible handprint around her wrist, and got to his feet. 'We'll talk tomorrow,' he told Tess coldly. 'Once you've had a chance to think about it.'

'There's nothing to talk about.'

Anger glittered brighter in his eyes but he nodded, then stalked away.

While a small part of her mourned the end of the relationship she'd wanted so much to work, another sighed with relief.

'Tess,' he called from the doorway, getting the entire room's attention. 'You're wrong. We belong together.'

She smiled blandly and shook her head.

'Psycho!' She recognised Joe's voice as he called to Aaron's retreating figure.

'Are you all right?' Indy asked.

'Yeah, I'm fine. Thanks.' But she felt the tremor in her hands and tucked them behind her back.

'Let me guess,' Callie said. 'That's the end of that?'

'One can only hope,' Indy muttered.

'Good, because honestly? He was beginning to creep me out.'

Tess stared at Callie in disbelief and shook her head. '*Now* you tell me?'

'Come on,' Indy said. 'I want you to fill me in.'

CHAPTER 16

Crash. The splintering noise woke Jared with a jolt. He leapt out of bed and stood just behind the door, listening. Through his window he could see morning sneaking into the sky, but the glow of the streetlight still illuminated his driveway. It was early, not the sort of time he'd expect a break-in. He carefully checked around the corner to the hallway. Beyond, in the lounge room, the curtain was drifting on its railing. He tiptoed out further, looking everywhere, reached the back of his leather lounge and looked over it. There were glass shards on the floor. The curtain flapped again, revealing the shattered window. On the carpet in front of it was a paper-wrapped rock. He knew not to touch it, but something was written on it in large black letters. He nudged it with his toe, flipping it over.

BACK OFF. OR ELSE.

Back off? He stepped around the glass and looked outside, scanning the street for any sign of movement, but everything was still and quiet. Whoever it was had made their point.

Jared snuck into the meeting room and put his coffee down next to Indy's. She paused, eyebrows raised in a clear but silent *Okay?* He nodded briefly, so she took a sip from her coffee then continued.

'We know Wilde was down here on business, looking into plans for a mega resort on the edge of Wellington Park. The *Mercury* ran a story on Wilde's arrival and her planned attendance at a big benefit at the casino that night. She attended with Sash, left around eleven-thirty and went straight back to the boat. This is what she was wearing.' Indy showed them the newspaper image. 'Note she's dripping in jewellery. None of that was found on board, nor was any cash or other valuables. So, whether it was the main motive or not, robbery was involved. Our main suspect is still this man.' She pointed to the sketch. 'And our skipper is still missing.'

'Our POI shot Sash and attacked and stabbed Wilde,' Constable Roberts commented. 'Wouldn't that suggest Wilde was the main target?'

Indy looked at Jared. 'Possibly,' he said. 'He shoots Sash, wants him out of the way. Then he takes his time with Wilde. Rapes and stabs her, but just once in the neck, lets her bleed out. That suggests personal. We know that although he likes to get his victims into bed, up until now that's been consensual.'

'So we're sure it's him?' Constable Perry asked.

'We've got a positive ID on our sketch from our four recent robbery victims,' Emily said. 'All had hooked up with this guy, all had taken him home within two weeks of the robberies. I have all the details.'

'And forensics have managed to remove a partial print on the knife found at the crime scene,' Indy said. 'It matches those found on the gate of last week's break and enter. Also, we've confirmed the knife used to kill Wilde was the same taken in that robbery.'

There was a round of murmurs.

'Our POI faultlessly got past the security system on the boat,' Jared said. 'It ran off a phone app. Wilde's phone is missing, however we know from her chauffeur that she had it on her when she returned from the benefit, therefore we believe that the phone our POI used must have belonged to Fitzgerald. We've tried tracking his phone, but we're not getting any signal from it. We have to assume there's a strong possibility he's met with foul play.'

'What if he was in on it?' Senior Constable Perry said. 'I'm wondering why Wilde didn't scream. Why didn't she make enough noise to raise an alarm? Why didn't she make it off the bed? Could Fitzgerald have been working with our POI?'

'That's certainly something to consider,' Indy said. 'But I believe it's unlikely. Fitzgerald's partner will be down shortly to help us with our enquiries. If anything you need answered stands out, let us know.'

'Anything from the door knock?' Jared asked.

'No witnesses have come forward,' Constable Johns said. 'We've covered the local streets, and we did find an older couple that had been sleeping on a boat moored at the other end of the marina that night, but they don't remember hearing anything.'

'How could they not hear gunshots?' Roberts asked.

'There was a silencer attached to the weapon. A dodgy homemade job but it did what it needed to,' Jared said.

'There's a possibility night fishermen might have seen or heard something,' Jared said.

'Night fishermen?' Indy asked. 'Would they be out that way?'

Jared shrugged. 'There's plenty of boats around out there. Could be.'

'Worth checking out. Anything else?'

'I've chased up the threat to Sash regarding his development,' Roberts said. 'They're a noisy bunch of locals but after looking into them, I highly doubt they're murderers. And none resemble our POI.'

'Okay,' Indy said. 'We're going to need to ramp up police presence at pubs and clubs this coming weekend.'

Jared looked out the window of the meeting room and saw a couple being led into an interview room. Wilde's parents, he guessed from the state of them, and sent Indy a look. She followed it, nodded.

'Anything of importance crops up, let Detective Denham or me know straight away. Thanks.' Indy got to her feet and stretched, then picked up her coffee and drained it. 'Someone threw a rock through your window?'

'Yeah. Warning me to back off.'

'And of course you processed the scene properly. Bagged the evidence?'

'Got forensics to do it. I had to get ready for work.'

'Someone doesn't want us on this case.'

'Yeah, well, next time they might throw a rock through your window. Or worse. Be careful.'

'It's a lot harder to get to me out at Calico Mountain than to you just down the road. It doesn't reassure me that whoever this is knows where you live. We'll put regular patrols out that way, keep an eye on the street.' She indicated the interview room. 'You ready for this?'

'Yeah,' he decided. 'Let's get it done.'

They walked into the interview room where a man in a navy business suit and a woman in a rose-coloured skirt suit got to their feet. Jonathan Wilde had silver hair and a lined yet strong face, with cutting pale-blue eyes, a large straight nose and a mouth that turned down at the edges as though used to carrying a dour expression.

Elizabeth Wilde was petite, with a chic bob, fine bone structure, set jaw and red-rimmed eyes the same colour as her daughter's had been.

'Mr and Mrs Wilde,' Indy said, shaking each hand in turn, 'I'm Detective Inspector Indiana Atherton and this is Detective Senior Sargent Jared Denham. We're sorry for your loss.'

'Have you found him yet? The man who killed my daughter?' Mrs Wilde asked, an edge of desperation to her voice.

'We're working on it, Mrs Wilde.'

'You must have a suspect!' Mr Wilde said.

'The bodies were only discovered twenty-four hours ago, Mr Wilde. We're still compiling evidence. Could you tell us if you know of anyone who might have been a danger to Madison? Did she have any enemies, any recent altercations with anyone or have any threats levelled at her?'

'No. Absolutely not. She was a very special person. Everyone loved Madison.'

'Except Bryce,' Mrs Wilde said, shooting a look at her husband.

'Bryce?' Jared asked.

'Madison's ex-husband,' Mr Wilde explained, then said to his wife, 'He's still in prison, darling.'

'For what?' Indy asked.

'Money laundering and embezzling funds from our company. He went through a period of gambling too much and taking drugs. His habit set him on a downward spiral and their marriage didn't end well, but he wrote to Madison several times, apologising for his behaviour. This all happened almost ten years ago. He's up for parole next month, I believe.'

Jared pulled the sketch of their suspect out of his folder and passed it across the table. 'Have either of you seen this man before?'

'Who is that?' Mrs Wilde's voice trembled.

'He's a person of interest. Do you know him?'

She shook her head, glanced at her husband.

'No,' he said. 'Why?'

'He's been linked to a number of recent local jewellery thefts and we believe one of his possessions was found on the boat.'

'Was her jewellery taken?' Mr Wilde asked.

'There was no jewellery found on board. As your daughter had been wearing several pieces, we believe that, yes, it's been taken.'

'That boat's security was state of the art; no local thug is getting past it the way that bastard did,' Mr Wilde said.

'Our person of interest has a history of beating security,' Indy told them. 'On that, I imagine your skipper had the app for turning on and off the boat's security system in his phone?'

'Yes, of course. The police that came to see us in Melbourne didn't mention him. I assume he's dead too?'

'We don't know. He's missing,' Jared said.

The couple exchanged glances.

'You think he could have had something to do with this?' Mr Wilde asked.

'We're not ruling out anything yet,' Jared said. 'Was anyone else capable of accessing the boat's security system?'

'My wife and I, the security company. That's it. Detectives, no disrespect intended, but I want you to tell me honestly, are you up to this? I can't imagine this sort of thing happens too often down here and I have the means and the contacts to provide assistance.'

'I promise you we're more than capable of handling this case. A very thorough investigation is underway,' Indy told him calmly.

Mr Wilde said nothing for several seconds as he considered that. Eventually he nodded. 'Make it fast, detectives. I want to know who killed my daughter, and I want him to pay.'

'Understandable,' Jared said. 'Again, I'm very sorry for your loss.'

After seeing the Wildes out he went back to his office and worked his way through the remainder of the morning, barely lifting his head until Emily alerted him that Fitzgerald's boyfriend, Matthew Stiles, had arrived.

'I've got him waiting in room two,' Emily said.

'How does he seem to you?'

'Miserable. Worried. Scared. I offered him a tea or coffee but he's too wound up.'

'Thanks.' Still shaking off the Wildes' misery over their dead daughter, he got up to face his second interview of the day.

CHAPTER 17

'Thanks again, everyone,' Craig Suitor, the Search and Rescue team manager, said. 'It was a short meeting but necessary, so I appreciate everyone coming out. See you all in a month, if not before.'

Tess dropped her head to one shoulder then the next and breathed a sigh of relief. She'd gotten through the meeting without any difficult moments with Aaron. She snuck a look towards him, noted he was chatting to Craig and, seeing an opportunity, threw her bag over her shoulder to make a quick exit. She slipped out the glass doors of the building onto the street and decided, as her stomach growled, that the Macca's across the road would do for dinner. She'd get drive thru, which would get her home earlier. She'd had a full day and was tired, and had been tempted to skip the meeting altogether.

She'd just made it to her car when she heard: 'Tess! I need to talk to you.'

Damn. So close, she thought, hand on her car door. 'If it's about us, we've covered it, haven't we?' she asked coldly.

'This is something you're going to want to hear.'

'Really?' She doubted it.

'I know you will,' Aaron said, enthusiasm in his tone. 'Okay, look, I'm sorry about the argument. I accept what you said and I really would like us to be friends at the very least. Which is why you need to hear this. Can we grab some dinner so I can tell you about it?'

Friends? Did she want to be his friend? And did she believe him? After everything that'd happened, not really. She pulled her jacket more tightly against her as a gust of icy wind whipped down the street.

'I really just want to go home. It might be better if you give me a call tomorrow?'

Aaron's mood deflated but he shrugged and nodded. 'Sure. But I'll call in. I want to tell you in person.'

Why? She wanted to say no, she wasn't interested. But she'd be back out on rescues soon and that would mean working together. She was going to have to make some effort or it was going to be impossible. 'Okay. Fine,' she said, opening her door. 'See ya.' She sent him a dismissive smile, climbed in and did up her seatbelt. As she turned on the engine, her phone rang. Indy. She pulled onto the street, because Aaron was still standing where she'd left him, watching her leave. She sighed, then answered the call.

'Hey.'

'I'm assuming Aaron was at the meeting. How'd it go?'

'Fine. He was completely reasonable. I, on the other hand, am a bitch.' She heard familiar noise in the background. 'Are you still at work?'

'Hmm. I'm thinking about food. Are you still around the corner?'

'Yeah, just pulling into Macca's. I was going to drive through. I'm stuffed.'

'You and your cheeseburgers. Come into the station, would you?'

'Why?'

'Because in five minutes I'll be free to eat some proper food and it will be more fun to find out why you're a bitch than eat alone at my desk.'

Tess's empty stomach rumbled again and she stifled a yawn but—'Okay. See you in a minute.' With a sigh, she steered the car back out onto the road and into the next street, finding a park outside the station. She walked inside, said a quick hi to Emily, who was sitting at the reception desk, and let herself through to Indy's office. 'You owe me for this,' she said on her third yawn in as many minutes.

Indy looked up from her computer and smiled. 'Sorry to keep you up. It's … not even nine. Wow. You should be in bed, Grandma.'

'Shut up,' Tess said with a grin and dropped into the spare chair opposite. 'Why are you all still here?'

'Bit of overtime on this case.' Indy lifted her arms above her head and stretched. 'Have you got enough energy to wander down the road to that little Japanese place? I feel like their noodles.'

'I just told Aaron I was too tired for a restaurant. Taking four lots of activities at the lodge today has worn me out.'

'He wanted to take you out after you just broke up with him?'

'He has something to tell me. Something exciting, apparently. And I'm a bitch because he's all for getting over it and being friends and I'm struggling to be nice at all.'

'Tess, don't be naïve. He's not the type to let go that easily. He's come up with some way to lure you back in. Or at least he thinks he has.'

'Well, he's going to have to let go. I'm over it.'

'I can tell. Besides—' Indy smiled and there was a definite teasing quality to it, '—according to Callie, you've been eyeing off Jared.'

'She's still on about that?' Tess really didn't need this right now, but it was probably better to make light of it. 'So what? Jared's good to look at.'

'Thanks, so are you,' Jared said as he walked in and dumped his things on the floor. 'Hi, Tess. Indy.'

'Hi, Jared. Long day?' Indy asked, burying a smirk.

'Yeah. Just packing up.'

Oh God. Tess felt heat flood her cheeks so she turned away, pretending to be busy finding her phone in her bag. When she dared glance up, Jared was yanking at his tie with a slight scowl. He dragged it off then he undid the top button of his shirt. She took in his tousled appearance as he tossed the tie into his bag and rolled up his sleeves.

'If you need to talk about the case,' she said to Indy, in a desperate attempt to run away, 'we don't need to worry about dinner.'

'Dinner?' Jared asked, grabbing his jacket from his bag. His eyes hit hers with a bit more than their usual punch and she felt a pleasant jolt.

'We're thinking Sakura,' Indy said. 'Wanna join?'

'I haven't eaten since this morning, thanks.'

'Then let's get out of here.'

'Jared?' Emily said from the doorway. 'Sorry, I know you're off shift but Tank Finlay was hoping to speak to you for a sec?'

'We'll deal with him on the way out,' Indy said.

Tess followed them to the front desk, where a large tattooed bikie type stood with a young woman Tess supposed was his daughter.

'Hi, Tank,' Jared said. 'And Riley, right? What can I do for you?'

Tank lifted a bag. 'I've had some jewellery come in. It looks a bit like some of the photos you showed me last week. Got held up in the office doing paperwork, but thought I'd drop in on our way home for you to look at tomorrow. Didn't think you'd still be here.'

'You just caught us. Let's take a look,' Indy said, taking the bag. 'Em, have you got those inventory photos handy from the break-ins?'

'Sure. I'll grab them.'

'We'll be back,' Indy told Jared and followed Emily into another room.

'Sorry to hold you up,' Tank said.

'No worries,' Jared said. Then to answer Tank's curious stare, he continued, 'This is Detective Atherton's sister-in-law, Tess. The one I mentioned the other day. She takes hikes out into the national park.'

'Nice to meet you,' Tank said to Tess with interest. 'Riley's heading out there in the not too distant future with her friends. What's the name of your guide, Riley?'

Riley pulled off a perfect teenage huff. 'Aaron Jackson. Not that we need a guide for the South Coast Track, right?' she asked Tess.

'That depends entirely on your experience,' Tess said.

'Which is next to none,' Tank said. 'Detective Denham seemed to think this Jackson was all right. Would you agree?'

Tess kept her face carefully blank. 'Yeah, Aaron's very experienced.'

'That's good to know. When Riley said he'd take them when no one else wanted to, I did wonder.'

'Probably because of the time of year.'

'So it's winter, but so what?' Riley asked. 'That just means it's a bit colder, right?'

Tess wasn't keen on getting too much more involved but both Tank and Riley were watching expectantly. 'It's not the best time of year to do that kind of trek. It'll be cold, most likely wet and muddy and the daylight hours are shorter. If you wait until spring you have a much better chance of good weather and you can enjoy the beaches and the views, and you'll be more comfortable walking and camping. The weather can turn in an instant at any time of year but in winter it's at its worst.'

Riley's face closed into an annoyed frown. 'The weather forecast doesn't look too bad.'

'Since when can you trust a long-term weather forecast?' Tank said. 'You're not going for another couple of weeks yet.'

'Regardless,' Tess said with a shrug, 'that area has its own weather. On average out there it rains every second day—in winter, often more than that. You could be lucky and get a week of sunshine, but it's unlikely.'

Doubt crept onto Riley's face. 'But it's not impossible, right? I've been looking on the internet. Lots of people have gone in winter and had okay weather. And there's not so many people walking the track. We could have it almost to ourselves if we go now.'

'Also true. You could get lucky with the weather and if you're fit enough, you won't have a problem making the distances in the shorter daylight hours.'

'And at the end of the day we camp around a nice warm open fire and—'

'Nope,' Tess cut in. 'The national park is fuel stove only.'

'You really sure you want to do this after hearing all that?' Tank asked Riley.

'Of course,' she snapped. 'We're all fit and prepared for the worst. And we're from around here. We're used to the weather. It's the only time we can all fit this in. Besides, I can't believe our guide would agree to take us if it was going to be that bad.'

'I'm a bit surprised he did,' Tess said. 'He doesn't normally do that hike mid-winter. But good luck,' she added with a smile. 'I'll keep my fingers crossed for you.'

'Thanks,' Riley replied coolly as Indy and Emily reappeared.

Indy handed over the case. 'This isn't what we're looking for, but thanks for checking.'

'I didn't think the owner looked the type but you never know,' Tank said. 'How's it going, anyway? Any closer to finding out who's responsible?'

'We're still looking into it,' Jared said.

'You must have some idea.'

'Why the interest?' Jared asked.

'Tell the truth, I'm getting sick of second-guessing everyone that wants to pawn something—more than usual anyway.'

'Well, you haven't found anything stolen,' Indy said. 'But thanks again for coming in, we really appreciate it.'

'No problem. Would you let me know? If you find the bastard? Bad enough he's stealing, but the murders are something else.'

'We're not sure they're connected yet,' Jared said.

'Of course. Bye then. Thanks for the chat, Tess.'

'Right,' Indy said. 'Are we ready to go? Tess?'

'Huh? Oh. Sure.'

The casual restaurant wasn't busy so near to closing and their meals came quickly. 'So there wasn't anything interesting in that stuff Tank brought in?' Jared asked Indy.

'It really didn't look much like what was stolen at all,' Indy said after swallowing a mouthful. 'Did you leave him photographs?'

'Yeah. I thought he seemed unusually interested in the case.'

'A bit. But it's understandable he's worried about accidentally taking on stolen goods. And we've been breathing down his neck.'

'Yeah, that and Darren thought he saw our POI in his shop. I still think something's off about that kid Tank's got working there.'

'Perhaps. But we shouldn't be talking about this outside the office,' Indy said.

'Don't mind me!' Tess said, lifting her eyes to a row of large lanterns hanging from the ceiling. 'I'm just trying to eat the meal I was conned into waiting forever for. I could have been home in bed by now.'

'Don't be offended,' Jared said. 'Indy's just doing her boss thing.'

'Boss thing?' Indy repeated, brow raised.

'With great power comes great responsibility,' he said.

'Voltaire?' Tess asked in amusement.

'Uncle Ben. *Spiderman*.'

He sounded so indignant she laughed. 'Right. But I can't quite picture Indy in a Spiderman suit. I see her more as a fighting for truth, justice and the American way kind of girl.'

'I'm Australian now,' Indy pointed out, but she was ignored.

'Ah, Superman—make that Supergirl,' Jared continued. 'She was blonde, wasn't she?'

'True. Okay. Wonder Woman?'

'You two are hysterical,' Indy said, deadpan, but Tess caught the humour lurking in her eyes. Then, noodles halfway to her mouth, Indy groaned and grabbed her buzzing phone. She glanced at it, frowned. 'I need to run back to the station for a sec. Won't be long.'

Now what? Tess wondered. She smiled at Jared, feeling strangely awkward. Probably due to the stupid comment she'd made back at the station about him being good to look at.

'How come you were in town tonight?' he asked.

'Special Search and Rescue meeting. Some shuffling going on. Indy just happened to call at the right time to catch me.'

'So … you run a guided hiking business, help run a guesthouse and cattle stud, and volunteer with Search and Rescue. What do you do with all your spare time?'

She grinned. 'It's never boring.'

'Any other interests?'

She shrugged, shifting slightly under the weight of his full attention. 'Lots of things. I also like training and competing with horses when I have a chance. Why?'

'Curiosity.'

'Tess.'

Her stomach sank. He had to be kidding, she thought as she turned in her chair. 'Aaron? Hi. Where did you come from?'

'I hung around talking to Craig for a bit after the meeting, called in for takeaway.'

She decided he probably wasn't following her; he did like the food here. But his voice was as full of accusation as she'd ever heard it, and she remembered she'd told him she was too tired for a meal.

'Right. Ah … you know Jared.'

'Yeah. Hi.' Aaron's tone was one degree above frosty and his eyes barely flicked Jared a glance before returning to Tess. 'I thought you were going straight home.'

'I was. Then Indy called and needed to see me and we were both hungry so she suggested we grab something.'

'And yet you're eating with Detective Denham.'

Hell. 'Look, Aaron. This wasn't planned. Indy's just ducked back to the station. You must have walked right past her.'

'That's funny, I didn't see her.' The amount of venom dripping from his tone rendered Tess momentarily silent.

'I hope you're not calling Tess a liar,' Jared said. The words were casually and quietly spoken, but there was an underlying threat that stopped both Aaron and Tess in their tracks. She looked from one man to the other and back again. They were an impressive pair as they faced off. Except Aaron suddenly seemed smaller, less sure of himself, and for several seconds, he didn't appear to have an answer. She almost felt sorry for him.

Then he turned hate-filled eyes back on her. 'You got him jumping to the rescue now?'

'No. Aaron—'

'Tess isn't the kind of woman to need rescuing,' Jared said in that same, quietly loaded tone. 'You should know that.'

Aaron straightened to full height, his face furious. 'I think I'll find somewhere else to eat.'

As he approached the door, he almost bumped into Indy coming back through it.

'Aaron! Hello,' Indy said.

'So there,' Tess muttered under her breath when he turned surprised eyes her way before pushing through the door.

'He really wasn't expecting to see her, was he?' Jared said. 'Sorry if I've made things more difficult.'

'Don't be,' she said. 'We're not seeing each other anymore. That's over. And even if we were, I still wouldn't be doing anything wrong.' She didn't want to have this conversation. The entire situation was embarrassing. 'He'll get over it.'

'I thought you said he was okay about the break-up,' Indy said, sitting down. 'He didn't particularly look it.'

'He came in for takeaway and thought I'd lied to him, blown him off to have dinner with Jared.'

'Ouch. Unlucky coincidence.'

'I should have just had a quick meal with him, heard him out. But now that I've called it quits, I see him coming and I want to run the other way. That's horrible, right? What's wrong with me?'

'You keep asking, I keep saying …' Jared muttered.

She felt a little jolt of pleasure over the guilt. 'It's just that he'd said he was fine with it, but needed to talk to me. Now he thinks I'm lying to him.'

'And I have no idea why you care,' Indy said. 'How's the wrist? The one your *friend* just about broke when he had the shits in the bar?'

'He what?' Jared asked sharply.

'He was upset,' Tess told Jared. 'He wanted to marry me, but I called it quits.'

'Stop making excuses for him.' Indy gathered up the last of her noodles. 'You bent over backwards to make it work. It didn't. You're better off without him.'

'Can't argue with that,' Tess said. 'I don't know why I thought I needed to find anyone. I've decided I'm happier on my own.'

'Shame.' Jared sat back from his empty plate with that half-smile of his on his face. 'If you ever change your mind …'

Indy choked on her final mouthful, couldn't seem to stop coughing. Tess barely noticed. Jared's eyes had locked on hers with an intensity that said, *I'm not joking.*

The buzz of awareness that shot through Tess seemed to jumble any words she wanted to say. She glanced away to get her head back in the right space. Did he mean it, or was he just trying to make her feel better? Despite her rather stunning physical reaction to him, the break-up with Aaron was still raw, his nastiness echoing in her head. She was feeling too hollowed out to say anything witty or flirty in reply. She wasn't exactly proficient in those sorts of conversations at the best of times.

A charged silence had descended on the table. She needed to say something. 'I'll keep that in mind.'

Jared's smile widened, eyes warm and amused.

'I don't mean to interrupt,' Indy said with a roll of her eyes and a check of her watch, 'but we should get going. Ready?'

CHAPTER 18

'Fitzgerald spoke to his partner Stiles around 11 pm,' Jared told the team the following morning. 'Fitzgerald said he was cruising the town for a nightclub. He sounded intoxicated and Stiles believes he was alone at the time. We need to check surveillance, try and track him down. Emily, you'll get on that asap with Johns and Williams.'

'Will do.'

'We also need to keep up the surveillance on the nightclubs. Roberts, how are the rosters for extra patrols this weekend?'

'All done. There'll be a big presence in and around the hotspots and out on the street.'

'Great. We had one possible sighting of our POI at the Quick and Easy Cash pawn shop on Harrington Street. Keep your eyes open.'

'Are we releasing the sketch to the media?'

'On the morning news as we speak. Expect a flood of calls and false sightings. You'll be wading through them for days but we only need one to be on the mark. The Wildes are understandably pushing for answers and the media aren't going to let up, but don't let the pressure get to you. We'll catch this piece of shit, just do what you do.'

As everyone collected their things and left the room, Jared stared at the sketch. 'He'll go to ground,' he told Indy, 'once he sees his image in the media.'

'There's not a lot of choice. We've shared the picture around already. If we don't release a statement and image officially, the media are bound to still get hold of it.'

'True.'

'Autopsies are set for this morning. I'm going to attend.'

'You need me there?'

'No, you've got enough to do. I'll let you know the results.'

'Thanks. I'm going to do a bit more digging. I think Tank may have been lying. That kid, Jai … something's going on. I need to know more about him.'

Relieved at avoiding the autopsy, he looked up Jai Wharton, found nothing then got caught up chasing up some of the phone calls that had started filtering in over the morning news. Between that, squeezing in a quick lunch then discussing progress with members of the team, by the time Indy breezed in with coffee he wasn't really sure where the day had gone. He checked his phone, noticed it was after five.

'Go home,' she told him, dumping the cup in front of him.

'Yeah, there's just a couple more reports I'm curious about. How did you go at the autopsies?'

'Nothing unexpected. Anything at your end?'

'We got back a result on our partial shoe print from the boat. Size nine men's Volleys.'

'Whoever he is, he isn't spending his diamond money on shoes. Any decent tip-offs?'

He groaned. 'One claimed to have seen our POI dressed in a clown outfit outside her bedroom window, another saw someone a bit like him partying interstate last year, another one looked like him but with purple hair on a train in Melbourne and—hand to God—I got one stating he was Elvis.'

Indy chuckled. 'Some people think they're funny.'

'Some people need Tasering.'

She laughed again but it was followed closely by a yawn. 'I hope our POI's unhappy about seeing his picture on the news.'

'The idea makes me feel slightly better about the world. And on the topic of how we're all feeling, how's Tess today?'

'Haven't spoken to her.'

'That Aaron guy was completely out of line.'

'I'm pretty sure your blatant flirting helped drag her out of the dumps a bit.'

'Good to know.' Then he shrugged. 'It was a serious offer.'

'Yeah, you didn't leave a lot of room for doubt on that,' she said with a smile. 'Okay, I'm heading off. See you tomorrow.'

'See you then.' Deciding calling it a day was a good idea, he got himself sorted and headed out. He deliberately drove past the pawn shop, noticed the lights were still on, but even though he slowed, he saw no one inside. He wondered if their POI had caught the news, what he'd be thinking of doing next if he had. He continued on, wound his way past the historic buildings of Cascades, and had begun the gradual climb up towards his simple two-bedroom house tucked into the base of Mount Wellington when his phone rang. Damn it, if he had to go back to work someone was going to pay with their life.

'Denham,' he answered reluctantly.

'I told you to back off,' a man's voice growled.

He wanted to pull over, record the conversation, but there was a car right behind him and nowhere safe until further up the road. 'Want to tell me why I'd do that?'

'You don't know who you're dealing with.'

'Why don't you tell me?' Keep him talking, Jared told himself.

'I'll kill you.'

'I highly doubt that.' He went around another bend. The car behind him sped up, levelled, then turned towards him. Jared swerved out of the way, hitting a power pole with a hard enough impact to set off the airbags. More angry than shaken, he grabbed his phone and jumped out of the car as his attacker spun their tyres and disappeared.

'Damn it!' He'd missed the plates. As he called Indy, he looked down into the darkness of a ditch only centimetres from where his car had hit the pole and decided he was happier to be up here than to have ended up down there.

'Yeah, it's me,' he said unnecessarily when she picked up. 'I think you're right. Someone's unhappy about seeing their picture on the news.'

CHAPTER 19

The knock on Tess's door came early, and when she spotted Aaron through the peephole, she wondered whether she could simply pretend she wasn't home. She discounted the idea and gathered her courage. She'd told him she'd see him, so it was probably better to just get it over and done with. She opened the door, not really knowing what to expect, and blinked twice when she saw the enormous bunch of red roses.

'Hi.'

'Hi, sorry for the early visit but it's nearly impossible to catch you otherwise. These are for you.' He pushed them at her so she stepped back as she took them, which was all he needed to invite himself in.

'What are these for?' she asked, realising what a dumb question it was as soon as it was out of her mouth.

'To apologise, of course.' Aaron walked further into the apartment, and into the kitchen. 'Is that coffee hot?' he asked.

'Yeah—okay, I'll make you one.' She'd already had a coffee but drained the pot to make enough for two and took the cups to a small table. She wondered why he would buy flowers. It was a sweet gesture but red roses didn't scream 'simple apology'.

He sat at the table, eyes searching her face. 'I acted like an idiot at the restaurant. I'm sorry.'

'Yeah, you did,' she said.

'I'm ashamed to admit I was jealous.'

Frustration welled in her chest. Tread carefully, she reminded herself. She sipped her coffee and thought about how to say what she needed to say. 'I don't want us to reach a point where we can't be friends—or at least, friendly,' she began tentatively. 'But just at the moment—'

'Tess, hold on. Before you go any further, you need to hear this. I'd been looking into something before we had that argument and I've just had confirmation, so … I've made travel plans, big ones.'

'Travel plans? You're going somewhere?' The relief that swept over her was immense and instantaneous. This was going to make things so much easier.

'Canada. To work for a wildlife adventure group over there. It's going to be amazing.'

'Sounds like it.'

'I have a couple of loose ends to tie up here. And I've got a hike booked. Shit time of year but the money won't hurt.'

'I heard about that. Jared introduced me to Riley.' She swore silently at the accidental mention of Jared. 'I did wonder why you agreed to take them in July.'

He scowled. 'That group are all teens, aren't they? A bit young to be Jared's friends, surely.'

'Jared knows Riley's father—Tank, I think they call him—through work. I think the story was Tank won't let them do it without a guide and this is the only time of year they can fit it in. Lucky for them you needed that money or they'd miss out. I wouldn't be keen to head out there right now.'

'Yeah, they might not feel real lucky if the weather doesn't hold,' Aaron replied, still scowling. 'So, you found all this out when you were with Jared … when?'

She controlled her temper. He was being childish. 'The same evening. Tank and Riley called in at the station over a police matter just as we were heading out to get dinner.'

'Right.'

'I told you what happened. I can't force you to believe me but I have no reason to lie. We're not together anymore.'

'And I told you,' he said, his scowl replaced with a guilty smile, 'I can't help being jealous. But okay.' He held his hands up then dropped them to hers, squeezed, smiled into her eyes with excitement. 'I don't want us to argue. Let's just put it all behind us. Fights, silly break-ups, they don't matter. I want you to come with me.'

'What?' She jerked her hands from his. 'Come with you … *to Canada*? Why would you think I'd do that?' He couldn't possibly believe she'd say yes, could he? But the animation in his voice, his expression, suggested he did.

'Think about it, Tess. You said you want adventure, independence. Over there you'd be being paid to hike some of the most beautiful country in the world.'

She shook her head slowly. 'I already hike some of the most beautiful country in the world. I have a home here, a business, a life. I couldn't just leave it even if I wanted to. And I don't.'

'Why not? The surprise I mentioned, I asked about a position for you, too. They're an expanding company, looking at hiring three or four more guides. They're more than willing to interview you and there's no way they won't take you if they've taken me. They've practically said yes already. The money's great. Just think about the adventures we'll have.' He sat back, beaming, as though he'd already sealed the deal.

Canada. She knew she'd love it. At a different time in her life she might have seriously considered doing a stint there. But not now. And not with Aaron. His irrational behaviour was scaring her. They'd broken up. What didn't he get about that?

'I know you're thinking about it,' he said after a moment. 'Say yes.'

'No.' She softened her gaze when his face fell. 'It's a great opportunity. A wonderful idea. But I'm already living my dream, right here. I can't just take off, drop everything I've worked so hard for. I'm happy for you—thrilled for you. But I'm not coming with you.'

'Tess,' he said gravely, 'I've said I'm going. I can't back out.'

'Of course not. Why would you?'

He stared in disbelief, then his mouth turned into a bitter sneer. 'Nothing I ever do is enough for you, is it? I look out for you, I take care of you, I offer you a stake in my business, I've forgiven you for the rubbish over the break-up, turned up with roses after you went out with another man. And you don't care at all, do you?'

Tess's heart thumped uncomfortably in her chest. A part of her had known the temper was coming. It was becoming too regular an occurrence. 'That's not true.'

Aaron pushed back his chair and stood, anger emanating from him, and shoved a finger in her face. 'You know, there are only so many chances that come around in a lifetime. How many do you think you have left? You're making a mistake.'

'I don't think so.' She fought to hold her nerve as that pointed finger became a fist, and tensed. She didn't trust him not to lash out, but he pulled it back, glared at her with nothing but disdain. How had she ever thought she loved this man?

'I guess that's it then. I tried.' He strode to the door. Paused. 'Good luck in Search and Rescue without me. And try and remember you're supposed to be saving lives, not putting them at more risk. Don't go falling off any cliffs.' He laughed nastily.

As far as parting slaps went, she'd score that a nine. If she'd cared a bit more about him, it could have hit eleven.

Tess sat there shaking and fuming for several minutes. Tears welled in her eyes but she refused to let them fall. He wasn't worth it. Thank God he was going away. She could only hope it was soon.

When she'd had enough of feeling sorry for herself, she pulled on her jacket and stormed out of the lodge to the equipment storage shed. She *hated* that Aaron had made a good point. If she was going to be a liability on a rescue, she was better off not being there. She had to be able to tackle heights; allowing herself to remain frightened of them was not an option.

She picked up a bag of abseiling equipment and checked its contents. Everything was there, so she tossed it in the back of her car and drove out onto the bush trails.

It only took a few minutes to reach the lodge's abseiling area. She parked the car off the main track, swung the bag over her shoulder, then walked along the short trail to where a large shelf of rock looked out over the tops of trees. There were three stations set up. At the closest end the drop was small, barely twelve feet. The beginners rock. She'd do that first. She went up the steps cut into the side of the bank, unloaded her equipment and got to work setting up. It wasn't until she was harnessed up, ready to descend, that she felt the fear close in. It disabled her.

Damn it, she thought, impatient with herself. Complete beginners tackled this all the time. A simple, easy descent. She got close to the edge, cursed herself, cursed her trembling legs. Nerves sent tiny pinpricks through her still painful fingers, weakening them; her chest seemed to close up, refuse to let in any air. As she tried to focus on where to put her feet, she caught sight of the ground below her and her vision tunnelled and swam.

She took several quick steps back from the edge and sat to try and calm herself down. It was hardly Fedder. She could—had—done this in a single jump hundreds of times.

She got up again, told herself to just do it. *Just lean back, just step out.* She forced a trembling leg back, but her foot slipped an inch. Heart in her throat, she scurried back to safety. With a growl of frustration, she ripped off her gloves and undid the harness, kicking it off. As she shoved everything back in the bag, her phone rang.

'Hello?'

'Oh—is that Tess?'

Tess rolled her eyes at her unprofessional answer. 'Yes, sorry. It is. Can I help you?'

'I called you a couple of weeks back about the possibility of doing a trek in the Southwest National Park. I was just calling in case … well, I suppose I was hoping you might have changed your mind.'

She sighed. 'You know, Par Avion do some truly unforgettable tours better suited to this time of year. Perhaps you should think about taking one of those.'

'We really had our heart set on a long trek.'

She remembered Aaron was taking Riley's group out. She was angry, over it, but it might get the woman off her back. 'I know someone who could possibly take you with another group. I'll give you his number.' She rattled it off and was lavished with gratitude.

When she ended the call, a text came through. Indy. She'd called in at the lodge for lunch. Where was Tess?

Tess hesitated, then, because she felt just that pathetic, answered, *Sitting on a rock in the bush feeling sorry for myself.*

She dropped the phone and stared ahead. It was just her and the small cliff. She should try again. But what was the point? She knew she wasn't getting down there today.

Her phone rang again. Another unknown number. She frowned, wishing everyone would just leave her alone for five minutes. Then she answered.

'Do that often?' Jared asked.

'What?'

'Sit on a rock in the bush.'

'How did you know?' she asked in surprise.

'I'm having lunch with Indy and Logan, but I'm feeling like a bit of a third wheel. I don't suppose you're hungry?'

She pressed a hand to her jittery stomach. 'I'm not really sure I can fit anything in at the moment,' she answered honestly, then worried that sounded like a brush-off. 'I don't want you to think I don't—' *want to have lunch with you?* Was that too much? It was a call-in lunch with Indy and Logan. It's not like he'd planned a date. 'I would, if I was there. But I'm only going to hold you up and you're probably busy.'

There was a pause, then, 'Where is this rock?'

She laughed, because when he said it, it sounded so silly. 'I'm at our abseiling area.'

'Ah, abseiling. Now it makes sense. See you soon.'

'What makes sense? Jared?' She heard him end the call. It had sounded for all the world like he was on his way. How did he even know where their abseiling area was?

When he turned up five minutes later she figured Indy must have told him. And there it was again, that little jump in her belly she would have thought impossible after all the drama over Aaron.

'I brought food,' he said. 'In case you changed your mind. And because I'm hungry. Mind sharing your rock?' He looked completely out of place in his suit, holding paper-wrapped rolls. On top of the undeniable attraction, Tess felt a tug of something more.

'Thanks. You didn't have to.'

'I know. Here.'

She took the roll and peeked at it. 'Hey, my favourite. How'd you know?'

'I've solved tougher cases,' he said.

'You had a source.'

'I did. Callie.'

She fought the urge to roll her eyes. Callie would be loving this. 'Weren't you with Indy?'

'And Logan, yeah. So.' He began unwrapping his food. 'Come here often?'

'All the time.'

'Pretty spot.'

'There's plenty of them out here.'

'Oh, yeah? Where else do these trails lead?'

'All over the place.'

They ate as they talked, and when they were finished, Jared brushed off his hands, took the rubbish and stood.

'So, you want to tell me what's wrong, or can I guess?' he asked.

She got to her feet and shook her head. 'It's stupid. I don't seem to be able to get down there.'

'Down … there?' he asked, pointing to the edge.

'Yeah.'

He took her hand, turned it over in his, then turned it back. 'Still sore?'

'They're not the problem.'

'Then what is?'

'It's in my head. I can't do it. I can't go over the edge. How can I do what I do if I'm going to be scared of heights? I was so ticked off at Aaron, but he has a point.'

A frown touched Jared's features and his tone cooled. 'And what point would that be?'

She blurted it out, about Canada, about the rescue—all of it.

'I think what he would have said,' Jared told her after a moment, 'had he been feeling more reasonable, is that you should give yourself some time, work your way back up to it.'

'Yeah, but how do I know I will get over it? I feel like a coward.'

He grinned at that. 'You're the woman who charged into a police station with a serial killer in the building and saved my life. The woman who risked her life on a mountain in a thunderstorm with no safety gear. Tess, you went over a cliff. You nearly died. If your brain isn't telling you to avoid heights, there's something wrong with you.'

She dropped her gaze. 'Perhaps.'

'Would you teach me?'

It took her a moment to catch up. 'Teach you what? How to abseil?'

'Yeah,' he said with that half-smile. 'Unlike you, I've never been comfortable with heights. I got out of abseiling at school camp when I was fourteen by pretending I had a stomach ache. I'm a complete wuss. Teach me.'

'When?'

'Now.'

'Now? You're wearing a suit.'

He picked up her harness and shifted it around in his hands, trying to figure it out. 'So what do I do?'

'First of all, you're not wearing that one. Hold on.' She went back to the bag, took out a men's size and found him a helmet and gloves.

He climbed into the harness, followed her instructions on fitting everything properly and slipped on the gloves when she offered them. 'Right, what's next?' He walked over to a couple of neatly tied lengths of coloured rope. 'We attach one of these?'

'The blue one.'

'Why not the red one?'

'Length,' she said with a flick of a smile. 'The shorter one is fine for this but it's important to make sure your rope's long enough to make it to the bottom of the cliff.'

'Okay,' he said. 'Show me how you attach it.'

'Know how to make a figure-eight knot?'

'You know what, I think I do.' He had a go.

'Perfect,' she said. 'Now we attach it to this ring bolt like so ...' She threaded the knot into a heavy metal ring bolted deep into the rock. 'And add a stopper knot so the rope is secure. Now we do it again. Never use just one anchor point. Three's a good number.'

'I'm guessing they're not going to move.'

'This abseiling station is set up here permanently. This is my beginners rock for guests. Tried and tested. Nothing is going to move.'

'Okay, cool. What's that?' he asked of a metal clip she'd picked up.

'This is your belay. We just have to loop the rope through it like this, then attach it to your caribiner like so ... then clip you onto it here.'

'That's it?'

'Once we've done the carabiner up,' she said, rolling it into place to lock it, 'yeah, almost. There's a couple of different ways we can do this, but because you're a beginner, I'm going to attach a prusik knot as an extra precaution.'

'Extra precaution. Sounds like a plan.'

She wrapped the prusik knot around the rope, hooked it onto another clip on his harness and checked it all over. 'Okay. You're ready. Now you just need to—' She swallowed. Nerves bouncing, she tried to focus while he took a good look at where he had to go.

'It's not too far down if I stuff this up. Right?' he asked.

He really was unsure of himself. It helped her mind switch back into instructor mode. 'You're not going to stuff this up. I'm not going to let you. Watch.' She edged closer and looked everywhere but down. 'The belay uses the friction of the rope against itself to control your speed as you let it out, but if you do happen to slip, or let go, the prusik will tighten around the rope and stop you from falling.' She heard the reassurance in her voice, knew the truth of it, and felt even more stupid for not getting down that small drop herself. 'You need to hold the ropes like so … great. Now just take some weight on the rope and lean out to about a forty-five-degree angle.'

He leant out. And just seeing him heading over that drop, no matter how small, put Tess back on Fedder and filled her mind with Charlie. She dropped to her knees, stunned at the inability to breathe against the sudden tight knot in her chest.

'Why forty-five?' he asked, still poised as though he couldn't see her fighting not to pass out.

'What? Jared, I'm sorry. I can't do this.'

'You're not. I am. Why forty-five?'

'Um …' She made herself look at him, refocus. Slow her breathing. 'Not enough lean, you'll face plant the rock; too much, you'll end up upside down. How you are right now, that's good.'

'So what next?'

'Now you …' She cleared her throat, tried again. Another deep breath. 'You slide the prusik down the rope as you let it out. Good. Make sure your feet are spread wide enough to keep you stable. You don't want to tip to either side. That's it. Then you just …'

'Start walking?'

'Yeah.'

'Got it.'

He took a few steps, until she could just see his face over the rock. *What if he falls?* 'Jared—'

'Hey, once you're over the edge, it's great!'

'Just go slow and steady. Please.' She got her legs under her and hurried down the slope at the side of the drop to watch his descent from below, but he had the hang of it and beat her to the base.

'Too easy,' he said with a grin. 'Can we do the big one next?'

She pressed a hand to her head where it hurt from tension. 'Ah … I suppose so. But not today. Indy will need you back, right? We should get you out of the harness.'

'You did it. You wanted to pass out, but you got me down. You're not a coward, Tess Atherton. Forget about Aaron. He's just bitter.'

'And good at scoring points.' Another deep breath had her feeling almost back to normal. 'I don't know why I assumed he'd just let go without a fight. I'm sorry you got dragged into it. Stupid thing is there isn't even anything for him to be jealous about.'

'Would you like there to be?' he asked. 'The offer still stands.'

Would she? She couldn't believe she was even considering it. She liked Jared, and she certainly felt better when she was around him. But …

'I know your head's full of your break-up with Aaron,' he said as though reading her thoughts. 'But if you feel like going out and just forgetting about it for a while, let me know. No pressure, okay?'

Perhaps it was what she needed. Maybe it would take some of the focus off Aaron. Make it all seem less important. But she needed some clarification. 'If what you're suggesting is some sort of sympathy date, forget it.'

'Sympathy would have nothing to do with it.' The words and their warm delivery did anything but loosen the knots in her stomach.

'Well, in that case … You're not clingy, are you?'

Jared's smile became a laugh. 'You can find out Saturday night.'

CHAPTER 20

'Abseiling?' Indy asked in disbelief as they drove back to the station. 'You hate heights!'

'I'm not sure Tess wants it broadcast to her entire family, but she's having a bit of a hard time with them herself.'

'Yeah, I know.'

'I thought it might help if she instructed me on it. Got back into the swing of things.'

'Does she not expect it to take time?'

'Aaron is the one who has her stressing over it.'

'Aaron? He just won't go away! What did he do this time?'

'He asked her to go to Canada. I'm sure she'll tell you about it. But when she said no, he made some stupid parting shot about her being useless because she had a moment over the height at the last rescue she did.'

'The one where he nearly knocked her off the cliff, you mean?'

'He did *what*?'

'Accidentally. Apparently.' Indy sighed heavily. 'I'm just glad she called it off so I don't have to pretend to like him anymore.'

'You didn't like him?'

'I know, I know. Everyone likes Aaron. How could I not like him?'

'Everyone likes that guy? Really? I must be missing something.'

'He's a bit of a hero in Search and Rescue circles. He's done some great things since he arrived a few years back. If you believe his stories, he was just as successful doing a similar job over in the UK.'

'I see. Tess obviously liked him enough to start seeing him in the first place.'

'He can be thoroughly charming. And he's easy on the eyes. Brave, dedicated and shares a similar lifestyle. And he absolutely adores her.'

'I sense a really big *but* coming.'

'I don't like him. Tess is a capable, independent person. She was willing to compromise on a lot of things to give the relationship a chance and he just kept reeling her in tighter and tighter. He had her questioning everything she did. Anyway, he's gone.'

'Or soon will be. What was that phone call about as we were leaving?'

'Wilde's pushing for answers—his lawyer was giving me a rocket up the backside. I'm copping pressure from all corners.'

'Don't let it get to you.'

'I won't. Oh, I meant to say, the phone you were called on during your drive home last night was a prepaid job. We haven't been able to trace it.'

'I didn't expect our POI to make it too easy.'

'And he left no fingerprints or other evidence after the rock-throwing incident. You don't seem to be taking the threat very seriously. He could have killed you.'

'He wants me to back off. I'm not backing off.'

Emily was waiting for them when they entered the station. 'I think I've found something.' She took them back to her desk and gestured for them to look at her monitor. 'Does that look like Fitzgerald to you?'

'Yeah, that's him.'

'Good, because I've spent most of the morning chasing him on every available camera. In your notes from your interview with Stiles, he said Fitzgerald had visited a pub with a direction and coordinates in its name. I figured it had to be Tavern 42 Degrees South. He's leaving the pub here, safe and sound, next picked up on CCTV crossing Macquarie Street and again south on Liverpool Street. I'm guessing he was most likely heading towards Flamingos because I think, though I can only see the back of him, this is him entering the club. The footage is quite a distance away.'

'Clothing looks right. That's a different location to our POI's usual haunts.'

'It's a gay and alternative bar.' Emily flicked to another screen. 'I think this could be Fitzgerald leaving at around midnight. There was a big crowd that poured out at once and the camera angle's not great.'

'Hold up. Go back to the first lot of footage and let it run.' He scanned the screen, spotted it. 'There!' He pointed to another figure in the background, heading in Fitzgerald's direction. 'Is that the same guy who was behind him when he left Flamingos?'

Emily opened another screen. They all looked closer.

'Could be …' Indy said. 'Go back to the Macquarie Street footage. Keep it going after Fitzgerald has moved on.'

A few seconds ticked by. The other figure came on screen, following Fitzgerald from a distance.

'It's the same guy,' Indy said. 'He's stalking him. How clear can we make that face?'

'Better, but probably not great. It's only a partial and shadowed.'

'Pass it over to tech, see what they can do.'

'Why is he just wandering around after him?' Emily asked.

'The later it gets, the more bars he goes to, the drunker the victim,' Jared said. 'And the less likely he is to fail.'

'This is different from the others. Our POI would pick up women, learn how to get in to their houses, wait a few days at least, then break in.'

Indy nodded. 'He might not have been able to get near Wilde. Besides, he only needed to pick up the paper to have known she was worth the hit. But he needed to get in. So I'm guessing he watched the boat, the routine, worked out the security was linked to their phones. Then he followed Fitzgerald around until he was as drunk as he was going to get and jumped him for the phone. Take another look at them both leaving the club. They're practically side by side but there's no interaction. Fitzgerald wasn't involved in this and he never made it back to that boat.'

'Em, can we get an analysis not only of the guy's face, but his approximate size?' Jared asked. 'We know Fitzgerald was five-eleven, so this guy's huge.'

'Okay, I'll find out.'

'Thanks. Because I can't see a guy like that fitting into a size nine shoe.'

'You're right,' Indy said and cursed under her breath. 'There's two of them.'

Jared picked up his jacket and car keys.

'Where are you going?'

'I'm going out there. I'll try Flamingos and the yacht club again, then head out on foot between the two if nothing new surfaces.'

He drove to the nightclub first. The streets were packed with shops and businesses and he knew it was well lit at night. He checked every nook and cranny he could find, before deciding the relatively quiet streets surrounding the yacht club contained many more likely sites for Fitzgerald to have been attacked. They'd searched the immediate area. He'd have to extend it, look again.

The yacht club sprawled out along the roadside. He walked slowly around the clubhouse, checked out boats and cars and bins. At the furthest end of one carpark, a shipping container caught his eye. He wrestled with the handles and opened it. Nothing. Damn, where *was* Fitzgerald? In the water? Had they missed him?

Jared walked along the waterfront to the park, up and down the rock wall and stopped at some boat sheds, trying to figure it out. His foot kicked a bottle lid. He watched it roll away and hit the wall. Something had leaked out from under one of the roller doors next to where the lid came to a stop. He walked over and bent down to take a closer look. Noticed the smell. He tried the door. It was unlocked or broken, because it rolled straight up. He took several steps backwards.

Fitzgerald's body had been carelessly dumped in the corner. He was wearing the clothes he'd left the club in, crusted in blood that had run from a wound to the back of his head. But from the way his bloodshot eyes seemed to be popping from their sockets together with the angry wound on his neck, Jared was going with strangulation as cause of death. A few feet away a leather wallet sat open, but there was no sign of a phone. He pulled his own phone from his pocket as he turned away to drag in a couple of deep breaths of fresh air, and call it in.

Because Indy had taken the first two autopsies, Jared put his hand up the following day for Fitzgerald's. He didn't enjoy them the way a few cops he'd worked with did, but he could understand and appreciate their fascination for the process, the giant jigsaw puzzle of evidence that constituted a homicide victim's body. He still walked out feeling sick to his stomach.

'How'd you go?' Indy asked as he arrived back at the station.

'Fitzgerald was struck over the head before being strangled with a copper wire. Traces were found embedded in his skin.'

'The initial blow knocked him out?'

'There's no evidence of a struggle or defensive wounds so it doesn't look like he ever knew what hit him. The heels of his shoes were worn in a manner that suggests he was dragged some distance over a gravelled surface.'

'That was risky,' Indy said. 'If he caught a cab back to the yacht club, that's what? Couple of hundred metres to the dumping point?'

'At least. He could have just dragged him to a car.'

'Most likely. Knocked him out, dragged him into his car, drove him round, strangled him in situ. Roberts reported earlier that they'd found what they believe to be the remains of Fitzgerald's phone washed up under the jetty. It was completely destroyed, which is why we couldn't get any kind of a signal off it to track it down. I wonder if the copper wire was found at the scene.'

'Not that I know of. I didn't notice it, either.'

'Hmm.' Indy chewed on her pen, stared into space.

'Something else is bothering you,' he said. 'What is it?'

'Does this really seem like an amateur burglar turned killer to you?'

He sighed. 'I have some issues with it.'

'Our second POI could account for this massive jump in behaviour, but it still reads to me like Sash was murdered just to get him out of the way, and Wilde was the main target. I've been looking into her ex.'

'Bryce Cochrane, the full of remorse, money-laundering druggie. And?'

'He's been in prison almost a decade, due for a parole hearing. That money laundering Mr Wilde mentioned was a business agreement Cochrane had with a local motorcycle club. He was running their drug profits through the casino for them, handing it back over in chips they would then cash in as clean money.'

'And?'

'It was quite profitable—to the tune of several million. The money was never recovered, apparently all blown on Cochrane's extravagant gambling habits and failed business ventures.'

'Hence the divorce.'

'No, that came about after Madison found social media pics of him having a little too much fun one night in a brothel he had a stake in. She had him followed by a private investigator and when evidence of criminal behaviour came to light, got the police involved, which brought the rest of it out in the open. Bryce initially swore she set him up, that Madison was angry enough to want him to pay for cheating on her, that she swiped money from the business herself and bounced it through his accounts, before making it vanish.'

'And yet Mr Wilde suggested Cochrane was apologetic.'

'In the last couple of years he sent them both written apologies, blaming his behaviour on a drug habit, debt and simply getting in over his head.'

'A big turnaround. You think it was to look good to the parole board?'

'Maybe. Timing's about right.'

'What makes you think he had anything to do with her murder?'

'There were some threats early on. They were pretty vicious. Jared, what if we've been looking at this the wrong way around? Instead of thinking of our POIs as local thieves who have graduated to rape and murder, what if the hit on Wilde and Sash and the five mill in diamonds was the goal all along, orchestrated by Cochrane?

The other minor break-ins could have been designed to throw us off track, give our POIs an idea of police presence, response times, some easy cash while waiting for the main target to arrive?'

'I'd say that pointed to a well-planned, well-executed crime by someone who knows what they're doing.'

'I've organised for Mr Wilde to come back in this afternoon. I want to ask him a few more questions about his former son-in-law.'

'You think Cochrane's somehow set this up from prison?'

'Correct. Feel like a trip to Melbourne first thing Monday?'

'To interview Cochrane? I'll book the flights now.'

'Great. But don't be late. You and Tess are still doing something tonight, right?'

He laughed out a sigh, almost told her in the nicest possible way to mind her own business. 'Yeah. Why?'

'Just playing the nosy sister-in-law. Have fun.'

CHAPTER
21

He got away from work almost on time, only to find a missed call from Tess on his phone and a message. *Hi Jared, sorry, I need to rain-check. We've got a horse down with colic and Logan's at a comp. I'm going to need to stay put.*

He was disappointed, but weighed appearing clingy against putting in some effort, then called back. 'Hey, just got your message.'

'Yeah. Sorry again. I can't go anywhere.'

'That's okay. Favourite takeaway?'

There was a pause, then, 'I could really go a cheeseburger and a seriously big vanilla shake.'

Though he cringed at her choice, he yielded. 'Macca's it is.'

Forty-five minutes later he drove through Calico Lodge's impressive main gates and down the long, winding drive past the guesthouse to find Tess standing in a floodlit round yard outside the stable block, patting a small black and white patched pony. He parked nearby then, gathering the takeaway, kicked the door closed with his foot and made his way across the grass.

'Hey,' he called.

'Hi!' Tess said, stroking the pony's face. It was hot and bothered, its ears were pinned back and it was stomping, kicking at its stomach.

'He looks pretty upset at the world.'

She unclipped the lead and walked across to the gate. 'He's impacted, in pain. I've stomach tubed him and given him some painkillers. Hopefully they'll help with that. I've just got to keep him moving, or at least on his feet. I don't want him rolling around.'

'Here to help.'

She tipped her head to the side, smiled. 'You're forever bringing me food. You didn't have to come all the way out here, you know.'

'Yeah, I did. You want your burger?'

She took another long look at the pony before nodding and slipping through the gate. 'Just a sec.' She disappeared into the stable block.

Almost immediately, the pony pawed at the ground, dropped his head and buckled at the knees. Jared placed the takeaway on the ground and jogged across the yard. 'No, no. You're not supposed to do that,' he said as it lay down and kicked its feet in the air. 'Come on, buddy. Get up.' He pulled on the halter and the pony fought the tug, dragging Jared forward a few steps before reluctantly getting up. 'Good boy, now stay on your feet, okay?' He let the pony rub on him, stroked a hand along its sweaty neck and talked about silly things because his voice seemed to hold the pony's interest.

Tess came rushing back in. 'Sorry, I was just getting a couple of chairs.'

'It's no problem. He's cooperating. Sort of. Come on, bud, let's move.' The pony began walking. 'Why don't you go eat your food?' he said to Tess. 'We've got this.'

She hesitated. 'But you—'

'Predicted this was going to be a tag-team effort and ate my quarter pounder on the way over.' The look she sent him made the indigestion worth it. 'Go, eat.'

'Okay. Thanks.' She went back to the gate and slipped through, opened up the folding chairs she'd brought out of the stables and sat in one before digging into the bag. 'How much do you know about horses?' she asked as he walked the pony past.

'A bit. My mother showed ponies.'

'Do you ride?'

'Not since I was seven and discovered dirt bikes,' he said.

'Bikes are fun. Horses are better.'

'You ride bikes?'

'We've got some Yamaha 250s in the shed.'

'Is that another one of those activities you take visitors out on?'

'Occasionally. Along with mountain bikes, kayaks, hiking, quad-bikes, skiing …'

'What can't you do?'

'Abseil,' she answered immediately.

He laughed but shook his head. 'Quit giving yourself a hard time, Tess. You've—'

Her gaze swept away from his to the pony. 'Stop.'

'I think you need to hear it.'

'No, I mean stop walking,' she said with a laugh and put down her food, coming back into the yard and around to the side of the pony as it groaned and lifted its tail.

Jared heard a splat, then another, then an explosion of it.

'Good boy!' Tess crooned, coming to the front to stroke the pony's face and kiss his forehead. 'Good job. I bet that feels better.' She turned her face up to Jared's and gave him a massive grin. 'He pooped, yay.'

'Evening highlight? You did say it was never boring.'

'Feel free to leave in disgust now if you like. I won't hold it against you.'

'I would but … I haven't finished my shake.'

Still smiling, she walked back to the gate. 'I should keep an eye on him a bit longer.'

He followed her, picked up their drinks. 'Well, it's not the sort of thing I'd usually toast to, but we can celebrate the explosion,' he said and handed her a large shake, tapped it to his. 'Cheers.'

'Cheers back.' Her expression softened, warmed. 'Jared … thanks.'

He took a chance and reached out, tucked some escaped tendrils of hair back behind her ear. 'Not exactly a romantic first date.'

'Actually, driving all the way out here to feed me a cheeseburger while I wait for a horse to poo is probably the most romantic thing anyone has ever done for me.'

'Then you've had rotten dates.'

'Honestly, I hate fancy restaurants. I mean, other than ours at the lodge, I don't feel comfortable in them. I'm not a wine and dine, flowers and chocolates type. If that's what you're after, I'm not it.' She looked so damn anxious about it all of a sudden he felt the need to get her to lighten up.

'I think I just fell in love with you,' he said, then laughed at her expression. 'Turn off the cling-o-meter, Tess. I'll restrain myself from proposing.'

She grinned, relaxing back into her chair, and lifted her shake in the air. 'Keep this sort of thing up, it could be you running for breathing room.'

He looked into her sparkling eyes and decided he wasn't messing with her quite as much as he'd made out. 'I highly doubt that.'

The moment was broken by the sweep of headlights and the approach of a car. 'Sorry, guys!' Indy called out. 'Jared, we've got a report of a break and enter. I thought you'd want to know.'

'It's only just after seven!' he said.

'You want to take the chance it's a different POI? House belongs to a single white female.'

He looked at Tess apologetically. 'Sorry.'

'Nah, don't be. Go get the bad guys.'

'We'll have to do this again sometime.'

She flashed him a big smile. 'Minus the sick horse, and you're on.'

'Bye.'

'Bye.'

'Jared!' Indy called.

'Yep,' he said, dragging his attention from Tess to jog to his car. With difficulty he got his head back in the game. 'Where?'

'Follow me.'

He did, and Indy drove fast. It took less time than it should have to get back into the suburbs, where they pulled up at the end of the street behind a parked police car. Surely by now it was all over and done with? But Roberts got out and approached them, showing no sign any arrest had taken place.

'You said to watch and wait. We have cars at either end of the road and a man watching the house, and two on the street behind in case he takes off over the back fence.'

'He's still in there?' Indy asked. 'Are you sure?'

'Yep. Got a report a couple of minutes ago of movement inside.'

'What the hell is he doing?' Jared said. 'I'm going in.'

'I'll go front, you go back,' Indy said.

He approached the house, noticing a light was on somewhere inside. As Indy went up the front step a sensor light illuminated the front veranda. Jared hurried around the back, his foot crunching on broken glass from a window. He looked up just as someone barrelled through the window and straight into him, knocking him to the ground. He got a hand on the offender's shirt and copped what might have been a fist or an elbow to the face but managed to pull the offender under him.

'Stay down!' he ordered, hearing Indy's footsteps running to his assistance.

'Okay! Okay!'

The voice was remarkably familiar, the fumes coming off her pure spirits.

'You've got to be joking!' Jared snapped and dragged the thief up with him. 'Ruby, what the hell are you doing?'

Ruby lifted her head just enough to see the team of police surrounding her and threw her arms up in the air, almost smacking him in the face in her haste. 'All this for me?' she cried out. 'Guns! Why do you have guns?'

Jared cuffed her, too pissed off to be gentle. 'You're under arrest.'

'I just needed some cash,' she said as they followed the narrow concrete path back around the side of the house to the waiting police car. 'And they had this chockers bar. JD and Johnny, just sitting back with a coupla drinks, whole place lights up outside like Christmas. Had to get going, legs didn't wanna cooperate. Just needed some cash. Wasn't hurting anyone.'

He helped her in, sent her back to the station with a couple of officers.

'She's really in for it this time,' Indy said, watching the car disappear. 'Sorry to ruin your night.'

'The pony was recovering when we left. I think it's going to be okay.'

'Nice date.'

A neighbour emerged from the house across the street. 'I called it in,' he explained. 'Did you get the guy?'

'Yes, thank you.' He didn't bother to explain the guy was a woman.

'Was it the one from the news?'

'Too early to say. Thanks for your assistance.'

'I'll meet you back at the station,' Indy promised, and took off ahead of him.

He went into the house, made sure everything was under control and left Roberts in charge. By the time he got back to the station, Indy was already grilling Ruby.

'You know how this looks, Ruby?' she asked as he walked in. 'We've got a spate of serious break-ins in the area over the last few weeks and we've already caught you with stolen goods you claimed landed in your lap.'

'I never stole nothing else!' Ruby was in tears, her face flushed and damp. 'I just needed some cash fast. I got to go back to court on Tuesday 'cause you arrested me over that other thing. Lawyer reckons I could be lucky, get a suspended sentence and a huge fine. But if I can't pay it, I have to go to jail. I can't go to jail!'

'I think you'll be going to jail, Ruby,' Jared said. 'After this, anyway.'

'Oh come on, Detective Handsome! *Please*. Can't you cut me a break? I shouldn't have got stuck into the JD. But I needed the cash. I gotta stay out of jail! I'm no thief, you know that!'

'Evidence is pointing to the contrary,' Indy muttered.

'I panicked. That's all. Not fair—if you've got money, you can pay your way out of this stuff.'

'Sometimes,' Indy said, 'life's not fair.' She indicated with her head for Jared to join her outside.

'I'll charge her. You should ice that eye.'

'I got hit by a very small woman who can't punch. I'll live.'

'I can see it bruising.'

'You don't really think this is anything more than what she's saying, do you?'

'Nope. Different time of night, different method of entry. No gloves, no hiding her tracks and only after cash. If I could charge her with it, her biggest crime would be stupidity. There's no point both of us hanging around. Go.'

'Fine. Thanks.'

Bloody Ruby. What a waste of a night. He'd been enjoying his unconventional evening with Tess more than he'd expected to. It was certainly more memorable than a simple dinner in town. Even as he told himself not to push, he wondered when he could see her again.

Instead of heading for home, he turned onto the road that led to the waterfront, made another stop when he noticed a hunched figure emerging from a carpark off to the side of the yacht club. The man had a canvas bag slung over his shoulder, a fishing rod in one hand and a plastic bucket in the other. He stopped and watched Jared suspiciously as he climbed out of his car and approached.

'Evening!' Jared called out. 'Detective Jared Denham. Nice night.'

'Bit windy. Is there a problem?'

'You'd have heard about the murder that happened on a boat moored out here last weekend?'

'Heard something about it.'

'I'm looking for witnesses. Were you out here early last Sunday morning, between one and four?'

'I'd been fishing out the end of the rowing club. Packed up my stuff about two or a bit after. I'd parked in the carpark by the beach over there,' the man said with a wave of his fishing rod. 'Did see a couple of young hoons having some fun spinning their tyres as I went back to the car. Didn't see or hear any trouble on any of the boats though. Bit far away.'

'Hoons, huh? Did you get a look at them?'

Old guy screwed up his face. 'Nah. I don't know. One sat a lot taller in the car than the other.'

Jared showed him the sketch of their suspect. 'Did one look like this?'

'Maybe. Not sure. But could be they lost their boat. Saw a little dinghy floating out on the water. 'Less they pinched it. Often get the kids street racing and the like. Bit of a shitbox of a car though. Orangey colour, I think. Little hatchback. Week before kids came round in a hotted-up Datsun. Much nicer wheels. Did some decent donuts. Little shits.'

'Right. Thanks. Hey, if you remember anything else, would you give me a call?' Because the man didn't have a free hand, Jared slipped his card in the fishing bag. 'Thanks for your time.'

He considered calling Indy with the new information, but it was late. Maybe tomorrow. Or maybe he'd call in to the lodge, speak to her in person and see if Tess was around while he was at it. He'd have to work out a way to make his early exit up to her.

CHAPTER 22

Tess sat down hard against the enormous buck the filly performed as two steers barrelled past to avoid the portable yard. 'Steady, madam,' she murmured. 'We'll get 'em next time.'

She brought the edgy filly back to a walk around behind the watchful steers. As they took off again, the filly lunged after them, ears pinned back, then spooked when one spun around to face them. Tess clung to the saddle and laughed. 'Oh yeah, you're so brave. Not.'

'You okay?'

At the sound of Jared's voice, she pulled the filly up and turned around. He was standing by the gate. 'Fine! She's amazing. Just young. She thinks she knows what to do, then isn't so sure when it doesn't go the way she wants it to.'

'That's a nicer explanation than the one I had in my head.'

What was he doing here? Had he thought about last night, decided to tell her in person he'd changed his mind about them? She'd been half-expecting something like that all morning. She moved the filly in his direction and he opened the gate to let her through.

'She's pretty.'

'She is. I have to think of a name for her.'

'She's new?'

'Logan gave her to me. Thought I could use a new challenge. Flash is getting on and I'd like to have another go at putting her in foal.' She slipped from the saddle, patted the filly's neck, then smiled up at him, trying to read what was on his mind. 'Hi.'

'Hi. Don't let me stop you.'

'That's okay, she's had enough.' They walked back to the stables and she began unsaddling. 'You should have let me know you were dropping in,' she said. 'I could have finished quicker. And—' she looked down at her filthy clothes with a grin, '—changed.'

He leant back against a stable and watched her work. 'I don't expect you to drop what you're doing just because I felt like calling in.'

'Appreciated.' She put her gear away and came out to find Larissa talking to Jared as he stroked the filly's neck.

'She's a bit of a sook,' he said.

'A hot and sweaty one. Let me clean her up.'

'I can do that,' Larissa offered. 'Logan wanted me to give her a proper bath this weekend anyway.'

'Okay then, thanks.' Then to Jared, Tess said, 'Do you want to come up to the lodge? I could use a cold drink.'

'Sure. I have my car. I'll drive us back.'

She got in beside him and decided she had to know. 'So what brings you out here?'

'I've been speaking to Indy about the case. She told me you were down here with your latest love so I came down to chase whoever it was off.'

Tess laughed, and part of it was relief. 'And I was just getting used to her.'

'Then I guess we'll have to timeshare.'

'I'm a bit surprised you came back,' she admitted. 'I thought maybe last night might have been enough reality for you.'

'I had a great time. Sorry again for having to rush off.'

'There's nothing to apologise for. It's your job.'

He pulled over in the parking area by the lodge. 'It takes more than a sick pony to scare me off,' he promised her. 'How is it doing?' he asked.

'Much better, thankfully.' They walked up the path to the front steps. 'He's a legend with nervous kids. He's getting on in age, but hopefully he's got a few more healthy years ahead of him.'

When they got back inside she realised her mistake. 'Ah … there's a guest birthday going on down here. You might not mind the dusty jodhpurs, but the well-dressed party at the bar might. Sorry. I've got drinks in my apartment?'

'Fine by me.'

Because she hadn't been expecting company, she walked in first and performed a nervous sweep of the area. The kitchen, which flowed into the lounge and dining area, was relatively clean, her favourite handcrafted bowl on the kitchen bench containing most of the mess. In the lounge area leaf-green cushions sat tidily on the deep mocha sofa, and the dining table wasn't too laden with horse equipment.

Jared came in behind her and headed straight for a line of large prints along one wall, a series of her riding Flash: Flash flying after a trio of steers; Flash crouched in a tight turn as she spun around after another.

'These are incredible photos,' he said when she came to stand nearby. 'I think I've heard of the photographer. How did you get these?'

'Mia's a friend of Indy's. She and her husband Ben spent a week down here when Indy and Logan got married. That huge framed one of Calico Lodge down in the foyer's another one of hers. It was their wedding present.'

'The subject is pretty impressive too.'

Not sure what to say, Tess ran her hand lightly over the glass framing the horse and deliberately misinterpreted him. 'Yeah, this new filly's going to have to work hard to be a touch on Flash.'

'I meant the rider.'

The simple compliment had her momentarily tongue-tied. 'The amount of riding I've been doing lately, I've got some serious work to do too.'

'Then what? You'll go to campdrafts with Logan?'

'Some. I used to compete all the time.'

'I'd like to see you in action.'

She smiled, took a deep breath and walked back into the kitchen. 'I only have the basics, I'm afraid. Lemon squash, juice, sparkling water, tea, coffee?'

'Whatever you're having is fine.'

She took out a couple of glasses from the cupboard. 'So, you're off to Melbourne tomorrow?'

'Yeah, Indy told you about it?'

'Sort of.' She opened the fridge, took out the sparkling water and a lemon. 'She has a way of keeping everyone up to date without actually giving much away.'

'Job requirement.'

'I get it. The job's not always easy.'

'Last night it completely sucked,' he said, stepping close. His gaze moved over her face, and she had a strong suspicion his eyes knew way too much about what was going on in her head.

'But hey, you got the woman, didn't you?' she said, a little unsteadily. God, he had her trembling just looking at her. She wanted to jump him. How had she ever thought what she'd had with Aaron was anything other than mundane?

'Not the right one.'

'Oh.' She held her breath as he lowered his head. The kiss buzzed through her system, the feel of his hands lightly resting at her waist seared into her skin and sent pleasant little jolts radiating through her entire body. She touched her hands to his chest to steady herself, felt the heat emanating from him and moved closer to slide her arms around his neck.

A knock on the door jolted her back to reality. She wanted to ignore it but Jared had already stepped back.

'Damn,' she muttered.

'My thoughts exactly,' he said, taking a deep breath and exhaling.

She opened the door. 'Hi,' Callie said, coming in. 'I know you just came back from the horses but—oh, Jared. Hi.'

'Hey, Callie,' Jared said, then stepped around her. 'I should leave you ladies to it.'

'Don't go on my account!' Callie said. 'I'll work something else out.'

'What's to work out?' Tess asked reluctantly.

'I was hoping you could take four guests out on kayaks. Matt's been held up at Cradle Mountain.'

Tess looked apologetically at Jared.

'Go on,' he said. 'I'll see you soon. I have something I need to do today, anyway.'

'Okay. Bye.' She closed the door after him slowly, then leant against it with a sigh. 'Callie, your timing sucks.'

'And you have no idea how sorry I am,' Callie said dramatically. 'None. So?'

'Do you think it's wrong to be feeling like this about someone so soon after breaking up with someone else?'

'Not at all.'

She eyed Callie suspiciously. 'Why not?'

'Because you were never crazy about the first one, you just *wanted* to be. This is much more of a real deal, I can tell. And real deals don't wait for perfect timing, they just happen. So …' Callie smiled widely and dropped into a chair. 'The kayakers can wait five minutes. Tell me everything.'

It was windy on the waterfront, not as peaceful as the first time Jared had visited the yacht club. The boats were restless, bobbing and tossing at their moorings. He drove slowly, past the yacht club, a sports field and the rowing club in the elbow of the coastline. The carpark the old fisherman had indicated was a long line of spaces facing a small, sandy beach. He pulled up in the farthest space and climbed out, then dragged on a jacket against the sharp sting of the wind blowing off the water to look around. The chances of him finding that dinghy were slim, but he hoped by some miracle it might have washed up somewhere close by.

To his left a fence ran either side of an inlet. He could see a couple of little boats pulled up on shore and decided to start there. It wasn't going to be easy to get across with the high tide, so he changed tack, headed over a footbridge and onto the street. The houses that flowed up the steep hill were immaculately kept heritage-style homes on large blocks, most with wide verandas designed to take in the ocean views. Among them was a sprinkling of modern designs and, as though in mutual agreement, the residents all kept their little piece of the roadside gardened to near perfection. Just one building stood out, right on the corner by the water, an old barn-like building, weathered and rustic, with peeling paint and splintered, sun-worn wooden panelling. It belonged to one of the more modern residences and beyond it he spotted boats sitting upside down on a grassy verge between land and water. He found the gate to the front door and pressed the intercom.

No one answered, so he trekked the length of the street, knocking on doors and speaking to the few people who answered. He didn't mind this sort of footwork usually, but he was freezing and he was getting nowhere. He tried the house at the bottom of the hill a second time on his way back to the car, just in case. Nothing. He'd have to go back to the station and—

'Can I help you?'

A woman stood behind him holding the leash of a small spotted terrier. He absently dropped a hand to pat it as it excitedly sniffed at his trousers.

'Morning. Detective Jared Denham. I was hoping to speak to the owners.'

'I hope everything is all right?'

'Yes, no problem. I'm looking for a small boat that was spotted out on the water several days ago. Was going to ask if any of theirs had gone missing, or if perhaps they'd acquired one by accident.'

'A boat?' Her gaze sharpened. 'Wasn't a little blue and white dinghy, was it?'

'Ah … possibly. Why?'

'My grandson and a few of the other local kids fished one out of the rivulet on Monday after school. Poor Jett took half the skin off his knee trying to climb down to get a rope on it, then they dragged it all the way from the Balmoral Street bridge back out to the beach and up to our place, 'cause we're on the water just up the street. It's nothing special, but you know kids. It's the fun of the find.'

'Do you think I could take a look at it?'

'Course. Just sitting on our lawn.' She turned back up the street and he took that as a cue to follow. 'Keith—my husband—wouldn't let 'em clean it up or play with it until he was sure no one was going to come looking for it. He put an ad in the local paper this weekend.'

Her house was another pretty older-style building looking out over the ocean. The front yard was surrounded by a white picket fence. BOAT FOUND ENQUIRE WITHIN was painted in black on a piece of ply tied to the fence. She led him through the gate and down a narrow side path decorated with a pretty purple-flowered climber and gold pebbles to a terraced backyard. More gardens, and at the bottom of a couple of small sets of steps was a grassed area complete with a soccer net, netball ring and trampoline. By a small metal gate that led to the waterfront was a white fibreglass dinghy with a blue interior laid on its side.

'That's it there,' she said unnecessarily.

He looked it over. It did look as though it had seen better days, but it was sturdy and just large enough for a couple of men. The oars were inside and one carried a suspicious brown stain on its handle. 'Mrs?'

'Oh, sorry. Hilary Kemp.'

'Mrs Kemp, some people are going to have to come and take a look at this boat. I think it may be the one I'm looking for.'

'No problem. Kids might be disappointed, but you can't just assume finders keepers, right? And Keith will be relieved. He didn't want an old thing like that around. Was it stolen?' she asked, eyes curious.

'It's part of an ongoing investigation.'

He called it in, then waited at the property until it was taken away for forensics to examine and went home. No one was going to look at it on a Sunday. He'd have to wait. Besides, he had an interview with Bryce Cochrane to prepare for.

CHAPTER 23

Bryce Cochrane looked a lot like Jared had anticipated: a few years past his best with a cocky, boyish grin and a haircut he should have grown out of ten years ago. A charmer, Jared suspected, who used to have the looks to back up the attitude. But the eyes didn't match the easy smile and relaxed demeanour; they were dark, calculating and cold.

'S'pose you're here about Maddie.'

'You heard then.'

He sniggered. 'Mate, it's prison not another planet. Besides, Wilde came to see me.'

'Wilde did? Why?'

'Poor guy's devastated. Came to tell me what's going to happen to me when I get out if I had anything to do with it.'

'Did you?'

Cochrane huffed. 'As if. I don't s'pose you got the bastard that done it yet, either, since you're here talking to me.'

'Suppose you're right. Have you got any ideas on who'd want to kill Maddie?'

'Who'd want to kill her?' He laughed humourlessly. 'Seriously, mate, no one would want to kill Maddie. She was a doll. A bloody legend.'

'That's a generous attitude. Considering.'

Cochrane dragged his hands over his hair. 'I stuffed up. Got caught up with the wrong people. In over my head with that money-laundering business. It was only meant to be a one-off, then an occasional favour. Before I knew it, I couldn't get out of it.'

'Yeah, isn't that what they all say?'

'I'm saying I deserved it, okay? I don't blame her for any of it, that's why I dropped the assault charges. She fractured my jaw,' he added as though proud of her. 'Gentlest person I've ever met and she swung a tyre iron like a pro baseball player when she caught me outside the brothel. Guess she really did love me.'

'Whatever you say. Do you recognise this man?' Jared showed him the photo of their main POI.

Cochrane reached for it, looked closely. 'Seriously? I've been in here for eight years. That guy looks like he still woulda been in school back then.'

He had a point, so Jared nodded, put the photo away. 'Thanks for your time. And just a friendly warning: if I find out you're impeding a police investigation in any way whatsoever, you won't be getting that parole.'

He turned to leave, heard, 'Wait!'

'Yes?'

'I said I didn't know anyone who would want to hurt Maddie. But maybe I might know of someone who'd kill her to get their hands on the diamonds.'

Jared pulled a face at the wall and sat back down. 'Go on then.'

'There's a guy down that way that did some work for me—unofficially. I didn't always launder with casino chips, detective. Sometimes it was gems, and he was always pretty good at moving them for me.'

Jared concentrated on keeping the urgency out of his expression. 'And who is this mystery man?'

Cochrane sat back, smiled. 'When my parole goes through, I'll let you know. I just, ah … hope it goes through fast. So you get him first.'

Jared leant on the back of the chair. 'First? What does that mean?'

'It means Wilde and I had a similar discussion. If he hasn't figured it out, I'd be shocked.'

'If Wilde's figured it out, and anything happens to our POI because you withheld information, you can forget about getting out of here.' Jared saw the smug expression slightly waver. 'So for your sake, I hope you're wrong.'

'I want my whiskey,' Evan told Jai for the second time, his voice rising.

'You've had it, Pop. It's time for bed.'

'Liar! I need my whiskey!'

'Pop, you—okay. Fine.' He poured a dash more into the cup. 'Here.' He knew it wasn't good for Evan to drink much, but what was one more nip in the scheme of things?

'Thanks,' Evan muttered, and settled into his recliner.

Jai went back to the kitchen to lock the bottle away, then sat at the table and considered pouring himself one.

'Hey.' Pax's voice floated in through the window.

'What are you doing here?' Jai demanded. He got to his feet and let Pax in.

'Just got a call. Cops are getting too close. Boss is pissed. I need you to do something for me.' Pax took his backpack off his shoulder and dumped it on the counter. He took out a small black velvet bag. 'I need you to take this to the shop tomorrow, put it in the front drawer under the till. Got it?'

'Why?'

'I'm keeping the cops off our back, okay?'

Jai snatched the bag and opened it. A stunning diamond bracelet fell into his hand. It had to have come from the boat. He shoved it back in. 'By putting the stuff where I work? Do you think I'm a complete idiot? Forget it. You're setting me up!'

Pax's expression was genuine confusion. 'Huh?'

'Like not giving me gloves at that first break-in. The cops found my fingerprints, and the gun you got me to shoot—where is it?'

'Didn't want to hold on to it—if it's found on us, we're toast. Wiped it clean before I left it there. This is Tank, right? Putting ideas in your head.'

'Yeah, like the one about the knife, and the other one where you tricked me into shooting that Sash guy.'

'And because you did, the rest of what's in here's for you.' Pax pushed the backpack across the bench. 'Look at it.'

Jai eyed Pax with suspicion before pulling the bag open. Cash. Hundred dollar notes in thick, neatly packed rows. It was more money than he'd ever seen in his life.

'That's twenty grand for knocking off the boyfriend,' Pax said. 'Boss is very happy with you.'

Twenty thousand dollars? He couldn't believe it.

'So you ready to cooperate?'

Was he? Would Pax take the money back if he said no? 'Yeah, maybe, but I still don't get it.'

'You don't need to. Just do what you're told.'

Guilt and worry nudged his conscience over the light-headed elation of holding twenty thousand dollars in his hands. Putting the bracelet in Tank's shop made no sense. Was this going to come back on Tank? Damn it, he wanted the money. He needed it. But … 'I'm not doing anything else until you tell me why!'

'Oh, right. You must think I'm kidding.' Pax pulled a gun from the back of his jeans and stalked into the lounge room where Evan had passed out in his chair. He put the gun to Evan's head.

'No!'

'I'd keep my voice down if I were you. If he wakes up and sees me, I'll have no choice.'

'He won't remember you five minutes later, he has dementia!' Jai hissed as desperate panic curled in his gut.

'Not taking the chance. You're going to agree to do what you're told or I'm going to start repeating myself. Every time I have to do that, my voice is going to get louder and louder until dear old Pop wakes up, understand?'

Jai's heart sank as Evan stirred, but he didn't open his eyes. 'Yes! Please leave him alone.'

'If you don't do this, if you stuff it up, I will kill you. After I kill him. And Riley. I'll do Riley like I did Madison. You know I can. I will. Got it?'

Jai wished he could believe Pax was bluffing. But he didn't. He knew what Pax had done to Madison and how easily he'd brushed it off. The guy didn't have feelings. Didn't care. So he nodded, desperate for Pax to leave.

'Good. Make sure that stuff's where it's supposed to be when it's supposed to be there. Or else.'

Jai sat staring at the velvet bag long after Pax left, barely slept and took it with him to work in the morning, still not sure he should follow through. Tank could be a bastard, but he'd helped him. Jai had a feeling this wasn't going to end well. Then again, that twenty grand was a lifesaver, and if he didn't do it, he had no doubt Pax would follow through with his threats. What choice did he have?

'Morning, boss,' he said as Tank walked in.

'Jai. Mind the front for me, would you? I've got some work to do in the office.'

'Sure. Let me just put my stuff away.' He raced into the office, grabbed the key to the locked drawer he needed to access and slipped it in his pocket.

He'd almost made it to the till when Riley burst through the door. 'Hi,' he said, instantly worried by the look on her face.

'Aaron has pulled out of the hiking trip!' she blurted.

'What! Why?' He wanted to sound sympathetic, but he could feel the nervous trickle of sweat down his left temple. The bracelet was burning a hole in one pocket, and the keys he was worried Tank would realise had gone missing were burning a hole in the other.

'I don't know. He just said something came up. He sounded like a complete jerk. Said I should ask Tess Atherton to take us.'

'The one who gave you a hard time over the hike at the police station?'

'Yeah.' She sighed heavily. 'We're screwed.'

'Maybe—maybe it's just not meant to be.'

'How can you say that?' Riley cried, her eyes suspiciously wet. 'We've been planning this forever!'

'I know.' He needed to give her a hug, but his pockets were full of stuff that shouldn't be in there. 'Why don't you go talk to Tank about it? I'll be there in just a sec.'

'That's it?' She looked incredulous. 'You don't care, do you? You never really wanted to go!'

'That's not true,' he lied. Because regardless, he would have gone—for her. But the odds just kept stacking against them. 'And I'm not giving up yet. I'll finish what I have to do here, then I'll be in the office. We'll call Tess Atherton and see what she says. She might be able to help, right?'

Riley still looked deflated but nodded. 'I suppose.'

Without having time to worry any more about what he was doing, he opened the drawer under the till and shoved the jewellery inside.

CHAPTER 24

Jared glanced at the time and stifled a yawn. Half an hour left of his shift. He had plenty of work to do, it just wasn't getting done fast enough. And it wasn't what he wanted to be doing. Tess would be here soon and they were heading out to dinner. He was looking forward to it. When a string of emails came through he checked for anything interesting and clicked on lab results. He scanned them, then took them to Indy's office.

'They found traces of blood on one of the oars of the dinghy. It's a match to Sash. No matching prints. Some made by kids. Likely the smeared marks on the oars were made by gloves. Anything back on Cochrane?'

'It's going to happen. Should be signed off on by close.'

'What's in the package?'

'Huh? Oh, don't know. It came in while you were out earlier, so I signed for it. It's for you.'

He opened the Express Post pack and pulled out a chocolate box wrapped in ribbon. 'Interesting.' He looked for a card, shook the bag, but found it empty. 'Who'd be sending me chocolates?'

'Don't know, but if you don't want them, pass them over.'

He grinned and opened the box. 'What the—' He picked up a handful of photos. In the first he was at work, walking towards the office from his car. In another he was at home, pruning back the old wisteria vine. But the one that really got to him had been taken at Calico Lodge as he'd stood by the sick horse with Tess. In the bottom of the picture he could see the barrel of a gun pointed in their direction. As he put the lid down he noticed *I won't tell you again* written on the inside.

'Indy.'

'Yeah?' She looked up, her expression freezing as he tipped the box to show her.

'He's been following me.'

She got up to look at the photos scattered on the table. 'Scare tactics. He wants you to drop the case. We're getting too close.'

'Yeah and now he's involved Tess.'

'His first attempts didn't work, so second option is to focus on people you care about, see if that works. You're making him nervous enough to go to a lot of trouble.'

'So first the rock through the window, then I'm run off the road, and now this. There's two of us running this investigation, why concentrate on me?'

'At a guess? Because for the most part I'm behind the scenes, I'm coordinating, I'm putting things together and making things happen, but you're out on the street, you're talking to people, you're the face behind whatever lead has got him running scared.'

A brief knock announced Emily's arrival. 'Hi, Tess is here,' she said, as Tess walked in behind her. Jared had been hanging for her to arrive, but her timing couldn't have been worse. Before he could get around the table, both Tess and Emily's gazes went to the box. Tess stepped closer, her face reflecting shock, then confusion.

'Tess.' He stepped between her and the photos. 'Don't worry about it, okay? We're sorting it.'

'I have no doubt. Am I allowed to know who wants me dead?'

'This is not about you. It's about me and the investigation.'

'I'm so sorry,' Emily said, looking paler than Tess. 'I shouldn't have charged in like that.'

'We need to bag all this for evidence,' Indy told her.

'Yeah, of course.' Emily left the room.

'Tess, let's get a coffee,' Indy said.

When Tess didn't move, Jared touched a hand to the small of her back and guided her to the tea room after Indy.

'Did the guy who ran you off the road send that?' Tess asked.

'Makes sense,' he said. 'Trying to scare me.'

'Did it work?'

'No. I'm not scared, just aware I'll need to be more cautious.'

She nodded slowly and stared at the table, glancing up with a weak smile when Indy put a coffee in front of her. 'Thanks. So … is he by any chance a serial killer?'

'Heading in that direction,' Indy muttered before returning to the kettle to pour two more coffees.

'Only heading?' Tess said. 'I've faced worse then. Are we still grabbing dinner? Maybe you can tell me a bit more about what's going on.'

'I'm sorry, Tess,' he said. 'It's not safe. You should probably steer clear of me until we've got this guy. He might not be making empty threats.'

Her eyes flashed with anger. 'Right, except that picture there with me in it clearly says this arsehole knows who I am and where I live. So maybe I'm better off sticking close, right?'

'She won't back down,' Indy muttered into her coffee.

'Do you carry a gun everywhere?' Tess asked him.

'No, of course not.'

'How about you start?'

He smiled at that, then waited while she answered her phone.

'Tess Atherton.' Tess's hand slapped her forehead and her eyes focused on the ceiling. Went round. 'He said what?' she asked, voice deadly. After a brief pause, a string of easily decipherable swear words poured silently from her mouth. 'That's not true. I understand that but I already told you … Mmm hmm, okay, yes, yes, I would be prepared to discuss it with you, if for no other reason than to talk you out of it. Tonight? Now? I'm not at the lodge right now. I'm in town. Possibly. Hold on.'

Tess covered the receiver. 'I need to go talk some kids out of a mid-winter trek. Long story. I might have to skip dinner after all.'

'Is that Riley?' he asked. 'Are you going to her place?'

'The shop. Wherever that is. They're all there.'

He exchanged glances with Indy. He still wasn't sure about Tank and Jai nor if or where they fit in to the investigation. 'I'll run you over.'

Tess nodded and told Riley she'd be there shortly. Then she thumped the phone down hard on the table and expelled a long, angry breath. 'I don't like the F word. I don't use it. I think it sounds terrible but very occasionally, very, very rarely, there's just nothing else appropriate. There's just not. What a *fuck*wit!'

'Aaron?' Indy guessed.

'He pulled out of the hike. Told Riley to talk to me because I had nothing better to do. That as I was such good mates with you,

Jared, and you were such good mates with Tank, not only would I be happy to take them, I'd most likely do it at mates' rates.'

'Uh-oh,' Indy muttered.

'Damn right uh-oh. If he hasn't already left for Canada he'll be lucky to make it.'

'He's just annoyed you turned down his offer to go with him,' Indy said calmly.

'I tried to be nice about it! Even as I thought, whoa, not a chance. I said I had a life and a career here. I was still calm. I was. But then he said something along the lines of how at this stage in my life I should think about taking some chances before they run out.'

'Hmm.' Indy frowned into her coffee.

Jared opened his mouth to ask Indy what she was thinking, but Tess barrelled on.

'And I don't care if perhaps he has a point. Because he was so damn patronising and sure of himself, like he was offering me this great opportunity and I was going to wither away and die an old maid if I didn't take him up on it. At that point I should have trodden a little more carefully.' She fell back heavily in her chair. 'I should have made him feel better about the fact I was thinking really scary things about his state of mind. But I just wanted him gone. I was so relieved he was going to the other end of the world.'

'And if I know you at all, by the end of the conversation he was well aware of that,' Indy said with a small smile that had Jared relaxing a little; he'd been sure he'd seen worry flare in her expression a moment ago. 'Seriously, just forget it. This whole spiel he fed Riley is just his parting shot, his ego soother.'

'He already had that! Made me feel like a liability to Search and Rescue. That was his parting shot. I gave it a nine, mostly for delivery, and I sucked it up.' Her face darkened into a sneer. 'This time I want to twist his balls until they snap off and shove them so far up his butt they work as breast enhancements!' She pushed to her feet and snatched her phone off the table. 'But first,' she said and this time the deep breath she took was a calming one, 'I need to politely address this group. Are you sure you want to come with me?' she asked Jared.

He nodded. 'Absolutely. Let's go.'

'Jared,' Indy said. 'Make sure she goes straight home after dinner.' Then, less intensely, 'Tess, don't make me arrest you. Let Aaron flee the country.'

'Let's just see how the next half-hour or so pans out,' Tess said. 'I'll let you know.'

He let her seethe on the way there, or perhaps calm down. Whatever she was doing, she was doing it quietly. Watching her handle seeing that photograph had really impressed him. She'd kept it together, kept her head. He supposed that's what she'd done all that time ago in the police station. But he couldn't quite shake the earlier conversation with Indy. Something had occurred to her, had bothered her. He wanted to talk to Tess about it, but as he saw the shop come into view, he decided to tackle it later.

'Here we are,' he said. The shops were mostly closed, but a few cars were clustered in front of Tank's place, so he parked a little way off. 'You ready?'

'Yep.' Tess undid her seatbelt but she didn't move to get out. 'Jared, sorry about earlier. I was mad but I think I was mostly hurt. Because I've tried really hard to go easy on Aaron's feelings and he just keeps going for the kill shot. You don't think …'

'Think what?'

She sighed and shook her head. 'It's just the way he's been carrying on, a part of me wouldn't be surprised if he was the one who wanted to point a gun at me.' She laughed at herself. 'Saying it out loud makes it sound even more ridiculous than in my head. Forget it.'

Jarred felt ice settle over his skin. Perhaps they were going to have that conversation now, after all. 'Has he threatened you?'

'No, he wants me back, not dead.' She laughed it off again. 'Seriously, he's just been a bit intense. You're chasing a murderer who wants to shut you up. That's been going on longer than my issues with Aaron. Sorry. It was a stupid passing thought.'

Jared considered her in silence for several seconds. Tess's concerns for her safety—even just in passing—on top of Indy's comment had him rethinking what he thought he knew. 'When does he leave?'

'I'm not sure exactly.'

'I think I'll make a note to find out.' He looked into her worried eyes and smiled. 'Come on, let's get this over with.'

'Right.'

'So what's the plan?' he asked as they approached the shop. 'Are you going to take them on this hike?'

'I haven't decided. First, I want to make sure they know what they're getting into.'

'I thought you made it pretty clear the other day.'

'So did I. And yet.'

He held the door open for her and followed her inside.

Tank looked up from his position behind the counter, receipts and other papers spread out around an open laptop. 'Tess, nice to see you again,' he said before turning his attention to Jared. 'Detective, didn't know you were coming.' His tone was friendly enough, but curious.

'Tess and I are planning on grabbing some dinner after this,' Jared said.

'I see. The kids are in the office at the back. I've been kicked out here to work while you discuss the trip. Thanks for coming.'

'No problem,' Tess said. They headed down a row of shelves with power tools on one side and electrical equipment on the other. The office came into view as they reached the end.

Riley stood in the doorway, spotted them and smiled, waving them in. 'Hi, Tess, Detective Denham.'

'Hi,' Tess said. Several other young people were watching them with interest.

'This is Jasmin and Brock.' Riley introduced an attractive young couple sitting closely together in one corner. 'They're coming with us, along with Alex in the blue jumper and Chris on the floor,' she said of the two leaning their backs on the wall. 'Sorry, we don't have many chairs.'

Brock got up and offered his to Tess then dragged Jasmin onto his lap to share hers.

'Hi,' Tess said again. 'And thanks.' She sat while Jared leant against the wall, arms folded, relaxed. 'So I know you're hoping to do the South Coast Track next week?'

'The fifteenth,' Riley said. 'You said you'd take us, right?'

'I said I'd talk to you about it,' Tess clarified. 'I want to make sure you know what you're getting into.'

'We do,' Riley said. 'We've read all about it and Aaron sent us a heap of information with an itinerary and gear list.'

'Okay, well I can supply any of the gear you would have hired from Aaron, just tell me what you need. But before we get to that, like I said to you at the station, you haven't picked a very good time of year to do this.'

'We can handle it,' Brock said. 'A bit of rain won't hurt us.'

'If the pretty lady can do it,' Alex said with a sideways smile for Chris.

Tess studied the wiry beanpole of a teen with shoulder-length waves of gold hair and the shorter, keg-like Chris before answering. 'The difference is experience. With rain comes mud and lots of it. You'll be wading through water, sinking through kilometres of muddy track, slipping and sliding up and down mountains.'

'We've done some extreme stuff,' Chris told her. 'Cross-country skiing, mountain biking, abseiling. Only one we haven't done is the Gordon Dam. It's lined up though.'

'The tallest commercial abseil in the world, baby!' Alex said enthusiastically, with a high-five for Chris.

'I've done it,' Tess said. 'Twice.'

'No way!' Chris said, eyes wide. 'I want proof.'

Exasperation crossed her face. 'Fine.' She dug out her phone and scrolled through, tapped the screen and dropped it on the table. Jared watched over her shoulder as a video played, showing Tess and two others leaping out over the edge, the rope skimming through their fingers as they flew down the dam wall in long fearless bounds. Then he remembered Tess cowering from the small drop at her abseiling station and thought that, sometimes, life sucked.

'That's sick,' Alex said almost reverently.

'In case anyone else wants to question my qualifications I've also completed every track in Tassie more than once, have successfully led people into and out of wilderness areas professionally for many years, completed advanced training in wilderness survival and I'm an SES Search and Rescue volunteer.'

'Wait …' Chris said, eyes narrowed, '*you're* the hot lady we heard about that nearly died on Fedder, aren't you?'

'I'm not sure who referred to me that way, but you can call me Tess.' She paused. 'It's not the wisest move to be heading out at this time of year.'

'It's an adventure, right, guys?' Alex said. 'Gotta have some stories to tell the grandkids one day.'

'If you go into this unprepared, offspring of any kind will cease to be an issue. I need to know a bit about your experience and how prepared you are. And you two—' she pointed at Chris and Alex, '—you should probably shut up and let the others talk, okay?'

They exchanged glances, then Chris nodded, looking at Tess with a new kind of awe. 'Yeah. Sorry, go ahead.'

'What hikes have you done?' she asked the other four.

'We've been on heaps of hikes,' Riley said.

'What's the longest you've been out?'

'We did an overnight in the Tarkine rainforest,' Jasmin said.

Tess's brow shot up. 'You mean the one with the meals, accommodation and short guided walks?'

'Yeah, but we can tent it. No problem,' Jai said.

'Tent?' Jasmin repeated sharply with a glare at Brock. 'You said it would be just like the Tarkine.'

'It's an established track with designated campsites,' Brock told Jasmin. 'We're not bush bashing. You'll be fine.'

'Actually, the track can be difficult to follow,' Tess said, 'especially if the weather turns, which it can, in an instant. The fog can be so thick you can't see your hand in front of your face, the roaring forties can blow you off the Ironbound Range, the rivers, the beaches, the boat crossings can be hazardous to the point of uncrossable, and that's if you make it through the deep mud and heavy forest. It's bound to rain at minimum every second day, probably more. You could get sleet, possibly snow, and the low temperatures can freeze you quicker than help can come to the rescue. If you can't so much as properly set up a tent, you might not make it.' She pinned them all with an impressively serious stare. 'This is not a stroll in the countryside. It's a serious trek. *Especially* at this time of year.'

'Not helping,' Brock muttered to Tess with a glance at Jasmin's concerned face.

'Actually, helping is exactly what I do. And yes, I nearly died recently because of someone who didn't take the wilderness seriously enough. I ended up swinging out over a six hundred metre sheer drop by someone's jacket sleeve after trying to rescue a young

"I can handle anything" guy who thought he'd be "fine". He wasn't fine. He's dead.'

There was utter silence while everyone took that in.

'Tess, can I talk to you for a minute?' Tank asked from the doorway.

Tess walked out and Jared decided to follow. 'This is insane,' she told Tank. 'I can't prepare them for this in a week.'

'Pay no attention to Alex and Chris. They're just kids,' Tank said. 'And you are hot. You don't think you're going to make a goofy teenage kid feel awkward? Come on, this means a lot to them.'

'Look, I met those kids five minutes ago and I'm ready to bet they can't even be in civilisation without causing an accident. You really want to set them loose in thousands of hectares of harsh wilderness?'

'Riley—'

'Riley's fine. I'd say she and Jai and Brock would all make it okay. But the others? They all need to be fine out there. All of them.'

'If you really think it's that dangerous …'

Tess's shoulders dropped, her tone calming. 'Under most conditions it's not too dangerous if you're properly prepared; not compared to a lot of the other southwest wilderness hikes, anyway. But it could be really uncomfortable and difficult and they have to be prepared to follow instructions. They're not heading out there to be miserable, they want an adventure. A good one. If they get sick of it, they can't just call a taxi and go home. They're fit and strong and capable, so I'll take them, if they're set on it, if the weather forecast stays mild. But Jasmin especially needs to realise this is not glamping. She might be better off staying behind.'

'She'll be okay,' Riley said from behind them. 'And we're sorry if we didn't sound like we were taking you seriously. We're just really keen to go. We'll listen, we'll do whatever you think we need to do to prepare.'

'Okay, then,' Tess said. 'We should run through some scenarios.' She stepped back inside the office and Jared slipped in behind her. 'What are you going to do if you get separated from the group, get lost?'

'Call for help?' Riley said.

'What if you don't have reception? Have you ever used a sat phone?'

'No,' Riley admitted.

'What about a PLB?'

They all looked at each other. 'We don't know what that is,' Jai said.

'A personal locator beacon. You all need to carry one so you can activate it if you get lost or hurt.'

'We kind of just assumed Aaron would take care of that stuff,' Riley said.

'You still need to at least know what these things are and how to use them. Let's run through a few more.'

Jared listened with interest as Tess talked to the group. He was so engrossed he cursed in surprise when his phone rang. He stepped outside the office to answer it.

'Denham.'

'Are you still at the shop?' Indy asked. Her urgent tone had him making sure no one could overhear.

'Yeah,' he said. 'What's happening?'

'Cochrane just got his deal. He gave up the name. It's Tank Finlay.'

'Shit,' he muttered. 'Do you believe him?'

'He did four years for theft in Melbourne. Diamonds. And he did some work for Cochrane. We know that because he testified against him at his trial in return for immunity from prosecution for his role in Cochrane's money-laundering operation.'

Jared glanced at Tess, catching her eye. She frowned slightly.

'Are you on your way?'

'Yeah. Jared, do me a favour and get Tess out of there before we arrive. Just in case.'

CHAPTER 25

Tess was torn between making absolutely sure the group was prepared and not wanting to keep Jared waiting forever. They had to have been almost an hour already. She glanced back and saw him talking on the phone. He looked serious. Whatever he was saying, it wasn't an easy conversation. Or was he just getting sick of waiting?

'So that's about it. Oh—there was another couple I believe may have booked in to go too. I'll have to check on that.'

'Yeah, we know. That's fine,' Riley said. 'Tess, we really appreciate it. Thanks.'

'The wilderness out there will rival anything you'll experience anywhere in the world. It's truly magical, stunningly beautiful, and I really want you to have an unforgettable experience. You'd just have a better chance of that in the warmer months, that's all.'

'Tess,' Jared said, entering the office, 'sorry but something's come up. We need to go.'

'No problem, we're done. I'll be in touch regarding gear hire, Riley.'

They walked to the front of the shop, the rest of the group following. The window shattered and glass rained down. Before either of them could even fully take that in, gunshots cracked.

'Get down!' Jared's voice, his body over hers as he tackled her.

From her position on the floor under Jared, Tess saw three men in balaclavas with guns coming into the shop. Beyond the shattered window, a car slowed, the driver staring. Another car pulled over sharply, the driver already on the phone.

'You need to get everyone back in the office, understand?' Jared ordered.

Tess nodded and rolled out from under him. To her right, Jasmin and Brock were huddled together behind a set of shelves. She gestured for them to go to the office, where Chris and Alex were peeking around the door, then another crack had her ducking behind the shelter of a display cabinet.

'You bastard!' one of the masked men growled, and dragged Tank by the scruff of his neck out from behind the counter. He pushed him to his knees and pointed what looked like a sawn-off shotgun at his head.

'Dad!' Riley raced past Tess towards the gunmen. Tess lunged and dragged her back. She saw a gun aimed in her direction, then a gunshot hit the wall somewhere behind their heads.

'No! Dad!' Riley screamed.

The man who'd shot at them pointed the gun again. His eyes landed on Tess's. Time seemed to slow as she grabbed at Riley, hoping she might have dragged her further back, but all the room in her mind was taken up with one thought: *He's going to shoot me.* She knew she had to think, to do something. But she couldn't.

Jared stepped into the gunman's line of sight with his hands raised, blocking them from harm. 'Take it easy, mate. Don't do anything stupid. Why don't you put the gun down, tell us what you want?'

'Shut up!'

'No one's been hurt, you can still get out of this. The cops are on their way so—'

'I said shut up!' The gunman looked over his shoulder at the sound of more glass shattering. The third man was rifling through the jewellery cabinet.

'Where are the diamonds?' the first gunman demanded.

'I don't know what you're talking about!' Tank said.

'Take whatever you want,' Jared said, louder. 'No one's going to try and stop you. But take the gun away from his head. You wouldn't want to accidentally do something you'll regret.'

There was a splintering of wood as the locked drawer under the till was split open. 'What's this?' the third gunman called, and lifted a piece of jewellery that looked like a bracelet.

Instead of taking the gun from Tank's head, the first man shoved him with it. 'Where'd that come from, eh?' He kicked and Tank doubled over. 'Well?'

'I don't know!' Tank said breathlessly, shakily raising his hands up by his head. 'Please, I don't know.'

'Hey,' Jared said to the second gunman. 'You don't want this to go bad, okay? You should take off, now. Let the others take the fall for this.'

'Get back!' the gunman ordered urgently, but he looked strained. 'Don't take another step!'

Sirens, the flash and whine of them from somewhere in the distance, were rapidly getting closer.

All three gunmen looked at each other and the third stopped searching.

'We need to go!'

The one on Tank nodded, sneering, then lifted the gun. 'This is for Maddie!'

'No!' Riley screamed.

Jared sprung and the two rolled, the gun pointing up between them. The second gunman dragged Jared off, smacked him with the butt of the gun, and the third pulled the first gunman to his feet.

'Move!'

As they headed for the back of the shop, the first gunman aimed his weapon at Tank once more, sending Jared and Tank back behind the counter.

As soon as the assailants were gone, Riley pulled away from Tess's unsteady grasp and ran to her father, falling in front of him. 'Dad, are you okay?'

'Yeah,' Tank said, getting unsteadily to his feet.

'Good,' Jared said, gingerly touching his jaw where the gun had hit it. 'Tank Finlay, you're under arrest.'

'What?' Riley cried.

Police cars were screaming in, officers were spreading out, calling, some running through the shop in the direction the gunmen had gone, others scattering. It was chaos.

Tess got to her feet and went back to the office, where the others were huddled. 'It's okay, it's over.'

Jasmin's tear-streaked face was red and swollen, and she clutched at Brock like her life depended on it. Alex and Chris were already on their feet, watching the proceedings with mile-wide grins. She left them to it, walking as though in a daze back to the shop. She felt hands on her a second before she was pulled into Jared's arms.

'Are you all right?' he asked urgently.

She let the warm security of him soak into her for a moment before answering. 'Yeah. The others are too. They're still in the office.'

'Jared?' Indy came in, followed by several officers. 'Tess, are you hurt?'

Tess stepped back. 'No.'

'Thank God.' She turned to Jared. 'They've taken off down the street. We've got cars in pursuit. Does anyone need an ambulance?'

'No, we're all fine.'

'Great, I need everyone back at the station. Em will take Finlay.'

Tess sat nursing a cup of cold coffee. She'd been told she could go home hours ago, had even been offered a lift, but for some reason she hadn't been able to move. She'd wanted to stay at the station, with people and lights and movement and sound. With the look on the gunman's face as he pointed that gun at her still in the front of her mind, she needed all those things to remind her she was alive, she was okay. Back home in the dark loneliness of her bedroom, it would be too easy to fall apart and let the events of the night overwhelm her. She was alive. She was okay. That just needed to sink in a little longer. Brock and Jasmin had left, but Riley and Jai were still beside her. Jared and Indy were talking to Tank. She'd heard nothing on the gunmen.

She yawned and checked the time—1 am. She was getting restless, needed to move. Riley sniffed and Tess turned, smiling tiredly. Jai had an arm around Riley and was dozing lightly. 'Want me to get you anything?' Tess offered.

Riley shook her head. 'No, thanks. How could he do it?' she asked for the millionth time. 'How could he arrest Dad? He's the victim!'

'I'm sure there must be details we don't know,' she said, as she had each time Riley had voiced the question. 'We'll find out more soon.'

'I should have thanked you. That guy shot at me. You probably saved my life. I nearly got you shot, too, didn't I? I'm sorry. I was so worried for Dad.'

'I know. We're fine. It's over.'

'I don't get who Maddie is, either. I mean, what was that about?'

Jai opened his eyes and Tess caught something, some flicker of discomfort. 'Do you know?' she asked him.

'What? Oh.' Jai's eye contact fell away. 'Just, um … no, not really.'

Two uniformed officers stomped by, sparing them a quick look before heading down the hallway.

'Maddie,' Riley murmured. 'Hey,' she asked Jai, 'what was the name of that woman killed on the boat at the yacht club?'

'Can't remember,' Jai said.

'Madison Wilde,' Tess said. And then putting it together, she continued, 'So that's what this is about. The gunmen must have found some of her jewellery at your dad's shop.'

'The bracelet,' Riley said with a confused frown. 'The one the guy held up. I wonder how it got there? Dad's been so careful about any diamonds coming in.' She glanced at Jai. 'Have you seen it before?'

'Nah,' he said. 'Never.'

'Dad's been set up!' Riley got to her feet. 'I need to see him. Talk to the detectives.'

'Sit down, Riley,' Tess urged. 'They're several steps ahead on this, I'm sure.'

The door opened as she spoke and Jared came out. He seemed surprised to see them still sitting there.

'Dad's been set up!' Riley told him.

'Relax, Riley,' Jared said. 'We're just having a conversation. Tess, why are you still here? I asked Emily to take you home.'

'She offered but … I thought I may as well wait.'

'Are you letting my dad go?' Riley asked.

'We need to keep him a bit longer. Why don't you head home and get some rest? It could be a while. Tess?' He led her out of earshot. 'You must be exhausted.'

'No, I'm fine. I couldn't have slept earlier anyway.' She smiled self-consciously.

'It's been a hell of a night.' He tucked a loose strand of hair gently back behind her ear. 'You're allowed to admit you're shaken up.'

'Okay, I'm shaken up. But mostly I'm relieved it's over.' Then, because she had recovered enough that the sympathy in his eyes was starting to embarrass her, she changed the subject. 'Do you really think Tank had something to do with the murders?'

'I don't know. We didn't find any stolen goods from the theft or any evidence linking Tank to the murder. We can't hold him indefinitely based on a gunman's accusation and a missing piece of jewellery that may or may not have been the piece belonging to Madison Wilde. He's saying he was set up and maybe he was. We're going to hold him while we finish searching the shop and his house. If we don't find anything else, we'll have to let him go.'

'And the gunmen?'

'Still searching. You really should get some rest.'

'Okay. But I'll drive myself back.'

'If you're sure. Hey, how about we get that dinner tomorrow night?'

'Sounds good. I'll sort it.'

'Detective Denham?' an officer called.

She smiled again at his worried expression. 'I'm fine. Go get the bad guys.'

CHAPTER 26

'I'm really not sure we should have left,' Riley said as they got out of Jai's car. 'Dad might need us to go get him again at any time. They can't hold him forever.' She slammed the door hard, shattering the silence of the street. 'The whole thing is a joke.'

'Hey, take it easy, okay? The police have to do their job. It might help them find the guys that did this.' His nerves prickled at his words. Though his system had long stopped firing on overload from the attack, his gut had continued to churn with guilt. He'd had no choice, he told himself. But it didn't make him feel any better. Hurting Tank was bad enough, but Riley could have been killed tonight. She didn't deserve any of this.

Riley checked her phone as they walked to the front door. 'But what if he needs us?'

'Then we'll go back and get him.' He pushed through the door where the agency nurse was waiting with a coffee in the kitchen.

'Hi, are you guys all right?' David asked, getting to his feet.

'Yeah, thanks for staying back,' he said.

'No problem. It was on the news. What happened?'

'Do you mind if we talk about it tomorrow?' Jai asked, glancing at Riley. She had large dark circles under her worried eyes. 'We're wiped.'

'Yeah, of course,' David said. 'Still want me here at eight-thirty?'

'If that's okay.'

'Yeah, I can do it.'

He saw David out and turned around to see Riley checking her phone again. 'Come on, up to bed.'

'I feel like I should shower,' she said as she reached the staircase, 'but I just want to sleep.'

'Then sleep,' he said and wrapped his arms around her, kissed the top of her head. 'I'm going to go check on Pop. I'll be up in a sec.'

'K.'

He watched her trudge upstairs and told himself everything would be okay. But he didn't really believe it. Evan was sleeping soundly, one arm thrown across his face, snoring quietly. He hadn't changed out of his clothes. Looks like David had lost the shower argument today. What was going to happen to Pop if he was caught? The guilt welled up again and threatened to overwhelm him. There was at least a small chance Tank would be left with no choice but to dob him in. He closed the door and smacked hard into Pax as he turned to go upstairs.

'And he's back,' Pax said. 'Took ya long enough.'

'Where did you come from?' The anger was instant and violent. 'You want to tell me what tonight was about? Did you organise that?'

'No,' Pax said. 'I followed orders. Remember our talk?'

'They were going to shoot him! Who was it? Wilde's people?'

'I certainly hope it looked like that. I told ya I'd get this off our backs. I know what nights Tank works back late. Problem was, ya failed to mention you were all going to be there.'

'I didn't know what was happening because you wouldn't tell me! And I don't have a phone number to contact you. Besides, if we hadn't been there to see it, what was the point of the show?'

Pax shrugged carelessly. 'I planted a witness on the street, mate. So what's the story? What do the cops think?'

'I don't know. Tank's not saying anything as far as I can tell.'

'Nah, he wouldn't.'

'I don't know why. If you're going to get him killed, what's he got to lose?'

'Riley. And you. He doesn't want to drop ya in it. I wonder how he'd feel if he found out you'd planted the stuff in the shop?'

Jai dragged his fingers through his hair restlessly. 'You didn't give me a choice! That's Riley's dad! He's been good to me. What's going to happen now? Why didn't you leave the bracelet behind if you wanted him to take the blame for everything?'

'I wanted him to take the blame and be dead. Cops charge him now, he's out of reach.'

'You can't kill him!'

'I just do what I'm told.' Pax bent down to get in Jai's face. 'So do you, understand?'

'I did, didn't I?'

'Yeah, and ya need to do something else.'

His stomach lurched, his temper spiked. 'You've got to be—'

Pax put a bag in Jai's hand. 'Ya lose this, ya life is over, got it?'

'What's in it?'

'Doesn't matter. I was supposed to hold on to this until the boss got out of prison, but my face everywhere is making him nervous so he's got someone coming to collect it. Ya need to deliver it to him on Monday night.'

'Why Monday?'

Pax's look was impatient. 'Just details, mate. They don't concern ya. Put the bag in ya backpack and go to this address.' He put a piece of paper in Jai's hand. 'Go through the gate, knock three times, leave it on the doorstep and pick up the one waiting. Drive away. That's it.'

'Where will you be?'

'I've got a few other loose ends to tie up.'

'So I do this, but that's it, right?'

'It's not over until you're told it's over. Anyway, I've got another shitload of money for ya. It'll be in the backpack ya pick up when ya drop off the bag.'

Jai felt the tug of wanting that money. But he still had some principles left. 'Okay, but tell your boss to back off Tank. He's not gonna talk. I'll do what you want, what your boss wants, but he leaves Tank and Riley alone.'

Pax smirked. 'Sure, big guy. I'll pass on the message.'

'Good,' Jai said with more bravado than he felt. 'Are we done?'

'Yeah, we're done. For now.'

Pax let himself out of the house and Jai locked up behind him, then went upstairs and put the bag on his chest of drawers. Curious, he opened the bag and found a jewellery box. Inside was a diamond ring. He put it aside and pulled out a mobile phone. Strange.

Riley sat up. 'Everything okay? I thought I heard more voices down there.'

'All good. Just talking to Pop.' He quickly shoved everything into his top drawer and scattered his clothes over the top. He'd put it back together tomorrow. Then he crawled onto the bed next to Riley and was asleep in seconds.

The press of Riley's lips on his woke him. He only felt as though he'd slept a few minutes but sunlight was pouring through his window.

'Morning.'

'Morning,' he muttered, then noticed she'd showered and was dressed for the day. She was smiling at him: a big, blow-you-away smile he couldn't quite figure out.

'Did they let your dad go?' he asked, sitting up and rubbing his eyes.

'Yep. We need to go pick him up as soon as we're ready. He asked if we'd go to the shop, help him clean up. The glass guys are coming with replacement windows in a couple of hours.'

'Okay, yeah, of course. That's great.'

'David's here. I let him in and threw Evan's clothes in the wash. I put away the load in the dryer.'

He remembered the state of his grandfather's clothes, frowned. 'You didn't have to do that.'

'It's fine.' She kissed him again before hugging him hard. 'Even when everything is as bad as it can get, you make me happy. I love you.'

'Okay …' he said slowly. 'I love you too.'

'Everything's going to be fine. Isn't it?'

'Yeah,' he said with more conviction than he felt. 'Everything's going to be great.'

As soon as she left him alone he went to his top drawer. Clean socks and undies were folded at the front. The jewellery box had been carefully placed in the corner. *Oh shit.* He scrambled through the drawer, found the small bag and phone still tangled in his things further back. Relief came first, before understanding hit him hard. Riley must have seen the ring. She must have thought—no wonder she was bubbly. He opened the box. A large diamond sat amid a cluster of smaller ones. Expensive. And shaped like a classic engagement ring. Hell. Now what? What was she going to do when he didn't give it to her?

He snapped the lid closed and returned the ring to its place in the drawer. Riley was expecting a proposal.

CHAPTER 27

Jared walked into the station in time to see Indy dismiss everyone from their morning meeting. 'Sorry, I got held up talking to Madison Wilde's father. Did you get any sleep?'

'A couple of hours. You?'

'Yeah about that much. Wilde's denying any knowledge of the attack on Finlay.'

'Do you believe him?'

'I don't know. Wilde says Cochrane never told him anything. He did remember Finlay from Cochrane's trial though.'

Indy tapped a red fingernail on the folder in front of her. 'I ran Finlay's prints against the ones we lifted from the robbery and the dinghy. No match on prints, shoe size or physical description, and he has an alibi for the night of the murders. He's not our second POI. He might have been handling the diamonds, but he's not one of our killers.'

'Sorry,' Emily said, knocking on the door. 'We've had a report of a burnt-out car. Orange hatchback. Witness can't see anyone inside. Looks like it's been rolled into a ditch and lit on purpose.'

'Orange hatchback?' Jared repeated. 'We may have found our missing escape vehicle.'

'Let's go and find out.'

The car was at the bottom of a steep ravine on the side of a timber track. The area had been cleared and the burnt-out shell sat in a wet, muddy hole.

'Plates have been removed,' Indy noted.

Jared wrestled with the hood, shaking it and kicking at it until it came apart. 'Serial number's been scratched out.' He looked closer. 'Might be able to make out one or two numbers, so may be possible to ID it.'

'Call it through now. Tell them we need it back asap.' She turned and looked back up to the trail. 'Em, how many people have scrambled up and down this slope?'

'The logger that called it in went down to check no one was in the car. Otherwise just us. I've marked out a boot print that doesn't match the tread of the set the logger made. It's about halfway up. Forensics are on their way to cast the print and go over the car. Doubt they're going to find anything useful in that wreck.'

'Great work,' Indy said.

'How long do you think that numbers check will take?' Jared asked.

'Your guess is as good as mine. Why? In a hurry?'

He shrugged. 'Just wondering whether to hang around.'

'Your date with Tess isn't until tonight.'

'It's not about—' He resisted the urge to sigh. 'How do you know?'

Indy's eyes danced with humour. 'She booked in at the lodge's restaurant. The *good* restaurant.'

'I didn't think she liked that sort of thing.'

'She likes it occasionally. When it's her idea and our restaurant. Wear your suit.'

He nodded, liking that Tess could surprise him. Indy was giving him a strange look. 'What?'

'I'm happy for you two. Honestly. I just think it's hysterical that you breeze past each other for years without a second glance then suddenly you can't get enough of each other.'

'Maybe I breezed past,' he said, 'but who says I didn't glance?'

Indy chuckled. 'It'll do her good to get her mind off Aaron.'

'I wanted to ask you about that. Something's been bothering you.'

'Aaron's been bothering me. He doesn't seem to want to take no for an answer since they broke up. One minute he thinks she's just mad, that she'll calm down and they'll be fine, the next he's hurling abuse at her and possibly even threats.'

'You mean the comment about her taking a chance before they run out?'

Indy shrugged. 'I keep telling myself I'm reading too much into it. That he was trying to soothe his ego—he's hurt and upset and not many people take break-ups well. But since Tess mentioned that shove on the rescue after they'd fought, I can't quite get the idea out of my mind that he could be more dangerous than we give him credit for.'

'It crossed Tess's mind that he might have sent me the photo of us out at her place. She said she felt silly for mentioning it, but the thought still got in there.'

'He's due to fly out a few days after she returns from that hike she's doing. Let's hope that's the end of it.' Her phone rang and she answered it. 'Great, send it through.' She ended the call and said to him, 'There's an orange Hyundai i10 with those numbers registered to a Mary Ted. Not reported stolen.'

'Ted?' The unusual surname stuck in his mind, taking him back to his visit to Tank's shop. 'Old lady, widowed.'

'How would you know that?'

'If it's the same person I'm thinking of, she was at the pawn shop one day when I was there talking to Tank.'

'Interesting. I've got an address. Let's go chat to her.'

Jared looked back up the slippery, muddy bank he'd just negotiated his way down and nodded in resignation. 'After you.'

At Mary Ted's house, he hit the doorbell once, twice. Waited. 'No one home,' he said unnecessarily.

Indy was frowning. She walked around the side so he followed, noticed her staring at the windows. 'Do you think it's odd that all the blinds are closed?' she asked.

'An old woman living alone might be a bit paranoid, I suppose. But yeah, I do.'

'Hello.' An elderly man appeared at the side fence with a hose in hand. 'Looking for Mary?'

'Yes,' Indy said, moving around to him. 'We're police. Have you seen her around today?'

'Oh, I haven't seen Mary for a good couple of months now. Wife and I took the caravan up north for a trip, came back and she was gone. She's moved in with family. Terribly old and lonely she was. So nice they came and got her.'

'Do you know where we can find her then?'

He shook his head. 'No, didn't ask. The grandson's a very nice chap though, I'm sure he'd be happy to help. He's been coming and going, looking after the place for her.'

Jared exchanged looks with Indy and jogged back to the car, got the picture of their POI and brought it back. 'Have you by any chance seen this man around?' he asked the neighbour.

'Why yes, that's him. That's Mary's grandson. Nothing's happened to him, has it?'

'We're not sure,' Indy said. 'When was the last time you saw him?'

'Day before yesterday, I think.'

'Did you ever see a second person?'

'No …' the man said slowly, seemingly thinking back. 'No, just him.'

'Do you know if he's in there now?' Jared asked.

'Couldn't tell you, sorry.'

'Harry! Lunch!' was shouted from somewhere in the neighbour's house and he smiled. 'Sorry, that's me.'

'Thanks for your time,' Jared told him. 'Appreciate it.' Then to Indy, he said, 'What do you want to do?'

'I have grave concerns for Mrs Ted's safety, and reason to believe our POI may be inside. That's good enough grounds to go in, check it out.'

'Let's do it.'

The front door was locked, but they found a back one open.

'Stuffed lock on the laundry,' he noted. 'Fits our POI's preferred method of entry.'

They carefully searched each room, finding no one home. 'There's milk in the fridge—still in date,' Indy said. 'And some recent takeaway food.'

'We should get out of here, keep watch on the house.'

'Agreed. Hey, does it look like this space is missing something?'

He looked at the carpet under their feet, saw it looked cleaner and a shade or two darker than the carpet around it. 'Missing rug.'

'Didn't see it anywhere. Let's go.'

Outside, Jared hesitated at the door to the garage. When he turned the handle, it opened, so he stepped in. The sickly sweet smell was familiar and overwhelming. Indy came in behind him, gagged and stepped around him, hand over her mouth and nose. She pointed to the dim back corner of the space. He saw a floor rug, rolled. The toes of a stockinged foot were just visible protruding from one end.

'Son of a bitch!' He abruptly turned and walked out.

Indy closed the door and stood beside him, dragging in air. 'Murdering a defenceless old woman. Our POI just officially scraped the bottom of the barrel.'

'We need to get this bastard off the street. What are our chances of getting the scene processed before our suspect returns and the media get hold of this?'

'Absolutely none.' Indy walked a few steps away and called it in. 'I'm convinced this guy came down here specifically to carry out the attack on Wilde and Sash.'

'A local would have his own place,' Jared agreed, 'not need to hijack someone else's, and he obviously has no problem killing. He's cold, calculating and knows what he's doing. A murderer capable of pulling off a theft, not the other way around. He's a pro. But what about our second POI?'

'The one leaving evidence wherever he—or she—goes? I don't know. I haven't made sense of that yet but I'm guessing it's a local he's picked up along the way. Not as polished.'

By the time other police vehicles arrived, the majority of the street was watching. Teams of officers traipsed in and out, and the local papers had got wind of it and were hanging around taking photos and demanding details.

'There's no way the guy's stupid enough to return with all this going on,' Jared said to Indy.

'I doubt he was planning on coming back anyway, hence the dumped car. He's taken off again. Job's done, he's cleaning up.'

'Makes sense. In which case I bet we won't find a single print, or any other evidence.' They'd lost him just when they'd thought they were going to finally catch him.

'Let's hope you're wrong. Nothing came back on your chocolate box, did you know?'

'Yeah. No reason he'd start getting sloppy now.'

'Detectives?' It was the neighbour again—Harry. 'What have you found? What's going on?'

As the body bag was going to be brought out shortly anyway, Jared decided he might as well break the news to the guy. 'I'm afraid Mary was at home. She's deceased.'

'Oh—oh, no. What a shame. Just when she and her family …' Harry studied Jared's face. 'That grandson didn't have something to do with it, did he? You hear of young ones knocking oldies off for their inheritance, but he seemed so nice.'

'I don't think he was her grandson.'

The man's face fell even further, the creases deepening impossibly in his forehead. 'That's terrible. Terrible news. To think he was swanning in and out of here … the lying little bastard! He was annoying, you know, in some ways. Used our mower more than once, put his rubbish in our bin. But I thought it was so good of him to help out, I let it go. I fell for it!'

'There's no way you could have known but …' Jared glanced at Indy. 'How recently did he put rubbish in your bin?'

'A couple of days, I think. It hasn't been emptied yet.'

'We'll need to take that rubbish into evidence,' Indy said. 'And take a look at your mower.'

Tess checked her appearance in the mirror and wondered if she'd gone overboard. She'd booked them a table at the restaurant. Not the casual buffet, but the lodge's two-hat restaurant, and she'd put on one of her few special dresses for the occasion. She'd told Jared she didn't particularly enjoy this sort of thing, so perhaps it was the wrong move. But she wanted him to see her dressed up like a woman, not just a horse-riding, outdoor activities manager. She didn't think too much about why that was suddenly important to her, she just did it. And then he knocked on her door and a wave of crippling doubt crashed in on her.

She peeked through the peephole first, saw he was wearing his suit and, relieved, opened the door. 'Hi.'

'Wow,' he said in return. When he slid an arm around her waist and pulled her in she held her breath, her system humming when he kissed her.

'You're wearing makeup,' he murmured against her lips.

'Yeah, just to prove I own some.'

'And a dress.'

'Same goes.'

'It looks almost as good as your jodhpurs.'

She laughed, relieving some of the tension in her chest. 'Thanks. I think.'

He stepped back, keeping their fingers linked, and looked her over from head to toe for several excruciatingly hot seconds. 'You're stunning.'

'Thanks.' It was all she could think to say. 'I hope you like the restaurant. I had a small moment of panic because I hadn't told you where we were eating.'

'Indy mentioned it.'

'She did?'

'Yeah, your sister-in-law enjoys keeping tabs on us.'

'She should mind her own business,' she replied, unoffended.

'She has a point about how long it took us to get this far,' he said, brushing her hair back from her face. 'Really should have got here sooner.' His expression promised all sorts of things and anticipation built inside her.

'Things just keep … getting in the way.' She stepped back to get her purse and keys. 'This is our third attempt at dinner.'

'On that, I meant to thank you for the other night,' he said. 'Hanging around with Riley at the station.'

'That's okay. She was going to keep at you otherwise and the boyfriend wasn't all that helpful. He got a pretty big scare when Riley almost got shot.'

'Yeah. You gave me one when you dived after her.' He stepped in to touch her again, the back of his fingers drifting lightly down her cheek. 'Bullets hurt, you know.'

'I wasn't vying for the experience,' she objected, skin tingling. 'I thought she was going to get herself killed. And you're in no position to criticise. You walked straight out and started chatting to them!'

He grinned, lifted his other hand and swept it under her hair to the back of her neck. 'My job. Besides, he was pointing that gun at you.'

'Mmm, and all I could think was I was going to be kneeling on another hard floor trying to stop you bleeding to death. Again.' Her words trembled out. Breathing was getting complicated. She didn't want to relive it, not now. She didn't want anything to interfere with this moment.

All traces of amusement left his face as he backed her into the bench. 'You're incredible, Tess. Even petrified, you do what needs to be done. I never thanked you properly for saving my life.'

She pressed her hands against his chest, sliding them over his shoulders and around his neck as he closed the last inch of space between them.

'I'm not letting anything interrupt us tonight,' he murmured against her lips.

Her body ignited. 'You know, one of the perks of living at the lodge is that dinner can be delivered … later,' she suggested, then shivered as his lips grazed her neck.

'I think we're supposed to make it through at least one official date before we—'

'Do you want to wait?' she asked, tugging at his ear with her teeth. 'Do you want to risk another interruption by leaving this room?'

'Is that really in question?' He swept his hand up her ribcage, brushed his fingers across her breasts. 'I'm having trouble figuring out why we haven't already—'

She heard the purr erupt from her throat. 'Maybe because you talk too much.'

'You're right. I should just shut up.' He put his mouth to better use, devouring hers while his hands traced the lines and curves of her heated, pulsing body. She wondered if she'd been too forward, too fast, then, as the need between them pushed them on, decided she didn't care. His hands slid under her thighs and lifted her off the ground as he turned around and pressed her back against the wall. She wrapped her legs around his waist, gasped at the intimate contact of being plastered so fully against him.

'Lock the door,' he muttered against her mouth and she reached out blindly to the lock.

'Phone?' he asked, destroying her ability to think as he moved against her.

'Purse. Bench.'

He held her in place with one arm long enough to pull his phone from his pocket, dropping it next to hers. 'Bedroom?'

'That one.' She pointed. When he carried her through the door, she kicked it shut. Tonight the world was going to have to survive without them.

CHAPTER 28

Tess struggled out of the supermarket, arms loaded with her regular groceries as well as extra supplies for the hike. It was coming up fast, and her head wasn't really in the right space for it at all.

She'd finally said goodbye to Jared just before 2 am. When she'd closed the door she'd already been looking forward to seeing him again. And she'd been sleepy, sated. Then she'd picked up her phone to set her alarm, and that's when she noticed the messages. Aaron needed to talk to her. He needed to make amends. He didn't know what had come over him. He was sorry. They couldn't leave things like this. Would she give him a chance to apologise? Could he pop over for just a few minutes? Could she at least call him back? She'd left her phone muted and ignored the buzzing while she caught a few hours' sleep. But more messages had been waiting for her when she woke up, and they hadn't stopped.

She reached the car and popped the boot. When her phone pinged she pulled it from her bag. And here was another one. Why hadn't she called? He'd been waiting all day. She scrolled back through his messages. Uneasiness washed over her. This wasn't right. Wasn't *rational.* Maybe she should call him, just to tell him to stop.

'Tess!'

The sound of Aaron's voice behind her had her spinning. 'What? Are you following me now?' she asked, incredulous.

'Huh? No, of course not,' he replied with a smile that was too warm. 'I was getting petrol. Spotted you from across the street. Any reason you've come into Hobart to do your shopping?'

'I needed a couple of things for the hike I can't get anywhere else. Why?'

'The hike I passed on? Riley Finlay?' he asked as though surprised. 'I didn't think you'd go for it.'

'That's not the impression you gave them.'

'You'll have to be careful out there. At this time of year—'

'Aaron, I really have to keep moving. I've got more things to do.'

'Can't you just spare a minute?' he asked hopefully. 'I've been trying to talk to you. You're not still mad and ignoring me, are you?'

'Not exactly. But I don't know what else there is to say.' As she bent to pick up the last of her groceries, he swooped and loaded them in, then straightened to stand just a bit too close.

'I thought we'd agreed to be friends,' he said gently. 'You ignoring me doesn't really fit with that.'

She stepped back to shut the boot, smiled coolly. 'I'm sorry. I've been busy.'

'Oh, yeah?' His voice dripped with accusation. 'Busy last night, were you?'

Her stomach flipped nervously. Here it was again, that lightning-fast shift from overly warm to spitting rage. Now what? She took another cautious step back, but she wouldn't cower. 'I don't appreciate being bombarded with messages late at night,' she said, voice not quite as strong as she would have liked. 'I'm certainly not going to answer them at two in the morning.' She turned her back on him to get in the car.

'Well, I wouldn't want to interrupt anything, would I?' His hand shot out, holding on to the door as she climbed in to prevent it from closing. 'You lied to me, Tess.'

A chill ran down her spine at the tone, the look. 'I never lied to you. And what I do now is my own business. Goodbye, Aaron.' She reefed at the door handle and it shut with a bang. She started the car with trembling hands, put it in gear and drove away as calmly as she could.

Aaron had seemed so sure of himself. How could he know she'd been with Jared last night? There's no way. Not without spying on them.

'Don't be stupid, Tess,' she muttered as she weaved her way out of Hobart. Aaron was guessing. Jealously imagining, perhaps. And he was leaving, so there was no need to worry about the mood changes, the insinuations, the accusations, or the look that had come over his face that had made her want to shrink back and run. 'Stop it.'

The incident at Fedder, the gunmen at the pawn shop, this nastiness with Aaron were all turning her into a nervous wreck. She needed to get away from it all. Some time in the wilderness on the hike she'd been worrying over might just turn out to be a blessing in disguise.

A slow-moving truck in front of her had her glancing in her mirrors then over her shoulder to change lanes. She pulled out, did a double-take and checked her rear-view mirror. Was that Aaron's car?

Shit.

Coincidence? He did come this way to get home, so probably.

But right behind me?

She kept driving, slowed to below the speed limit, but he never passed her, just stayed a few cars back. Because her mind was going crazy with unsettling thoughts, she called Indy.

'Hi, sorry, are you busy?' she asked when Indy answered.

'Just waiting on Jared to tie up a couple of things for the day, what's up?'

'Probably nothing. Are you on your way home soon?'

'Okay seriously, Tess, what is it?'

'Again, probably nothing, but … Aaron's acting a bit unusual. I've had about a hundred messages from him since last night, he ran into me at the shops earlier apparently by accident, and now he seems to be following me. Look, I know it's quite possible he really was just getting petrol and spotted me, and now he's on his way home too. That's probably exactly what's going on.' She laughed hollowly. 'Maybe I'm just on edge in general.'

'Perhaps. What did he say when you ran into him?'

'He—Indy, I think he's been watching me. He knew I'd seen Jared last night and he wasn't happy about it.'

'Okay. Are you going straight home?'

'Yeah.'

'Good. No stops. If he follows you past his turn-off, call Logan. Make sure he's waiting at the guesthouse for you. He'll deal with Aaron.'

'Yeah, okay.' The idea was a comforting one. 'I will.' She was already feeling better just telling Indy, was starting to feel silly.

'I won't be far behind you anyway. Jared's just walked in, I've got one thing I absolutely have to do, then I'll ditch the rest, come find you at home and we'll talk about it, okay?'

'Thanks.' Tess ended the call as the towns gave way to hills and river, and the pretty stretch of the Lyell Highway took her closer to

New Norfolk. She really hoped Aaron would turn off. She'd rather feel silly than deal with any more upset.

The car's temperature alert went off, dragging her attention to the dash. 'Shit!' It was too high. She looked closely at the bonnet and noticed thin wisps of smoke from the engine. She looked for somewhere to pull over. The highway might be pretty but there wasn't a lot of room for getting off the road. She wasn't far from Murphy's Flat. There was a rest stop nearby.

Another thought had dread stacking on dread. Where was Aaron? She was about to stop in the middle of nowhere. She couldn't see him, so she called Indy again, got voicemail. 'Call me back,' she managed. 'Something's wrong with the car.'

The car limped off the highway just as the sun was touching the tops of the mountains, reminding her it'd be dark soon. Indy had said she wouldn't be far behind, and she was still closer to Hobart than home. But if Indy didn't call back in the next minute or two she'd try Logan. She climbed out, swiped at the smoke coming from under the hood and took a few steps away from it. There was no way she was getting any closer to the engine for the time being. She rubbed her arms against the chill of the late afternoon and looked around. Hills to the left, wetlands and the river to the right. A car shot past, another not too far behind. Since she was on the main road almost everyone took from Hobart to anywhere in the northwest, she was far from isolated, but at that moment it felt like it. And Aaron couldn't be too far away. Stuff waiting for Indy, it wouldn't hurt to call Logan too.

Before she could do more than think it, tyres crunched on the road behind her, and the hairs on the back of her neck stood up. She knew who it was. She slowly turned around, swallowed her nerves.

'What's happened?' Aaron asked, getting out of his car. 'Radiator?'

'What are you doing here?' she asked, ignoring the question.

'Heading home. Lucky I spotted you,' he said.

'Yeah, you just ran into me … twice in one day.'

'Yes, and I could have left you here to fend for yourself after the way you spoke to me earlier. But I didn't. Because someone has to look after you.'

She managed a tight smile. 'Thanks, but I'm fine.'

'It's getting dark and it's freezing. Lock your car and hop in mine. I'll give you a lift home.'

She didn't trust him anymore. Couldn't do it. 'I don't want to leave my car out here like this,' she said. 'I'd rather wait for a tow.' She opened the door to get her phone out.

The car door slammed shut before she could lean in, startling her. She stumbled backwards several steps, staring at Aaron in disbelief.

'That's not a good idea,' he said with a slow shake of his head and a dangerous gleam in his eyes. 'The car could catch fire. Explode. You need to stay away from it.'

'It's not going to …' She wanted to tell him not to be stupid. The car wasn't going to explode. But he clearly didn't want her calling anyone. The realisation had her heart thudding in her chest. Another thought slammed into her mind. Had he done this? Had he done something to her car then followed her, waiting for the car to stop?

'What did you do?' she whispered.

His eyes remained cool, detached. 'It's dangerous out here on the side of the highway. You never know who might come along. Or why. Get in my car, Tess. Now.'

CHAPTER 29

Jared walked into Indy's office and found her on a call. She spotted him and lifted a finger. He'd been hoping to sneak off a few minutes early—a stint at the morgue watching Mrs Ted's body being disassembled in the autopsy room had his stomach feeling queasy and his head pounding. The look on Indy's face suggested that wasn't going to happen.

'Tell me this is good news?' he asked.

She turned her monitor around to show him a picture. 'Paxton Orvist,' she said triumphantly. 'We found a partial fingerprint on a toilet roll in the neighbour's rubbish. Twenty-seven years old, spent some time in the army, dropped out. Served most of his young-adult life in the same prison as Cochrane on sexual assault and attempted murder charges. He was only released a month before our first break-in. Height and build match our POI.'

'I imagine you've already got everyone in creation looking for this guy?'

'Of course. And there's something else. Orvist and Cochrane didn't just spend time in the same prison, they were friends. According to one of the guards, they spent a lot of time together in the lead-up to Orvist's release.'

'So Cochrane knew both men, one good at moving stolen diamonds and the other capable of murder. Orvist is seen in Finlay's shop, jewellery most likely belonging to Madison Wilde is discovered in the shop … Finlay's been lying. He knew Orvist all along. They've been in on this together.'

'Which is why I've already got him waiting in Interview 2. Let's go talk to him.'

Tank Finlay scowled at them from his seat as they walked in. 'About time. You want to tell me why you're talking to me again instead of finding the little bastards who broke into my shop?'

'Cut the bullshit, Tank,' Jared snapped. 'We know exactly what this is about, so why don't you start again?'

Tank dropped his head and stared at the table. 'I don't know who broke into my shop.'

'If you don't start cooperating,' Indy said, 'we'll just go ahead and charge you for your involvement in the murders of Madison Wilde and Brendan Sash. We'll have to assume that you were intent on selling the diamonds from the robbery and—'

'Look, okay. *Okay*. It's not what you think. I had no choice.'

'Keep going,' Indy said, leaning back and folding her arms.

Tank took a deep breath. 'You know I rolled on Cochrane. I did it because I didn't want to go back to prison, because my wife had died and I needed to raise my daughter. I made a stupid mistake getting tied up with my gang again and the cops gave me a way out. I came down here to get away from it all. I hoped he'd let it go, wouldn't look for me. But he found me.'

'And he very kindly gave you your old job back?' Jared asked.

'No, of course not. He sent Pax down with a note saying he was there for a job, that all I had to do was provide him with some cover and pull apart whatever jewellery he brought back. Cochrane said if I did that, he wouldn't come after me or Riley. I couldn't believe it. Of course I went along with it. I'd been worrying about the day he walked free for years.'

'So it's okay with you if someone else's daughter is murdered as long as it's not yours,' Indy said in disgust.

'No!' Tank growled. 'I never, *never* knew that Pax was going to kill Madison and that other poor bugger. I never agreed to murder.'

'Pax and who?' Jared asked. 'He didn't commit those murders alone. Who's he working with?'

Tank's gaze hit the table again. 'Dunno.'

'Why should we believe you?' Jared asked.

'I'm not bullshitting. If you want me to guess, I reckon that whole thing in the shop was a setup to make me look guilty then shoot me so I couldn't talk. Shoulda known they'd use me to cover their tracks.'

'Yeah, you should have,' Jared said. 'So where are the diamonds?'

'I handed them over the afternoon of the break-in.' Tank's expression was strained. '*Please*. I'm just an old piece of shit, but Riley's a good kid with her whole life ahead of her. He would have killed her. Pax still might, if he thinks I'm talking to you.'

'Let us worry about Riley,' Indy said.

'I'll do the worrying myself if it's all the same.' His expression was tortured. 'I'll cooperate fully and go a step further. There's a whole lot more I can say about Cochrane, about the criminals he dealt with. Some of the names you won't believe. But I'm not doing a thing, or saying a thing, until Riley and her friends are miles away in the wilderness where nothing can touch them. And I don't want her coming back until this is all over. Do we have a deal?'

'Jared?' Indy nodded towards the door and he got up and followed her into the corridor.

'What do you think?' she asked.

'I don't think he's in much of a position to be calling the shots.'

'There are a few crucial details of this case that might rely on his testimony. If protecting Riley is going to make him feel more inclined to talk, I think we should give him those couple of days to see her off on her hike with her friends. Pick up from there.'

'Then let's do it,' Jared said and checked his watch. 'Pin him down and threaten him with everything in our arsenal then cut him loose for two days. We might even get away from work on time for once.'

'That would be nice …' She trailed off as she checked her phone, then listened to the message. 'I'll leave you to do that last bit. Gotta go,' she said, already hurrying away.

'I said, get in the car, Tess.'

'And I said, no.' Tess stood rigid, not fully able to believe that the man she'd dated, slept with, shared a history with, could really be a threat, but at the same time unable to ignore the alarm bells ringing in her ears. She backed up warily as he approached.

'What are you going to do, Tess, run all the way home?' His words were chilling in their quiet delivery.

'Why are you acting like this?' she asked desperately.

'Like what?' He was moving slowly, not letting her put too much distance between them. 'I've been nothing but caring and considerate. You're not doing so well without me, Tess. You're losing the plot and I'm here to help. Just get in my car and everything will be fine. Trust me.'

She backed into her car and saw Aaron tense as though ready to spring.

A car came in fast off the highway. Indy. Relief flooded through her. Aaron turned, smiled then waved as though the last few moments hadn't taken place.

'Okay?' Indy asked, jumping out.

'She's fine, just a radiator issue, I think,' Aaron said. 'Hello, Indy.'

Indy ignored him. 'Tess? Are you okay?'

Tess stared hard at Aaron, then nodded. 'Yeah.'

'I was going to give her a lift home, but she was worried about her car.'

'Thanks, Aaron,' Indy said coolly. 'We'll be fine from here.'

'No worries.' He got in his car and wound down the window. 'Oh, Tess. Almost forgot. I have something of yours.' He held a large envelope out the window.

She hesitantly walked to the car. When she tried to take the envelope he held on to it and looked her in the eyes.

'It's very important that you make the right decision.' He let the envelope go, called out, 'Bye, Indy! Nice to see you!' then started the car and drove back out onto the highway.

Tess stood staring after him. What would have happened if Indy hadn't shown? Just what exactly had he had in mind?

'Tess?'

'Sorry,' she said and walked unsteadily back to Indy's car.

'What did he give you?' Indy asked.

'I don't know.' She opened the envelope and pulled out the contents. A lump of lead landed in her stomach. 'He's bought me a ticket to Canada.'

CHAPTER 30

Jai woke in a sweat. Riley was no longer tucked up beside him and he wondered when she'd snuck out. After the way he'd slept, he was surprised he hadn't felt her leave the bed. Guilt hung over him. He'd wussed out of taking Evan into the respite home himself, instead calling for a patient transport van. He'd followed him in, of course, made sure he got settled into his room. But none of it had gone smoothly. Evan didn't want to be there and he'd made sure everyone knew about it. He'd pleaded with Jai not to leave him there and it had taken two male nurses to restrain him when Jai had to leave.

He got up and stood under the shower, wondering how his pop was going this morning. It wouldn't hurt to call and find out. Once he was dressed, he found Riley in the kitchen with coffee and toast.

'Morning!' She jumped up, planted a kiss on his lips. 'I wanted to let you sleep. You were tossing and turning all over the place last night.'

'Sorry.'

'Don't be. Want me to make you some toast?' she asked.

He wasn't the least bit hungry but his smile was genuine. Just having her there brightened him up. Pop would be okay, and Jai just had one more hurdle, one more thing to do and this might be over once and for all. 'Yeah. Yeah, that'd be great, thanks.'

She hummed as she placed the bread in the toaster. 'I was thinking maybe I should spend some time with Dad tonight. He's been through a heap. Want to join us?'

Relieved, because he was wondering how he'd been going to sneak off if she'd insisted on staying, he shook his head. 'That'd be nice but I'll go see Pop, then I wouldn't mind an early night.'

'Okay. Ah … might we be going to do something special together soon?' She had that look on her face again. With everything that had gone on he'd almost managed to forget she'd seen the ring.

'Of course,' he told her, mirroring her smile. 'Count on it.'

After breakfast, he watched her happily drive away, wondering how he was going to tackle the ring issue. Who the hell else would he be buying a ring for? Could he say it was an old one of his mother's? That wasn't going to work. He trudged back upstairs to make sure it was still where it was supposed to be—he had a suspicion she'd checked it out more than once—and found it still tucked in the corner of his drawer. Why had Pax put it in a brand-new box from the local jewellers? Jai recognised the name of the shop he walked past nearly every day. He was sure Riley would have too.

He took the ring out and had another look at it. A simple raised diamond, a couple of smaller ones either side. A gold band. Traditional design. Pretty. He had a bit of an eye for valuing jewellery from working for Tank and he wouldn't have put it at much over eight or nine grand. Why would anyone kill for it? Especially a bunch of millionaires. He rolled it between his fingers and noticed a small symbol engraved onto the inner edge. Shrugging, he put it back in the box. It didn't matter, because an idea had struck. He dived into his wardrobe, found the backpack and counted out some cash. He'd spend it on a ring for Riley. If he bought one from the same shop as the box this one was in, if it was similar enough, hopefully she'd never know the difference.

He sent Tank a text saying he had to duck in to see his pop's doctor before work, hoped he wouldn't hassle him over it, and twenty minutes later was standing in the jewellery shop.

The woman looked up from her phone as Jai walked into the warm interior of the shop. Dawn, according to her nametag, frowned slightly, looking him up and down before plastering a polite but cautious smile on her made-up face. 'Can I help you?'

'Hi, yeah, I …' He had a sudden worry that Riley might see him in the shop. Shit. He glanced around, decided she'd probably have gone straight to uni. No reason to think she'd be on the street. When he returned his attention to the sales woman she was clutching her phone, looking nervous. His behaviour probably had as much to do with that as his appearance. 'Sorry—just don't want my girlfriend to see me in here,' he attempted to explain. 'I want to buy her a ring.'

The woman's features lost some of their tension. 'Oh, an engagement ring? Do you have an idea of budget?'

'It's really just about the right ring,' he told her, feeling good about having the cash in his wallet. 'I have a design in mind. I've been saving some cash.'

She smiled as he approached a cabinet and looked at a few designs. 'Sorry if I seemed a bit off. You know about the recent robberies, those poor people on that boat and then the shop down the road? Can't be too careful.'

His stomach felt like lead but he nodded a bit, smiled through it. 'Yeah. Terrible. I was hoping to find something like this one here, but with a couple more diamonds around the edges.'

He walked out half an hour later with his choice. He needed to compare it to the original just to be sure, but he was fairly certain it was going to be similar enough. If it was a bit different, Riley would be bound to think she'd remembered it wrong, rather than considering there could possibly be two.

He couldn't quite keep the grin off his face for the rest of the day. He went in to see Evan, spent some time simply being with him as his grandfather lay glued to the small television set above his bed. It wasn't until he got home that his good mood evaporated as he remembered what he had to do next.

He took the ring straight upstairs to compare with the original. They were so alike, he had nothing to worry about.

'Hey!' Riley said. 'What are you doing?'

He jolted, dropping the ring in the drawer with the other one. 'Hey,' he said as warmly as he could. 'Aren't you spending the night with Tank?'

'Yeah. I got dinner ready super early and wanted to surprise you by leaving some in the oven for you. I didn't think you'd be home from visiting Evan yet. How is he?'

'Good. I didn't spend too long there. He was watching telly.'

'Okay … hey, are you all right?'

'Yeah, I just—' She hugged him and he heard the bag from the jewellers scrunch in his pocket. 'I just got home and really need to go to the bathroom. Hold on.' He went into the bathroom, took the bag and receipt out and stashed them under the sink, then hung around another minute or so before flushing the toilet and coming back out. 'Sorry, hi.' He drew her in and kissed her. 'And thanks. Dinner will be great.'

'You're welcome.'

She'd made some sort of pastry-wrapped meat with a drizzly sauce and roasted vegetables.

'Well?' she asked, putting a plate in front of him.

'Looks amazing,' he said. 'Smells amazing.'

'Hope it tastes amazing. I'd better get back before I ruin the rest of it.' She kissed him again. 'I miss you already. See you tomorrow.'

He waved her off, thought he should try and eat some of the delicious-looking meal she'd cooked for him. He really wasn't sure about how the whole engagement thing was going to go down with Tank. A sudden crazy whim suggested he call Tank, let him know in advance there probably wasn't anything to worry about. That the way his life was going, the ring was never going to amount to anything more than a gesture. Something for Riley to remember him by.

He forced a few mouthfuls down. It was good, but his stomach was in too many knots to properly enjoy it. He sat on the kitchen chair, leg jiggling up and down as he thought about the drop, the instructions he had to remember. Pax hadn't actually given him a drop-off time, but he didn't think he'd meant this early. Did it matter?

He got on Google Maps and had another look at the address. South Hobart, just a quick drive. No big deal, right? But the need to get it done sat heavily on his chest. *Stuff it.* He grabbed the ring and tossed it in his bag, picked up his keys. Tough luck if it was too early, he wasn't sitting around any longer.

He parked on the main street, where his car became just one of several others outside locked-up houses. A quick scan of the area revealed no one about. The street sign on the corner pointed to the correct NO THROUGH ROAD. 'Okay,' he muttered. 'Let's get it over and done with.'

He climbed out, slung the backpack over his shoulder and decided against locking the car. If it went bad, he might need to get in quick.

He walked as casually as he could down the freezing street. His breath came out in billowing clouds, his sneakers squeaked quietly on the path. He made the turn onto the road. The streetlights were few and far between, the buildings old. Graffiti marred a low brick wall that led to a demolition site, homes sat behind tall wooden paling or chain link fences and high shrubbery kept them hidden from sight.

Headlights swept into the street along with a crunching of tyres that followed his progress before pulling up just ahead of him. His heart rate picked up when he identified the car. Cops. Shit. Tank's talk of Pax using him as a scapegoat echoed in Jai's head and he felt himself start to sweat and shake. Had all this been a setup? Should he run?

The cop in the passenger side of the car stepped out and looked Jai up and down with the kind of stare he thought cops must learn at police school. 'Evening. Mind holding up there for a second?'

'Uh, why?'

'We're conducting some extra patrols in the local area due to some recent break-ins. Got some identification on you, bud?'

Jai pulled his wallet out of his pocket, showed his driver's licence and tried to act like it was no big deal. When the short stubby nails on the hand holding the backpack began to cut into his palm he forced his fingers to relax.

'Thanks, Jai,' the cop said, reading his licence. 'Can I ask your reason for being out this evening?'

Jai wasn't sure, could he? 'Just, um, heading home.'

'You live around here then?'

'Ah, yeah.' *Shit*. The cop knew he didn't—he'd just seen his licence. 'I mean, I'm … going to a mate's place.'

'What's in the bag?'

'Nothing.' He swung it off his shoulder, opened it. The ring and phone were in the front section, the main one was empty.

'That's fine, thanks, bud, don't need to see it. Just wondered why you put your wallet in your pocket when you had a bag handy.'

'Habit.'

The cop nodded. 'Have a good night. Appreciate your cooperation.'

Cooperation? Like he'd had a choice. He was pretty sure they couldn't just bail people up like that. He reminded himself it was at least partly his fault they were doing the extra patrols. But what now? The cop had returned to his mate in the car. They were still watching him.

The house was at the end of the street. He couldn't keep going past it because the road ended and if he didn't go somewhere the cops were going to know he was up to something. So he ducked in through the front gate and took a second to lean back against it and catch his breath. He heard the car drive off.

'Oof!' The sound erupted from his lungs as the fist buried itself in his gut. *Smack*, his jaw exploded with pain. He stumbled sideways, tripped and landed heavily on a patch of wet grass, was dragged roughly back to his feet, then slammed against the wall. A gun barrel was pressed to his face.

'Stop! You fucking idiot!' a deep voice growled. He recognised it—the gunman who'd tried to shoot Tank. 'The cops are on the street! They'll hear the shot.'

'Fuck,' the one holding the gun muttered. The gun dug painfully into Jai's cheek.

'What are you doing?' Jai spluttered. 'I … had to bring …'

The bag was ripped from his shoulder and tossed to the second man, who rifled through it until he found the box, opened it, pulled out the phone. 'It's all here.'

'So what do we do with him?'

'I'm supposed to get paid. Pax sent me.'

'You really are a clueless sook.' Another punch to the gut, then large hands wrapped around his throat.

Everything hurt. He tried desperately to breathe, lashed out, kicked. The man's evil eyes bulged with the effort of crushing Jai's windpipe. As dizziness and pain and desperation took over, Jai got his hands up to those eyes and pushed his thumbs in hard.

The relief of that first breath was painful and overwhelming. He got a hand on the gate and fell through onto the footpath. The hands he expected to drag him back didn't come as he staggered up and started running. What was that about? He was pretty sure they'd been going to kill him. But Pax had said—he should never have trusted Pax; he wanted Jai dead, just like he wanted Tank dead. *That's* why Pax had sent him here. He was cleaning up his loose ends.

CHAPTER 31

Tess dropped another jumper on the pile of clothing littering her dining table and took stock of what else she might need. Food and equipment were spread out on her kitchen bench and her lounge and an assortment of shoes had been tossed carelessly on the floor. She couldn't wait to get out on the trails, have some time away from all the recent drama, be somewhere Aaron couldn't find her. But she had found herself wishing Jared was coming with them. She was going to miss him.

She returned her concentration to her gear. She didn't think she was missing anything, so she stood her pack up and started organising in her mind. Then a knock on her door had her stepping around the pack to open it. 'Hi,' she said to Jared.

He dropped a kiss on her lips and smiled down at her. 'Hi. I know it's late, but I've been trying to get out here all day.'

She wasn't surprised at his amused grin. She knew how she looked: her hair was bundled on top of her head in a messy ponytail, her tee had been chosen purely for comfort and her cargos were too well worn. She led him further into the apartment and waved her hands at the mess. 'Welcome to chaos.'

'You can't possibly be carrying all this stuff,' he said.

'You'd be surprised what will fit in a pack. I'm preparing for two weeks, because we could get held up and even if we don't, someone's bound to not take enough or wildlife will pinch something somewhere along the line. The packs start off heavy, get lighter as we eat our way through supplies.'

He looked at the table covered with packets of dried foods, wraps, Cup A Soups, instant noodles, muesli bars, chocolate and some glucose lollies. 'Most of this stuff doesn't look very appetising.'

'Trust me, after hours of slogging through wilderness, Easy Mac never tasted so good.'

He touched her face gently. 'Indy told me what happened with Aaron. If I'd known, I would have been there.'

'I know. She didn't tell you at the time because she was worried about a confrontation.'

'She's one to talk,' he scoffed lightly. 'How are you holding up? You've had a lot thrown at you lately.'

'I'm … looking forward to some time in the wilderness.'

'What's it like out there, really?'

'It's the best place on earth,' she said without hesitation. 'There's nowhere else like it in the world. I don't want them to get caught up in how wet and cold and muddy and difficult it can be, which is why I pushed for going at an easier time of year. But it'll still be an unforgettable experience.'

'You really love it,' he said.

'I wouldn't do it otherwise,' she said with a grin. 'Too bloody difficult.'

'You want some help?'

'I need to double package all the food, do a final check of my equipment, get everything in my pack … yeah. Thanks, that'd be great.'

As she gave him a quick lesson in packing supplies, the light rain that had been hitting the window became a heavier, almost thunderous, sound.

'Are you sure you're taking enough comfort food?' he joked. 'Because one bar of chocolate and a few jelly beans just doesn't seem enough.'

She pulled a face. 'I should make you come with us.'

'I would,' he said and pulled her to him, 'but there's this killer running around making a nuisance of himself, and someone's got to catch him.'

'Hmm.' She linked her arms around his neck. 'Shame. Little tent, long dark nights …'

His fingers convulsed against her waist. 'That's just cruel.'

She rubbed her lips against his. 'I think you should be reminded what you're going to be missing.'

He chuckled. 'That won't get your packing done. And it's getting late.'

'Didn't I tell you?' she asked, looping her arms around his waist. 'I'm a pro. Packing won't take long at all.'

'No, but I might,' he said against her lips. 'Once I get started with you, I might take a really, really long time.'

How was she supposed to think about packing when he made that sort of promise? 'You'd better get started then.'

Tess woke and slowly stretched, feeling every wonderfully sore muscle. Jared was still sleeping beside her. Neither of them had meant for him to sleep over, it just hadn't seemed worthwhile him going home by the time they were done with each other. Somewhere in the middle they'd managed to eat and get her packed up. She closed her eyes tight, opened them again, just to make sure it wasn't a dream. He looked so peaceful in sleep.

Outside, light rain fought with thick fog, just the sort of swirling, cold conditions created for lazy mornings indoors. She wanted to burrow deeper in the covers, but she was going to have to get up. She considered waking Jared, decided that could complicate the getting-out-of-bed process and fought back the temptation to do it anyway. She extricated herself carefully from the blankets, headed straight for the shower.

She'd just gotten out when her phone rang. The voice on the other end told her all flights had been grounded until the weather improved.

'What's happening?' Jared asked in a gravelly, sleep-filled voice.

She sat on the bed and he dragged her down for a lazy kiss. 'There're no planes today. Weather conditions aren't good enough. It's supposed to clear in a day or two. So no Melaleuca until then. If we're still going to make it back on Riley's schedule I'm going to have to push them harder than I would have liked.'

'Damn,' Jared muttered.

'It's not that bad, is it?' She ran a finger lightly down his chest.

He caught it, kissed it. 'I need Riley safely out of the way so Tank will talk. I'll have to figure out something else.'

She considered that, saw the worry in his face. Sighed heavily. 'Okay, look. Bearing in mind I would generally *never* suggest this because who wants to walk in the pouring rain and the mud, but under the circumstances, I suppose we could go in from the other end. Start at Cockle Creek and hike out to Melaleuca.'

Jared's concern only increased. 'You were the one who said it was too dangerous to head out there in bad weather.'

'We'll go slow and steady, hope the rain clears quickly. We've got a couple of extra days up our sleeve so we can bunk down out there if we have to. Riley and the others will still be out of the way and on the track.'

'No. I don't like it,' Jared said. 'I'm not going to be responsible for you putting yourself and those kids at risk.'

What was left of Tess's good mood evaporated as every argument she'd ever had with Aaron came flooding back. 'You're *not* responsible. I am. I said I'd take them out, I've told you I can do it safely!' She heard her voice rise, lowered it. 'This is what I do. We'll be fine.'

Jared swung up into a sitting position, face grave. 'Tess, you can't—'

'Yes, I can!' she snapped. 'God, you're all alike! Do this, don't do that, yes you can, no you can't! It's like the second you sleep with a guy he thinks he owns you.'

Jared rubbed his forehead, sighed. 'That's not true. I just don't want anything to happen to any of you because you're trying to do me a favour. I'd prefer you didn't liken me to Aaron.'

'And I'd prefer you didn't act like him.' She huffed out a breath. 'I'm sorry, but I really need you to be different.'

'Tess, I am.'

He didn't quite grate it out, but she could see the temper, and was too frustrated and angry herself to care. 'Great, prove it. It's a three-hour drive to Cockle Creek. Get up. I need someone to drive the shuttle bus.'

Jai heard the footsteps on the stairs moments before Riley burst into his room.

'You're ready!' she said.

'Yeah. Of course.' Of course he was ready. He'd spent what had remained of last night in the backyard shed, petrified Pax's thugs would turn up and murder him in his bed. But they hadn't come, so maybe it had been a mistake. Maybe they hadn't been meant to kill him. But he didn't quite believe it. The sooner they were out of here, the better.

'Excellent. Wait—what happened to your face? Who hit you?'

'Oh, um … no one.' He'd rehearsed his excuse after seeing himself in the mirror just a moment ago. 'I climbed up on the footstool to get my sleeping bag from the back of the linen cupboard and the damn thing slipped. Whacked my jaw on the shelf.'

'Did you ice it?' she asked. 'It looks so sore.'

'Yeah, yeah, it's fine. Looks worse than it feels,' he lied. Then he pulled her in for a kiss, pressed the box into her hand and covered it with his own. 'Happy birthday, Riley.'

'Thank you!' She opened it excitedly. And damn, she started to cry.

'You don't need to worry about anything,' he told her. 'I'll take care of you. I'll always take care of you, no matter what. I want to marry you. I do want to wait just a bit—until I have some more money put away so you can have a beautiful wedding and the house by the beach and everything you want. But that ring's a promise. It's a promise that that's what I'm working towards, saving for. I love you, Riley.' He took the ring and slid it on her finger.

She flung herself into him, held tight. 'I don't need a big wedding and I can help save money, too. The school I'm interning at love me. I'm sure when a position comes up I'll get it. We'll have more than enough. Besides, I don't want anything else right now. Just you.'

He held on to her for several moments and let himself believe that one day he'd be able to keep his promise. But he'd had to say it, even though he wasn't sure. In case he didn't get another chance. If something did happen, she'd know what she meant to him. And that was important.

He stepped back and brushed the tears from her face. 'Let's go hiking.'

She gave him a watery smile. 'I had a moment last night where I thought maybe we shouldn't. I know you don't really want to leave Evan in respite, and I wasn't sure I should leave Dad with everything that's been going on. I told him we could stay home, forget the whole thing.'

'What did he say?'

'That we had to go. That he was putting his foot down. That we both needed a break and he'd paid a heap of money he wasn't getting back. He practically kicked me out the door.' She stared at the ring in wonder. His own gaze dropped to it. He frowned, looked closer. His heart stopped.

No. That was impossible.

'Let me see it for a minute,' he said, sliding it back off her finger.

'Why? What's wrong?' She almost snatched it back.

His heart pumped viciously in his chest as he saw the small marking on the inside. Not Riley's ring—Madison's. 'I think it might be a bit loose,' he managed through his own panic. Pax was bound to come looking for him. He'd leave it on the table and Pax could take it. Hopefully he'd leave them alone. Jai had enough cash to buy her a replacement. 'Why don't we pop it away until after the hike and I'll get it altered?'

'No way! It's a perfect fit.' She took it from his shaky fingers and slid it back on. 'It's never leaving my finger again.'

'You shouldn't take it on the hike,' he said more sharply than he meant to. 'It could get lost.'

'It won't get lost. I'll take care of it. Jai, what's wrong with you?'

Maybe Pax's boss wouldn't notice. The rings were almost identical. The dickhead that had taken the ring hadn't realised the mistake last night. He could be panicking for nothing.

He looked down at the mixture of confusion and hurt on Riley's face. If he was going to tell her, now was the time. But how could he tell her without telling her all of it?

'Nothing,' he finally blurted out. 'Nothing I just … would hate for you to lose it.'

'I won't,' she promised. 'I know how hard it must have been for you to afford this. I'll treasure it. Always.' She groaned when her phone rang. He watched her face fall as she answered and he wondered what else could possibly have gone wrong this morning. But then the worry lifted and she was smiling into the phone.

'Our flight's been cancelled because of the rain,' she told him a moment later. 'But Tess said we can walk the track from the other direction.' She took another happy look at her ring. Sighing, she held his face in her hands and kissed him again. 'This is going to be great.'

He checked out the window several times while they waited for the shuttle bus, expecting Pax or one of the gunmen to turn up at any moment. A million miles from nowhere had sounded like a nightmare up until this morning. Now he couldn't wait to go out there. Now it seemed like the only safe place on earth.

The shuttle turned up at nine and Tess and Jared helped them load their gear. There was a weird vibe between them, and when he'd repeated the lie about his bruised jaw to Denham, he wasn't sure the guy believed him. Why had the detective come, anyway? Riley had said she'd thought he and Tess were a couple, but they weren't acting much like it.

Brock, Jasmin, Chris and Alex were already on board, as well as a middle-aged couple who introduced themselves as James and Libby, a couple of local lawyers. James had a serious face and a head of perfectly cut greying ginger hair, a bit of a stomach protruding over the belt of his jeans and the soft appearance of someone who spent all their time behind a desk. Libby was willow slim and had a fragile appearance. Makeup. Who wore makeup on a hike? But she had a kind smile, which he returned as he introduced himself. Riley quickly greeted the couple on her way to the back of the shuttle, straight to Jasmin. The two girls gushed over the ring while Brock moved to take a seat next to him.

'You're keen. Trying to make me look bad?' he joked.

'Nah,' Jai scoffed. 'Riley and I have been together forever. You and Jasmin are a new thing.'

'Might feel like forever but, mate, are you sure? There's heaps of time to worry about marriage and stuff later, right?'

'You never know,' he replied, thinking about Pax, and about the man who'd already made the hike more uncomfortable than it needed to be by almost getting him killed.

The bus headed out of the city through suburbs and bush and farmland, and beyond, where rainforest occasionally parted to show the sparkling blue water and white sandy beaches of the coast. The surfaced road became gravel as they approached their destination and campsites popped up, some with tents and campervans inhabiting them. Then they were crossing a bridge and pulling up at a small parking area overlooking more coastline. Jai wished he was in the mood to appreciate the scenery and winced when he realised he'd chewed a fingernail too short. If Pax didn't kill him, his own nerves might.

'Here we are!' Riley turned her attention to Jai as she got up from her seat. 'Ready?'

He managed a smile, a nod. 'Let's do it.'

Tess and Jared climbed out first to unload the gear. Jai grabbed his and Riley's packs, moved them out of the way, and noticed Riley and Jasmin were further away reading a sign. It was a visitor's notice: YOU'VE REACHED THE END OF THE ROAD. He thought it was probably right in more ways than one.

CHAPTER 32

Tess felt the first raindrops hit her as she gathered the group together. 'I'm guessing we might be held up at least once, maybe more,' she told Jared stiffly. 'I'll be in touch if our schedule changes.'

'Good luck,' he said in much the same tone. They hadn't spoken more than was necessary since the argument. She'd felt the disapproval pouring from him as they'd picked up the hikers and loaded the bus, and hadn't she had enough of that from Aaron? Still, she'd expected more objections as the morning progressed. Aaron would have insisted on being right, gotten nasty or at least patronising. Jared had done none of that. He'd kept whatever thoughts he had to himself and brought them out here anyway. She was all too aware he didn't agree with them going, that he was annoyed at the way she'd spoken to him and that had gotten her back up even further, but ... perhaps he had a right to be. She'd probably overreacted. A part of her really wanted to talk about it and clear the air. But there was no chance to talk about it now, so she smiled briefly and stepped away.

'All right, does everyone have their waterproof covers on their packs? Water handy? We're going to head over to the registration shelter first, sign on. Grab your stuff, let's go.'

They crossed a boardwalk and signed on. Tess noted no other hikers had logged on in the last couple of weeks. That wasn't surprising for the time of year, and almost everyone that was going to brave the hike did it from the other direction.

The group were chatty as they began the walk that took them through light forest. The walking here was easy, a mix of rocky path and boardwalk and the rain was holding off, making the trek more pleasant. But as if she needed reminding of the cold, the surrounding ranges came into view, dusted heavily with snow.

Libby and James walked with her, while Riley's group was a few metres back.

'So you've done this walk a few times?' James asked.

'This particular one I've done four times, though never from this direction. I've always flown groups in, come back. But I know the way, don't worry.'

'We were so glad you could take us,' Libby said. 'It's just what we needed.' She slipped her hand into James's. 'Right, hon?'

James's smile didn't quite reach his eyes. 'A long walk with a heavy pack in the freezing cold? Absolutely.'

Libby's expression became hurt. 'You said—'

'Yeah, I know,' he said. 'Sorry. I'm sure it'll be great.'

'We've been working on our marriage,' Libby admitted. 'Our counsellor said to do something together away from the office. It's not easy running a business, living and working long hours under each other's noses, and well … we just need to take some time to remember why we're together in the first place.'

'I hope it works out for you,' Tess said, not only for their benefit but for the hiking group in general. Having two people at each other's throats the whole way wouldn't be fun. It would make for a long nine days.

They continued to where forest opened up to the wet, button-grass plains of Blowhole Valley before the track darkened again with scrub and fern.

'Oh, is that the ocean I can hear?' Libby asked.

'Yep. It's still a fair way off, but we'll get there.'

She kept them going until they reached the black, sloping cliffs of an exposed bluff.

'Where are we?' Riley asked, catching up to gaze out over the incredible view. The ocean was wild in the turbulent weather, but the wind wasn't as bad as Tess had feared. 'This is South Cape Bay. Over to the left is South East Cape which is the southernmost point of Australia, to the right is Lion Rock. If anyone wants to stop for photos, this is a good spot.'

'How much further today?' Jasmin asked, dropping her pack to rub her shoulders.

'It's not a long walk today. We're about two-thirds of the way to our campsite already,' Tess said. 'We're going to follow the cliffs a couple of hundred metres further, then take some stairs down to the beach. But once we get back up off the beach, there's going to be some steep and muddy uphill trekking through the scrub before we make it to our campsite at South Cape Rivulet.'

Jasmin rolled her feet around in her boots. Tess stared at the boots. They looked brand new.

'Did you wear those boots in?'

'Wear them in?' Jasmin asked blankly.

'As in do some walking in them before today.'

'No, I only just got them two days ago. They're expensive. I didn't want to wreck them before we started.' She wiggled them. 'Nice, huh?'

'Hmm.' Tess briefly wondered if anyone had done any of the reading she'd given them or if it had all been left in the shop following the break-in. Perhaps she should have chased that up. By the end of the day or tomorrow, tops, Jasmin's blistered feet were destined to be the next drama and who knew what was to come after that?

'Did you bring bandaids?'

'Yeah. I brought everything.' Jasmin laughed.

'Hey, Tess,' Riley called. 'Can you take a picture of us?'

'Sure.' She waited for them to hand over cameras and phones and bunch together. Alex, Chris and Brock shuffled around by the edge, looking over the cliff. Chris shoved Alex, grabbed him and pulled him back. Tess's heart leapt into her throat.

'Don't get too close to the edge,' she warned them. 'It's too dangerous.'

'We're fine!' Alex said, still messing around as though determined to do the exact opposite.

Here we go. 'National Parks have posted signs at different places along the track. If you don't want to listen to me, at least read them, okay? I'd rather not have to perform any rescues or explain to anyone's families why they didn't make it back.'

Jasmin spotted the sign Tess was talking about and jogged over. '"Cliff edge can collapse without warning",' she read. '"Severe hazard area"!'

'Yeah, yeah,' Chris said. 'They have to post those signs to protect themselves from idiots. Don't worry about it.'

Jasmin shook her head. '"Severe risk", "use caution", "the area is only for experienced visitors" … You should come and read this!'

'Lighten up, Jas,' Brock called, then said jokingly to Tess, 'Now you've done it. I'd be surprised if she doesn't want to go back and we've only just started.'

'She's not the one who should go back,' Tess snapped at him. 'I said I wasn't taking anyone out who wouldn't listen and follow instructions. Make up your minds. Because unless you're prepared to do what I tell you, when I tell you, I'm not taking you any further.'

The boys stared at her for several seconds before their smiles dropped. Alex said something under his breath she couldn't catch but they all smirked at each other.

'Fine,' Brock agreed, annoyed. 'Can we just take the damn photo and get going? You know, away from these dangerous cliffs?' he said, wide-eyed and sarcastic.

'Pull your head in, Brock, and smile,' Riley ordered without heat.

Tess took their photos for them, handed their phones and cameras back and hoped the three boys would settle down once they got further on their way. 'Okay, let's get moving.'

Jasmin took her camera from Tess, then as she stepped back, almost tripped over her pack. James grabbed her arm to steady her.

'Are you all right?'

Jasmin looked up into his face, flushed pink. 'Yeah, thanks.'

'Everything okay?' Brock asked, staring at the hand on her arm.

'Yeah, I'm just a klutz.' Jasmin laughed, but her eyes returned shyly to James's. "Thanks.'

James chuckled, his smile fading as he caught sight of Libby's face behind Jasmin's. 'You said that already. No problem.'

Uh-oh, Tess thought, seeing the open admiration in Jasmin's eyes and the simmering resentment in Libby's. The pretty young blonde with no sense falling for the much older marriage-in-trouble guy could mean problems.

'Don't worry about the guys,' Riley said, catching up to Tess as they moved off. 'They're just showing off. And Brock's pissed off because Jasmin hasn't been able to take her eyes off that James guy. She flirts with everyone she comes in contact with. It's just the way she is.'

'Trying to play alpha male to win her attention back while he's out here is stupid. And maybe have a quiet word to Jasmin about toning it down with James. Jasmin might not mean anything by the way she behaves but it could be damaging.'

'Right. Sure. Of course.'

Riley fell back and Tess felt a small tug of guilt at her sharp tone. She could only hope getting that out of the way would make the rest of the trip smoother. A light drop of rain hit her face, then another. Well, they wanted an adventure, she reminded herself as she thought about the steep, muddy incline to come. They were going to get it.

CHAPTER 33

Jared finally got back to the station around mid-afternoon. 'Shuttle buses are not designed for comfort,' he told Indy, entering her office to swap keys. She'd driven his car to work and was taking the shuttle bus back to Calico Mountain after her shift.

'Thanks. They all got off okay then?'

'Yeah.'

'Uh oh,' she said, eyeing him. 'Tess was huffy this morning, and your tone suggests likewise. What's up?'

He shrugged. 'I stupidly suggested she should rethink heading out in this weather. Now I'm Aaron.'

Indy's face screwed up. 'She's going to be a bit touchy about that sort of thing for a while. She acts all practical and on top of everything but all this crap with Aaron has hit her harder than she lets on. And if there's one thing I've never known her to do it's make the same mistake twice.'

'Oh, great—now I'm a mistake.' He immediately lifted a hand in truce. 'Sorry, shouldn't bring this stuff into work. Has Finlay shown up yet?'

'After the shop closes. With Jai away, he hasn't got anyone he can ask to watch the place.'

'Right.'

'You might want to talk to Roberts, too. You'd asked them to keep an eye on Jai's place during their patrol?'

'I didn't think it would hurt. Why?'

'Jai went out last night. Roberts and Perry followed him to South Hobart, where he parked on one street, headed off on foot to another with a backpack. When they stopped him, he told them he was visiting a friend, then showed up a couple of minutes later looking worse for wear and out of breath. For some reason he'd left his car on the main road.'

'Strange. Right, I'll go talk to Roberts.' He headed for the door.

'Okay. Jared?'

'Yeah?'

'I'm sure she just panicked. Tess is head over heels about you or she wouldn't have considered getting wrapped up in anyone else so soon after Aaron. She knows you're different. You'll work this out.'

He hoped so. It niggled in the corner of his mind as he spoke to Roberts, then filled in the rest of the day catching up with work. By six he was tapping his pen on his desk in impatience to get the day over with.

'Tank said after work,' he said to Indy when she came in. 'I assume that meant just after five.'

'I would have assumed the same thing,' she said. 'So call him. We've gone along with his request and now we need to hear what he has to say.'

'Agreed.' He called Tank's mobile and then the shop but both numbers rang out and went to voicemail. He tried again, waited a few minutes and then tried a third time. When he still couldn't get through to Tank, he went searching for Indy. 'I can't get him on either of the numbers we have so I think I'll go looking for him.'

'I hope he hasn't done a runner,' Indy said. 'If he has, we've made a massive mistake.'

Jared didn't think so. 'I can't see him leaving Riley. I'll let you know when I locate him.'

He drove out to the shop. It was closed, so he went to Tank's home and noticed the car in the driveway. Annoyed that Tank had come home instead of going to the station, Jared knocked on the door. It opened under the weight of his fist and swung in to reveal a mess: a lamp had been pulled over, the coffee table was on its side, a curtain had been ripped from the window. He quickly checked the rest of the house, but found no sign of Tank.

He called Indy as he checked the backyard, the garage. 'I'm at Finlay's house. Looks like a struggle's taken place. I think someone's taken him.'

He heard the muttered oath, then, 'Hang there for me, would you, while I get some people out to go over the place for evidence.'

'Yeah, you bet. Damn it, Indy. Riley talked to him this morning. We're just too late.'

In the two days since dropping Tess and the others off on their hike, Jared had done everything he could think of to locate Tank, on top of assisting Indy in managing the ongoing manhunt for Orvist. Tank's house had revealed no clues, nor had the shop. In desperation and with barely enough basis to deserve it, he managed to get a warrant to search Jai's house. 'I'm at Wharton's house with Emily and Roberts now,' he told Indy over the phone. 'I'll let you know if we find anything.'

'It doesn't make any sense,' Indy said. 'Someone was definitely looking for something. But what? Tank said he'd already handed over the diamonds.'

'Maybe he lied. Shot through with them.'

'Or someone caught up with him and well, that's not going to have a happy ending. I'm worried. He was so genuinely concerned for Riley's welfare. I just can't see him bailing.'

He ended the call and walked into Jai's house. It looked no better than Tank's.

'They've been here too,' Emily said unnecessarily.

Jared left Emily and Roberts downstairs and found Jai's bedroom. He went through the already opened drawers, looked under the bed, moved to the open closet. There were a couple of backpacks and a few boxes of junk on the floor. One backpack was light, empty, the other was open, cash spewing out of it. 'Hello,' he said. 'Hey, Henry!'

Henry Roberts came bounding up the stairs. 'Yeah, what—whoa!'

'Is this the bag you saw Wharton with?'

'Nah, that one was empty. I would have noticed if it was suddenly full.'

'Maybe it shouldn't have been. You said he came out looking like he'd been in a fight. Something must have gone wrong.'

Roberts nodded thoughtfully. 'Could have been us, I suppose. If he was up to something underhanded, having the police out the front questioning you wouldn't go down too well. Someone broke in here and didn't take all this?'

'It's not what they were after. Do you remember that address you saw him go into?'

'Of course.'

'Get Em. We'll go take a look. I'll get Indy to meet us out there.'

They arrived at the house at almost the same time, and he got out of the car to meet Indy a couple of properties down from their target.

'Anyone about?' she asked.

'Not sure yet. Haven't heard anything. Obviously can't see much,' he said and gestured to the wooden paling fence with the overgrown shrubs that somehow even managed to obscure the view of the second storey. 'Em went around the back. It's not a block-out fence on that side, looks more like a security fence designed to keep people out—you know, one of the spiky ones we're not going to be able to get over, with a big padlocked gate.'

'Seems like overkill.'

'Depending on what they're doing in there, perhaps not.'

'Tell Emily and Henry to stay where they are in case anyone makes a run for it out the back.' She sized up the property again. 'Are you armed?'

'Yeah.'

'Then let's go find out what requires this much security.'

They slipped quietly through the gate to the front door. Music was on and the smell of stale cigarette smoke lingered by an overused ashtray. Indy's step squeaked on the decking and she froze, but no one emerged. She indicated for Jared to move to the window. He looked inside, squinted through the space between the almost closed curtains. A small front room had a doorway into a kitchen. A shadow moved across the wall. At least one person was in there. He signalled that back to Indy then ducked under the window and took a look from another angle. In the corner of the room sat Tank, tied to a chair. His body was limp, his head lolling. Cuts and bruises covered every visible area of his body.

He turned to make Indy aware and saw her eyes widen, her gun level at something behind him. 'Put it down!' she ordered.

He ducked just in time to hear a bullet whiz past his back. Another shot, this one from Indy. A thud. He spun around to see the gunman lying on the ground.

'Damn, you're fast. Thanks,' he said.

Indy was already moving past him to check on the man lying on the ground. She swore quietly, talked to Emily and Roberts on her radio, then headed for the door. When it didn't open, she kicked it in. He followed, watching her back. A man appeared from a back room and sprinted up the stairs when he saw them, ignoring their commands to stop.

'I'll go. You check Tank,' he said, and took the stairs cautiously. He found the guy in the master bedroom, dragging a window open.

'Don't move!' he ordered. 'Step away from the window, hands—'

The man threw his legs over the window ledge and leapt.

'Damn it!'

Almost immediately the screaming from outside suggested the jump had gone wrong. Jared checked and saw the guy hanging upside down from the security fence.

'He's impaled himself!' Emily called out, as she and Roberts attempted to take the man's weight.

Jared rushed back down the stairs and through the empty block next door to the outside of the fence. He got his shoulder under the screaming man. The man was pierced through his thigh, close to his groin. By the amount of blood he'd already lost, he'd damaged a major artery.

'Step out,' he told Emily, 'go help Indy with Finlay. And let the ambos know we're going to need cutting equipment.'

'Get me down!' the injured man demanded. 'Get it out!'

Jared recognised the voice as belonging to one of the gunmen from Tank's shop. Tank had been right about being set up.

'We can't do that. Sorry,' Roberts told him.

'You sick bastards, let me down!'

'If we pull you off that thing we could do a whole lot more harm than good,' Jared said calmly. 'We have to wait for help.'

'Then call them!'

Jared decided to use the man's desperation to his advantage. 'Why don't you tell me exactly what's been going on here?'

'Nothing!'

'Geez, you're getting heavy. Is he getting heavy, Henry?'

'Really heavy,' Roberts replied.

'Yep. Not sure I can keep the pressure off.' Jared wasn't kidding. The awkward position wasn't easy to hold and the threat was followed up by an involuntary shift.

'Argh! Not telling you shit!' The wail of the ambulance as it came around the corner had the guy all but sobbing.

'That ambulance is for Tank. They don't know about you yet,' Jared told him.

'Oh, man. Please. He played Cochrane.'

'Who did? Tank? He didn't hand over the diamonds?'

'Yeah, yeah. He did. But it was never about the diamonds.'

'Keep talking.'

'Cochrane wanted to make Maddie's death look like a robbery gone wrong, so all her stuff was pinched during her hit. But all he really needed was her ring and her phone. Only the kid gave us the wrong ring. Kid's a sook, so Pax reckons he's run to Tank and Tank's swapped 'em over for leverage or payback. But the stupid old bugger won't tell us where it is.'

'Why are Maddie's ring and phone so important?'

'I can't—I—where's the ambulance?'

'I'm still deciding if I'm going to let them know you're here.'

'The ring has an NFC chip in it!' the guy said desperately. 'An electronic key. You tap her ring to her phone and—boom—you're into all her offshore accounts and shit. Millions. Man, I'm gonna pass out.' He was as damp and pale as anyone Jared had ever seen. A trickle of sweat dripped from the guy's cheek and ran down Jared's hand.

'Okay, just take it easy. The ambos are coming, all right?'

He saw the paramedics running around the corner and tried to shift aside enough to let them work.

'Rescue truck is coming with the equipment,' one paramedic said.

'I'm gonna need protection,' the guy managed.

'I'll protect you, buddy. Until you testify, you're my new best friend.'

The guy's head fell back in semiconsciousness. Pained gasps escaped his lips. His eyes widened when he saw another paramedic arrive with an angle grinder. 'You gonna cut my leg off?'

'No. No, of course not. Relax, okay? They're going to cut the spike off,' Jared said calmly. 'They can't remove it until you get to surgery.'

'What?'

'You're going to be okay,' Jared said. The words 'hang in there' came to mind, but as he already was, there didn't seem to be much point saying them.

CHAPTER 34

Tess huddled in her jacket and stared out from their elevated position at the Surprise Bay campsite past the twisted branches of the trees to the wide rivulet that cut through the broad expanse of beach. Beyond, islands of vegetation stretched into jagged fingers of ancient rock that defiantly speared out into the ocean.

This was one of her favourite places on the track. In better weather, the sunset reflected everything the eye could see in gold, crimson and vivid orange. Tonight the sky was leaden grey, the view hazy with heavy fog. There was beauty in its wild, untamed nature, but the time of year was costing the group more than they knew.

'It's still lovely, isn't it?' Riley said, coming to join her. 'Even when it's at its worst.'

Tess smiled at her, appreciating the observation. 'I love it. I'm not saying I also wouldn't love a hot shower and a warm, dry bed …'

Riley laughed. 'Me too. We could get a better day tomorrow though, right?'

'Not sure.' Yesterday's walk from South Cape Rivulet to Granite Beach had been relatively smooth, but the weather had been uncooperative. Beach walking had been hard going, with the wind doing its best to knock their legs out from underneath them, and the bush walking today, wading through water and mud and negotiating difficult, slippery sections of track, had been tiring and time consuming. 'The forecast is suggesting it could clear.'

'I hope so.'

'So do I. I took a look at the rivulet below us earlier. It's not promising. If we can't cross it, we'll be stuck here until it lowers.'

'At least we've got a good spot.' Riley looked out over the view as Tess had done. 'We're going to turn in soon.'

'Good idea.' She went to her tent, and as the others were making tea, decided to have one. Tents close together in a circle, they sat at the entrances, happily comparing sore muscles, blisters, scratches and scrapes.

'How am I going to walk for another week in these boots?' Jasmin complained as she examined the raw red skin of her toes and blistered heels.

'You should have worn in your boots,' Riley told her. 'There was a big section of Tess's notes telling us how to prepare.'

'Oh I … think I left the notes at the shop,' Jasmin admitted. 'It got a bit out of control, remember?'

Tess set water to boil on her fuel stove and added a sachet of chocolate to her mug. 'You're going to need to take good care of those feet,' she told Jasmin. 'Antiseptic, gauze and keep them as dry as you can. You should undo your boot laces, open the boots right up and hope they dry out a bit.'

'In this on-again, off-again drizzle?' Riley asked. 'How? Everything's wet. Even this cost-a-fortune waterproof jacket doesn't seem to be able to handle this weather.'

'Getting your shoes out of the weather will help,' Tess said, with a pointed look at the boots tossed haphazardly on the wet ground.

'Can't we start a fire?' Jasmin complained. 'Just long enough to stick the boots in front of to dry?'

'Sorry,' Tess said. 'No open fires.'

Jasmin finished tending to her feet and put away her bandaids, then pulled a notebook from her pack.

'Oh, here we go,' Brock said.

'What is it?' Libby asked.

Jasmin opened the book up and sat it on her legs. 'All sorts of stuff I found on the area.'

'Bullshit stuff,' Brock muttered with a smirk.

'Take it easy, mate,' James said.

Brock inhaled loudly, his face tight. 'You know, I'm just about sick of you having an opinion on everything I say to my girlfriend.'

'Whoa-ho-ho!' Chris exclaimed loudly, elbowing Alex. 'Look out, it'll be on in a minute.'

'Better than the game of cards we were thinking of playing,' Alex said.

'Brock, don't,' Jasmin pleaded. 'Let's just have a nice evening.'

'Yes, thanks,' Tess said with a sharp glare for all of them. The tension between Brock and James had increased since the beginning of the trip. Jasmin's refusal to leave James alone and the bickering between her and Brock hadn't given the growing animosity any opportunity to calm down, and Chris and Alex seemed to enjoy inflaming it. 'Why don't you tell us what you found, Jasmin?' she prompted, feeling a bit like a kindergarten teacher.

Jasmin dragged her eyes from Brock and smiled thinly. 'Strange stories, unexplained stuff … I like that sort of thing.'

'Oh, so do I,' Libby said enthusiastically. By the look that passed between Libby and James, Tess suspected the tone was more about changing the subject than any real interest, but Jasmin's smile became more genuine.

'I can tell you some?'

'Go for it. The only thing I found was that a mystery sailor drowned and washed up on a beach out here somewhere,' Libby said.

'True,' Tess said. 'There was a sailor who drowned off the coast and washed up not too far from here. Deadman's Bay is named after him.'

Jasmin nodded. 'They say his ghost still haunts the place, trying to get home. People have seen unexplained lights on the beach at night.'

Tess bit back the smile. 'I've never heard of anything paranormal related to him. Who says that?'

Jasmin shrugged. 'It's stuff I've read on the internet. I printed out some photos of orbs and weird zig-zagging lights.'

Tess took the offered book and looked closely. She suspected most of what she was seeing was the result of raindrops on camera lenses but didn't say anything, simply handed it back.

'Poor guy. I wonder what happened,' Libby said.

'I believe he was a whaler, but I don't know a lot of details,' Tess said.

'Even though I'm the one that can't swim, drowning is actually your worst fear, right, Brock?' Jasmin asked. ''Cause you nearly drowned once, as a kid.'

'No one likes the sensation of not being able to breathe,' Brock snapped, as though annoyed she was threatening his tough-guy image. 'I'm sure they've got one too,' he said, looking pointedly towards James.

'I hate snakes and spiders,' Riley admitted. 'They're my worst nightmare.'

'Worse than fire?' Jasmin asked. 'I can't even stand to burn my fingers eating hot chips. Imagine being burned alive.'

'No thanks,' Riley said. 'What about you?' she asked James.

'Dunno,' he said with a lift of his shoulders. 'I'd just want it to be over quick.'

'Not sure either,' Libby agreed, then playfully she wrapped an arm around James's shoulders and squeezed. 'But as long as we end up together, forever, it wouldn't be so bad, right?' She kissed him noisily on the cheek and he chuckled, turned his face to kiss her properly.

'Sure,' James agreed.

'Boredom!' Chris said with a smirk. 'Dying of boredom. Kind of like at uni.'

'Agreed,' Alex said emphatically. 'Hanging around doing nothing all day when you could be doing something extreme.'

When they high-fived each other again, Tess decided they reminded her of characters from some old movie Connor and Logan had made her watch years ago. *Bill and Ted* something or other, she remembered. That movie was probably older than they were, but it could have been modelled on the two idiots.

Riley bumped Jai, who'd gone quiet. 'Well?'

'Falling,' Jai decided. 'Knowing you're going to die and just waiting to hit the ground.'

Tess's stomach flipped. 'Have to agree with you there,' she muttered.

Riley bumped Jai again, harder, then glanced meaningfully at Tess.

'Oh, shit—sorry, Tess,' Jai said. 'Didn't mean to bring that up.'

'Bring what up?' Libby asked.

'A near accident, that's all,' Tess said, then fought for a smile. 'This is all very morbid. Why don't we change the subject?'

'Sure. What else have you got in there, Jas?' Riley asked.

'Okay, so actually there's lots of reports of strange things in the sky.'

'Look out, she's got the aliens coming after us now,' Brock said, but without any of the snap of earlier.

Jasmin smacked him playfully. 'You never know.'

Jai whistled a few bars of *The X-Files* theme and the group laughed. After barely being present for the last couple of days, Tess was relieved to see him relaxing and joining in. She knew about his grandfather being in respite and thought it must be difficult having to leave him in a place he didn't want to be.

'And there's the guy who lived out at Melaleuca all alone until he died,' Jasmin continued. 'Some people reckon he never left.'

'If Deny is still there,' Tess said, 'I hardly think he'd be wasting his time scaring away tourists when he was renowned for his incredible hospitality.'

'Who was he?' James asked.

'An amazing man who almost single-handedly made Melaleuca what it is. He was an outstanding bushman, naturalist and environmentalist, and he's a big reason this place is a world heritage area. He was a legend. If anyone's made up any rubbish about him, I don't want to hear it.'

Jasmin looked at whatever else she had on the page and very pointedly turned to the next one. 'How about those escaped convicts that ate each other?'

'Well, that's more like it!' Chris said enthusiastically.

'Are you serious?' Riley asked.

'Alexander Pearce,' Jasmin said. 'He was an Irish guy sent to Australia for seven years for stealing some shoes, but he escaped and ended up with a worse sentence in an even worse prison. They reckon the place drove the prisoners mad. Anyway, in 1822 he and seven of his mates escaped but they got lost in the bush and were so starving they ended up drawing straws to decide who they were going to eat.'

'Ew!' Riley exclaimed.

'Serious!' Jasmin said. 'And they just kept eating each other until Pearce was the only one left. He got caught again and the authorities didn't believe the others had been eaten. They thought the other prisoners had escaped and he was covering for them. But then he escaped yet again with another prisoner and when he got caught that time they found parts of the other prisoner in his pockets.'

'This conversation just gets better and better,' Libby said with a shudder.

'What happened?' Riley asked.

'They hanged him.' Jasmin looked around. 'Imagine being lost out here and being starving enough to eat each other.'

'Actually, that was further north,' Tess said, amused. 'They weren't ever in this part of the wilderness.'

'No, but the seven of us are,' Alex said in a spooky voice.

Everyone groaned. 'Wouldn't you rather sing campfire songs or something?' Tess prompted.

'I know what I'd rather be doing,' Libby said. 'Snuggling up in a warm sleeping bag. I'm exhausted.'

'And on that note,' James said. 'Goodnight, everyone.'

Tess wished them goodnight. If nothing else, this trip may have saved a marriage. She got to her feet and walked away to take one last look over the ocean. The moon had made a tentative appearance, struggling for space between the heavy clouds. Perhaps tomorrow would be a better day after all. She heard the waves, the ferocious *smash, smash, smash* against the shore. It was powerful yet soothing in its regularity. A branch snapped nearby, then another. Someone was still up, probably visiting the pit toilet before bed. Cold, she walked back to her tent, noticing torches were out and tents carefully zipped up. What she'd heard must have been an animal. She hoped everyone had done a good job of double bagging and protecting their food. It was amazing the damage some of the wildlife could do while scavenging.

Though the morning sky had broken with streaks of blue and the wind had dropped back to a breeze, the tannin-stained water of the creek in front of them was still restless and angry, spewing froth and tossing debris in swirling patterns out to the ocean.

'Can we cross it?' asked Jai.

Tess looked helplessly at the line of hopeful faces. She wasn't keen to try. 'Look, even at knee depth on a good day this water has got a strong flow about it. I'm not sure—'

'We can't stay here forever,' Brock said.

A currawong sang in the branches above them while she considered that. 'It's dropped its level since earlier this morning,' she said. 'We can wait it out, hope it continues to go down. I warned you this might happen.'

'What if we form a chain?' Chris asked. 'Strongest help the weakest?'

She shook her head. 'Best way to cross is to use your poles, face upstream and watch your footing—it's difficult to tell in the dark water. I'm pretty sure we should let it drop a bit more first.'

'Okay, well, it's a nice morning, so how about we get some photos?' Riley suggested.

'Good idea. Will someone take some of James and me?' Libby asked.

'Of course,' Tess said. 'How about over there? Brock!'

Brock had moved further upstream and was wading into the water. 'It's fine!' he called out. 'Not too strong.' But the water was pulling at him, eddying in a deep groove behind him as it dragged at the top of his thighs. He stumbled once, righted himself and braced. He held out his hand. 'Come on, Jasmin.'

'Brock, if you're set on crossing, it's actually better to be down here, closer to the ocean,' Tess called out.

Jasmin looked from Tess to Brock, chewing her bottom lip. 'Maybe you should do what Tess says.'

'Jasmin, I'm standing in it. It's fine. Trust me!'

'Jasmin can't swim, remember?' Tess snapped. 'Don't be stupid!'

Brock ignored her. 'Last night you told me you trusted me, Jas. You said I was being stupid worrying that I wasn't enough for you. Prove it.'

'Seriously? How juvenile can you be?' Tess demanded.

'Yeah. Come on, man,' Chris surprised Tess by calling out. 'Even if we can do it, it doesn't mean Jas should.'

Tess had a quick moment of guilt over the mean things she'd said about him in her head last night, then noticed Jasmin heading reluctantly towards Brock. 'Don't do it, Jasmin,' she called. 'By this afternoon there's a good chance it'll be much safer.'

Jasmin looked from Tess to the others. 'Brock, I think I'd rather wait.'

'Fine!' he snapped. 'You're full of shit, Jas.'

'Okay! Okay wait.' Jasmin sent Tess an apologetic smile and hurried into the water.

'Jasmin, undo your belt clip and chest strap!' Tess ordered, and was relieved when she did that, at least.

Jasmin waded in. She was a foot shorter than Brock and the water reached her waist. She was moving backwards, being pulled down the beach more than across the rivulet. Tess dropped her pack and reached the water's edge closer to the inlet, watching, tense, as Brock sidled towards Jasmin. He took her hand and they went slowly, inching their way across. Obviously deciding it was safe, Chris and Alex went in after them.

'Watch your step just ahead,' Brock called. 'There's something in the water.'

'Right, thanks!' Alex called back.

Brock threw a smug look at Tess over his shoulder. She fought the urge to sneer back before a wave of panic hit her. A dead tree came at them fast in the strong current, its branches twisting and tossing in the water. She opened her mouth to warn them but it was too late. Brock and Jasmin seemed to rise out of the water before being pitched violently forward, disappearing underneath it. Jasmin's pack slipped from her shoulders and a moment later she rose to the surface, coughing and struggling. Brock's pack was still attached, making it difficult for him to surface. He fought desperately against the weight of it, but Jasmin was being carried away quickly by the strength of the water.

'Damn it!'

Tess went in. It was difficult keeping her feet under her. As Jasmin was carried right at her, Tess felt the impact smash into her and lost her footing, struggling to get it back as she held Jasmin's jacket in one hand and dragged at the water with the other to keep upright. Then Jai was there, and James. Somehow they managed to get out, back on the same side they'd started from.

Jasmin collapsed on the sand, coughing and shaking, crying.

Brock had gotten himself out on the other side. 'Jasmin! Are you all right?'

'No,' she shot back, then coughed again.

'You just won't listen!' Tess snapped. 'I'm so sick to death of men who think they know better! The last one is dead. You're lucky not to be!'

'Give me a break! If it hadn't been for the log we would have—'

'Shut up!' she yelled. 'Just shut up!'

He looked as shocked by the outburst as she was for having made it. She was trembling with adrenaline, angry, but she knew she shouldn't behave that way. Telling herself to find some control, she bent back over Jasmin. The girl was freezing.

'We need to get you into something dry.'

'My pack. It's gone.'

Tess looked around. 'There's a chance we might get it back but everything is going to be soaked. You'll have to borrow some of my clothes, and we'll dry off the ones you're wearing.'

'And use some of mine, too,' Riley offered. 'Between us we'll have enough to go around.'

'Come on, up you get. We all need to get dry.'

It was lunchtime before Tess managed to coax Jasmin safely across the creek. The water level had dropped and with Jai on one side and James on the other, she made it without too much trouble. Brock had waited on the other side, alone, for hours. He had everything out of his pack, drying. He'd somehow also managed to salvage Jasmin's pack and her things were laid out with his.

'Never miss a chance,' Brock muttered at James for helping Jasmin out of the water. Tess had trouble biting her tongue.

James walked up to Brock and punched him in the jaw. 'Grow up.'

'Hey!' Tess snapped. 'That's enough!'

Brock was brought down on one knee by the force of it. He stayed there, head down. Then he nodded, pressing his fingers to his eyes. 'I'm sorry.' He stood up, his jaw red, his lip split. 'Jas, I'm sorry. We would have been okay—'

'Yeah, well, we weren't.' Jasmin walked past him up the beach and started shoving her things haphazardly into her pack. 'Are we going?' she asked Tess.

'In a minute,' Tess answered. 'Once Brock's packed up.'

Without argument, Brock limped over to his things. Tess frowned. 'What have you done?'

'Just a small gash from that tree. It's not bad.'

'Want me to take a look? We're really going to have to push ourselves to get to the next campsite before dark.'

'I said it's—no. No, thanks. It's fine.'

'We'll help you pack up, bro,' Alex offered.

Brock kept up along the beach, even ascended the timber stairs that led back into the bush without slowing them down. Tess took that as a good sign and relaxed about whatever injury he'd sustained. They continued along a track dominated by beech trees, the otherwise grey landscape broken by the startling lime green of native grasses. Then the track opened out into more muddy plains where they slogged through shin-deep mud, the earth suctioning their boots and making walking exhausting. The light, scrubby bushland beyond was a welcome relief.

'Hey, is this our campsite?' Libby asked when they reached a clear area of ground.

'It's a campsite, but not ours,' she told her. 'Unless Milford Creek is uncrossable. But we should stop here, take a break.'

'How much further?' Riley asked, taking a long, thirsty drink.

'About four k's.' Tess saw Brock rub his leg, his face reflecting discomfort. 'If it's too much, we can stay here, but it'll mean a more difficult day tomorrow.'

'No,' Brock said, catching her watching him. 'Four k's is nothing.'

'The last part of today's track is a difficult climb up some dunes. But whatever you say.' She gave them ten minutes, her own calves aching. Then she got them on their feet. 'We don't want to be setting up tents in the dark. We're going to have to move fast.'

CHAPTER 35

Tank was sitting up in his hospital bed. One eye was completely swollen shut, bruises covered his face and arms, and a long row of stitches marred his left temple. The skin that wasn't bruised was sallow and he looked older, softer. But his one good eye sharpened when he saw them. 'Detectives.' Even his voice sounded weak.

'Tank,' Jared said. 'Good to see you awake.'

'Thanks for coming to get me. Not sure I would have ever woken up if I'd been there much longer.'

'Can you tell us what happened?' Indy asked.

'I went home to freshen up to see you two about what we talked about and got jumped. They wanted to know where the ring was. Told 'em I didn't have a clue what they were talking about.'

'And did you?' Jared asked.

Tank took a sip of his water and shook his head.

'Did you know Jai Wharton was working for them?' Indy asked.

Tank dragged his fingers over his head. 'Jai isn't one of them.'

'He delivered a ring to them,' Indy said. 'Except it wasn't the right one. Cochrane seems to think you told him to swap it for another one.'

'I don't know what they're on about! Real one, fake one … And if Jai took something to those morons, it was because Pax blackmailed him to. The bastard couldn't leave him out of it. Got him all wrapped up. Poor kid was a mess.'

'I hope you're not covering for him,' Jared said. 'Because he's out in the middle of nowhere with your daughter.'

Tank scowled. 'You could torture that kid to within an inch of his life—he'd never hurt Riley. Never hurt anyone on purpose. I'm telling ya, he's a good kid.'

'That good kid had more than ten thousand dollars stashed in a backpack in his wardrobe,' Indy said.

'That's what Cochrane does. Throws money at you to get you in, keep you quiet. Did Jai go out and buy a new car, flash it around? He wouldn't have asked for that money, but he was desperate enough to keep it. What's he spending it on? His pop's care, no doubt.'

'Just how wrapped up did Jai get?' Jared asked. 'And what is it you think Orvist could blackmail him about? Is he the other killer?'

Tank shifted gingerly and reached for a glass of water. When he sighed heavily, he seemed to age ten years. 'It was an accident. Look, I told you I'd tell you all of it and I will. Sit down.'

Jared took notes. 'So Cochrane's belief the ring was being held as a bargaining tool is off base?' he asked when Tank had finished.

Tank shook his head. 'I didn't have a clue what they were on about. And Jai wouldn't have the guts to muck them about. He was scared of Pax. He wasn't about to go screwing over Pax's boss. He was a trainwreck over those murders. Looked like death warmed up, couldn't eat, sleep or think. That's not the type to go up against Cochrane. Pax is a conniving little prick. He's the one you need to find.'

'Yeah and you're going to help us do that.'

Jared was still on edge when they walked out. 'I'm not happy about this kid being out there with Tess and Riley. He might not have meant to kill anyone, but he's made mistake after mistake. He's a time bomb.'

'And do we want him to explode out there?' she asked. 'I don't want to spook him. It might push him over the edge.' She looked at her phone, read a text. 'Melbourne Police have just located Cochrane. They're bringing him in for you. Can you get up there right away?'

'You know I will.'

Cochrane was seated with his lawyer but he got to his feet as Jared came in.

'You want to tell me what this is all about, detective?' he asked. 'Cops won't tell me anything. This is not legal. You can't just arrest someone and not—'

'Be quiet and I'll fill you in. You're under arrest because you sent Paxton Orvist down to murder your ex, her partner and the boat's skipper. You involved Vince Finlay in order to throw us off-track with the investigation. You wanted us to think the murders were about the diamonds and set him up by sending your men in to discover some of the missing jewellery. Except what you were really after all along, on top of paying back your ex and Finlay for their roles in putting you away, was Maddie's phone and the NFC chip in her ring.'

'That's bullshit!' Cochrane laughed uncomfortably.

'You cheated on your wife in every way possible. Personally and financially—you wanted in to her accounts. And then you killed her.'

Cochrane's face reddened in fury. 'Oh sure, poor Maddie. I fucked a few whores and stole her money.'

'Twelve million or so. What happened to it?'

'If you believe the lawyers and the cops, I frittered it all away with my extravagant lifestyle. Gambling addiction, whores, elaborate money-making schemes that never quite got off the ground.' He leant forward and glared. 'But she had it all along.'

'Bullshit.'

'I'm not lying! She stashed the money away so it'd look like I'd lost it. The bitch framed me to pay me back and put me away. All that missing cash has been siphoned into offshore accounts. *Her* offshore accounts.'

'And all you need to access those accounts is the phone and the electronic chip in that ring, right?'

Cochrane hesitated for the first time, sitting back in his chair. He seemed to regret what he'd given away and glanced at his lawyer when the man cautioned him about saying anything more.

Jared pressed on. 'And you didn't mention any of this right through the trial or for the last eight years in prison.'

'Eight years inside. Could have been twenty-five. Not so bad. If I'd brought it up, she would have just removed the evidence.'

'And you wouldn't have been able to get your hands on it when you got out. That was the plan all along, wasn't it?'

Again, Cochrane's lawyer interrupted. Cochrane closed his mouth on whatever he'd been about to say, then shrugged.

Jared got to his feet. 'You're going to spend the rest of your life in prison.' He looked from Cochrane's furious face to the window and shook his head. 'So close, Bryce. You were so close.'

CHAPTER 36

'Why are we heading down to the beach?' Jasmin asked Tess as they reached a wide expanse of water. They'd spent the night at a nearby campsite, so Tess couldn't really understand how this part of the itinerary had escaped Jasmin's attention. Then again, she'd gone to bed early last night, generally pissed off. Perhaps she'd just forgotten to mention it and no one else had, either.

'This is New River Lagoon,' she told her. 'We need to cross it.' The snaking lagoon was calm. The blue sky sparkled on the light ripple of waves created by the breeze across its surface, the first real sunshine they'd seen since beginning the hike. She pulled off her boots and socks, and the sand was cool but soft under her feet.

'That?' Jasmin asked in terror. 'How? Isn't it deep? We don't have to swim, do we? I can't.'

'There's boats, Jas,' Riley said, catching up and removing her own shoes. 'Just over there.'

'One on this side, two on the other,' Tess said, already heading for it. She looked across the lagoon. 'At least, there should be three, but I can only see two. Doesn't matter. There's going to be a few trips involved anyway. We need to make sure we leave at least one boat on either side of the lagoon, so once we're all across two of us are going to have to row back again in both boats, leave one and row back together in the other.'

'Not a problem,' James said. 'I'll do a couple of trips.'

'Thanks.'

'I don't mind,' Brock and Jai said at the same time.

'Thank, Jai,' Tess said, because she was sure Brock had been struggling with his injury.

'Fine,' Brock mumbled.

James, Jai, Chris and Riley went across first. When James and Jai came back with both boats, Brock climbed in with Alex and Jai.

'Let's go, Jas.'

Jasmin ignored him and climbed into James's boat.

'Oh, really mature. You're going to have to speak to me again at some point, you know.'

'What makes you think that?' Jasmin asked.

'It was an accident!'

'No, it was ego. You needed to show what a tough guy you were and wouldn't listen to Tess, then you used what I feel for you to manipulate me into going along with it. Blame the submerged inanimate object all you like—whatever it was, it still outsmarted you!'

'If that's how you feel maybe I should just leave you all to it!' He stepped out of the boat again.

'Whatever.'

'Get in the boat, Brock,' Jai said. 'She just needs a bit longer to cool down.'

'So this is fun,' Libby said to Tess before climbing in with James and Jasmin. Tess had to agree. She stepped into Jai's boat. It was a quiet trip across, and a tense several minutes standing around with Brock and Jasmin waiting for Jai and James to take the boats back and return in one.

'Okay,' Tess said, putting the oars back in the plastic pipes beside the boat. 'Packs on. We've got a long stretch of beach ahead of us. Ready?'

'Hey! Hello!'

Tess spun around to see an older couple waving at them from the end of the sandbar.

'Looks like we're waiting,' Tess said. 'Drop your packs again if you like.'

Riley dropped her pack and wandered a short distance away, head down, looking at the sand. 'Hey, Tess. What are these?' she asked, pointing to tracks in the dune.

'That's wombat,' she answered, 'and the one over there looks like wallaby.'

'That's so cool. They're everywhere.'

'Most of the wildlife here is nocturnal, so we don't see them. But there's plenty around.' She looked up and smiled politely as the couple caught up to the group. 'Hi.'

'Thanks for waiting,' the man with a head of dishevelled silver hair and a tired but smiling expression said. 'We didn't realise you were ahead of us.'

'We weren't,' Tess said. 'We're going the other way.'

The man's face fell, the woman with her bright crop of silver hair looked concerned. 'Never mind then,' the man said. 'Have a good walk.'

'Is there a problem?' Tess asked, sensing trouble.

'Nope, we're fine,' he assured them.

'He hurt his arm,' the woman blurted. 'Trying to help me up a slippery bit of track. I fell awkwardly on him. He's worried about rowing.'

'I see,' Tess said. 'I'll have to—'

'I'll take them,' Brock cut in.

'Thank you,' the woman replied with obvious relief. 'I'm Belinda, this is Richard. We really appreciate it.'

'You all go ahead,' Brock told the group. 'It won't take me all that long to take them across and back.'

'We'll be waiting here,' Tess said.

'No, Tess!' Then he said, in a lower voice, 'I need some space. I *really* need a few moments to myself.' He glanced sideways and when Tess followed suit, noted Jasmin glaring at him. 'I don't even want to be here anymore. Please, *please* just go ahead.'

She sighed. 'There's a five-k walk along the beach ahead of us. That's all you get. We'll be waiting for you there. I'm not heading back up into the bush without you.'

'Great. Thanks.'

'Brock,' she said quietly, 'I'll talk to Jasmin. It was a stupid mistake, but we've all made them, okay?'

'Yeah. Tell her that.'

He untied the boat without a backwards look.

Tess picked up her pack. 'Right. Let's go.'

They walked across the sandbar and onto the long stretch of Prion Beach, James and Libby attempting to keep up happy chatter. Jasmin stopped once to look back when the crossing was out of sight.

'Do you think I was too hard on him?'

'I think he's learnt his lesson,' Tess said. 'I can't tell you what to do, but the trip would be much nicer for everyone if you weren't at each other's throats the whole time.'

She looked along the beach. Prion was one golden strip of sand—Brock should have been visible by now. If he was sulking, it was going to cost them valuable time.

She took them as far as Grotto Creek, where a tumbling of stones and a trickle of water turned the trail inland, then stopped and took off her pack.

'Still no Brock,' Libby said, dropping her pack next to Tess's and stretching her back.

'Nope.' Damn it, she was going to have to go back and find him. There was no point waiting. 'Let's take a break.'

'You want us to go back?' Alex and Chris offered.

'No, but thanks. I'll do it.'

Adding another several kilometres to an already long walk didn't improve her temper. By the time she crossed back onto the sand-bar, she was fuming. It took all of two seconds to see Brock hadn't returned. Two boats were on the wrong side of the lagoon. The third, which she hadn't been able to locate earlier, was drifting near the opposite shore.

'Brock!' she called. Nothing. 'Brock!'

Perhaps he'd got caught up helping the couple, hadn't dragged the boat onto shore quite far enough. It would be difficult to remain angry if that was the case. She looked around. He'd taken his pack. Why would he take his pack across the lagoon?

I don't even want to be here anymore, he'd said, and had pushed them to keep going. A sinking feeling sat heavily in her gut. He'd left them on purpose. 'Stupid irresponsible dickhead!' she muttered loudly. She stood a couple of minutes longer, hoping by some chance she was wrong, that he'd reappear. When he didn't, she began the trek back to the rest of the group.

'What if I swim across?' Jai offered when she broke the news. 'Try and catch up to him?'

'Are you kidding?' Riley said. 'Remember how far it is!'

'Can we walk around it? Head out over the sand to the narrower crossing?'

'Not realistically, no,' Tess said. 'It's high tide and the banks are unstable. The outlet changes course all the time and it's like quicksand to walk on.'

'I think I could swim it,' Jai said again. 'Then I'll row one of the boats back.'

'And then what? We lose a day and he doesn't want to come back anyway? No,' Tess decided, 'I'm not having anyone else risk anything stupid. He made his decision. He's with that couple so he's not alone. He has a PLB if he gets into trouble, as well as all his rations and gear.' She took out the sat phone and called Indy. When the call went to voicemail she left a message letting Indy know what had happened, and because she was keen to get going, asked her to call National Parks to let them know about the boats. They'd sort it. She put the sat phone back in its waterproof bag and back into her pack. 'Okay, let's go.'

'Tess, you've already done an extra ten k's today, do you want to break here for the night?' Riley asked. 'There must be an alternative campsite.'

'There's a small one at Deadman's Creek about three and a half k's away, but the better one's only a couple more kilometres on at Little Deadman's Bay. We'll make it. Jasmin?'

'Sorry,' Jasmin sniffed, wiping at tears. 'I've ruined everyone's walk.'

'You haven't,' Riley said, throwing an arm around her. 'Brock was a tool, but he's gone back with those oldies. So now we can get back to having a good time, right?'

'Really? I feel bad.'

'Well, don't,' James said. 'I'm glad he's left. Come on, Libby and I have been saving a small block of chocolate for just such a day. Let's get to the campsite.'

Despite her legs feeling like lead, Tess kept them going. The group made good time through the coastal forest and creek crossings, small gullies and stretches of beach. It was a shame there wasn't more time to stop and take in the incredible scenery, but they reached the pretty, sheltered cove of Little Deadman's Bay with daylight to spare, making their fast pace worthwhile.

Despite the cold temperature, Tess was hot and sweaty. 'This is the campsite,' she told them, letting her pack fall from her shoulders with relief. And though they were by the river, Tess wanted the beach. 'I'm going to set up my tent, then wander down to the beach. Anyone want to join me?'

'Sounds like heaven!' Riley agreed. 'My feet are killing me! I want to soak them.'

'It's rocky, bring your shoes.'

They set up quickly and went down to the beach.

'This is better!' Jai said, rolling up his hiking pants and tossing off his jumper to wade into the water.

'Shame it's too cold to swim,' Tess said, 'but paddle and soak your legs. The cold water will be good for them.'

'Hey, a bath would be good for all of us,' Jai said, and bravely jumped right in. 'Come on, Riley!'

'Are you crazy?' Riley asked, navigating her way over the smooth rocks on the shoreline to the water's edge.

'Not kidding. If I'm clean, you'll only smell worse, and we have to share the tent, remember?'

'I've been washing!' Riley objected, but as she got close to Jai, he pulled her in. She went under and came up spluttering and squealing at the cold.

Alex bolted into the sea with a 'Woo hoo!' and dived. Chris followed.

'Oh, what the hell,' James said and, scooping up Libby, ran in. Libby shrieked, laughed, then they both submerged.

'Tess! It's not that bad,' Riley called, dragging her loose hair from her eyes. 'Jas, come on!'

'I think they're lying,' Jasmin said with a grin for Tess.

'Can't be the only pikers,' Tess said.

'But we're low on clothes.'

'We'll make do.'

Despite the teeth-chattering temperature, the five or ten minutes they all braved it out were worth it. Then they rinsed themselves and their clothes off in the creek, got dry and hung their wet clothes on the branches of nearby trees to dry.

'I think it's actually colder when it's not raining,' Jasmin said as they ate their dinner.

'Yeah, but it's nice to see the stars,' Libby said, looking up.

'If you're not supposed to have open fires here, how come there's a stone circle just by my tent that looks like it's been used as one?' Jasmin asked Tess. 'It's not like anyone's going to wander in during the night and fine us.'

'Which is why not everyone does the right thing,' Tess said. 'But we do.'

'Hey, look!' Jai whispered and pointed. A spotted-tail quoll came into view, boldly foraging around the edge of Tess's tent.

'Cute,' Tess said, 'but up to no good. Make sure your food's safely stored tonight, or it might be gone in the morning. Those things can chew through tents.'

Tess had been asleep a couple of hours when she rolled over and caught an orange glow through the lining of her tent. She jumped up, unzipped the tent and checked outside. Jasmin was sitting by the fireplace she'd mentioned, a small fire burning.

'What are you doing?' Tess demanded. 'Put it out!'

It was only when Jasmin's surprised face turned in her direction that she realised the girl had been crying.

'I can't sleep. I needed something to stare at, to keep warm.'

'What's going on?' Riley's and Jai's heads appeared at their tent flap.

'I just needed to think,' Jasmin said, her voice catching. 'I wish Brock was here. I shouldn't have been so mean.'

Not this again ... 'Then think without the fire,' Tess said with a yawn she couldn't quite stifle. 'I'm sorry you feel bad, but you need to put that out.'

'Oh, come on, it's only a little one,' Chris said, appearing. 'She's upset.'

Tess silenced him with a look and he ducked back in his tent.

'Okay,' Jasmin said reluctantly, and began heaping dirt on it. Tess saw the glow dull to nothing and, satisfied, went back to sleep.

Screaming woke her. There was a terrifying light. She leapt up and out of the tent at the same time as the others fell out of theirs. Jasmin's tent was almost completely engulfed in flames. One side had collapsed and smoke poured out of the other. Jai tried to get inside, somehow managed to get a hand on Jasmin's burning sleeping bag and, with James's help, pulled it out and away from the tent. Tess patted desperately at the flames while James unzipped it, ripping it off the still-screaming Jasmin. Riley, Libby, Chris and Alex busied themselves putting out the flames already crawling towards the nearby bushland.

'She's burnt!' Jai said, an edge of panic in his voice. 'It's bad.'

'Get her down to the creek!' Tess ordered. As the tent had been completely devoured, the faintest hint of pre-dawn light was all they had to see by. The men moved fast and Tess scrambled after them and when they gently placed Jasmin in the water, the screams that had dulled to whimpering began again.

'Tess!' Riley called out. 'We can't put it out!'

'Jai, help them, try and sweep away any leaf litter, cover the embers in dirt.'

Tess moved around to where Jai had sat, cradling Jasmin's upper body. 'Shh,' she crooned. 'The water will help. I know it's cold, but you'll be okay.' She swept a gentle hand over Jasmin's forehead to lift the hair from her face. It came back sticky, the hair stuck to Tess's hand. Dread and horror hit her at once. Just how badly burned was she? It was almost impossible to see. 'I need a torch,' she told James, 'and my sat phone.'

'Okay, you got her?'

'Yep.'

'I put it out,' Jasmin managed. 'I put the fire out like you said.'

'I know,' Tess said, doing her best to keep hold of Jasmin as uncontrollable shudders racked her body. 'I know you did. An ember must have caught. Tell me where it hurts most.'

'My head, my legs. The tent fell on my face and I couldn't get out of the sleeping bag. It caught on fire.'

James returned, handing the torch to Tess.

'James, I also need my first aid kit—where's the sat phone?'

'I couldn't find it. Just the torch. I'll take another look when I get the first aid kit.'

'Okay, go,' she said when he hesitated. If this was bad she didn't want Jasmin to see the look on his face when he took in her burns. He left, and Tess sucked in a breath and switched on the torch. One side of Jasmin's face was a mess, her ear unrecognisable. Her clothing was burned to her skin but completely gone from her legs, which were blackened and blistered in large areas of her thighs and shins. Tess's lungs clogged with panic. Her basic first aid kit was not going to come close to helping. She lowered Jasmin further, tried to rest most of the burned area of her head in the water without it entering her mouth or nose.

'Dear God,' Libby exclaimed under her breath as she slid down with her own torch to join Tess. She dragged her gaze from Jasmin. 'I've been through your pack and your tent. The sat phone's not there.'

'What?' How was that possible? Jasmin started coughing. Tess raised her up into more of a sitting position. 'We need to get water on the injured areas of her face. Can you get me a cup or a bottle?'

'Yep.'

'James!' she called as Libby raced off. 'Activate one of the PLBs!'

'On it!' he said.

Riley appeared. 'Chris and Alex are mopping up the last of the embers, but it's basically all out.' Then, 'Hey, Jas. Feeling a bit better?'

Jasmin didn't answer. She was shivering and shaking and her breathing was raspy.

'Is she going to be okay?' Riley whispered urgently.

'Of course she is,' Tess said with a look that told Riley to shut up. Jasmin might have passed out from the pain, or she might be hearing everything they said.

Libby reappeared with a water bottle. Tess took it and started pouring the cold water gently over Jasmin's burns.

'Tess, I am seriously so sorry,' James said, 'but where are the PLBs?'

A sick feeling washed over her. 'You all have them in your packs. You were all given one. They're there. Check again.'

'I couldn't find ours and we'd been through your stuff for your sat phone, so I know yours isn't where it's supposed to be.'

'That's impossible,' she snapped in disbelief.

'I'll get ours,' Riley said. 'I know where I left it.'

'It's not there either,' Jai said. Then, to Tess, 'Fire's out.'

'I can't understand how it was still alight,' Riley said. 'We saw her put it out.'

'Obviously not well enough. An ember must have blown onto the tent.'

'After all that time?' Riley asked. 'It's almost six in the morning.'

'I don't know, Riley. Right now it doesn't matter.' Tess heard the strain in her voice, but she couldn't help it.

'Tess, what can I do?' Libby asked.

'How's your first aid knowledge?' Tess asked as quietly as she could. 'Because I know burns are supposed to be cooled where possible in running water. She has so many the only viable way to do that is to lie her in the water. It's probably colder than it should be but what can I do? But I also know when a patient is in shock you should keep them warm with their legs elevated. Right now, she's freezing cold with her legs down in the water and her head up because she can't seem to breathe lying down. I'm winging it here, because what we should be doing is getting her airlifted out as quickly as possible to a hospital and no one can find any of the devices we brought with us for just such an emergency.'

Libby put a hand on her shoulder. It felt warm enough for Tess to realise how cold she was. 'You're doing great. You're doing everything you can. What does your gut tell you?'

'I think it's too cold. I think the shock might be more dangerous at this point than the burns.'

'Okay. So we pull her out, and then what?'

'Dress the wounds, keep them clean. Monitor her vitals. She can have my tent. We'll set her up in there.' She was starting to wonder whether all the shaking was coming from Jasmin. 'Okay, I want to get her out of here.'

They got Jasmin to Tess's tent. Tess had expected the crying to start up again but got no more than weak whimpers. Those were much, much scarier.

Jai changed into dry clothes and sat by the side of his tent making hot chocolates. Alex and Chris were with him; for once both were quiet and solemn. Libby and James were sipping tea and talking in hushed voices he couldn't quite catch. There was another heart-wrenching wail from Jas. Tess was with her. He wanted to help, but he wasn't sure how.

Riley came out of the tent. When she sat, he pressed a cup into her hand. 'Here, drink this.'

'Thanks.' She took it and swiped at her tear-stained face with her free hand, her eyes moving straight to Tess's tent when Tess emerged, face tortured. 'How is she?'

'I'm doing everything I can. She wants me to let her try and sleep.'

'Tess,' James said after a moment. 'If this was an accident, how come our sat phone and PLBs are missing?'

'I don't know how they could all have gone missing,' Tess said. 'Even if I was able to convince myself that we'd somehow not packed them—which is ridiculous—I know I had my sat phone. I can't understand it.'

'I'm wondering just how well these guys know Brock,' James said.

Jai shifted uncomfortably. 'Brock's a mate,' he said.

'Is he a vindictive one?' James shot back.

'Wait,' Alex said. 'You're saying you think Brock did this?'

'He couldn't have,' Tess said. 'He was already on the other side of the lagoon when I used the sat phone to call Indy.'

'Was he?' Libby asked. 'The third boat wasn't tied to the shore. For all we know he came back and set it loose to drift across the lagoon.'

Riley snuggled closer so Jai put an arm around her. 'Brock wouldn't do that!' she said. 'It's more likely an animal raided our bags or something.'

'An animal gets into our bags, leaves the food and goes for the PLBs and the sat phone? Are you joking?' James scoffed. 'How well do we ever really know anyone? Any one of us could be a murderer.'

Jai flinched, looked away. 'Not Brock.' He thought about Pax, about the complete lack of emotion he'd shown when he'd been about to rape and murder that woman on the boat. About how excited and hyped up he'd been afterwards.

'Oh, trust me,' James said, 'we've seen it all before. Friends, brothers, sisters, spouses testifying they can't believe this person or that person could do something terrible. But it happens. In our line of work it happens every day.'

'Then it could have been any of us,' Chris argued.

James shook his head. 'The only chance anyone would have had to take our stuff was while we were down at the beach. No single one of us has been up here alone, none of us sitting here have had a chance to do this.'

'There's something else,' Libby said. 'You can't really believe it's a coincidence that the other night Jasmin said her worst fear was burning to death and now this. She said that right in front of him, right after she'd pissed him off.'

'This is ridiculous,' Riley said, but her tone was less than convinced.

Besides, they were right. This wasn't an accident and someone other than the people sitting around their fuel stoves had to be responsible. Someone who most likely had heard that conversation. Why wouldn't they suspect Brock? Again, Pax's face seared into the front of Jai's mind. Even if Pax did figure out Jai had handed over a different ring, he wasn't going to have followed them all the way out here over one piece of jewellery. Not when he knew he could just pounce on Jai when he got back. Besides, Pax would have gone after him, not Jasmin. No. This was something else, he reassured himself. This was not about a ring. What happened to Jas was not his fault.

'I don't know what's going on,' Tess eventually said. 'But I'm leaving you guys here and heading for help.'

'What?' James said.

'No! You can't leave us!' Riley begged, straightening.

'You can't get back across the lagoon,' Libby said. 'Even if you do and you make it back to Cockle Creek, you've got no phone. How will you contact anyone to come and get you? Unless maybe you catch up to that older couple.'

'I'm not going to Cockle Creek,' Tess said. 'I'm going to Melaleuca. It's closer and I can halve the time it takes to get there if I go alone. I could be lucky and meet other hikers walking back, or flag down a plane load of day tourists on the airstrip. When the weather's clear there's flights going in and out all the time. There's a good chance a plane will get there before ours is due for one reason or another. Worst-case scenario: I meet ours. It'll still save days waiting here for a rescue no one knows we need. You'll just need to ration your food a bit in case Mother Nature doesn't cooperate, and try and keep Jasmin's bandages clean and dry.'

'But—and I still don't believe Brock did this—what if whoever did it comes back?' Riley said.

'We don't know what's happened,' Jai said. 'But if we stay together, we'll be fine.'

'Yeah, but Tess won't,' James said, looking up from the map he'd pulled from his pack. 'There's no way I'm letting you go alone, Tess. Apart from anything else, it's irresponsible. If something happens to you, we're all screwed. We wouldn't even know. Libby and I have already discussed this. We'll go ahead *together.* It's three days and, looking at the map, I believe we can do it in two.'

Tess seemed to consider that, but she didn't look altogether happy.

'James is right, Tess,' Jai said. 'No one should go alone and we need you to help us take care of Jas.'

'Okay,' she said after another hesitation. Then to Libby and James, 'Let's get you packed up. The sooner you get going the better.'

As the couple got ready, the sun slowly emerged, shining streamers of bright light through coloured cloud. It was finally a perfect morning, Jai thought absently. Except it wasn't.

'Anything we need to know about?' James asked Tess.

'A couple of k's or so from here you'll hit some steep terrain. At the bottom there's an old track. It's closed. You have to cross the creek to pick up the proper one. Be careful when you come to crossing the Louisa River. There's a rope but it can still be dangerous. Keep an eye on the depth and flow. Other than that, it's pretty straightforward. Just don't take any unnecessary chances.'

'We can do it,' Libby promised, lifting her pack onto her shoulders. 'Be safe.'

'You too.'

Jai watched them go, then scanned the trees. Was someone out there, watching, waiting? With a shiver of apprehension, he turned back to camp.

CHAPTER 37

'I missed the call, but they're fine,' Indy told Jared. 'Tess sounded pissed off that the kid had high-tailed it off with the other hikers but there was no indication she was worried about anything else. I did try and call her back but couldn't get her. I'd say she's only turning the phone on when needed to conserve battery power.'

'Makes sense.'

'Everyone's here,' she said and pushed through the door to the meeting room. 'Morning. We've talked to Finlay. Several weeks ago he received a letter from Cochrane, which we now have in our possession, telling him to give Orvist a job to help him fit in to the area while he prepared for what was supposed to be a simple robbery. Also, that he was to break down the jewellery Orvist brought back and in return Cochrane would leave Finlay and his daughter alone for good.'

'So where does Wharton fit in?' Roberts asked.

'Orvist took advantage of Wharton's desperation for cash to drag him into the theft and murders.'

'But Wharton delivered the wrong ring to Cochrane's men,' Emily said. 'Are we sure he didn't collude with Finlay on this? Does one of them still have it?'

'Finlay claims he knows nothing about it,' Indy said. 'We need to speak to Wharton, who is currently out on the South Coast Track with Finlay's daughter, four of his friends, Tess Atherton, and a couple from Sandy Bay.'

'How long until they finish their trek?' Roberts asked.

'Unless we hear from them to say they've been held up, a plane is due to pick them up from Melaleuca in three days.'

'Is going in after them an option?' Emily asked.

'That option would involve knowing their exact location and getting police to them without alerting Wharton of our presence. We believe he's just a desperate kid who's got himself in over his head but that doesn't mean he's not a threat. If we start something out there, there's a high risk of the situation becoming dangerous.'

'So we don't panic him,' Roberts said. 'Let him continue to think he's safe, then pick him up at the plane where we can have a good police presence waiting.'

Indy looked questioningly at Jared.

'Makes sense,' he said.

Indy nodded. 'That's settled then. In the meantime, Finlay will remain in hospital under police guard.'

'We never completed that search of Wharton's property. Is it worth going back in?' Emily asked.

'I'll get it sorted,' Jared said.

'Great,' Indy said. 'How are we going with Orvist?'

'Nothing,' Parker complained. 'It's like he's just vanished.'

'No one just vanishes. He's very much alive and well somewhere.'

'Do you think he's managed to get back to Melbourne?'

'It's possible, I suppose. No matter how much we monitor everything, there's always a chance he's gotten through.'

'He was staying at Mrs Ted's place.'

'Yeah, and?'

'He was doing those break-ins before she was murdered. She was still alive when I dropped in on Finlay after the break-ins had started. So where was he staying before that?'

'I think that might be a question for Finlay,' Indy said, eyes lighting up. 'You want to go ask him?'

CHAPTER 38

Tess woke up to the sound of strong wind and light rain on the tent. She had vague memories of it being more akin to torrential through the night. Why hadn't Riley or Jai woken her? Alex had volunteered to share Chris's tent so she could have his, and they'd all organised to take turns watching Jasmin.

She opened the tent and bullets of rain hit her with force. Outside was chaos. The ground was soaked. Strong wind gusts had blown branches and leaf litter over everything that had burnt the night before. The slim coastal trees surrounding the camp swayed, bending alarmingly when another ferocious blast of wind battered them, the sound a whistling moan. Over that, a loud snapping sound caught her attention. She looked across to Alex and Chris's tent. The fly sheet was flapping madly in the wind, torn from its rope. But for all the commotion, the wind was taking with it the remnants of last night's storm, and blue sky was chasing away cloud.

Jai was huddled in his jacket and bent over his fuel stove, trying to boil water. 'Morning.'

'Morning. You didn't wake me.'

'We decided to let you sleep.'

Another crack of the fly had her shaking her head. 'How are those guys sleeping through that?'

'No idea. I'm a bit peeved they crashed before I came out again to take over with Jas though.'

'They what?' she asked, instantly annoyed. 'Damn it. How was she last time you looked in?'

'She's sleeping. I think the painkillers are helping. She was talking quite normally for a bit last night.'

Tess found that hard to believe. If infection wasn't setting in it would be a miracle. 'I'll look in on her now.'

She dragged her arms into her coat and stepped out into the Antarctic blast. She blew into her hands as she went to Jasmin's tent and unzipped it before ducking in quietly. Jasmin's eyes were closed in sleep, but she was trembling, wheezing. A pained expression crossed her face with every involuntary movement.

'Jas?' Tess whispered. She gently touched the undamaged side of Jasmin's face, felt a clamminess that was somehow hot and cold at the same time. Sitting back on her heels, Tess chewed her lip, wondered what else she could do for her. She could only hope help wasn't far away. Deciding not to wake her, she crept out again and checked that, unlike Chris and Alex's, the tent was still secure. Thinking of the two, her temper resurfaced. She went to their tent.

'Hey!' she called, hammering on the fabric. When no one answered she opened the flap and found it empty. 'They're not in here,' she said to Jai. Worry immediately began to churn in her stomach as all sorts of possibilities flashed through her mind.

Jai carefully tipped hot water into two cups, his expression closing into a frown. 'I'm sure they're fine, just visiting the pit toilet or something. Riley and I have been up since five but in and out of the tent. It's possible they ducked off and we didn't see them. Grab a coffee and give them a minute. There's enough water here for a third cup.'

Tess took another long look around before nodding reluctantly. 'Okay, but if they're not back after coffee, I'm going looking.'

Riley came out of the tent still in the process of zipping up the final of several layers of clothing. 'Morning.' She flopped down next to Jai. 'You know, the guide said it can be boiling hot one day and snowing the next, but I didn't really believe it. Now I do.'

'The weather's clearing,' Tess said. 'Hey, you haven't seen or heard from Alex or Chris this morning, have you?'

Riley's hand froze midway with her mug to her lips. 'They went back to the tent before we got up. Didn't they?'

Tess shrugged. 'They're not there.'

Riley's mug hit the ground, hot coffee sloshing over the sides. 'We should find them! We should—'

'Give them a couple of minutes in case they're on their way back,' Jai cut her off. 'Riley, you need to be calm.'

'Calm?' she repeated, dragging the hair out of her eyes. 'Brock's missing, Jasmin's hurt, all means of communication with the outside world has been stolen and we don't have a clue who's out there or why. Now Chris and Alex vanish and you're sitting there drinking coffee like there's nothing in the world to worry about?'

'They're two strong, fit guys together,' Tess said. 'Surely—'

'But I'm not sure they were together,' Riley interrupted. 'When the guys came out at one to take over, Chris sat with Jas while Alex ducked off to pee.'

'I forgot about that,' Jai said.

Tess put down her coffee. She was too wound up to enjoy it now. 'You're right, I won't feel better until I see them back here in one piece.'

'Okay, you know what?' Jai said, and got to his feet. 'Stay here. I'll give them a shout.'

'No way. I'm coming with you,' Riley said, clutching at his arm.

Tess watched them head up the hill. Jai was calling loudly, but much of the volume was blown away with the wind. She paced, watching for anything out of the ordinary. She heard Jai's voice getting closer, and damn it—she needed to pee. She quickly ducked into the scrub just far enough, eyes darting everywhere for any sign of danger. The longer Jai called without answer, the more nerves jostled in her stomach. Why weren't either of them answering? And why was that nearby tree creaking so loudly? Branches rubbing together in the wind? She got up, risked going just a bit further away from camp to check it out.

Came face to face with Alex.

She didn't realise she'd screamed until Jai and Riley came pounding through the scrub calling her name.

'Tess!'

'Here.' It hadn't been branches creaking, it had been the rope gouging the tree branch as Alex swung lifelessly from it. She swallowed back the horror, tried to make sense of what she was seeing. Who could do that? Who could kill a big, strong, healthy man and get him up there? She couldn't seem to speak, couldn't take her eyes off him, so she felt rather than saw Jai and Riley stop behind her.

Jai swore. It came out raspy, as though he couldn't quite drag in a breath. Riley was silent for several seconds, then dropped to the ground beside Tess and began to sob hysterically. Jai backed away slowly, then spun.

'Chris!' he called. Then again, more desperate, more broken: 'Chris!'

'Jai, wait!' Tess managed. She swallowed with a dry throat and tried to think over her own shock and the sound Riley was making. Couldn't. 'Make her stop,' she said, pressing her fingers to her eyes. 'Riley—stop!' she said louder.

'Hey, babe, come here.' Jai dropped shakily down beside Riley and wrapped his arms around her, speaking to her while she quietened.

'Okay.' Tess heard the wobble of threatening tears in her own voice and cleared her throat. 'We'll look for Chris together but we need to stay within earshot of each other and at least one of us needs to be able to see Jas's tent at all times.'

Jai got to his feet and helped up the now quietly crying Riley. 'Should we get Alex down?' he asked.

Tess tried not to look into Alex's lifeless eyes as she shook her head. Nothing inside her wanted to leave him like this, but she knew they had to. 'We shouldn't touch him. We need to back away and try not to disturb the scene any more than we already have. When the cops get out here they're going to need to go over all this for any evidence. They're going to want to hope there's something here to help them catch whoever did this.'

'You don't think—he didn't do that to himself, did he?' Riley sniffed.

'No. I don't think so,' Tess managed. 'I don't believe in coincidences. Someone's doing this to us. We need to find Chris.'

They searched for an hour, then two.

'It's hopeless!' Riley complained when they gathered near camp. 'He could be anywhere. We could step right over him in some of these places and not see him.'

Tess didn't add she was thinking it was too late anyway. Even if he couldn't reach them, he'd be able to answer their calls, wouldn't he? She looked through the trees to the campsite. 'I want to check on Jasmin,' she finally said. 'She's been alone too long.'

They traipsed quietly back and found Jasmin in much the same condition she'd been in when they'd left. Tess tried to wake her, to get some water into her, but Jas fought the water bottle. Giving up, Tess stepped back out to take a cup of coffee from Riley. 'Thanks.'

'This is not Brock, Tess,' Riley said. 'It's just not. So who is it?'

Jai sucked in a deep breath when Riley's gaze left Tess's to meet his, then released it slowly. The idea it could be Pax wouldn't leave him alone. It was just guilt, he told himself. Why would Pax go after all the other hikers and not him? But … maybe he should tell them anyway. Because keeping the story to himself was eating away at him.

'Do you think Libby and James will be close to Melaleuca by now?' Riley asked Tess.

Jai watched Tess's gaze drift in the direction the couple had taken. Her face had lost all of its colour and tension was written in her frown lines. 'Should be,' she said. 'If …'

If they're alive. It wasn't difficult to interpret her thoughts. He was thinking the same thing. 'We need to widen the search.' He got up and wrestled through his things, pulled out his knife.

'And what, we're going to take Jasmin?' Tess said. 'Whoever this is has already tried to kill her. Do you honestly think he'll hesitate if we leave her completely alone?'

'He only attacks at night. Gutless bastard!' he all but shouted out to the tree line.

'Jai—don't!' Riley pleaded.

'I'm going alone,' he told them more bravely than he felt. 'You stay with Jas.' Then to Tess, he said, 'If Chris was dead, we would have found him.'

'If Chris was alive, he'd be back,' she replied. Her gaze landed on his heavily. 'If he couldn't get back, he'd hear us calling and answer. If he's alive and too far away to hear us, you're not going to find him anyway. Don't go out there alone, Jai. Don't risk it. We can't lose anyone else.'

Riley got to her feet and placed herself in front of him. 'Please don't, Jai.'

He wanted to go. But even if this was Pax, talking to him, promising to give him the ring might not stop him killing him. Then Pax could go after Riley for the ring and Jai couldn't protect her. And if it wasn't Pax? He could be risking his life for nothing when he should be protecting Riley and Tess.

'Okay, fine,' he mumbled, sitting back down. 'So what do we do then? Do we stay? Go?'

'Go?' Riley gasped. 'Libby and James are telling help where we are. They could be just a few hours away.'

'I've been thinking while we were searching,' he said. 'Whatever's going on only started when we reached this place. I don't think we should stay here another night.'

Tess dropped her gaze to the ground, and some of her strength seemed to ebb. 'Even if we wanted to leave, we can't. This next part of the track … it's the most difficult. We can't stretcher Jas over it. And I'm not leaving her. Besides, I'm not so sure it's this particular spot, because I'm not sure Brock went home.'

'What?' Jai and Riley said together.

'I thought you said you didn't think Brock was responsible,' Riley reminded Tess. 'I'm telling you he couldn't do this!'

'I don't know Brock well enough to say. But we need to consider something else. At the same time Jasmin said she feared burning, she also mentioned Brock was scared of drowning.'

They were silent for a moment, then Riley's eyes went wide. 'You think something happened to him too? On the boat? You think he drowned?'

'I don't know.'

'You don't think that old couple could have anything to do with it?' Jai said. He knew he was grasping, blaming a small woman and an older guy with a dodgy arm.

'I don't know!' Tess said again. 'But when Chris joked about not wanting to die of boredom—'

'Alex said something about hanging around. Oh my God.' Jai's stomach sank. Tess was right. 'I remember.' He dragged his hand through his hair. 'Shit!'

'What did I say?' Riley whispered. 'Was it snakes? Spiders? I can't remember what I said!'

'Riley, it doesn't matter,' he told her, hugging her to him.

'Of course it matters! It might be about to matter more than anything. Jai, you said falling.'

'And I agreed,' Tess said quietly.

'Then we stay away from heights,' Jai countered in an attempt to be brave. 'But Chris said boredom. You can't really die from that, right?'

'He's gone. Whatever's been done, it's done,' Tess said, then dragged in a deep breath. 'We need to gather firewood. The driest bits we can find.'

'What?' Riley exploded. 'After what happened to Jas and all your preaching, now you *want* to start a fire? What will it do to Jas to wake up and see flames?'

'I know, okay?' Tess snapped.

'Riley, Tess is doing her best,' Jai said quietly. 'Listen to her.'

Riley nodded and sat, eyes downcast.

'This could be life or death,' Tess said. 'We don't know who and we don't know why but we can't assume one of us won't be next. How will you feel tonight, sitting around in pitch-black darkness not knowing if whoever's responsible for all this is miles away or right behind you?'

'You're right,' Jai said. 'Why would he stop now?'

'Oh, God. We're going to die.' Riley buried her head in her hands while fresh, silent sobs racked her body.

'No, we're not,' he promised her, meaning it. 'I'm not going to let that happen.'

CHAPTER 39

Jared walked into Indy's office to find her chewing on her lip, staring into space. 'Something wrong?'

'I just thought I'd try Tess again. Not being able to contact her is bugging me.'

'You were the one who told me not to panic, remember? We know she was fine yesterday.'

'I know. It's just all that new information about Orvist has me on edge again. We've got to find him.'

'I don't think Finlay's lying about not knowing where Orvist was staying,' he said. He'd gone out to the hospital yesterday, quizzed Tank again, but it had been a waste of time. 'Orvist wouldn't want that sort of information to be general knowledge.'

'I know, but I'll feel better when—hold on, that's Emily,' she said, checking her phone. 'She and Roberts are out at the Wharton property.' She answered and put the call on speaker. 'What's up?'

'We found a receipt screwed up in a plastic bag under Wharton's bathroom sink. It's from the jewellers down the road from the pawn shop. For a six thousand dollar diamond ring.'

'That's an expensive ring,' Indy commented.

'Must have been the engagement ring,' Jared said. 'The group were bubbling on about Riley and Jai getting engaged on the bus trip down to Cockle Creek.'

'For a kid that's supposedly been struggling, he sure seems to have a lot of cash to throw around. Why would he buy something so expensive?'

'Young love?' Jared guessed. 'I spent half the trip down to the drop-off point shaking my head at how eager they were to tie themselves to each other for the rest of their lives.'

'Ah, and on a morning you were fighting with Tess, too.'

'You two had a fight?' Emily asked.

Jared glared briefly at Indy before answering. 'Just a small difference of opinion.' Then it hit him: 'Wrong ring.'

'You had a difference of opinion over a ring?' Emily asked slowly.

'No.' He breathed out a laugh. 'Our impaled guy said Wharton had given them the wrong ring. Do we have a picture of Wilde's ring?'

'We had one of Wilde wearing it blown up that gives us a pretty good impression,' Indy said.

'Great. Em, come back to the station via the jewellery shop. See if you can get a detailed description of the ring Wharton bought.'

'On it.'

Indy ended the call. 'You're suggesting Wharton's ring went to Cochrane's men, and Riley Finlay is wearing Wilde's?'

'It's just a thought.'

Indy swung back in her chair, tapping her pen to her lips thoughtfully. 'Why would he swap them? With what we've learnt, I would have bet Orvist wouldn't have confided that the original ring contained a chip.'

'And it's useless without the phone anyway. Let's think more simply. He might have thought Wilde's was more valuable?'

Indy's face screwed up dismissively. 'Say Riley was on to him—she spent a lot of time at his place, right?'

'From what we can gather, sure.'

'Maybe she found it.'

He considered the implications of that. 'And he couldn't tell her the real reason he had it.'

'Unless she's in on it ...'

'If we assume for a moment she's not, Riley discovering the ring would place Jai in a very difficult predicament.'

'And he would have had to spend whatever it took to get an almost identical ring.'

He nodded thoughtfully. 'Then he's handed that one over, hoping they wouldn't know the difference.'

'Ballsy move.'

'We don't have a better theory at this stage.' He got to his feet and shook his head. 'It just seems so stupid to risk a run-in with Orvist and Cochrane over a piece of jewellery.'

'Like you said—young love.'

He resisted the urge to roll his eyes. 'I guess it's too bad. If he's worked so hard and risked so much to keep her in the dark, the whole thing's about to come crashing down around him. I wonder how he'll explain us waiting with handcuffs as they step off the plane?'

CHAPTER 40

Tess knelt by Jas's side for so long her legs went numb. The delirium had gotten worse through the night and though Jasmin had been restless, muttering and wheezing, she was weaker, senseless. Tess had spoken to her, quietly murmuring anything soothing that came to mind. She'd stayed with her, refusing Jai's offers to take over, and she'd been relieved when, just before dawn, Jas had finally quietened, knowing she desperately needed the relief a deep sleep offered from the intolerable pain. Exhausted, Tess had shifted position, put her head on her bent knees and slept lightly.

She'd been awoken not long later as Jas jerked in her sleep, dragging in a few noisy breaths before the tension seeped out of her again. Tess had gently tucked her back in against the early morning cold, and caught another short nap.

The next time she awoke the sun had risen higher in the sky, and Jas was still. Too still. Her eyes half open in death.

Another death was just too much.

Tess had been unable to do more than remain by Jas's side while grief, anger and fear rendered her helpless, but voices outside were slowly penetrating the shock. They interfered with the loop her mind had been playing in her head since realising Jas was gone: *This can't be happening. How can this possibly be true? How much more can I take?* She wanted to cry but the tears wouldn't come. All she felt was a painful lump, like concrete in her chest. It weighed her down, kept her from functioning, from processing, almost from breathing.

Another sound from outside. A billy being set up for hot water. It dragged her further back to reality. Riley asking for hot chocolate, not coffee. And as reality finally broke through she knew they had to move. Or they were all going to die.

Pins and needles in her legs and feet erupted painfully as her weight shifted. She needed to tell them. That was first. How was she supposed to tell them? Another friend gone, a beautiful young life snuffed out. 'I'm sorry, Jas.' It was a whisper through barely parted lips. 'I'm so sorry.' The tears did come then, a trickle that quickly became a deluge, running down her cheeks and soaking the knees of her pants. She waited until there were no more to shed, then she wiped them away and staggered out of the tent.

At Jai's concerned frown she shook her head. 'She's gone.'

'What? She can't be gone.' Jai lunged over and checked for himself, emerged a moment later, devastation etched onto his features. 'God, no.' His voice cracked. He sat back down, stared into nothing.

'What's going on?' Riley asked, emerging from the tent.

'Jas is gone,' Jai said, pulling at his hair.

'You think she got up?' Riley straightened and turned in a circle. 'I didn't think she could.'

'She didn't get up, Riley,' Tess said flatly. 'She died. Passed away.'

Riley's face dissolved in pain. 'No! She wasn't that bad! She wasn't!' Then, 'Do you think he came back, killed her?'

'No. I was with her. No one got to her.' *At least, not again.*

'But they were just burns! Painful and infected, but how could she die? How?'

'Shock? Sepsis? Organ failure? Something else? I don't know enough to give you the right answer. I'm sorry.'

Jai and Riley held each other, heartbroken and scared. Tess walked away. Anger and bone-deep sorrow had already emptied her from the inside out. She'd never felt so helpless, so alone. So tired. But the others were looking at her to lead them, to stay in control. Was she still capable of it?

She walked aimlessly towards the river. She wanted to scream, to yell, to hit something. Fedder, the gunmen, Aaron, now this? It was too much. She couldn't handle anything else. She wanted to crawl into a ball on the ground and be swallowed up by oblivion. As she thought it, she stared into the water and her eyes were drawn to a smeared imprint in the mud by the water's edge. A boot print. Her eyes swung further around. There was another behind it. Her sense of survival once again kicked in.

'Jai!'

He appeared at a run, Riley at his heels. 'What? Are you okay?' he asked, his red eyes darting around, scanning for danger.

'Is this yours?' She pointed to the heavy print.

Jai didn't answer, just stepped beside it. When he lifted his foot, the mark his boot left was smaller, different patterns cut into the muddy surface.

'It's him,' Riley whispered. 'The killer, he's—God, that's him. It's actually him! He was here. He was—'

'Watching us through the night,' Tess said. An icy trickle of apprehension slid up her spine and adrenaline snatched away the fog of grief. She welcomed it. She needed it. Now was not the time for self-pity.

Libby and James were expecting them to be here when they returned with help. *If* they returned with help. She didn't want to think that terrible thought, the one where Libby and James might not have made it, but she had to be practical. She wasn't spending another night out here hoping for the best. She couldn't wait around for whoever was doing this to make his next move.

'Okay, that's it. Pack up.'

'Agreed,' Jai said with relief.

'We're just going to leave her? What about Chris? We can't!' Riley cried.

'They're dead, Riley!' Tess snapped.

'No. You don't know Chris is dead! You're just scared.'

'Even if he is alive, we don't know where to look,' Jai said quietly. 'We need to get help. We need to stay alive and get teams of people out here to find him. Come on, Riley, you need to pack up your stuff. Now.'

Instead, Riley sank to the ground. 'What's the point?' She glared at Tess. 'If you really believed Libby and James were getting help you'd stay put. You reckon they're dead too, don't you? I think—'

'Stop it,' Tess ordered as firmly as she could manage. 'Stop falling to the ground in a heap, stop whining and crying and giving up! You don't have to think, you just have to follow instructions. When all this is over you can fall apart, but you don't get to do that yet. Now get up!' She bit down on the tremble in her voice and stalked back to camp to pack up.

They walked out of camp like a funeral procession, each one looking back more than once, but as soon as the campsite and Jasmin's tent were out of sight, Tess forced every thought from her mind except what had to happen next and spurred them on. 'We're going to move as fast as we can. When we come across water we'll fill up, keep going. We'll camp when it gets dark, wherever we happen to be. It's not going to be easy. Pick up the pace.'

They headed off through coastal forest, trekked down into a muddy gully and waded through a wide creek before beginning a long and difficult ascent up the Ironbound Range. The rainforest was thick with mud and vegetation. They walked, climbed and crawled for kilometres up a near-vertical trail riddled with tree roots, deep mud holes, jutting rocks and clinging vines.

Tess looked around often but saw no one. Were they being followed? She had to assume they were. The footprint kept reappearing in her head. Someone bigger than Jai, heavier. The tread of the boot was one she'd seen many times before, like the ones Aaron always wore. Or did they all look like that? Jai's hadn't. She should have taken a photo of the print for the police. She wasn't thinking logically, but one thought struck home. *There are always consequences for our actions, Tess.* Aaron's words. Taunting her.

Aaron. He was the last person she wanted to be thinking about right now. The photo of her and Jared and the gun barrel flashed into her mind. *Jared's case, Jared's bad guy.* There'd been other photos that had had nothing to do with her. Aaron's threatening behaviour on the side of the road after her breakdown still gave her the creeps, but Indy had decided after looking at the car that the radiator crack could have occurred for a number of different reasons; there was no way to pin it on Aaron. Besides, he might have been acting like he'd lost the plot, but he wasn't some sort of mass murderer. Was he? No, of course not. Her mind was wandering too much. She needed to stay alert.

When they finally broke through to the grassy heights of the Ironbound Ranges, it was to buffeting gales that pushed and pummelled, knocking them from the track more than once and making progress slow, close to impossible at times.

'Take a break!' Tess shouted over the thundering winds. Beneath them the coast stretched out to show off magnificent views, but what caught Tess's attention was the weather coming in off the ocean. It looked like hell was about to descend upon them. She took a thorough look around. The vegetation was low here, the track exposed. No one was close by.

'I can't keep going,' Riley said, puffing heavily. 'I feel like I'm going to get blown right off the mountain! How much further is it?'

'You've gotten through the worst of it. Rest for a minute.'

They sat and drank from their water bottles, caught up in the wilderness around them and the urgency of escaping it.

'How are we going for time?' Jai asked.

'We've knocked a couple of hours off what the guidebook says,' she said with a tight smile.

'What are those mountains?' he asked, pointing north.

She followed his gaze to the outline of jagged, ancient mountains, where one peak in particular dominated the skyline. 'The Western Arthur Range and Federation Peak.'

'Federation Peak. It's incredible. That's where you …'

'Yeah. That's it,' she finished for him.

He looked at the sky. 'The wind sounds like jet planes flying over us. It's so loud!'

'It's the roaring forties. Grown men with full packs have been picked up and flung off the track. We should start heading down. Are you okay, Riley? Can we get moving?'

'Yep.' Riley got to her feet, had some trouble lifting her pack back onto her shoulders but she managed.

'We're going downhill,' Tess told her. 'It's steep. Most of the nine hundred metre descent is done in about five k's. Use your hiking poles to steady you against the worst of the wind. Hopefully we can beat the weather and the darkness to Louisa River.' She looked all around them as far as she could see. 'And keep an eye out for anyone who might be coming behind us.'

'Goes without saying.' Jai pressed his lips into a thin line and looked back down the track as far as he could see. 'Stay in the middle, Riley. Let's go.'

CHAPTER 41

Jared stood with Indy at the reception desk of the fifth caravan park they'd visited that morning, while yet another park manager denied having anyone by the name of Paxton Orvist renting accommodation. He wasn't surprised. Orvist would have to be an idiot to use his real name.

'He may have used an alias,' Indy said, slipping Orvist's photo across the desk. 'This is the man we're looking for.'

The manager, who, according to his gold name badge, was Matthew, squinted at the picture and shook his head. 'No, can't say I've seen anyone like that.'

Jared's phone rang so he stepped outside and answered. 'Denham.'

'Any luck?' Emily asked.

'Not yet. We've got two more after this to check. What's up?'

'I'm sending you something,' she said, and a moment later the ping came through on his phone. 'The first picture is Madison Wilde's ring, the second is the design Wharton bought from the jewellery shop. They're similar but there are notable differences, right?'

Jared looked at the photos closely. 'Yeah, hard to tell though,' he said.

'Right, now I'm sending a screenshot of an Instagram post I found. It's on Riley's account.'

He saw a photo of the group of hikers, Riley holding up her left hand to show off the ring. Underneath was the caption: *Crappy weather, a backwards trip and, oh yeah—I'm engaged! Wish us luck.* Riley had set the location as South Coast Track.

'Now in blown up form …'

Another photo came through.

'This is the ring Riley Finlay was wearing at the start of their trip.'

'Riley's wearing Madison's ring,' he said.

A teenager with a halo of blonde curls and a sunny smile stepped around him and into the office.

'Yeah,' Emily said. 'And I thought I should let you know straight away because she's told everyone where they're going, when and in what direction.'

'Good call. I'll let Indy know and—' His attention was drawn to the door when Indy strode out, lips pressed together, eyes alerting him something was up. 'Em, I'll call you back. Thanks.'

'The girl who just came in works for the manager. Said she thinks she knows Orvist. He checked in as John Smith. This is his second stay. Paid in cash. Van forty-two at the far end of the park. Said that other than at check-in, she hasn't seen him.'

'Let's go take a look.'

'Jared, this guy's not going to come quietly. We should call for backup.'

'He might not even be there. Em just called. Riley is definitely wearing Madison Wilde's ring and she's posted it and all the details of their hike on Instagram. If he's not here, he could well be there. How much time do we want to waste?'

Indy considered that, her cheeks puffing as she blew out a breath. 'All right, but we let Em know to get everyone on alert. Then we'll check it out. If he's in there, we do this properly. If not, we'll put it under surveillance while we go find Tess.'

'We're going out there,' he said with relief.

'If there's a chance he's on the track, we need to be out there too. Let's just hope he's home.'

The caravan was tucked away in a bushy corner of the park, away from the pretty waterfront cabins and larger, more modern, accommodation options. There didn't seem to be anyone in the surrounding vans and Jared guessed most would be out and about enjoying the sunshine and nearby towns at this time of day. Because the curtains to Orvist's van were closed, he took the chance of getting up close for a better look, while Indy kept an eye on the road. He tried to see inside. He could hear something—a television or a radio—but couldn't see in. He crept around the front. A crack in the curtains there had him cautiously peeking inside. He looked past a sink and cabinets to a bench seat that divided the tiny kitchen from the rest of the van. On the wall behind it was a television. Just over the top of the seat he could see the back of a head, reclining, feet up on the table in front of him. Orvist. A half-empty stubby of Tooheys Extra Dry sat next to his boot.

Heart pounding, wanting nothing more than to burst in, Jared reluctantly made his way back to Indy, waiting behind the next van.

'He's in there. Watching the bloody football with his feet up. Indy, we can take him.'

But Indy was shaking her head, phone already in hand.

At least he wasn't out in the wilderness chasing after Tess and her group, Jared thought as he tapped his foot, waiting impatiently for the rest of the cops to arrive. His vest was on, his hand resting lightly over his gun, his eyes trained on the door. He tried to will Orvist to come out, to show his face. To get this done. But he knew the guy wasn't going to. He wouldn't wander around out here in the daytime when people might see and recognise him. He was good at going to ground. At hiding. But not good enough.

Armed police came in stealthily, surrounding the van in various sheltered positions and waiting for further instructions. Jared got the nod from Indy and they approached the door. He knocked. He didn't announce he was police, knew that was sure to end in a gunfight or some other disaster. He wanted to catch Orvist off guard, if possible, have him down on the floor before he had a chance to react.

When there was no answer he knocked again. Nothing. 'Any movement inside?' he asked quietly over the radio.

'None,' came the reply.

That was odd. Orvist might have been suspicious but he should have got up, should have wanted to check. He stood back from the door anyway, just in case, and quietly tried the handle.

The door exploded with the crack of a gunshot, and something whizzed past his face, sending him tumbling back to the ground with Indy. Shots erupted around them, along with shouting and the movement of police towards the van. The door swung open and Jared saw the barrel of a shotgun aimed in their direction. He was about to drag Indy back again when he noted it wasn't held by Orvist, but had been rigged to the doorhandle.

Police swarmed into the van, shouting orders and warnings. Jared leapt to his feet.

'Detective?' an officer said as he stepped up into the entry. Two other officers moved out of the way to give Jared a look at what they'd found. Indy came in behind him. He heard the oath under her breath and followed it up with one of his own.

CHAPTER 42

The river came into view just on dusk as the first spots of rain began to fall. Tess found a sheltered spot, dropped her pack and rolled her shoulders, watching the tannin-stained river running fast and wild.

'Do you think we should cross it before this next lot of rain hits?' Jai asked.

Leaves spun and dipped in the water. On a regular hike she would have waited it out. But there was another, more serious threat to worry about and the closer they got to Melaleuca, the more desperate she became to get them there. She was doing her best to keep her own fear in check, but it was eating away at her, affecting her thoughts, her decisions.

'It's higher than I'd like but if that storm out to sea hits it's going to get worse. So yeah, I do. We've got maybe an hour of light left but how much further we get will depend on the weather and how much more you can take,' she said. She was fit and used to long treks, but bone-deep tired. She could only imagine how they were feeling.

'Riley?' Jai asked.

Riley looked exhausted: she was pale, her features drawn. 'Sure,' she said, earning a big dose of respect from Tess. 'Let's keep going.'

'Undo your packs and use the rope to steady yourselves. You know how this works by now. See those dead trees tangled up in the shallows against the other bank? Be careful getting over them. You don't want to trip and go for a swim. I'll go first, just in case.'

She took hold of the rope slung between the two banks of the river and edged carefully into the water. The speed of the flow together with the high water level gave it a good tow but they wrestled their way across its freezing expanse.

At the far end Tess stepped between two large logs, got caught on another submerged branch and tripped and fell forward. Water and mud soaked into her clothes as she crashed into the rocky bottom.

'Tess!' Riley said from behind her. 'Are you okay?'

She struggled against the pull of whatever she'd gotten caught up in, couldn't quite get her feet under her. Something was in the way. Jai stepped around Riley and offered his hand. She accepted it.

As she pulled her leg free, a long, pale arm and limp hand emerged with it to stick out of the water as though waving.

Riley screamed and Tess felt her own lock in her throat.

'Libby!' Jai gasped, staring down into the stirred-up water. 'It's Libby!'

'She said she didn't care how she died.' A man stepped out from a cluster of trees just ahead of them. He was huge, and dressed in camouflauge gear like a soldier. He wore a large knife on one hip, a handgun dangled from his right hand. 'As long as they were together forever, right? Now they are. You'll fall over him once ya step over her.'

'Pax?' Riley whispered in confused terror. 'What?'

Tess backed away, shocked into silence. This was the guy who'd been killing them and Riley knew him? Libby's arm disappeared back into the water. *He must have gone straight after them. They never stood a chance.*

'Hi, Riley, ya mean ya boyfriend didn't fill ya in?' The man Riley called Pax looked at Jai, amused. 'Thought you were smarter than that, pencil dick. Who'd ya think it was?'

'Why not just come after me then?' Jai demanded. 'What have you done with Chris?'

'Chris? Oh, boredom guy. Right.' Pax's face turned nasty. 'That was a tough one. Had a bit of an accident. Broke his legs. Then of course he had nothing to do but sit around waiting to die. That's as boring as it gets. Didn't take long though. Ya know how fast shock and exposure can kill a person out here.' He pointed his gun at them. 'But enough chit-chat. I want the ring.'

'I ...' Jai staggered back a few steps to where Riley was still clinging to the rope mid crossing. 'Riley, give me your ring.'

'What?' Riley looked at it. 'I—I don't want to let go of the rope. I don't understand.'

'He wants the ring. Give it to him. I'll get you another one.'

'You killed all these people for a ring?' Riley asked. 'Pax, what's wrong with you?'

'That's a twelve million dollar ring, sweetheart. The boss would like it back.'

'It's not, it's—twelve million?' Riley gasped.

Tess's mind was spinning. *Well, it wasn't Aaron.* The stupid thought struck her as she attempted to process what was going on. The man in front of them had murdered everyone for Riley's ring. Did this have something to do with Jared's case? Was this the guy who'd sent Jared those pictures?

'Now!' Pax shouted when Riley continued to stare, shocked into immobility.

'Okay. Okay.' Riley shuffled around in the water, braced herself against the current and let go of the rope to pull the ring from her finger.

All the guy wanted was the ring. The initial relief he might take it and leave didn't last more than a few seconds as more questions formed in Tess's mind. Why not bail them up earlier and demand it? Why kill everyone off one by one, leaving them until last?

'Right, pass it along,' Pax ordered.

If he really thought he needed to get the others out of the way before taking back the ring, why not just shoot them? Why put them through what he'd put them through, like some kind of sick game? She looked at his face. He had cold, empty eyes, his finger twitching on the trigger of the gun.

'Tess.' Jai was attempting to give her the ring.

Was a man who did all those unspeakable things really just going to let them go? Sick panic clawed at Tess. Why would he? He wasn't going to stop until they were all dead. But what could she do? She stared at the gun and her mind went blank, just as it had in Tank's shop. This time, Jared wasn't here to step between her and a bullet. This time, she had to do something. She had to think. She opened her free hand to take the ring, but fumbled as it touched her palm, almost dropped it. Her heart stopped until she managed to wrap her hand around the ring. If it fell in the river there'd be no finding it.

If it fell in the river there'd be no finding it. All Pax cared about was the ring. An idea came to her. It was a desperate one, and defying this guy terrified her, but what other choice was left?

'Pass it up to me,' Pax said.

Tess nodded but spoke to Riley and Jai before moving. 'Back up, you two.'

'Give it to me!' Pax ordered, leaning over the edge of the water.

'In a minute.'

'Ya want to end up as debris too, bitch?' Pax spat. 'Just fuck me around.'

Tess held the ring out over the water with a trembling hand as she used the rope to help her move back. 'I couldn't care less about the ring,' she said, voice unsteady. 'It's yours. But I'll be leaving it on the other side. You follow us in, or shoot at them or me, and I'll drop it in this very fast flowing, very dark river. It could end up anywhere. You'll never find it.'

'Ya stupid cow!' Pax snarled. 'Ya want to live, you'll give me that fucking ring!'

'I might have believed that if you hadn't already killed our friends. You want this ring, you stay there until we're across. Then you'll get it.'

Pax's gaze moved to Jai and Riley, returned to her. 'Off you go then,' he said. 'I'll catch up with ya later. Hurry up, I'm coming. And if ya do drop that ring, I'll shoot ya before ya reach the other side.'

He had her. She hadn't thought this through. She glanced across the river. Jai and Riley were nearly at the bank, but it was going to be a sprint to try and get far enough away from Pax before he could fire. Impossible for her. Her rope hand brushed the hiking pole sticking out of the top of her pack. It wasn't much of a weapon but …

Pax stepped over some debris and sank to his knee, taking his eyes off her for a second, maybe two, to look where to put his foot next. She used those seconds to slide the pole from her pack, smacking it as hard as she could against the fingers holding the gun. It connected with a loud crack.

'Fuck!' Pax's hand convulsed and the gun fell from his grasp with a splash.

Her heart leapt wildly in her chest. This was it. 'Go!' she ordered the others. As she dragged herself the rest of the way through the water, she expected to be caught or shot at any second. When she wasn't, she ran with them.

CHAPTER 43

'There are way too many dead bodies associated with this guy! Where the hell is he?' Indy marched through the doors of the police station just ahead of Jared. 'I hope everyone's ready for this meeting because I need boots on the ground in the Southwest National Park *now*.' Indy was fuming but under it, she was as bone-deep scared as Jared was for Tess and her hiking group. He caught up enough to open the meeting room door for her, but stayed silent. Along with the dead Mr Booth from caravan forty-one, they'd discovered receipts and sales tags in Orvist's van for camping equipment, non-perishable foods and a pair of Nikon Monarch binoculars.

Inside the meeting room, cops were mingling, some sitting in small groups with coffees, others staring at the board of photos and evidence, deep in conversation or silent and thoughtful. They all quietened and took seats or stood behind their colleagues as Jared and Indy entered.

'Thanks for being so prompt,' Indy said. 'Where's Emily?'

As she spoke, Emily rushed in behind them. She smiled apologetically as she caught her breath. 'I'm sorry, but Kit from National Parks just called. She and another ranger went out earlier to recover the boat Tess found on the lagoon.'

Jared's stomach clenched. He was waiting for bad news. Emily's face gave it away. 'And?' he asked.

'They found a backpack in the boat, so they did a search. They found a body.'

There was a moment when he didn't want to ask, didn't want to know who it belonged to. But the colour had drained from Indy's face. She didn't ask either.

'Who?' he finally said.

'The body belongs to a male, probably early twenties.' Emily showed them an image on her phone of a victim that had been in the water.

'It's Brock Hodgkins,' Jared said, recognising him.

'Poor kid.' Indy sat, rubbing her eyes. 'Murdered?'

'Kit said it looks like a drowning, but the victim has bruising to his upper torso that could suggest a struggle of some kind. They want to know what to do. They're … worried about animals disturbing the body.'

'Ask them to cover him if they can, but don't intrude on the scene any more than necessary,' Indy said.

'Will do.'

'And do we know if anyone has located the couple he started back with?'

'I'll find out,' Emily said, and disappeared again.

Indy stared at Jared for a moment, though he thought it might have been more *through* than *at*, as though she were preparing herself for battle. Then she straightened, her face all business.

'Right,' she said sharply and pushed back to her feet. 'Paxton Orvist. The sick bastard knows where Tess and her hiking group are, has the survival training to exist in the national park, kills for the hell of it and is after a ring Riley Finlay has on her finger. We now have a dead hiker and I'm going to assume there's a strong likelihood his death is the result of Orvist's work. Finally, Tess believes Hodgkins went home and we have no way of warning her or her remaining group what they're up against. We need to get out there and attack this area from every possible angle. First priority is bringing Tess and the others back safely, but we don't want Orvist slipping through our fingers out there, either.'

'We're not going to be able to fly out there tonight,' Roberts said. 'It's already too late. We can't search until first light, anyway. But I've begun coordinating with Search and Rescue on the best way to tackle this. We don't want civilians on the ground but the chopper pilots will take groups of us out and drop us at strategic locations along the track and the surrounding areas. Other teams can go in by boat. Aaron and Craig are on their way in to talk to us.'

Though Jared grated at the mention of Aaron's name, now wasn't the time for grudges. Hell, if the guy helped save Tess's life, he'd happily shake his hand.

'Okay,' Indy said. 'Let's make this happen.'

'Are you okay?' he asked her as the preparation began in earnest.

She nodded. 'Yeah. But … God, Jared, I feel sick. If this bastard—'

'We'll get them,' he replied as confidently as he could manage over his own churning dread. 'We'll find Tess and the others, and we'll get Orvist. I'm on the first chopper out there tomorrow and I'm not coming back until we do.'

CHAPTER 44

Jai crouched low in the trees with Tess and Riley and waited, watching. Darkness was falling quickly and the rain was doing its best to soak them through their raincoats. It was freezing, and he noted Tess was shivering badly, no doubt colder than he and Riley put together as a result of her earlier fall in the river. Sitting so still, too afraid to leave their hiding spot, wasn't good for keeping warm, either.

For as long as he lived he'd never forgive himself for this. If he survived.

Tess lifted a hand and, following her gaze he spotted movement: a slow, silent stalking. Pax. And he'd found his gun. *Would it even work?* Jai wondered desperately. He put a warning hand on Riley, hoped his expression read *Don't move. Don't breathe.*

Pax continued past them, stopping every few metres, waiting for what seemed like an eternity, before moving off again.

They kept still for another ten minutes, none of them trusting Pax not to double back, to be waiting just out of sight. Then, limbs cramping painfully from inactivity and cold, Jai slowly stood to peer into the fading light. Tess and Riley rose beside him.

'We need to get back to the rainforest on the other side of the Ironbound Range,' Tess said, her voice barely audible. 'And we need to do it in the dark. There's no cover up there.'

Jai couldn't bear keeping still, waiting to be found. He'd rather move. 'Okay.'

'Can't we just stay here?' Riley whispered, eyes desperate. 'Or keep going towards Melaleuca?'

Tess shook her head. 'We're sitting ducks—there's not enough forest here to hide in indefinitely and there's too much open ground between here and Melaleuca. Besides, he'll be expecting us to do that.'

'It was scary enough in the daytime, Tess,' Riley whispered desperately. 'I can't do it in the dark. It's too high, too windy. If we fall, we're dead.'

Jai was thinking something similar, but pushed the fear back to something manageable. He knew it was their only choice. He put a hand on Riley's shoulder and squeezed. 'We have to.'

'Keep a look out,' Tess ordered, and with the next gust of wind that rattled the trees hard enough to make some noise, she unzipped her pack. He watched as she quietly shoved food into her pockets, then emptied the contents of her pack onto the ground. 'Give me your sleeping bags and any ready-to-eat food you have,' she said. 'Hurry, but be quiet.'

They loaded up one pack, secured it. 'Now what?' he asked.

'As soon as it's full dark, we walk. Even in almost complete darkness the path stands out from the ground around it, and once we hit the boardwalk, we can use it to guide us. The rest, you're just going to have to trust me.'

'I do,' he said and looked at Riley.

Riley hesitated, then nodded. 'Yeah. Okay.'

★

Jai's legs were jelly, his feet stung viciously from blisters and his head pounded from stress and long periods of heavy concentration as they seemed to trudge forever. He was out of water, too, but he didn't want to bring that up. It had been tough, slow going and they'd been walking or crawling for what felt like the entire night. He shifted the pack and felt a cold chill where it unstuck from his back. He'd been taking turns with Tess to carry it. Riley simply couldn't anymore. They'd had to talk her over a lot of the worst of the terrain, places that had scared him witless. But he was pretty sure they were on the last of the dips across the top of the ranges. He tried not to think too much about how much further Tess intended on taking them, putting one painful foot in front of the other, until she suddenly stopped.

'We're heading back down into the forest,' she whispered. 'I'm going to need to risk turning on the torch. Keep your eyes and ears open, okay?'

They crept under the canopy of the trees and slipped and slid by torchlight just a few metres. To their right, a huge fallen tree lay just off the track and Tess headed for it. 'We'll get behind this thing. Going too far into this sort of terrain in the dark would be suicidal.'

'What we just did was suicidal,' Riley said. 'I think I almost died twice.'

'Hey, at least it stopped raining,' Jai said. 'Are you sure this is good enough?' he asked Tess as he slid over the tree to the far side.

'We can't risk injury going further. I don't think we'll be visible from the track.'

'I feel sick,' Riley said, awkwardly scurrying over the tree. 'Sorry, not trying to complain, just saying I don't think I can go any further anyway.'

'We can't set up a tent, but we'll make up a rough shelter and try and get some rest. Make sure you eat something.'

He was standing close enough to feel the tremors emanating from Tess. 'You're shaking. Are you still wet from the fall?'

'I'll be okay. We're all cold, right?'

He wasn't going to argue. His ears were aching from the wind on the range and he couldn't feel his face or fingers. But he helped rig up a makeshift shelter from a tent fly and was grateful for the relative comfort of his sleeping bag.

'So,' Tess asked once they were settled, 'anyone want to tell me how you two happen to have a—what was it? Twelve million dollar ring?'

'I wouldn't mind an explanation,' Riley said. Her voice was full of anger. He couldn't see much but he knew she was glaring accusingly at him.

'I don't know!' he said. 'I was sure …' Because he didn't know how else to explain, or where to start, he told them all of it: the break-ins, the murders he was tricked into being a part of, how Tank was set up, the drop that went wrong. 'I was so nervous, so worried about getting it done. I must have picked up the wrong box.'

'Jai, what were you thinking?' Tess asked. 'Why didn't you go to the police?'

'I just got caught up,' he said miserably. 'I was trying to get out of it.'

'Good job!' Riley lifted her head to snap.

'I'm sorry!' he said, and heard the crack in his own voice. 'I didn't know what to do. On that—' He took a deep breath. 'Tess, what you did back there was awesome. Thank you. He would have killed us.'

'You have to tell,' Riley said.

'I'll go to prison for murder!'

'It wasn't murder. You might have been holding the gun but Pax shoved the guy at you and it went off accidentally,' Riley said. 'This is Pax's fault.'

'I don't reckon the cops will see it that way.'

'It doesn't matter,' Tess said. 'Not now. All that matters for the time being is staying alive. Someone will come after us, eventually. We need to survive until they do. Get some rest. I'll take first watch.'

Light rain hitting her face woke Tess at first light. She sat up, frozen, almost convulsing with the tremors that racked her body. She'd somehow rolled out from under the shelter and quickly moved herself back under it.

'Morning,' Jai whispered. Riley was curled up against him, sleeping soundly.

'Morning,' Tess replied. She reached for her water bottle, but found it empty.

'Mine's all gone too,' Jai said. 'We should have filled up when we crossed that creek.'

'Hey,' Riley said, stretching and looking around. The thick canopy of twisted trunks revealed little about their location. 'God, it's freezing.'

'Pass me your water bottle,' Tess said. She kicked out of her sleeping bag, rolled it up and put it back in the pack. Then she pulled on her damp shoes. 'Yours too, Jai.'

'Where are you going?'

'Back to that creek at high camp—it's maybe half a kilometre. I won't be long. Pack up ready to move if necessary but don't leave this spot.'

'Got it,' Jai said, taking a muesli bar out of the pack. 'Tess, be careful.'

'Do you think there's a chance he's given up?' Riley asked.

'Twelve million dollars and six dead hikers,' Tess said. 'What do you think?' She looked down at the ring she'd slipped onto her finger so she wouldn't lose it. A twelve million dollar ring? Didn't look very special to her. But it was worth killing for, so she wasn't letting it go.

'We don't know for sure he killed Brock,' Jai said.

Tess pulled a face at him that she hoped told him what she thought of that. 'If something happens, if he finds me, I'm going to scream as loud as I can to alert you. If you hear that scream, you're on your own. You don't come for me. You hide, you wait it out here or somewhere else where you're not too far from open ground so when you hear the Search and Rescue teams fly over—and they *will* come—you can get out fast and flag them down. Okay?'

'Tess …' Riley began.

'Okay?' she asked Jai again.

Jai hesitated, then finally nodded. 'Yeah. Yeah, okay. For Riley. If it was just you and me out here, I wouldn't leave. I'd come to help.'

'Then we'd all die,' she told him. 'Stay safe.'

'Be careful,' Riley begged.

She smiled tightly and moved quietly up the track. There was a long stretch of open ridge between her and the shelter of the light forest directly surrounding the creek. She stood just inside the tree line, listening carefully as she scanned the area for any sign of Pax. Nothing. She crept out, tense, ready at any second to duck for cover. A little further, further again. Then she raced on aching legs, ate up the ground as quickly as she could and fell down into the scrub by the creek, breathing heavily.

She filled the water bottles then crept back through the trees, unable to resist looking around, checking for any sign they'd been followed. When she couldn't find one, she began the trip back, almost fell over the pack hidden in the leaf litter. Her pulse jumped. She spun around, around again. She waited, every sense hyper-alert. But she couldn't see anyone. Where was Pax?

She picked up his pack, took it back to the creek and quietly slipped it in. It would give away that she'd been here, but no food, no clothes, no warmth or shelter would have to make a big impact on how long he could survive out here, hunting them.

A piercing scream had her jolting upright and running for their camp. Every sense on alert, she approached the trees, skidding to a halt.

Pax had Riley and Jai bailed up by the tree.

'I'm not going to ask ya again! Where'd she go?' he demanded.

'She's gone for help,' Jai said. 'Left us here and kept going.'

'Fuck!' Pax yelled, clutching at his head. Then he thrust the gun at Jai's head. 'This is your fault! They're all dead because of you, got it?'

'It's not his fault, it's yours!' Riley yelled through streaming tears, clinging to Jai and shaking so hard she could barely stand.

'I didn't take the damn ring on purpose!' Jai said. 'What would I do with it?'

'Ya fucked me over!' Pax said. 'That's what ya did—you and Tank. Didn't think you'd have the balls, but there ya go. You were going to sell it back to Bryce, weren't ya? Get me knocked off?'

'He didn't know!' Riley cried. 'He meant to give you the right one.'

'Oh, well,' Pax said wryly, 'guess it was just one big misunderstanding then.' His voice rose sharply. 'I don't care! Do ya think Cochrane gives a fuck? I need the ring or I'm dead. I don't have time for this. Gotta catch up to Tess.' He swung the gun at Riley.

'No, Pax, please!' Jai launched himself at Pax and they both went down. The gun went off, startling Tess into action.

As Pax and Jai rolled down the hillside, crashing through scrub, Tess scrambled down to Riley and grabbed her, dragged her back. 'Let's go. Now!'

'No! Jai!'

'Damn it, Riley—stop!' she said when Riley shook herself free. She went after her and found Pax standing over Jai. Jai wasn't moving. Blood from a nasty gash to his temple was trickling down his face.

Pax looked up and lifted the gun. 'Enough games. Hand it over.'

Tess took the ring off her finger. 'You take those bullets out and toss them, and I'll hand it over.'

He shook his head. 'Ya think you're in charge? Yeah? Okay, how about this?' He kicked Jai hard in the ribs. Jai moaned, rolled. 'I don't have to kill him straight away. How much he hurts is up to you.'

'I'd rather him hurt than dead.'

'Great. I can draw this out forever.' He kicked Jai again, this time in the face. Blood poured from his nose. As Jai rolled again, he went over the small ledge. Riley raced past Pax to reach him, but was snagged and dragged to Pax's side, the gun to her head.

'You walk over here right now and hand me that ring.'

'I'm sorry, Tess.' Riley sniffed. 'He's gonna shoot me anyway. Run, Tess. Just go!'

The distinctive thud of helicopter blades broke her concentration. A helicopter flying that low had to be searching. Relief hit her even as she wondered if rescue was about to arrive too late. She needed to stall him.

'Hear that?' she asked Pax. 'The cops are here. We're right in the location they'd expect us to be today and they're going to search it thoroughly. Even if I hand this ring over to you now, you're not going to get away. I'm Search and Rescue, I know how this works, so I'll tell you. They'll have coordinated teams on foot checking from the ground while the chopper keeps an eye out from the air. You're already surrounded. If you want to have any hope of escaping, you need to run. Now.' She had to hope it was true, wasn't sure, but he seemed to be paying attention. She put the ring in her hand and took up a throwing position. 'Let her go. Put the gun down and back up. When she's out of range, I'll toss it to you.'

'Bullshit ya will! Why should I believe ya?'

'There's no time to argue, Pax! Hurry up!'

Pax growled and dropped the gun, shoving Riley forward. 'Now give it to me!'

Riley ran towards her. 'Get up the hill,' Tess told her. 'Get the chopper's attention.'

She threw the ring past Pax and ran. The incline was brutal on her already exhausted muscles but she kept going. Riley tripped and Tess helped her up and pushed her ahead.

She felt the jerk of her jacket as she was caught from behind.

CHAPTER 45

Jared's stomach flipped and dived as the chopper jostled and jolted in the bad weather. Beneath them was an endless landscape of grassy hills and plains made dreary by a leaden sky and wet, foggy conditions. A snaking white line of track devoid of travellers cut through the uninviting terrain.

'We would have spotted them by now if they were on any of the exposed areas of the track,' Aaron said.

'What do you want to do, detective?' the pilot asked.

He should fly back, assist with search coordination. He didn't want to. They had emergency supplies and enough gear to last them a night or two in the wilderness should it be necessary. He intended on using them. 'I need to know where we might have missed them if the hike is still going to plan, and where they're most likely to be hiding if it hasn't,' he said to the man who'd done little since they'd gotten into the chopper other than make his dislike of Jared as clear as possible.

'I still think they're somewhere in this area,' Aaron answered. 'Louisa Creek, Louisa River and Little Deadman's Bay all contain campsites in sheltered, forested areas, but at this time of day I wouldn't expect Tess to be there. They should be on the track.'

'And if they're hiding?'

'Unless they've made it further than I think and bunked down in one of the pockets of cover around Red Point Hills, I'm guessing they'll be somewhere back in that really dense forest on the other side of the Ironbound Range where it tracks up from Little Deadman's Bay. If I were Tess, I'd be there.'

'Should we fly back over them?' Emily asked.

'Those more heavily forested areas were covered in fog on the way in,' Jared reminded her. 'There's no point.'

'May as well go home and put our feet up then.' Aaron's voice dripped with sarcasm.

'I wish *you* would,' Emily barked.

Jared ignored Aaron. His temper was building by the minute. If he let loose even a bit, the guy was destined to end up a bloody mess on the chopper floor. Aaron had already put Tess through enough before he'd landed her in this situation out of spite. If he hadn't been so good at his job, Jared would never have allowed him on the chopper.

'My point is,' Jared said, 'we need to get in there. Is there somewhere in that area we can land?' he asked the pilot.

'I can't land anywhere here on top of the range, not in this weather, but I can probably set you down just above Little Deadman's Bay.'

'Great. We'll check out the campsite, head up into the covered area of track Aaron's talking about from there.'

'Then I'll have to take the chopper back, refuel and pick you up later.'

'You sure you want to leave the chopper?' Aaron asked. 'If they have gone off track, we could be in the wrong place entirely. They could be lost, or severely held up. Tess knows better than to bush-bash out here.'

'It's highly likely Orvist, a man who spent time in the army and has the skills to navigate and survive out here, has come after them. I'm telling *you*, if Tess is running from this guy, she wouldn't be stupid enough to wander around in plain sight.'

'So what if they haven't made it this far?' Emily asked.

'We've got a team heading in from the Lagoon Crossing,' Jared reminded her. 'They'll let us know.' In the distance he saw the other helicopter carrying Indy, Emily and Craig. Tess had to have spotted it or at least heard the activity by now. If Orvist was anywhere in their vicinity, he'd be on alert, too. 'They've got to be out here somewhere.'

'Unless she's already dead,' Aaron said bitterly, 'because you couldn't do your job properly and catch the bastard.'

Jared had been carefully keeping that thought pushed to the back of his mind since this began. 'Let's not forget why she's out here,' he couldn't help but say. 'We should have been looking for you.'

The chopper landed and Jared jumped out first, then helped Emily out. When Aaron followed, the chopper took off again and suddenly it was just the three of them in the vast spread of wilderness. The slash of stunningly cold wind cut through Jared's jacket and stung his face. It wasn't raining, but the atmosphere was damp and heavy. He adjusted his pack on his shoulders and looked through a smattering of trees to the choppy silver water of the coastline, then back around to the heavy blanket of rainforest heading up to what he knew was the exposed track over the peaks of the Ironbound Range. He suddenly felt too small, missing the chopper's height and speed. The enormity of the task frightened him. His priority was Tess. She *had* to be alive. If they could catch Orvist out here, that was a plus, but the sheer scope and size of the area was overwhelming. If someone didn't want to be caught out here it would be damn near impossible to find them.

'So where's the campsite?' he asked Aaron.

In response, Aaron turned and began walking.

Jared exchanged glances with Emily, who pulled a face at Aaron's back and followed.

They walked in silence to the campsite. As it came into view, an orange tent stood out against the grey and green and Jared felt hope leap in his chest. 'Tess?' he called, picking up his pace, almost racing Aaron and Emily to the tent. There was no answer and, he realised, only one tent. He tried again anyway as he approached it.

'Tess?'

'Jared.' Emily put a hand on his arm and for a moment he couldn't understand why she was holding him up. Then he got it. The insects. The sickly smell that meant death. He lunged forward when Aaron stepped back and got the flap open with unsteady fingers. He reeled back. At first he wasn't sure who he was looking at. The ruined face was all he could process. Then he saw hair, patches of it, sticking out of a burned scalp. Blonde.

'It's Jasmin,' he choked. He'd seen plenty of death, but knowing this beautiful young woman had probably died like this at the hands of a monster still caught him in the gut.

'They had a fire over here!' Aaron called out. 'Tess knows better!'

'I'm not sure it was Tess,' Jared said, stepping away. 'Jasmin's been badly burned.'

Aaron shrugged. 'Maybe it was an accident. They lit an open fire. She could have fallen into it.'

'Those burns are too severe, even for that. Look—over there. That's the remains of a burnt tent. And do you care? Because it sounds as though you're more upset someone lit a fire!'

Aaron's eyes heated. 'No fire, no dead girl, right? And there's a reason open fires aren't permitted. Imagine how much destruction this one could have caused to the natural environment. There's evidence at the edge of the camp that it got out of control. They've had to chase it.'

All. Morning. All morning Aaron had been an arsehole, but this was too much. Jared's fist curled as he took a step towards him.

'Jared! Over here!' Emily called. The urgency in her voice was the only thing that stopped the punch. He looked in disgust at Aaron, who was tense, expecting it.

'We don't know what happened here. But there's a dead girl over there and if that doesn't upset you, you shouldn't be out here. Don't open your mouth again unless you find Tess. Got it?' He strode away, knowing it was good he hadn't thrown that punch but wishing he had anyway. 'Em?'

'Here.'

'What— Oh hell.'

Emily was standing by a hanging body. Alex.

'We need more people out here,' Emily said, face devoid of colour.

He nodded once, fear for Tess and her remaining group making him nauseous, then he walked away and radioed back to Indy. 'Okay, let's go,' he called to Emily and Aaron once he was done.

'What are we doing?' Emily asked weakly, a hand pressed against her stomach.

'We're going to keep moving. There's only one tent here and all their gear is gone. The rest of them must have walked out.'

'What they've been through … what way would they even have gone? I can't help but see it. See them having to leave their friends like this and …' Emily said with a sob. 'I'm sorry, Jared. I haven't seen anything like this before and—Tess. She's my friend. I mean

I know her, and you two and— Oh God.' She put her hands over her face and tears dripped through her fingers.

'Em.' Jared stepped in and squeezed her arms. 'Hey, I know. It's bad. And I'm sorry. You're so damn good at your job I forget—we all do—that you've never had to deal with a lot of what we throw you into before. This is tough for me too and I've seen a lot more. You can't focus on what's done. You need to put all your energy into the next bit, then the bit after that. Right now I need that big brain of yours focused on finding the ones who are still alive. Okay?'

Emily sniffed and dragged her hands over her eyes. 'Sorry.' Then she took a deep breath. 'I'm okay. I just couldn't hold that in.' She took a couple more of those long, ragged breaths then forced a smile onto her face. 'I can do that. Sorry.'

'Don't be.'

'Are we just about ready to go, then?' Aaron asked.

Emily's teary eyes moved past Jared to where Aaron was standing and hardened. 'Jared, can I shoot him? It would really make me feel better.'

He saw the attempt at humour for what it was—an effort to get back to normal—and gave her arm one last squeeze. 'Come on, let's get going.' As much as he wanted to make her feel better, there was a very real urgency tearing at him to find Tess.

There were plenty of trees and lots of mud, and a creek crossing left him soaked to the knees. But those first few kilometres were nothing on the joke of a mountainside they began climbing after that.

'Is this even a track?' he asked Aaron, lifting himself up over a tangle of tree roots interspersed with deep mud holes, only to crawl under a fallen tree and get tangled in some sort of unusual vine.

'It's *the* track,' Aaron replied. 'You want to wuss out? Go back down. Wait for the chopper. I'll find Tess.'

'You right, Emily?' Jared asked, ignoring Aaron and giving her a hand up a steep rocky slope.

'I say we stick him in a tree hollow,' she muttered, then, as she went down to mid-calf in a mud puddle, 'or drop him down a hole.'

'I thought you wanted to shoot him.'

'Shoot him first, then hide him. I bet no one would ever find him.'

'You're probably right.'

It was rough going, frustratingly slow. Every second felt like a minute, every minute an hour. His leg slipped down the side of a large rock, jarred him painfully. He swore, resettled the gun in his hand and pushed off again. He was a lather of sweat by the time he spotted a clearing through the last of the heavy forest. He pushed on, hoping for a better look around. At least the wind seemed to have died down. A blur of movement to his right had his head spinning, gun forward.

Riley, he noted with relief, and dropped the gun.

She rushed over. 'Pax,' she puffed. 'Got Tess.'

The fear came back, sharp and fast. 'Where?'

'Down there, on the track looking for the ring.'

'I just came up there, Riley. They weren't there.'

Riley began sobbing, shaking her head. 'Tess threw the ring and we ran but I tripped and he grabbed her. I kept running. We'd heard a helicopter and she'd said to flag it down, so I came out here. I don't know where they went.'

He could hear it too. Indy was close. 'Where's everyone else?'

'They're all dead, except Jai. I don't know where Jai is, either. Pax hurt him. He has a gun.'

'Okay, all right.'

'Riley!' Emily came into view, Aaron on her heels.

'Em, calm her down. Pax has Tess. I'm going after them. Aaron, this guy is armed. You should stay with Emily and Riley until backup arrives.'

Aaron shoved him, hard. 'Tess is not yours!'

The stupidity of it stunned him. Disgusted, Jared shook his head. 'Do what you like. I just don't need another victim.'

A gunshot had them ducking. 'Emily, stay—' As he turned around to talk to her he saw her shocked expression, saw her drop to the ground.

'No!' The helicopter he'd heard appeared up over the range. 'Keep still.'

'Damn it!' Emily said. 'I'm fine. Hit the vest, just—ow!'

Out of the corner of his eye, Jared saw Tess being dragged into the clearing, Pax using her as a shield, his gun at her temple. His heart lurched and he straightened, fought to keep the anger that ripped through him under enough control to think clearly.

'I'm getting out of here!' Pax yelled over the noise of the chopper. 'She's coming with me. Get that helicopter on the ground!'

The chopper was hovering, dancing from side to side in the wind. Aaron was staring at Tess as though in a daze.

'Aaron! Get down!' Jared ordered. 'Aaron!'

'Tess?' Aaron called out. 'It's okay, Tess. I'm going to help.'

Pax took the gun off her temple long enough to point it at Aaron and fire a shot. Aaron crashed to the ground, avoiding the bullet. 'I want that chopper down!' Pax demanded.

Jared risked another glance over his shoulder, saw Indy's gun was trained on Pax but knew she wouldn't take the shot. It was too risky. The chopper was rocking badly and Tess was too close. He got on the radio to talk to them.

'He wants the chopper to land.'

After a moment Roberts replied, 'Indy said to tell him we can't land it.'

Jared thought with the wind so much less intense than earlier they should have been able to, but wasn't going to argue. 'They can't land it, Pax,' he called. 'Let her go. It's over.'

'It's over all right. If I don't get this ring to Cochrane, I'm dead anyway. Got nothing left to lose. What's to stop me taking ya all with me?'

'Cochrane's back in prison, Pax. He's not going to be getting anyone.'

'Nah, he's getting out. He's waiting for me to get him that ring.'

'That's not going to happen. Put it down. Let her go.'

'So ya can put me away for the rest of my life?'

'You've killed a lot of people.'

'Yeah. Yeah, I have. So what's a few more?' He fired again, this time at the helicopter. It pitched violently, rose. Jared's heart stopped as Pax pointed the gun back at Tess's head and sent him a smirk.

Jai, filthy and bloody, appeared behind them and slammed into Pax, sending him sprawling. Jared sprinted the short distance and got a knee in the small of Pax's back, wrestled his arm behind him and jerked it up, hearing the shout as he pushed it just too far.

'Okay?' he asked Tess, quickly looking her over.

She nodded once, arms hugging herself. 'Yeah.'

Riley ran to Jai and threw herself around him. Indy's chopper landed and she charged over as Jared pulled Pax to his feet.

'Ya said ya couldn't land!' Pax spat.

'We lied,' Indy said.

'I shoulda shot the lot of ya!'

'Have you read Mr Orvist his rights?' Indy asked Jared.

'Forgot,' he said, already looking for Tess.

'We'll take care of that for you,' she said, and handed Orvist over to the other officers. 'Emily?'

'Just bruised,' he said, and turned to see Aaron step back from Emily as she got to her feet.

Tess was with them. Aaron stopped her to speak but her eyes moved past him and hit Jared's. Her smile intensified. With a few more words, she stepped around Aaron and came to him. He grabbed her, taking some of her weight as she fell against him.

'Thank you,' she said.

He held her, breathed her in. Everything within him gave a deep sigh of relief. She was alive. She was okay.

Four more officers arrived—the boatload from Little Deadman's Bay, Jared assumed. Indy spoke to them before walking over.

'Jai needs a doctor,' Tess said. 'Pax really beat him up.'

'I'll take Orvist back with Roberts, get a couple more officers to take Jai back. I'm guessing Riley will want to ride with them. I'll send a chopper back for you two and the others can hike back down to the beach, go back on the boat.'

'Indy,' Tess said. 'I know you have to arrest Jai, but—'

'He'll be treated fairly,' Indy said. 'That's all I can promise.'

Jai and Riley approached them and Tess let go of Jared to hug Jai. 'Thanks. You've got a really good tackle technique.'

Jai grinned as much as his swollen face would allow, but it looked sad. 'Finally did something right.' Then he looked at Jared and Indy. 'I need to tell you … about what I've done.'

'We'll get to it,' Indy said. 'Once we've had you checked over. Get into that chopper over there, okay?'

Then the choppers were leaving and a small group were left alone.

'Apparently I'm walking down to the boat with the officers,' Aaron told Tess. 'I'm sure if you wanted to come there'd be enough room on the boat for you.'

'Honestly, Aaron, I don't think I have another walk left in me,' she said. 'But thanks for everything you did today.'

Aaron's mouth was a thin line as he looked from Tess to Jared. 'Fine. We'll finish this later, Tess.'

'Finish what?' she said as he stalked off and disappeared into the trees with one last unimpressed glance over his shoulder.

Jared sighed heavily and drew her back to him. 'Are you up to telling me what happened?'

'Possibly,' she said. 'Shortly. Not yet. Feel like a nice muddy stroll?'

'I thought you didn't want to go with the others. The chopper's coming back.'

'I just mean a few minutes in that direction.' She pointed the opposite way. 'I feel like sitting on top of the world for a bit.'

She was too calm, too quiet. Shock, he thought, willing the chopper to come quickly so he could get her warm, get her dry and have her checked out. A walk was the furthest thing from his mind. He looked around, frowned. 'Aren't we already there?'

'Follow me.'

She took him to a spectacular view a short distance away, overlooking if not the world, then a decent portion of it. They sat on the ground, wind whipping their hair from their faces and freezing the feeling from their skin as they looked out over the broad expanse of the Southern Ocean and the breathtaking sweep of foggy plains so far below. Tears began rolling down her cheeks. Not so calm now, not so quiet as the first choking sob broke from her throat. He held her while she fell apart, purged herself of the horror of the last few days, until her sobs quietened and her trembling eased.

'Thanks,' she said eventually. 'I can probably tell you the rest of it now.'

He kissed the top of her head as she snuggled further into him. 'Later will do.' Then, after a few more moments while he guessed hypothermia could well be kicking in, 'You ready to go back to find a bit of shelter somewhere?'

She nodded. 'I needed to ground myself for a moment, that's all. This spot … I love it.'

He flicked at a brown blob on his leg, and realised it was a leech when it didn't come off. 'I can see why.'

Though her smile was sad, she managed one. 'How can you top all this?'

'I'll show you later,' he promised. 'When we're both warm and dry. Somewhere in civilisation.' But he intended on coming back out here when he could appreciate it properly, the way a place like this deserved to be appreciated. 'We could be the only people on earth out here.'

'And in this weather, probably the only ones who would want to be,' she joked. Then her face fell. She was exhausted, dead on her feet. 'What he did—he's a monster.'

'He'll pay for it.'

She stared back towards the track. 'I don't know how I can ever go back.'

'You will. He can't beat someone like you. This is part of who you are.' The sound of rotor blades broke the silence and a chopper appeared in the distance.

'What do you know,' Jared said. 'They found us another one.'

CHAPTER 46

Jared sensed the moment she woke up: the change in the regularity of her breathing, the slightest shift of her body against his. He'd been enjoying his own first few minutes of wakefulness, blocking out the events of the week before and simply being in the moment. Being with Tess, in his home, his bed. He wondered at how easy it would be to consider it their bed, how quickly she'd become the most important thing in his life. She was lying against him with her hair fanned out over his shoulder and her breath on his chest, and he wanted it to last a little longer. But she was getting restless.

'Why are you awake?' he asked in her ear.

'It's Sunday,' she said sleepily.

'That's kind of my point.'

He felt her smile and stretch languidly against him before turning her face up to his. 'We're both busy today.'

'We're both busy every day,' he said, kissing her forehead. He reached over to his bedside table and picked up his phone, checked the time and groaned. 'Want some breakfast?'

'I'd take a coffee and an apple.'

'Nope.' He slid out of bed and dragged his fingers through his hair. 'We're up early on a Sunday, we have a proper breakfast. After the amount of time I've spent at the station lately, I'm starting to think of it as a second home, but I'm not living on bad coffee and the lunchroom's Anzac biscuits all day.'

She rested her head on her elbow. 'When do you think they'll set a date for Pax's trial?'

'Can't say yet. It's a bigger case than just the particularly horrible piece you had to go through. He's also wanted on some related charges back in Melbourne. He'll be tried up there, I'd say, alongside Cochrane's case. But the media attention should hurry things through.'

'Hmm. I think the media's as bad as anything else.'

'It's a big story. Unfortunately, the worse the crime, the more the interest it creates.'

'I know Pax won't ever get out of prison, but it seems too kind for him, too easy after what he put those kids through. They were only just starting their lives. I hope he at least wakes up one day and realises what he's done. Feels some kind of remorse.'

He saw the sadness enter her eyes and wished he could erase it. 'It's unlikely. People are either capable of feeling empathy or they're not.'

She nodded, sighed. 'I'm not looking forward to the funerals.'

'No, but I'm relieved we found Chris's body so his family can give him a proper burial. I'll be there with you. Come on, don't do this to yourself. You've been through enough.' He tipped her chin and kissed her lightly. 'Are you still catching up with Riley today?'

'Yeah. She wants to go for a trail ride. She's worried about Jai. The prosecution are going for twenty-five years.'

'I doubt that will happen. Jai made a mistake under exceptional circumstances, then he risked his life to save yours, confessed, is remorseful and is willing to testify against Orvist.'

She smiled, relieved. 'And it sounds like he has a couple of cops in his corner.'

'He'll go to prison. That's unavoidable. He's everything I just said but he still killed someone, someone innocent who didn't deserve to die. I'm not completely in his corner, but we'll weigh in. See what we can do for him.'

'Riley will stick by him. She was so angry, but those two have a bond that's almost unbelievable for their age.'

'They're going to need it if their relationship is going to survive what's coming next.' He pulled her up. 'I'll be in the kitchen making breakfast.'

He made her pancakes, something he hadn't eaten since he was about twelve years old. But she'd said she liked them so he'd gone and bought the kind you just add water to and shake. They turned out surprisingly okay.

When she left, he tossed the plates in the dishwasher and had a shower, his mind well and truly back on what he needed to do. Cochrane, who the team had taken to calling 'cockroach', had a damn good lawyer keeping them busy, and he doubted Orvist would ever talk. He got a text from Indy making sure he was on track to head in and he replied telling her he was. Then he grabbed his keys and stepped out the front door.

Pain exploded in his head, knocking him to his knees. A dark shadow moved in front of him and another strike came, hard, a kick to the gut. Again, again. There may have been more, but the world dissolved as he lost consciousness.

Tess sat in her apartment sipping her second cup of coffee with Riley. 'So you're still keen to have a ride today?' she asked.

Riley's eyes lit up. 'Absolutely! If you really don't mind. On the trails?'

'I want to take my new filly out anyway. It's much more fun with company.'

'Great. Later this afternoon I'm meeting Jai at the hospital. They're letting him see Evan.'

Tess's smile dropped in sympathy. 'I heard he had another stroke.'

'The day we got back. And he's gone further and further downhill. It's only a matter of hours, the doctors reckon.'

'That's so sad for Jai.'

Riley shrugged. 'He loves Evan. His whole adult life has revolved around caring for him. I was thinking—and I know it sounds terrible—but I thought that when Evan passed Jai would finally be free. Now it's just the opposite. He's going to prison.'

Tess wasn't sure what to say, then her phone rang so she picked it up, frowning at the caller ID. Aaron. Damn it, he hadn't contacted her since she got back. She'd hoped he'd given up and flown out already. She thought about letting it ring out, before deciding he might show up if she didn't answer. 'Fine,' she muttered and accepted the call.

'Hey, Tess,' Aaron said.

'Hi. I … thought you'd be in Canada by now.'

'I'm supposed to be flying out in a few hours. The thing is, a couple of tourists have gotten themselves disorientated in the heavy fog out at Mount Field. They're okay, just cold, wet and miserable and looking for someone to go out there and bring them back. They managed to hike up to a good enough spot this morning to get some reception to call us on a phone with very low battery. I reckon they've ended up somewhere by that nice little lookout spot over Lake Seal by the sounds of it.'

'It's almost impossible to get lost in that location. And what are they doing there, anyway? The circuit's been closed for maintenance for the last couple of days, hasn't it?'

'The problem is they don't speak English very well. I think they had as much trouble understanding me as I had them. And yeah, they shouldn't be out there.'

'So why are you calling me?'

'Because Craig had a bad asthma attack last night. His wife called from the hospital, asked if I'd man the phone until he got back to me. I said yes because what were the chances we'd get a call, right? And I thought he'd have been right to take over again by now but I can't get hold of him.'

Hell, she hoped Craig was all right. 'Then send out an alert, see who responds.'

'Look, Tess, I'm literally trying to walk out the door and by the time I get an alert out and responses start trickling in—if they do—it could take hours, and it's such a simple task. They're cold and tired and just need pointing in the right direction. I don't have any right to call you, I know, but I really need to make that flight. Could you please just run out there and grab them?'

She huffed. Her riding time was about to evaporate, but she relented because she wanted him gone. 'Sure, of course. No problem. What are their names?'

'I think the guy might have said Zhang. Thanks, Tess.'

'No problem. Enjoy Cana—'

'You know, I really do wish you'd decided to come with me. It could be the best move you've ever made. It's not too late.'

'It's not going to happen. Have a nice flight. Good luck over there,' she added, though she didn't really care.

'Shame. See you, Tess.'

'I hope not,' Tess muttered, ending the call.

'What's happening?' Riley asked.

'A couple of tourists need help getting back in off the Tarn Shelf Circuit out at Mount Field. Sorry, but I'll have to postpone our ride.'

'You're doing a rescue?' Riley asked, eyes wide.

'It's not a rescue as such, just a lift back to civilisation.' But she messaged Indy anyway, because it was habit to let someone know, then put her phone back in her pocket. 'I'd better get going.'

'How far is it?'

'At a tourist pace, the whole track can take anything up to eight hours, but it sounds like they're not too far in. I'll be back as soon as I can.'

'I'd like to come. If that's okay.'

'Are you sure?'

'I feel like I should go back out into some wilderness, but for a couple of hours, you know? Just to do it. And if we're helping someone else it'll give me something to focus on other than myself.'

'Okay.'

'So that was Aaron?'

'Craig's been sick. Aaron has been standing in. Almost feel sorry for him that this landed in his lap today.'

'But you're taking it.'

'Which is why I said almost.' She sighed and got to her feet. 'I'd do just about anything to make sure he gets on that flight and leaves the country. It's going to be cold. Let's get some gear.'

It didn't take them long to get out the door and onto the road. Patches of ice on the road to the park made their journey slow.

'I'm glad it wasn't this bad on the South Coast Track,' Riley commented.

'Higher altitude here. Further from the coast. That said, I've seen snow on the Ironbound Range.'

'It's hard to believe it doesn't just blow off. I nearly did.'

Tess grinned, pleased Riley was talking about the trip she hadn't been able to bring up since they returned. 'Okay,' she said, pulling up. 'Let's go get them.'

Tess grabbed her backpack of supplies and led Riley down the track.

'It's gorgeous out here!'

'One of the world's best day hikes. According to Aaron they could see Lake Seal so we'll go this way first, hope we spot them.'

They walked around a roadblock with a sign warning the track and ski tow hut were temporarily closed and kept going.

'Why do they call it Tarn Shelf?' Riley asked.

'A tarn is a mountain lake. There are loads of them up here. Mostly frozen right now.'

Riley was pulling ahead, enjoying herself. 'I thought it would be harder than this to go back out into the wilderness. But it's so lovely.'

'Let's see if you still think so a few more kilometres in,' Tess teased as the sharp sting of icy wind hit her face.

'I don't see a sign of anyone,' Riley said after a while. 'Maybe they found their way back.'

'Aaron thought they'd be in an area just ahead.'

They walked for another few minutes, then stopped.

'This is it. The lookout over Lake Seal,' Tess told Riley. They stood behind a pile of colourful snow-capped boulders and gazed at a vista of mountains with a long, snaking lake below them. 'It would have been handy to have a phone number but Aaron said their phone was almost dead,' she said, then, 'Hello!' she called.

Nothing.

'Tess, it's amazing out here!' Riley climbed up onto the tumble of rocks that overlooked the lake. 'Pass me the pack? My camera is in it.'

'Don't get too close to the edge, okay?' Tess warned with a shudder as she handed over the bag.

'Sure. Hey, maybe they headed for one of those buildings over there? Makes sense if they're cold and lost, right?'

'Yeah, it does,' Tess said. 'That's the Rodway Hut day shelter and the other one's a ski tow hut. We're heading that way. Take your photos and let's keep moving.'

'You sound worried,' Riley said. 'Aaron said they were fine, right?'

'It doesn't make sense.' Tess scanned the mountainside. 'They got lost on a perfectly good track.'

'They might be on a track but it's not difficult to get disorientated when there are tracks going in all directions,' Riley reminded her. 'And if they're not good with English, how are they going to know which way is back? They probably just panicked and decided to stay put and ask.'

'Sure, but where are they?'

They reached the huts and found no sign of anyone. Riley walked down the mountainside a bit, camera out.

'Riley, it gets stupidly steep down there, *please* come back.'

'Tess!' Riley yelled. 'There's a backpack here!'

On the side of the mountain, Tess thought with dread. Where else would it be? The mountainside was a series of steep vegetated slopes and rocky drops heading towards a pillared set of jagged cliffs. Her worry for the couple increased. This wasn't the simple job Aaron had suggested. She was calling it in, getting the police and other rescuers involved.

'I'll get it.' Riley dropped out of sight.

'Riley!'

'Be careful, yeah I know!' came from somewhere below. 'Hey, what are you—Tess!'

Riley screamed and Tess slid down the slope as fast as she dared. Heart pounding, stomach flipping, she skidded to a stop at a large boulder that seemed to have nothing but space behind it. She dropped to her hands and knees, ignoring the burning of the icy rock and the warnings in her mind screaming at her to *go back, go back!* She forced her arms and legs to take her forward. She edged further out, and on trembling limbs, looked over the edge.

CHAPTER 47

'Jared!' Indy's voice was distant. And annoying. He was pretty sure she had no right to be waking him up. Why did everything hurt so damn much? Even hearing her voice hurt.

'Jared, hey!'

'What?' He clenched his already closed eyes against the kick of a killer headache.

'Just keep still, okay? I've got an ambulance coming.'

'Ambulance?' He pushed up into a sitting position, regretting it when it felt like someone had jammed a hot poker in his side and his head did a long, nauseating spin. Then he realised where he was, and he remembered. 'Some guy jumped me as I came out to the car for work.'

'Yeah, I can see that. Just one?' she asked.

Squinting at her he could see the wry humour through her worry.

He tested his ribs again, decided they were probably bruised, not cracked. His head on the other hand ... well, he wasn't sure. Zigzag lights suggesting he had a decent concussion flashed in front of his eyes and the headache felt like a drill determined to reach the middle of his brain. 'I'm okay. No, I'm pissed off. Hurts like a bitch but if you think they're carting me off in an ambulance … Help me up.'

'I'm not sure I should.'

'Can you call off the ambos? Please? They have lives to save. I, on the other hand, will live.'

She did another quick study. 'Fine but only if you get in the car and let me drive you to the hospital. I reckon the lump on the back of your head's the size of a tennis ball.'

He prodded it gently and hissed out a breath. 'I'll live.'

Once on the road, he let himself close his eyes.

'Did you see your attacker?' Indy asked.

'If I'd seen him do you think I'd have let him do this?'

'Then how do you know there was only one?'

'My ego would prefer to believe there were two,' he said, then sucked in a sharp breath as he tried to shift his position. 'Maybe ten. Professionals.'

She smiled at him. 'Tough guy.'

'We should be looking for clues.'

'I've got a team headed out to your place. I called them when I was trying to bring you around. They'll go over everything, see what they can find.'

'I'm guessing this is something to do with Cochrane. I wonder why I'm not dead.'

'You should look in a mirror. They probably thought you were.'

'Ha.'

'Talk me through everything you remember,' Indy said.

'Ah … Tess was over. We got up, ate pancakes, she left to go for a ride with Riley. I was probably out the door fifteen minutes after her. Walked out, turned around—'

'Stop, back up. Think. Was there anyone around, any cars on the street, anything different to usual?'

He tried to remember, shook his head slowly. The pounding that had eased slightly kicked off again. 'There might have been a four-wheel drive a bit like yours parked a couple of houses down. Come to think of it, you're the first person I saw. Not holding a grudge, are you?'

'If I was, I wouldn't take you by surprise, or hit you from behind. This car—you haven't seen it before?'

'I don't think so. But look, I really wasn't paying a lot of attention.'

'Like mine, you said. A Prado? Dark grey?'

'I only think so. It could have been something else.'

'Hmm. Do me a favour and pull up my emails on my phone.'

'What am I looking for?'

'I may have done some digging into Aaron,' she admitted sheepishly.

'You *what*?'

'I know! Bad detective.'

He scrolled back several days. Stopped. 'Like an *Interpol* check?'

'Nothing turned up on the national database and I remembered him bragging over time he spent overseas. Anyway, with everything going on I haven't even looked at it yet. Read it, would you?'

He opened it, and as the zigzags had faded from his vision, scrolled through it. 'You wouldn't happen to have any aspirin or anything, would you?'

'You could have a bleed on the brain! I'm not giving you blood thinners! I do have paracetamol,' she relented. 'Glovebox.'

He dug them out, helped himself. 'So what exactly spurred this check?'

'The too-good-to-be-true Aaron, who as far as I could see was slowly taking over Tess's life, was becoming more controlling, more demanding, undermining her confidence, and at times showing glimpses of a nasty temper. Tess was so adamant she felt his hands shove her towards that cliff edge during the Cradle Mountain rescue after their fight that I wondered if there could be more going on under the surface.'

'Did you talk to Tess about any of this?'

'Not directly. I wanted to make sure it wasn't just my cop mind working overtime creating worst-case scenarios. Hence the background check, which was clear. But then he refused to take no for an answer after she attempted to break up with him. We can't prove he sabotaged her car but the fact he was following her at the time had alarm bells ringing. And buying her a plane ticket on top of all that was just wrong. So I decided to search further afield. Then this thing with Orvist blew up and I haven't gotten back to it.'

Jared's gaze returned to the report. His already uncomfortable stomach lurched. 'Stop the car.'

'Huh?' She pulled over, idling on the side of the road. 'What?'

'How many times have you told me to listen to my gut instinct—and then you don't listen to yours?'

'What? Why?'

'Aaron spent four years in the UK from 2011 to 2015.'

'I know. Hence the—'

'While he was there his then girlfriend filed stalking charges against him. Two months after the last offence, the woman was involved in a fatal accident. A fall. The parents blamed Aaron but there was never enough evidence to charge him. That's all the detail that's here.'

'That's enough.' He watched a range of emotions cross Indy's face, then she spun the car out into a fast U-turn. 'If I don't take you straight to the hospital, you're still gonna live, right?'

'Depends,' he said, only half joking. 'Are you going to keep driving like this?'

She negotiated a give way sign and headed for the freeway. 'Tess spends the night at your place, then someone clobbers you, puts the boot in, leaves you unconscious.'

'I know. I was there.' But he had a bad feeling settling in his already upset stomach. 'You think Aaron did this?'

'Aaron sent Tess on a call-out to Mount Field this morning. An off-books rescue. It didn't go through official channels. Also, Aaron has a gunmetal grey Prado. Now, I hope I'm wrong, but what are the chances? Call Emily. Ask her to find out if Aaron got on his flight this morning.'

He took Indy's phone and spoke to Emily, then dialled Tess. The call rang out. He tried again, gave it a couple of minutes and was about to try again when the phone rang.

Indy answered it on speaker. 'Yeah?'

'Aaron's flight out of Hobart doesn't leave until tomorrow morning,' Emily said.

Indy glanced at him. 'He told Tess it was today.'

'Drive faster,' he said, willing the pain in his head to ease so he could think. 'I'll get everyone out there.'

Police and Search and Rescue took almost two hours to gather at Mount Field. It felt like too long, and not long enough since Jared had felt this same terror at Tess's life being in danger. Aaron had too decent a head start.

Craig, the team manager, got straight to work as he climbed from his car. The large man with the balding head had one of those easy, friendly smiles that generally always belonged to a decent person, a trustworthy one. But now that smile was tight, concerned.

'Detective Atherton. Detective Denham—what's happened to you?'

'Nothing that won't wait. You didn't know anything about this call-out?'

'I can't understand this at all. I'm the one who receives any notifications, then I put an alert out from my phone. Nothing's gone through me this morning. You said Aaron called her directly? Sent her out here?'

'Yes,' Indy said. 'About nine.'

Craig shook his head. 'I don't know why he'd do that.'

'Unfortunately,' Jared said, 'we think we do. And we think Tess could be in real danger.'

'From Aaron?' Craig asked, obviously astounded. 'His flight was this morning, wasn't it?'

'No. And you're just going to have to trust us,' Indy said. 'We need to hurry this up.'

'Of course.' He spread a map over the bonnet of his car while other officers and volunteers gathered around.

'You don't have to do this,' Indy told Jared. 'We have plenty of people out here. I know I'm not going to budge you off site but at least rest in the car by the radio.'

'You are joking, right?' He grabbed one of the bottles of water someone from Search and Rescue had brought and impatiently stared at the map while Craig organised what teams should cover what areas.

'I'm going this way.' He indicated a signpost that pointed in the direction closest to what Indy said Tess had described and, needing to get started, walked away.

Indy spoke to Craig, then joined Jared and shoved a jacket at him. 'Put this on. It needs to go back to Craig later.'

He gingerly slipped it onto one arm, cursed under his breath as he twisted his painful ribs to get the other in, and shrugged it over his shoulders. 'Are we ready to go?'

'Four teams, all have at least one officer. Choppers are still in use elsewhere on an MVA and a boat rescue off the coast, but they'll get one here as soon as possible. Emily's grabbing us a pack.'

'I'm here,' Emily announced, jogging to catch up.

'Then let's …' A wave of dizziness washed over the pounding in his head.

'Jared,' Indy said, worried.

He widened his eyes then squeezed them shut. Blew out a breath as his vision cleared. 'Let's go.'

CHAPTER 48

Tess lay on her stomach, every nerve cell screaming at her to get away from the edge as she pushed herself forward. She had to see. She had to help.

Riley was about ten metres below, lying awkwardly on a protruding shelf of rock. The drop wasn't smooth, rather an almost vertical tumble of ancient boulders. Riley had caught some of them during her fall and a large gash ran down one cheek and blood dripped off her boot from an injury somewhere to her leg.

Riley moaned. She was alive. Thank God.

'Riley! Don't move!' Tess called out hoarsely over the fear that almost locked her throat closed. If Riley rolled the wrong way she'd plummet way too far to the next jut in the rocks.

'My leg!'

The panic in Riley's voice clawed at Tess's stomach, reverberated in her head. Riley tried to sit up and time seemed to slow down for Tess, as frozen, she waited to see if Riley would fall.

'Keep still!' she ordered. She heard her phone ring—from the bag she'd handed over to Riley earlier. The bag was hooked in some shrubbery close to where Riley had landed. Riley didn't seem to be listening—or comprehending—because she shifted again.

Tess gritted her teeth and ran through proper procedure. She should get help, go down with the proper gear. But the phone was out of reach, a run back for assistance would take too long and Riley's position was tenuous at best.

Another impossible decision. Charlie all over again.

She struggled with what to do as common sense warred with desperation. Then a large portion of Riley's ledge broke away and Tess realised the small bank wasn't rock, but made up of tree roots and mud.

There was no time. Tess saw a foothold, and another, and somehow she was working out in her head exactly where she needed to go, how she was going to get down that mountain.

'I'm coming!' she yelled. She swivelled around on her belly and, feet first, petrified and unsteady, she began to descend. Just one foot, then the next. Adjust weight, find the next handhold, shift again. The cold, hard rock scraped against her stomach, her fingers ached. She heard a crack and her stomach plummeted. Turning her head almost unbalanced her. Riley had dislodged more of her ledge.

'Tess, help!' Riley sobbed, her fingers clawing at the rock as she slithered back from the edge, dragging her damaged leg.

She was almost there, but there was no room for two people where Riley was perched, and if it crumbled again … Tess looked down, shuddered. They'd both be dead. She found another foothold almost level with Riley.

'You'll be okay, just keep still. I have to keep going, get the bag.'

'Tess.' There was a world of pain and terror in that one word.

'Just focus on your breathing. Keep calm,' Tess said. 'I'm going to get my phone out of the bag, get you some help.'

Riley's eyes were suddenly drawn above them to the top of the mountain.

Tess couldn't believe it. He'd come after all. 'Aaron!' she called out in relief. 'We need help!'

'No! No, he's not going to help us!' Riley sobbed.

'Of course he will.' But the expression on Riley's face had her stomach sinking. 'Why wouldn't he help us?'

'Because he's the one that pushed me over.'

A rock the size of a soccer ball bounced over the edge and crashed past them.

'Are you sure?' But her mind went back. Two hands on her back, a shove. *Oh my God.* 'Aaron! What are you doing?'

'There are always consequences for our actions, Tess,' he called back calmly. Another rock fell past her, barely missing her fingers.

Tess dug her feet into the rocky crevices and grabbed a snow gum jutting out of the mountain. Alive and strong, she had to hope it was anchored well enough to take her weight.

'What's wrong with you?' she yelled.

'If only you'd agreed to come with me. You chose Denham instead. I told you losing you wasn't an option. I warned you you were running out of chances.'

Another rock, bigger than the last, smashed above them and shattered, raining shards and dust over them.

'I'm sorry it has to end like this, Tess.' A rope dropped a few metres to their left. For a moment she thought perhaps he was going to help them after all. 'I knew you'd go down there after her, but you didn't fall. I'm gonna have to hurry this up. Don't want reinforcements arriving.'

'Aaron, please!'

Riley cried out again as another wad of earth disappeared from under her, leaving her with just enough ledge for one foot.

Tess leant forward, adjusting her grip on the tree. 'Riley, grab my hand.'

'You won't be able to hold me! How can you hold my weight?' Riley's eyes flicked back and forth from Aaron to Tess's hand.

'You need to trust me. You need to reach. *Try*, Riley. *Trust* me.'

There was a final snap, and the ground fell away. Riley screamed, snatched at Tess's hand, and Tess grabbed her firmly around the wrist. They both swung downward, the branch Tess was hanging from groaning against their weight.

'Don't let me go,' Riley pleaded.

'I am *not* letting you go,' she said, teeth clenched with effort. Desperation and resolve mixed in equal measure as she clung with little more than sheer determination.

'I think Tess might have the best job in the world,' Emily said as an area of track thickened with snow. 'I've lived in Hobart my whole life and never come out here.'

'It's beautiful,' Indy said, 'but hard work at times—hey, look!' She hurried ahead and pointed to where the track had a thin covering of snow. 'Footprints.' She got on her phone and let the other searchers know what they'd found.

Jared charged ahead, finding a break in the trees that looked out over a stunning view of trees and water. So much space. Where were they? 'I can hear something!'

A scream—Riley. Tess's shouted plea. He looked across to a ski hut, down to a blur of movement. Saw them.

'Oh no,' Indy whispered.

They ran, Indy shouting into her phone. Jared's pain was forgotten as he pulled ahead of the women, hoping the track would provide the quickest route to the scene. *Hold on*, he told Tess silently, repeating it like a mantra in his mind until, breathing heavily, body exploding with pain, he spotted the two huts, got his bearings and bounded down the hill.

Aaron was pulling abseiling gear from a pack. 'It's going to look like just another tragic accident, Tess. You tried to save someone else. Another stupid, heroic act, this time ending in a double tragedy. So sad. So predictable. You're reckless, Tess. You don't follow the rulebook. These things happen.'

Jared ran at Aaron with a fury so blinding his own safety became irrelevant. He grabbed the man from behind and spun him around. Ignoring the pain in his side, he landed one almighty punch to Aaron's jaw, which stunned him into falling at Indy's feet as she and Emily caught up. Indy was on him in seconds.

Jared leant out over the edge. 'We're coming, Tess! Hold on!'

'Jared!' Tess's voice wasn't much more than a strained sob. 'Hurry!'

'Craig's group is closest,' Emily said. 'Ten minutes off.'

'She can't hold on that long.' He picked up Aaron's abseiling harness and stepped into it.

'Jared, you can't,' Indy said. 'Let me try.'

'Have you ever abseiled?'

'No.' She looked worried, but he knew she'd try.

'I have. Once,' he said and gritted his teeth—he was pretty sure those ribs might be cracked after all. 'Okay, so figure eight knot …' He tried to think, to remember, while all the time his mind was screaming at him that Tess could let go at any moment. That he needed to be down there *now.* The prusik knot was beyond him; he was going down without it. He locked the clips into place. Tess had said three anchor points. Aaron had only set one. It'd have to do. He walked to the edge, leant out and took a couple of steadying breaths, then tested the rope against his weight. When it held, he started down.

'This is all because of you!' Aaron yelled at him. 'I told you to back off. I warned you so many times to back off! If you had, I wouldn't have had to do this!'

It'd been Aaron who'd sent those warnings, Jared realised distractedly. That made perfect sense now, but he had to negotiate a tree poking out of the rocks, a gap in footholds. This was not a nice smooth beginners slope, so Aaron's words vanished from his mind.

'I can't hold on!' Riley screamed.

'Almost there, sweetheart,' he promised. He was close enough to see the strain on Tess's face, the trembling, linked arms, and hell, Tess's fingers slowly slipping from the tree. He found a place to brace himself, tied his rope off and grabbed Riley, dragging her to his side. She collapsed into him with an ear-splitting scream and clutched at her leg.

'Tess?'

'I'm okay,' she said, but she sounded exhausted. It took her more effort than he knew it should have to struggle back up to a safer spot. Once there she sat and dropped her head back to the sky, breathing heavily and rolling her shoulder. Then she must have gotten a good look at him because her eyes widened in distress. 'You're hurt. How did you get down here?'

'I kind of forgot I was hurt when I saw you two swinging from a cliff.' He grimaced as his body protested. Now he was starting to remember, but he tried for a reassuring smile. 'Lucky you gave me that abseiling lesson.' His gaze swung back to study Riley's pale features. 'How are you going?' he asked gently.

'I'm okay.'

'Her leg's broken,' Tess said. 'Make sure she doesn't pass out and go over.'

'Not going to let that happen.'

'I won't pass out,' Riley said. 'Tess. You held on. You didn't let me go. Thank you.'

Tess smiled but behind it was a flash of pain. She was thinking about Charlie, he figured. He wasn't sure how she'd even managed to get herself over the edge. He wanted to tell her how incredible she was, get that smile back, but raised voices above them had him turning sharply. A scream. Emily's body flung out over the edge. She fell a few feet, slammed and rolled and, as his heart leapt into his throat, she wrapped a hand around some foliage and saved herself from a much longer fall.

There was a roar from Aaron, a shot. Aaron fell left of Emily, bounced limply off a jut in the rock and flew past them, almost over their heads. They heard him crash into the scrub somewhere below.

'Oh my God,' Tess whispered in horror.

Riley whimpered.

'Indy!' Jared called. 'Are you all right?'

She appeared over the edge, one hand covering her forehead, the other with her gun dangling from it. 'Bastard headbutted me then tried to strangle me with the cuffs. I had no choice—he was coming down after you, and taking us with him.'

Emily scrambled back up to the top. 'Well, shit, that was close,' she said.

He couldn't have agreed more.

CHAPTER 49

18 months later

Paxton Orvist sat in the prison's common room and stared at Bryce Cochrane and his entourage. Hate churned in Pax's gut, his mind demented by rage. He was inside because of Cochrane, but Cochrane wouldn't have a bar of him. He should have welcomed him with an invitation to his little gang. Instead he'd given him a black eye and a warning to stay out of his way. He'd stuffed up, Cochrane had told him. Was lucky he didn't get his men to end him for it.

Fuck them. Sitting over there at the big table, thinking they were all such tough arses, thinking they ran the prison and could treat him however they wanted. Nup. Things were going to change. He was in here long enough to make it worth his while to do something about Cochrane's current leadership. The months of hiding in corners were over.

He fiddled with the shiv he'd paid for with cigarettes. The point was razor sharp.

One of the gang, a big guy named Thug, stuck his foot out as Chesky, a weedy little prick without any real balls, walked past with his steaming cup of whatever it was. Chesky hit the ground, the caramel-coloured liquid bursting into a long, haphazard explosion on the epoxy flooring. Thug laughed, laid the boot in as Chesky righted himself. He went down again.

Pax scanned the room. No one did anything. They never did. Not that he gave a shit. It was just weird. On the outside, some stupid dick or other would have stepped in. Would have cared.

He continued to watch, to wait. At five, like clockwork, Cochrane got up, said something to the other dickheads and headed out to have his shower. Pax waited a few beats, got calmly to his feet and stretched, then took his time wandering out. He passed a guard, a couple of inmates coming in and, with a final glance around, ducked down the hallway to the showers and slipped inside. No one would bother them. Everyone knew Cochrane got the showers to himself at five. No one messed with Bryce Cochrane.

Until now.

Steam billowed from the shower stall as Cochrane lathered his widening girth in soap. He was humming. What the fuck did he have to hum about? Pax slid the shiv out of his sleeve and into his hand. This was gonna be good. He stepped into the cubicle. Hot water spat at his face and the scent of Cochrane's soap filled his nostrils.

'Hey, Bryce,' he said. 'Owe ya something.'

Cochrane turned in surprise, bellowed as the shiv flew up towards his abdomen. He managed to wrap one beefy hand around Pax's throat as the other reached out in an attempt to hold off the strikes.

The grip at his throat was blindingly painful, but Pax struck with all the feral determination of the caged animal he had become. Warm blood spilled over his hand and down his arm as he stabbed again, and again, and again into Cochrane's flabby belly. Cochrane's grip weakened and Pax managed to drag in an excruciating lungful of air as Cochrane slumped to a sitting position in the corner of the stall, staring down at himself in shock.

'Die, fuckwit,' Pax demanded, satisfaction swelling in his chest.

Cochrane looked up from the mess Pax had inflicted on him, his lips working into a twisted smile as his eyes shifted to something behind Pax. He swung around.

The room filled with Cochrane's men. They spread out and Thug roared. Pax scrambled back from the cubicle, raising the shiv in a useless warning attempt.

It was over in seconds. They left him on the tiles in front of Cochrane's slumped, naked body, not quite dead. Broken, unable to move, barely able to breathe, Pax held his stomach together and watched his blood mingle with Cochrane's as it ran into the drain.

His pain dulled, his vision faded out. And then nothing.

EPILOGUE

'Nearly there!' Tess said, excitement lacing her voice.

He could have kissed the ground at that proclamation. He scrambled up another narrow area of mountainside, refused to look anywhere but at the hand and footholds immediately in front of him. There was much less of 'up' than there had been for the last few hours, and an ever-increasing amount of 'down'. He pushed the thought from his head, in case he was tempted to look behind him again. Whenever he did, his stomach tipped and his vision swam. He wouldn't enjoy the view until he was safely on top of it.

'Step up that bit there,' Tess instructed. 'Yep ... okay. Come on!' She offered him her hand out of unity rather than necessity so that they took the last few steps together. 'You did it!'

'We did it.' Legs shaking more from the dizzying height than exhaustion, Jared walked out onto the rocky summit. And wow. It was stunning. The top of Federation Peak. There was more space up here than he'd thought there would be and, without a cloud to be seen, the peak showed off three hundred and sixty degree views of endless, breathtaking scenery. Mountains, lakes, ancient forests, sea. He breathed it in, absorbed it. He'd wanted to climb it for Tess, but now he decided it was one of the best things he'd ever done for himself.

The trek had been beautiful in some places, terrifying in others, and one particular spot he could only describe as insanely suicidal. He'd had a moment, thinking about Tess up there in a Tasmanian storm, in the sleet and wind and rain, talking down a scared tourist. That she was climbing this monster again after all that had happened was unbelievable.

And they'd made it up—together. Pride and a real sense of triumph rose inside him.

'You were right. It's incredible,' he said.

'It really is.' She looked at him with a blinding smile. 'Thanks for this. I would never have thought I could get back up here.'

'Honestly, it was you who got me up here. I wasn't sure I was going to make it.' His smile turned comical. 'I'm already a little scared of the getting-back-down part.'

She pressed her lips to his. 'We'll be fine.' She unzipped her pack and took out her phone to snap a photo of them. Then her smile fell and she pulled up another shot.

'Hey look, Charlie,' she murmured, holding up the phone as though showing the image on screen the views. 'We made it.'

'That's a nice photo.'

'Yeah. I got Indy to send it to the family.'

'I'm sure they love it. I know if I were his family, I'd want to see his last, happy moments.'

She dragged in an audible breath. 'It's been months, but it doesn't feel like it.' Then she shook her head a little, brightened. 'Do you want to sign the book? It's here somewhere.' She put the camera down and moved a few steps away to ferret around under a pile of stones, but he followed and pulled her back up to face him.

'In a minute.' He smoothed her hair from her face and kissed her, long and slow. He heard the hum of appreciation in her throat, felt the press of her body against his and got caught up in it, wondered what was going on when a rumble of engine noise broke through his consciousness.

Tess broke the kiss to look past him. A light plane was zipping around the side of the peak. It dipped its wings once, twice, in salute. Tourists' faces were plastered to the windows with large grins.

'Just about to start their hike,' Tess said with a smile and a wave. 'I hope they have a good time. A memorable one, for all the right reasons.'

'So do I. How about we make this more memorable for us for all the right reasons?' he suggested, lowering his head back to hers.

The plane looped again and was gone. Neither of them noticed.

ACKNOWLEDGEMENTS

I'd like to say an enormous thank you to everyone who worked with me on *Deadman's Track*. My special thanks to …

Shaun Brooks, manager of the Southern Tasmanian SES SAR team, and Charles Smith, longstanding member of Wollombi Volunteer Bushfire Brigade, for kindly providing the information necessary to write many of the more challenging scenes. I couldn't have done it without your assistance.

Sergeant Tony Jones, who repeatedly went above and beyond to answer or find answers to my very specific police procedural questions.

Jo Mackay, I can't thank you enough for the dedication you show to your authors and your ongoing belief in my writing.

Nicola Robinson, you're amazing. It's been wonderful working with you for the first time.

Annabel Blay, there are moments I'm sure everything would fall apart at my end without your amazing organisational skills and friendly email updates and reminders.

Thanks also to the design team for my fabulous cover and the sales team who take my books out into the world.

A further thanks to Kylie Mason and Annabel Adair for assisting in making the story the best it can be.

Tea Cooper, thanks as always for your brilliant critiquing and forever making yourself available for help and advice.

A very special thank you must also go to the people of Tasmania. You never cease to amaze me with your hospitality, advice and generously shared local knowledge.

And last by not least, to all my readers. Thank you for reading, sharing and reviewing my books.

talk about it

Let's talk about books.

Join the conversation:

facebook.com/harlequinaustralia

@harlequinaus

@harlequinaus

harpercollins.com.au/hq

If you love reading and want to know about our authors and titles, then let's talk about it.